THE GHOST ANTS
OF GRYLLADESH

By Clark Thomas Carlton

The Ghost Ants of Grylladesh
The Prophet of the Termite God
Prophets of the Ghost Ants

THE GHOST ANTS OF GRYLLADESH

The Antasy Series

Book 3

CLARK THOMAS CARLTON

HARPER

VOYAGER
IMPULSE

An Imprint of HarperCollinsPublishers

THE GHOST ANTS OF GRYLLADESH. Copyright © 2021 by Clark Thomas Carlton. All rights reserved. Printed in the United States of America. No part of this book may be used or reproduced in any manner whatsoever without written permission except in the case of brief quotations embodied in critical articles and reviews. For information, address HarperCollins Publishers, 195 Broadway, New York, NY 10007.

Digital Edition MAY 2021 ISBN: 978-0-06-242978-0
Print Edition ISBN: 978-0-06-242979-7

Cover design by Guido Caroti
Cover art by Daniel Liang
Maps by Paul Manchester

Harper Voyager, the Harper Voyager logo, and Harper Voyager Impulse are trademarks of HarperCollins Publishers.

HarperCollins is a registered trademark of HarperCollins Publishers in the United States of America and other countries.

FIRST EDITION

21 22 23 24 25 LSC 10 9 8 7 6 5 4 3 2 1

*This one is for Mike
aka The Best Boy in the Universe.*

CONTENTS

ACKNOWLEDGMENTS

Thank you to Matthew Goodman for helping me to keep it all straight these many years. Thanks also to Kelly Lonesome for pushing me toward the weirder—always glad to do that. And kind thanks to David Pomerico for being so patient while I was a patient.

TRIBES AND NATIONS

Free State of Bee-Jor—The new nation established by Anand, Queen Polexima, and the Laborers' Army in what was the eastern half of **the Great and Holy Slope**. It contains nearly fifty human inhabited ant mounds including Mounds Palzhad, Venaris, Cajoria, and Shishto with some falling in and out of control by the **Seed Eater Nation** to their east.

Britasyte Wandering Tribe—The Britasytes, also known as **the roach people**, are a wandering nation whose insects' repelling odors allow them to travel different nations without being attacked by ants and most other insects. Their tribe comprises three clans: the **Pleps**, the **Entreveans,** and the **Fallogeths**. A fourth clan, the **Pafentus**, are mostly extinct.

Bulkoko—The extinct nation of the **bee people** or **Bulkokans.** They were freed from one oppressor, the **Icanthix** tree dwellers, and then enslaved again by the **Hulkrites**. The bee people were brought into **Bee-Jor** to make their new home in an oak tree at its northern tip.

Holy Slope—Formally known as **the United Queendoms of the Great and Holy Slope**, it is also known as **the Slope** and **the No Longer Great Nor Holy Slope** as well as **the Old Slope**. It is the nation of leaf-cutter ant people after it has been partitioned following the war with the Hulkrites. On its eastern border is **Bee-Jor** and in its west is **the Carpenter Nation.** The Slope's northern border reaches the Buffer Zone of **Dranveria** and its southern border is along the refugee-occupied **Weedlands**.

Seed Eater Nation, also known as **the Barley Empire**—A nation east of **the Slope** ruled by Emperor Volokop. **The Seed Eaters**, also known as the **Barley people**, have domesticated the harvester ant.

Carpenter Nation, also known as **the Beetle people**—The Carpenter people of the western pine lands have parasitized both the wood-chewing carpenter ants as well as the ants' own parasite, the massive war beetles.

Dneep, also known as **the Grasslands**—A nation of light-skinned roach people east of Hulkren and south of the Seed Eaters and confined to an area of densely growing grasses. Known as the **Dneepers** or **Grass people,** they have arrived at the Weed-lands south of **Bee-Jor** and the **Slope** to claim their new country.

Collective Nations of Dranveria—A vast area of nations, tribes, and peoples with individual governments as well as a single intergovernmental body that unites them. Their capitol is the City of Peace. Dranveria's southern borders are surrounded by a **Buffer Zone** where various tribes and peoples occupy trees, groves, water areas, and scrublands.

Hulkren, also known as **Termite Country** and **the Dustlands**—The defeated empire of ghost ant riders who worshipped the Termite God, Hulkro. Hulkren is south of the Slope in a vast area of devastated forest that touches on many other nations that were absorbed into the short-lived Hulkrish Empire.

Kweshkin—The small nation of shore people on the southern end of the Great Brackish Lake. It is east of Jatal-dozh in the **Dustlands** and it was briefly absorbed by the Hulkrish Empire.

Ladakh/Ledack—A nation far to the south of Hulkren that was destroyed by the Hulkrites. Its people are known as Ledackis or the **Meat Ant people** for their domesticated insect, the meat ants.

League of Velvet Ant Peoples—A new nation of multiple tribes with a common language and ancestry. They are also known as **the United Tribes of Velvet Ant Peoples** and by their ancient name of **Greeyas**. They have recently united as a single nation to reclaim territory that was stolen from their ancestors thousands of years ago. The Greeyas have adopted the wingless wasps known as velvet ants and wander in the vast scrublands west of the **Carpenter Nation**.

Vundjeloos—Also known as the **Spider people**, they are a cannibalistic tribe who stain their skin green. Before they were refugees in the southern Weedlands of Bee-Jor, they were absorbed into the Hulkrish Empire.

THE CHARACTERS OF ANTASY

Aggle—A low caste Slopeish defector from the Slope to Hulkren. Promoted to captain by Pleckoo, Aggle was from Mound Culzhwitta. Deceased.

Anand (ah-nand)—The son of **Yormu**, an outcaste Slopeite of Mound Cajoria, and **Corra**, a woman of the Britasyte roach people. Anand is also known as **Vof Quegdoth** and **Commander Vof Quegdoth** as well as **the Roach Boy**, **Lick-My-Testicles**, **the Dranverite**, **the Son of Locust**, and **the God-King of Bee-Jor**. He is the military commander of the Laborers' Army of the new nation of Bee-Jor and rules with **Queen Poleximinator**.

Babwott—One of the Learned Elders of Dranveria.

Barhosa—An elderly chambermaid of Mound Palzhad. She has served **Queen Clugna** and **Queen Poleximina** as well as **Queen Trellana**.

Batra, Commander General—The commander of the army of Mound Cajoria of the Slope. Deceased.

Bejetz—A young Britasyte man and the eldest son of Chieftain Zedral. Deceased.

Belja—A military general of Dranveria and the wife of **Hopkut**. Belja is mother to **Dwan**.

Bevakoof—The eldest of Trellana's maidservants.

Brother Moonsinger—A eunuch and former tutor of Mound Loobosh. He travels through Bee-Jor as a professional storyteller.

Butterfly Goiter—A guard assigned to escort **Pleckoo**. His fellow guard is **Sewn Shut**.

Clugna, Queen—The elderly queen of Mound Palzhad. Her husband was **King Kammut**. She was the mother of **Queen Polexima** and the grandmother of **Queen Trellana**. Deceased.

Corra—A woman of the Britasyte Wandering Roach Tribe or roach people. Her common-law husband was **Yormu**, a Slopeish outcaste of Mound Cajoria. She was mother to **Anand** and a member of the Entrevean clan. She was sister to **Glegina** of the Plep clan. Deceased.

Da-Ma—A religious leader of the Britasyte roach tribe and member of the Plep clan. He/she is a priest/priestess of Madricanth, the Roach God.

Daveena—A young Britasyte woman formerly of the Plep clan and married to **Anand** of the Entreveans. She is a dancer in the Roach Spectacles and speaks the Seed Eaters' tongue.

Dolgeeno, Pious (dohl-jee-no)—Formally **His Ultimate Pious Dolgeeno**, the highest religious official of both the Holy Slope and Bee-Jor and all their mounds. He shares his title with **Terraclon**. He was formally **His Most Pious Dolgeeno**, the highest priest of Mound Cajoria.

Dorfen—The foreman of the blinders' caste of Mound Cajoria. His caste's job is to blind all newly hatched ants and to slaughter any ants born with wings.

Do-Tma—He/she is the two spirit or religious authority of the Entrevean clan of Britasytes.

Dumbree—A young man of the midden of Cajoria. He is Keel's second oldest son and brother to **Tal** and **Shimus**.

Durelma—A Slopeish young woman of Mound Palzhad who was captured and enslaved by Hulkrites. She has returned to her native Mound Palzhad and serves as an interpreter.

Dur Knazhek—A princeling of Durxict in the Seed Eater Nation. His father is the **Dur Gorodz** or Grand Prince of Durxict and is the brother of **Emperor Volokop**.

Dwan—A young Dranverite man and an albino. His mother is **Belja**, a Dranverite general, and his father is **Hopkut**, a fire master.

Dziddens, Captain—A light-skinned man from Mound Cajoria serving in the Laborers' Army as a pilot.

Edgeth—A Hulkrite who is second cousin to **Commander Tahn**. He was the captain/ruler of Jataldozh. Likely deceased.

Ejolta, Pious—The high priest of Mound Palzhad and formally known as **His Most Pious Ejolta**.

Elga, Elder—An elderly woman of the Kweshkite shore people. After the death of her husband, she became her people's leader following their expulsion from Kweshkin.

Elora—A girl from the scraping caste of Mound Cajoria who was forced to join the Fission pioneers of the new colony in Dranveria.

Ennochenzo, Pious—A priest who was once the supreme religious leader of the Great and Holy Slope. He resided in Mound Venaris and was succeeded by **Dolgeeno**. His formal title was **His Ultimate Pious Ennochenzo**. Deceased.

Esnock—The senior scout of the **Greeyas or League of Velvet Ant Peoples**.

Estaine, Pious—A priest of Cajoria, formally known as **Pious Estaine of Cajoria**. He is devoted to the oak tree god, Bortshu-Mox.

Fadtha, Captain—A captain in the Hulkrish army, originally from the Seed Eater Nation. He was the captain/ruler of Fadtha-dozh and his wife was **Muti**. Likely deceased.

Feegalo, Pious—Also known as **Old Pious Feegalo**. He is an elderly priest at Mound Palzhad.

Fewlenray, Queen—The young and beautiful sorceress queen of the border mound of Mound Fecklebretz of the Old Slope.

Flandeek—The younger sister of **Mulga**, a member of the servant caste at Mound Cajoria.

Frinbo, Pious—A young priest of Cajoria, one of Pious Dolgeeno's favorites. He rises to greater prominence at Mound Cajoria after the war with Hulkren and assumes the duties of highest priest of the mound.

Gafrexa—Formally the **Widow Gafrexa Chando**. Her husband was a lieutenant general in the army of Mound Cajoria.

Geweth (goo-eth)—The wet nurse to **Pareesha** in Hulkren.

Glegina (gle-jin-uh)—A Britasyte woman who is **Corra**'s sister and **Anand**'s aunt and a widow. She married into the Plep clan.

Glip—Foreman of the midden caste of Mound Palzhad in Bee-Jor.

Glurmu—The idols keeper of the midden caste at Mound Cajoria. He conducts religious rites for the outcastes.

Grillaga—A woman of the Plep clan of Britasytes who speaks the Carpenter tongue. She is the eldest wife of **Zedral**.

Hamlutz, Defender—The head of Anand's guard at Mound Cajoria and a veteran of the war of the Hulkrish invasion.

Hawjud—A Greeya and one of six captains of the League of Velvet Ant Peoples.

Hopeful—A baby boy rescued by **Pleckoo** after the War of One Night. Hopeful was adopted by **Princess Jakhuma** and **Kula Priya**.

Hopkut—A Dranverite man known as a fire master. His wife is **Belja** and his son is **Dwan**.

Inveedra—A woman of the Fallogeth clan of Britasytes. She speaks the Seed Eaters' language.

Jakhuma, Princess—Formally **Princess Jakhuma of the Meat Ant People of Ledack**. She was the slave of a Hulkrish warrior. Her servant is **Kula Priya**.

Jidla—A young woman of Dranveria and a flight instructor.

Jizzlane—A young woman of the midden at Cajoria. Her parents are **Keel** and **Splooga**. Three of her brothers are **Tal**, **Dumbree**, and **Shimus**.

Kammut, King—The king of Mound Palzhad and the father of **Queen Polexima**. He was married to **Queen Clugna**. Deceased.

Keel—The foreman of the midden outcastes who work in the trash heaps of Mound Cajoria. Three of his sons are **Tal**, **Dumbree**, and **Shimus**. His wife is **Splooga** and his daughter is **Jizzlane**.

Kep, Prince—A prince of Mound Kulfi and the identical twin brother of **Prince Maleps**.

Klonpak, Captain—An officer in the Laborers' Army.

Kontinbra, Pious—A priest of Mound Cajoria who accompanies **Queen Polexima** on her travels.

Kula Priya—A Ledacki woman and the personal servant of **Princess Jakhuma**, both of whom were enslaved by the Hulkrites after the conquest of Ledack

Ladeekuz, Queen—The queen of the Bulkokans or bee people. Also known as **zaz-Ladeekuz**.

Lagoradny, Crown Prince—The firstborn son of **Emperor Volokop** of the Barley Empire or Seed Eater Nation.

Lamalla, Princess—The crown princess of Mound Palzhad and Polexima's younger sister. Lamalla's parents were **King Kammut** and **Queen Clugna**. Deceased.

Lamonjeeno, Pious—Formally **His Most Pious Lamonjeeno**, the highest priest at Mound Shishto.

Lania, Queen—The sorceress queen of Mound Sloveck in Bee-Jor.

Maleps, Prince—A prince of Mound Kulfi and husband to **Princess Trellana**. He was briefly **King Maleps** of Mound Dranveria and of Mound Cajoria. His identical twin brother is **Prince Kep**.

Medinwoe, King—King of the Dneepers, the yellow-skinned roach people of Dneep, also known as the Grasslands.

Mereeno—A Britasyte man of the Fallogeth clan and a spanner to the Slopeites.

Mikexa, Defender—She is a skilled locust pilot of Bee-Jor.

Moosak—The young son of **Glip**, the foreman of the midden caste at Mound Palzhad.

Mulga—A woman of the servant caste at Mound Cajoria. She is **Queen Poleixma**'s personal attendant. Her younger sister is **Flandeek**.

Muti—A great beauty and the wife of **Captain Fadtha** of the Hulkrites. She is originally from the Seed Eater Nation and resides in Fadtha-dozh. Pleckoo named her his "**Entrusted**."

Naloti—The wife of **Glip** of the midden caste of Mound Palzhad.

Nimfa—A young priestess of Seed Eater stock at Fadtha-dozh. Her sister is **Soblazni**.

Nuvao, Pious (new-vay-oh)—He is Polexima's favorite son and a Slopeish priest. He resided in Mound Venaris and was recently crowned king of Mound Palzhad with his sister, **Trellana**. He is a locust pilot in the Laborers' Army of Bee-Jor.

Odwaznee—A boy originally from the Seed Eater Nation and a former Hulkrite. He was left to guard the Bulkokans at Halk-Oktish during the invasion of the Slope. He left Hulkren and lives among the Britasytes.

Omal, Defender—A locust pilot of Bee-Jor.

Omathaza, Queen—Formally **the Sorceress Queen Omathaza**, she rules Mount Shishto with her husband, **King Wahdrin**. Her cousin is **Polexima** and to **Trellana** she is known as **Auntie Omathaza**.

Ovoglock—The captain of the Orange Wasp Tribe of the League of Velvet Ant Peoples.

Pareesha, Princess—Polexima's youngest daughter,

a baby. Her older sister is **Trellana** and her surviving brother is **Nuvao**.

People's Agent—The highest elected official of the Collective Nations of Dranveria.

Pizhyot—A man of the lost Britasyte clan of Pafentus.

Pleckoo—A young man of the midden outcastes at Mound Cajoria and an older cousin of Anand. He is also known as **Pleckoo the Noseless**. In Hulkren, he was known as **Commander General Pleckoo** and as **the Second Prophet** as well as **Khali Talavar**.

Polexima, Queen (po-leks-i-muh)—The queen of Mound Cajoria, formally known as **Polexima the Sorceress Queen of Mound Cajoria**. She is originally from Mound Palzhad. Her husband is **King Sahdrin** and her daughters are **Princess Trellana and Princess Pareesha**. Her last surviving son with her husband is **Pious Nuvao**.

Pozlushny—A former warrior in the Hulkrish army of Seed Eater stock. He works as foreman of the workers in the ant queen's chamber of Fadtha-dozh.

Punshu—A Britasyte boy of the Entrevean clan. He was the driver of **Daveena**'s roach-sled in the Dustlands and fought with **Polexima** against the Seed Eaters.

Putree—A young woman from an unknown tree tribe. She survived being thrown out of a tree by the bee people of Bulkoko and was adopted by the Plep clan of Britasytes.

Queestra—A Britasyte woman of the Entrevean clan who speaks the Carpenters' tongue.

Sahdrin, King—The male ruler of Mound Cajoria, formally known as **the Warrior King Sahdrin of Mound Cajoria** and also known as **His Highness the Legless**. He is married to **Queen Polexima**.

Sametta—A chambermaid to **Queen Fewlenray** of Mound Fecklebretz.

Sebetay—A young soldier of the army of Ledack or Meat Ant people. He was captured by the Hulkrites and enslaved. After the fall of Hulkren, he was a refugee in the Ledacki camp in the Weedlands south of Palzhad.

Setcha Greeya—Also known as **Torvock-son-of-Koshvock**, he is the leader and uniter of the **League of Velvet Ant Peoples**. He is also known as **the Setcha** or the **Great Greeya**.

Sewn Shut—A guard assigned to watch **Pleckoo** along with another guard, **Butterfly Goiter**.

Shlovock—The oldest son of the **Setcha Greeya**, also known as **Shlovock-son-of-Torvock**.

Sinsora, Emperor—The ruler of the Carpenter Nation, also known as the Beetle people.

Soblazni—A priestess of Seed Eater stock at Fadthadozh. Her sister is **Nimfa**.

Splooga—A woman of the midden of Mound Cajoria. Her husband is the foreman **Keel**, and three of her sons are **Tal**, **Dumbree**, and **Shimus**. Her daughter is **Jizzlane**.

Stubby—A boy at Mound Cajoria with a deformed arm left in charge of guarding **Pleckoo**.

Tahn—The military and spiritual leader of the Hulkrites and the first prophet of Hulkro, the Termite God. He was also known as **Commander Tahn** and the **Prophet-Commander Tahn** and **the First Prophet**. Deceased.

Tal—The eldest son of **Keel,** who is foreman of the outcastes. Tal works the trash heaps of Mound Cajoria and is expected to succeed his father. Two of his brothers are **Dumbree** and **Shimus** and his sister is **Jizzlane**. His mother is **Splooga**.

Tappenwoe, Prince—The young nephew and heir of **King Medinwoe**.

Tellenteeno, His Most Pious—The high priest of Mound Fecklebretz.

Terraclon—A young man of the midden outcastes in Mound Cajoria and Anand's closest friend. He was given the title **His Ultimate Pious Terraclon** and he is the supreme religious leader of both Bee-Jor and the Holy Slope, a title that he shares with **Dolgeeno**.

Thagdag—The chieftain of the Entrevean clan of Britasytes.

Toothless—A Hulkrish warrior and one of the sober guards.

Trellana, Queen—The eldest daughter of **Queen Polexima** and **King Sahdrin**. She is **Queen Trellana of Palzhad** and was formally known as **Princess**

Trellana of Mound Cajoria. She was known briefly as **Queen Trellana of Mound Dranveria** as well as of **Cajoria**.

Treti Korolsyn—A young Seed Eater royal captured by Terraclon and brought as a prisoner of war to Mound Cajoria.

Ulatha—A Britasyte woman of the Entrevean clan who speaks the Slopeish tongue.

Utchmay, Defender—A sentry at Mound Shishto in Bee-Jor.

Vanka, Queen—The sorceress queen of Mound Smax in Bee-Jor.

Veltfock—One of the captains of the League of Velvet Ant Peoples. He is leader of the Red Wasp Tribe.

Vematta, Matron—The personal servant to Queen Fewlenray at Mound Fecklebretz.

Viparee, Pilot—A pilot of Bee-Jor descended from a crafting caste.

Vof Quegdoth—The name Anand uses for himself in Hulkren and as the military commander of Bee-Jor.

Volokop, Emperor—The ruler of the Seed Eater Nation or Barley Empire. He suffers from both grossly swollen and atrophied body parts.

Walifex—A war widow of Mound Shishto. Her husband was the Commander General of Shishto.

Wahdrin—Formally **the Warrior King Wahdrin** of Mound Shishto. His wife is **Queen Omathaza**.

Wartra—A middenite woman of Cajoria. Her son is **Terraclon** and her husband is **Zlok**.

Yormu—An outcaste man of Mound Cajoria, also known as **Yormu the Mute** and **Defender Yormu**. His corporal punishments have left him with an inability to speak. He works in the midden, or trash heap, as a salvager. His son is **Anand** and his common-law wife was **Corra**, a woman of the roach people.

Zalavock—Leader of the Yellow Wasp Tribe of the League of Velvet Ant Peoples.

Zedral—A Britasyte chieftain of the Plep clan.

Zembel—The chief of protocol for **Queen Polexima**.

Zherquees, Queen—The queen of Mound Shlipee in Bee-Jor.

Zlok—A middenite of Cajoria and father to **Terraclon**. His wife is **Wartra**.

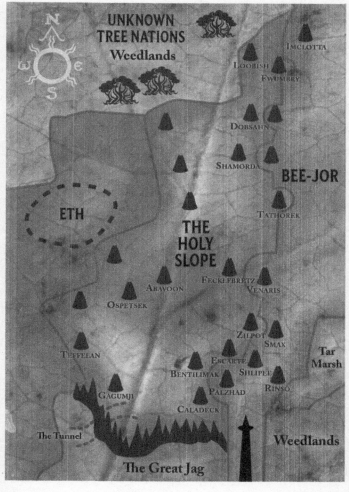

Mounds of The Eastern Slope
and Western Bee-Jor

THE GHOST ANTS
OF GRYLLADESH

CHAPTER 1

STRANGE ODORS

Anand held Daveena's hand as they looked at an uproar of wildflowers waving above the rain-spattered greens of a fragrant meadow. They gaped at the petaled towers of violet lupines and then at the orange cups of radiant poppies. Shining above them all were the stalks of whorled autumn daisies, blooming out of season, with each flower as bright and yellow as a tiny sun. The two climbed the stair-ladder of a viewing rock to take in the sight of an oak grove glistening in the distance. When they reached the rock's top, they saw a double rainbow with its delicious order of shimmering colors. "There's one for each of us," said Daveena. Anand turned from the dazzling spectrums to look at her darkly beautiful face, which reflected the blue of the sky. He looked into her eyes as she raised her chin and opened her mouth for a kiss. When he bent to touch her lips with his, her mouth dissolved and floated away like paint poured in a stream.

He grabbed her shoulders, which blackened, then crumbled into dust. The sky, the trees, and the flowers were all falling now, collapsing into blackness. Anand felt unsteady on his feet when he fell facedown in a shallow puddle. Shaking his head free, he realized he was dreaming and was coming out of sleep again in the boat he had stumbled into on the shores of the Barley Lands. All around him was a lightless dark. He wondered if it was still night or if he had gone completely blind.

"Blindness," he muttered to himself. Losing his sight was one of his worst fears: to be deprived of all that was beautiful to look at. And it meant being an object of pity, and worse, it ended life as a warrior—and Bee-Jor needed its warriors. "Or its *defenders*," he said, using his Dranverish.

We are not warriors, but defenders, he recalled as the first lesson taught to cadets at Rainbow Lichens. Anand hoped that during his sleep the boat had drifted towards Dranveria and not back to the Barley Lands, or worse, to the unknown eastern countries. A faint glimmer was in his eyes and he turned towards what had to be the East and the rising sun. The light grew stronger and his vision was filled with a ruddy softness and then the blurs of water sparkles as the lake and sky turned blue.

I'm not completely blind!

And then he heard it, over the lapping of the water—the voices of humans and the splashing of a craft coming towards him. He waved his arms. "Help me, help me! I'm blind!" he shouted in Dranverish.

Something flew past him and grazed his ear. A mosquito or a swamp fly? *Or a dart! Not a dart with the Living Death! Please, Roach Lord, help me!*

He dropped and knelt below the hull, head turned up. "I am a Dranverite! A citizen of the Collective Nations!" he shouted. The voices loudened and he heard the churning of water as the boat got closer. Were they cannibals or slavers or perhaps just curious? From the sound of tightening fibers, he realized that what had flown past him was a rope that had cinched the stern of the little boat, and after a rough jerk, they were tugging it towards their larger one.

Anand's head throbbed with panic when he realized the boatmen were not speaking Dranverish or any tongue he recognized as they boarded his craft and yanked him to his feet. He smelled their dank breath as they tugged at his cape and felt the silk of his tunic before they relieved him of it and the rest of his clothes—even his loin strip. Someone pushed his chin up for a good look at his face. They gripped each of his limbs and then hoisted him to the deck of a much larger boat with a noisy crew. The lid of a crate-basket was untied and he was pushed into it with a cold fish that was alive and slapping its tail. He felt the sharp scrape of the fish's fin against his thigh and then its hard mouth under his ear as it gasped for water. Sails snapped as they were raised up, then pummeled by the wind, and then he heard the sounds of choppy water as it was slashed by a prow.

The day spent in bobbing confinement with a stinking fish was an agonizing monotony, but finally Anand sensed the sun was sinking. The breezes had grown cooler as the boat reached the shore. He heard the crew jumping into the water's shallows to pull their boat through the shore muck and someone, perhaps the boat's captain, was shouting to a crowd on land. What the captain said excited them and they rushed to the boat to secure it to a docking rock. Anand heard the squish of mud and then the scrape of sand as, at last, the boat stilled. It felt good, for a moment, to be grounded and he sighed in relief when the crate-basket was lifted onto several shoulders, dipping and wobbling as it was carried into a throng. Around Anand were a mass of men and women who babbled in a wet tongue that sounded like it was falling out of their mouths and had to be sucked back in.

Anand realized that the slats of the crate were large enough to reveal him, and his naked body had to be on display. He worried his captors were cannibals and then doubted it because they would not have been tempted by his lean body, which was more bones and sinews than meat and fat. A gate was creaking open and then he sensed the shade of a roof overhead. The crate's lid was untied and they dumped him out. He stood, then slipped on the fish at his feet, falling on his bottom as fish scales cut into his soles. Women ran in, eagerness in their voices, to gather up the fish and carry it off. Someone pulled Anand in one direction, then guided his hand to a low table. He felt a drinking-bag and then pressed his fingers on top of something gooey and sour smelling, a platter of food of some kind.

Anand saw soft bars of diffused light and realized he was in a spacious cage. Through the gaps, he heard his captors gasping and giggling; he wandered up to the thick bars and took in their circular placement. Under his feet he felt a fine, almost powder-like sand that had been sifted for comfort. The throng stepped away from the cage and he heard the sound of crawling insects and the whipping of their antennae. Ants, of some kind, with long feelers were stroking him, searching for kin-scent. But he was no longer certain of what kin-scent he had—the Seed Eaters had doused him with that of their harvester ants and without his clothes he had little or no roach-scent. A moment later, he heard wet hissings, then smelled a stench he could not identify—it was like rotting earthworms and moldy barley with a whiff of a soiled diaper. Anand coughed and his eyes started tearing.

"Good Roach Lord," he said. "I'm in Stink Ant country."

He fell to his knees and rubbed his watering eyes and felt phlegm flying from his nostrils as he sneezed.

"I will survive this," he pledged to himself. "For Daveena. And for our children."

CHAPTER 2

THE EMPEROR TIDIES UP

"I'm mad with boredom," Daveena said out loud as she pivoted in the tiny space of the prison cell she occupied with Slopeish priests and royalty. The Slopeites to her right glanced at her now and then, this dark-skinned roach-woman talking to herself in a language that made them wince. On the left side of her were Slopeish corpses that no longer reeked but had dried, shrunk, and wrinkled during her imprisonment. She looked out the wall of clear quartz to the palace's courtyard where occasional strollers would stop and stare at her, but she was no longer a novelty. In the distance, she saw harvester ants returning from gathering food and climbing up to their mounds—this time they had some purple seeds of amaranth. Closer to her were bonneted gardeners tending potted pink thistles with long, wavy leaves and spikes that had to be sheared.

Daveena looked at the desiccated bodies wrapped in royal and priestly costumes, and knew she could move them and make more room for herself. "What else have I got to do?" she said aloud, and then picked one up and dragged it toward the wall when the Slopeites screeched in horror. She understood few of their words, especially when spoken in the royal dialect, but she knew they were telling her not to touch and pollute Slopeites—even dead ones.

Well, that is about to change.

"No, no, no!" she shouted, and stepped towards them, meeting their eyes as she clenched her fists at her sides. "I will make myself some room!" As Anand had taught her, she threatened to spit at them by feigning it at first. They backed away, their screeches turning to weeping as she set the corpses into neat stacks that allowed her to take a few more steps. Even better, it gave her room to lie down. As the one-eared Slopeites sobbed over the desecration of their relatives, Daveena lay on the tiles, stretching her arms and legs, and it felt just . . . extraordinary.

"Day sixteen," she said to herself as she stared at the ceiling, cringing as she recalled the moment when Anand was smothered in a poison-drenched blanket, then packed in a crate bound for Dranveria.

Had he somehow gotten there? And how? The Seed
Eaters were not boatmen and they feared the Great
Freshwater Lake, believing it to be the home of the
Demoness Water Spider, whose eight-legged daughters dragged humans to the bottom to drown, then
offer to their devouring mother. Even if Anand had
reached Dranveria, how would he be treated? Would
they target him with the Living Death? Force his
return to Bee-Jor? Or would they throw him in prison
or a pit?

Daveena's stomach rumbled and she felt a mild
kick from one of the babies inside her. "You must
be hungry too," she said, and patted her belly as she
looked out the window. The shadow on the plaza's
sundial indicated noon. "Breakfast soon, little ones,"
she said. Her eyes shifted east to some new strollers,
women and girls, who walked towards the cell with a
strange haste. They were followed by others and soon
there were hundreds of them, milling in their garments that bulged with excessive embroideries. They
glanced at Daveena but their sights were focused on
the noblewomen and the priests of the Slope. The
look on the strollers' faces was not the usual curiosity
tinged with condescension. They were angry, pointing at the prisoners, and shouting names at them.
Daveena could read their lips and knew the Slopeites
were being called "flea-cunts," "mosquito-fuckers,"
and "piss-royals."

What's happened? Something's happened!

The Slopeites were murmuring among themselves, shaken, when they heard the scrape of the chamber's door as it slid open from the palace's corridor. The warden's visits with the food delivery were one of the few bright moments of Daveena's day, but today his arrival brought more dread. The warden had admired her as a dancer in the Roach Spectacles and he always made sure that her box included a smear of cactus jam or evergreen cherry to help her keep her hair and teeth. He usually had a shy and admiring grin for her, but today his face was long and wan; he averted his eyes.

"Good morning, Good Warden," Daveena said, using the formal tongue as she spoke over the hubbub outside the cell. She saw the food cart had only a single box.

"For you," he said, making quick eye contact before pushing the meal towards her in the sliding compartment at the cage's bottom. She felt the glaring eyes of the Slopeites on her back as she picked up the box.

"No food for the others?"

"No," he said, looking at the Slopeites in contempt. "But they're getting a special . . . *treat* today. A visit from His Divine Grace Emperor Volokop."

"The emperor? Has he returned?"

The man nodded once, then looked away from her.

"Was he in Bee-Jor?"

"Young madam, you are a stranger in our land," said the warden. "It is best not to ask any more questions."

Daveena felt unsteady and then all went black as she fainted. She dropped her head until it filled with blood, and when she stood, she realized the Barley people had somehow waged, then lost, a war, despite her and Anand's attempt to prevent it. At the very least, their invasion had been repelled. *But how did Bee-Jor do it without my husband? Did Anand somehow get back there?* She no longer felt hungry but knew she must eat for the welfare of the ones in her womb.

The Slopeites stared at Daveena in angry silence as she peeled back the leaf cover to reveal the box's contents. Inside the box was a roach egg, one that had been close to hatching before it was killed with a puncture. Daveena raised up the meal to show the Slopeites after she peeled it. Although it was a pale brown corpse, they gasped in disgust when they realized it was a roach hatchling. She bit into it, and they heard the crunch of its delicate carapace. The prison mates were appalled and some wept or screamed. Daveena took another bite and exaggerated the sounds of sexual ecstasy. The Slopeites screamed louder, as if their toenails were being ripped out, which made Daveena laugh for the first time in her imprisonment—payback for all their haughty mistreatment of her. As she chewed, she wondered what message the emperor was sending. Was it a warning for the prisoners, or for her? When she finished eating, both her stomach and her womb were quieted but her mind was noisy with dark imaginings. As she had just eaten a roach, would she soon be bathed and then fed to one?

A short time later, the door opened again and the emperor's high priest of Lumm Korol entered with several of his under-priests. All of them wore their hair in a braided and lacquered stick that stood on end from their scalps. Their robes were a somber blend of black and blue checks that contrasted with the white, crud-encrusted braids of their beards. They had brought fresh shreds of sagebrush bound to the ends of sticks, which they used as mops to spread an aromatic oil over the floors and walls. After the scent cleansing, the priests pressed themselves to the back of the walls and looked up and chanted with raised palms to their moon god.

The emperor's guards entered in single file, lifting their legs without bending the knee. They wore ceremonial armor of various beetle chitins and carried lances with gold-wrapped blades of spider fangs. The soldiers parted to allow for the entry of the throne-sled drawn by shaven-headed boys that sweated in a group harness. Daveena heard the soft scratching of the sled's bristles over the floor and creaking when it came to a halt.

Emperor Volokop sat atop the sled dressed in

a cone-shaped cloak that hid both his body and his chair. The cloak was a reddish orange, a kind of cloth made from matted human hair. At the front of the sled's prow were two large locking blocks of marble with a hole drilled through their middle. Daveena was startled by the sight of these objects but was unsure of why they made her stomach flip. The emperor muttered something inaudible, then raised his spindly arm through a slit in his robe. In his hand was a two-handled saw with fine teeth made of black obsidian. The high priest took the saw and muttered a prayer as he raised it to the ceiling for a blessing from their god.

As the left side of Volokop's face was a clump of bulbous distortions, his expressions had to be surmised from the right where his mouth was downturned, in a scowl. His right eye was unblinking as it took in the faces of the Slopeites, all of whom had raised their chins in a mutual look of contempt. Along the back wall, the Seed Eater priests sang a group prayer in an ancient tongue that Daveena couldn't fully understand but she managed to make out the words for "offering" and "gift" as well as "pardon." The blocks of marble, heavy to lift, were set on the floor by the guards and one of the men placed a large and lidless basket next to them. The high priest left his prayer-trance and marched to the emperor, bowed deeply, then entered into a slit in the cone-robe. He returned with a compact idol of the moon god chiseled from lapis and rose quartz, which he set in a niche in the wall.

"Bring the first of the offerings," shouted Volokop in a voice weighted with grief.

Two of his guards bowed deeply, then marched to the cell and proceeded to lie in its sliding compartment. The warden grunted as he pushed the guards inside to the prisoners, who backed away in fright when the guards stood and threatened their swords.

"The offerings?" Daveena shouted at Volokop, and then regretted the defiance in her voice. "What are you offering and to whom . . . Your Divine Grace?"

"Silence!" Volokop shouted at her while pointing with the bony fingers of his atrophied arm. "You have not been spoken to, roach-woman. I will address my grievance with these thieving Mushroom Eaters, these silk-clad royals, and profane priests who will at last serve some purpose. I'll deal with you last." One of the guards shoved Daveena to the eastern side, forcing her collision with the corpse stacks that snapped and cracked and then imploded to send up a strange-smelling dust. *He must have suffered a terrible defeat*, she thought. *And is taking revenge on these prisoners!*

The guards grabbed the first Slopeite within their reach, a haughty priest of Mantis who resisted as he shouted prayers to his god. The priest was beaten with fists to his face and was stunned and gasping after a wallop to his throat. The guards forced him into the compartment and he was pulled to the other side of the bars, then pushed to his knees before the locking stones. The top stone was raised and then dropped over his neck and he squirmed and screamed when he realized it was a pillory. Two other guards took the saw by its grips and set the middle teeth on the priest's shoulders. He screamed for mercy as the saw was worked to rip up the skin of his neck before it cut through his spine.

Sprays of blood and flesh spattered on the floor and the bars. Once the head was severed, the emperor's priest raised it up to the face of the moon idol, then dropped it in the basket. The headless body was plucked from the pillory, then dumped in front of the cage as a gruesome torment to the Slopeites. They were clutching each other, weeping in fear as the next of them was selected for beheading. The next victim looked to be a graceful royal who had maintained something of a clean and neat appearance in once elegant clothing. Stunned with terror, she went quietly to the pillory, stumbling towards it on dainty boots with tapering heels. Her face had a dead expression, which remained unchanged after her head was cut off and presented to Lumm Korol.

Daveena turned away from the carnage, knowing there would be forty or more executions. She was dizzy and nauseated, and when she finally vomited, it was as if her body was trying to expel her stomach. She clenched her eyes shut and prayed.

Lord/Lady Madricanth, if this is my time, end my suffering and take me and my unborn children now. And please protect my husband.

"I love you, Anand," she said out loud.

She covered her ears as the sawing continued, but she could not block out the shrieks and screams nor the cheers outside the window as each severed head was raised to the moon idol. As the cell was emptied, she paced in its opening space, praying to Madricanth. When the last Slopeite was slaughtered, the silence that fell was a heavy threat. Shock gave way to shaking and sobbing. She turned her back to the emperor—an offense to him—as she heard him descend to trudge to the cage.

"Roach-woman," he said to her with his broken voice. "What would you know about our battle with the Slopeites?"

"As I have been a prisoner here, I have no news of *any* battle," she said over her shoulder, refusing to meet his eyes.

"Really. I thought Britasytes could see the future. One of them read my destiny from the shape of my ear once. She correctly predicted my transformation, as well as the escape of my third wife. She also said I would have no more children."

"As my husband tried to tell you, you will not have warred on the Slope but on Bee-Jor, a new nation that has no designs on your own. The Bee-Jorites were intent on returning more of your mounds that had been stolen by *Slopeites*."

"The Slopeites—or Bee-Jorites if you will—made allies of the Britasytes!" he shouted. His words were stretched and fractured with sadness as he screamed them. "Together, they invaded our nation on the backs of roaches! And on flying locusts! These cowards attacked us—from the sky!"

"As I said, I have been a prisoner in your palace," she said, her body and her voice shaking. "What I do know—the roach tribe does not declare war on any nation. Together they are made up of a few clans, perhaps thirty thousand people, whereas you rule millions."

"Your husband, a roach person, said he was a Bee-Jorite *and* a Dranverite. *All* of these nations joined to destroy us."

"All those nations are committed to peace," she said. "And would never invade another country. They *would* defend their own."

Volokop stared at her with his right eye and kept silent.

"What will you do with me?" Daveena asked, finally turning to him and staring into his good eye.

"How insolent you are!" he shouted. "A roach-woman asking *me* questions, the Emperor of the One Righteous Nation!"

He was wordless for a moment but Daveena heard

his breathing, heavy with rage. The strange sound of his body shifting overtook the room.

"You are pregnant, roach-woman?" he finally asked.

"I am."

"You will stay here in Worxict. We have a use for you. And as for your husband—this arrogant Anand of so many nations—he seems to care for you, deeply, to the point of weakness. Does he not?"

"My husband is not weak."

"I am eager to speak with him when he returns for you. After that, we can deal with this problem of . . . Bee-Jor. And Dranveria after that. He will return for you, yes?"

Daveena was unsure of how to answer and hesitated. "That remains to be seen," she said.

Volokop gave her one last look and then slowly turned his head with all its deformities in profile—it resembled earthworms squirming out of a pile of maggots. "We are done here," Volokop said to the high priest and the captain of the guard. The priest nodded and the captain clicked his heels.

The emperor made a slow ascent back to the chair on his sled. The under-priests rearranged his cone-robe, and as he was hauled away the harnessed boys sang a song of numbers that aligned their steps. The priests followed after in single file, and then the guards marched out in their clattering armor. Left behind in the silence was the tart smell of blood. The warden stepped away from a recess in the wall and walked carefully over the gore-spattered floor, trying not to slip and fall in the crimson globs. He was trembling, ill, and had not cleaned all the vomit off of his own tunic.

"Into the slider, madam. I am taking you elsewhere," he said, and Daveena obeyed him. As she lay at the bottom of the compartment, her eyes welled, tears streaming down her neck, and suddenly she was overwhelmed with a desolate sobbing she could not control. Gently, the warden pulled her to the other side of the bars and helped her to her feet. She was out of the cell but felt no relief as she looked in his face. He pitied her.

"Follow me," he said. "Please."

"Where are we going?"

"To join the women of the milkery."

"The what?"

"You are with child, yes?"

"I am."

"Then you will have milk once it is born. That milk will be taken from you and used in the making of delectables for the royals' table."

"Delectables?"

"Yes. It will be curdled and aged or sweetened and fermented. Sometimes it is left to clot and ripen after it's infused with tasty molds, what we call *zir*. Often enough the princesses drink it fresh or bathe in it to keep their skin as soft and moist as an infant's."

In all her shock, Daveena was sickened to imagine her milk being consumed by her captors . . . especially the emperor.

"But I will need my milk. What about my babies?"

"Your babies?"

"Yes. I am sure I carry twins!"

"Twins. I see." He was quiet a moment and went from grave to graver. "You might be able to keep one."

Her heart was racing. "One? And the other?"

He looked away from her, shook his head, and went silent. As they walked the long corridors to the royal kitchens, she looked through the walls of orange quartz and wondered how she might escape and get back to Bee-Jor.

Bee-Jor! How did they defeat the Seed Eaters? If Anand didn't lead them, who did?

CHAPTER 3

NEW WORRIES

The pulsing aches in Polexima's face kept her awake. The pain radiated from her nose, clogged with blood, and boxed her ears from within, and seemed to bounce within the breathing mask and her eye goggles. She was starved of sleep, but the roach-crawl home was not without dangers through the Barley Lands, and she kept her bow with its last arrow at the ready. Punshu, her driver, was just as fatigued and he had run out of kwondle bark to chew on for alertness. He had bleeding gums and weary limbs but was humming to himself as he steered their roach home. When they finally neared the border of Mound Shishto, she saw the last of the Seed Eater villagers, so weak and skeletal, scampering to hide in the grass or in their pebble shacks . . . or was it to retrieve weapons for one more desperate attack?

Bee-Jorite soldiers jumped off the train's roaches to disassemble the Seed Eaters' border wall, but then realized it was flimsy and low enough to allow for their passage since they had no sand-sleds. The riders at the train's front reached the top of the wall and unfolded a pole to raise the banner of Bee-Jor with its bars of red, brown, and yellow. Polexima saw their signal had been received with a wave of the same banner from above the Shishtites' wall. As the train crawled west over the neutral strip, she saw an entire section of the border wall retracting, sliding back like one of the drawers of her clothing chests. As she got closer, she saw the section, glued as a unit, was set on a palate with scale-lined rudders that men were pulling in with ropes. She realized that it must have been another of Terraclon's innovations and smiled when she remembered his fascination with her chests as he pulled their drawers out, then pushed them back in, something he had never known.

As they got closer to Shishto's housing rings, Polexima heard the sounds of a boisterous crowd descending from the mound. The roach train passed through a spicy-smelling stand of black mustard and over a rough carpet of its oily seeds before they arrived at Shishto's airfield. Tens of thousands had gathered to welcome Polexima with banners and idols of

Goddess Cricket, a sight both spectacularly beautiful and enormously comforting that sent waves of warmth through her arms and legs and tingles down her spine. Punshu looked over his shoulder at the queen with the same admiration as the crowd. As they shouted her name in synchrony, he managed a smile that revealed his bloody gums and missing teeth. *Oh, those teeth*, Polexima thought. *They had been so very beautiful.* As instructed, Punshu guided their roach out of the parade to the staircase of a Monument to the Eight Laws. Shishtites assembled before the monument to hear their queen.

Shishtite priestesses of Cricket helped Polexima off the roach and to the platform of the structure where they fastened crinkled antennae to her head, handed her the Staff of Night Singer, and then fastened her into a star-spattered Robe of the Evening Sky. The queen struggled to stand tall in the midst of her fatigue as she stepped up to the amplifying-cone.

"Bee-Jorites, let us offer thanks to Cricket, who has guided us in our defensive measure. May She ever keep our peace. Let us pray."

The priestesses stroked their cricket harps in a slow chirp.

"Queen of Night, Wisest of All, Kindest of Heart, and Bravest in Battle," shouted Polexima with eyes closed over clasped hands. "We thank You for your guidance, Your bounties, and Your help in defeating those who attacked our nation. May You temper us when we are tempted to war. May You remind us always that we are all members in the One Great Family."

She opened her eyes. "Bee-Jorites, turn to your neighbors, clasp their hands, and wish them happiness, peace, and prosperity for all."

The people were completing the prayer when Polexima heard a buzzing overhead and saw a small chevron of locust flyers. They released powder trails of red, brown, and yellow as a sign of friendly approach.

"Vof Quegdoth!" shouted a boy.

"It's Quegdoth!" shouted others as the crowd cheered in astonishment and smiles burst on their faces.

Polexima wanted to believe it was Anand—but how could it be? "Clear the field!" she shouted.

The people drew back to reveal the field's landing circles as the squadron spiraled down. It was not Anand who was landing but His Ultimate Pious Terraclon atop his white-striped locust. He sat erect, behind his pilot as she clenched a sensor prod in her mouth and splayed out the locust's antennae for a landing. The six legs of the locust clawed at the air before they caught the sand, then crawled to a smooth and dignified stop. Terraclon stood atop the locust's saddle, the amulet of his priestly office sparkling in the sun, and raised his chin as he turned to the crowd. The people pressed hands together in silent reverence to their New Ultimate Holy, even as the wind had whipped away his face powder to reveal his brown skin. He gracefully dismounted and raced up the stairs to Polexima. Upon reaching her, Terraclon bowed and then spoke through the cone.

"Bee-Jorites!" Terraclon shouted; Polexima heard the thrill of victory in his voice. "I wish that it was Vof Quegdoth who had returned instead of me. But our Righteous Commander is still on his mission in the Barley Lands . . . a mission where he will insist on the recognition of our nation of *Bee-Jor* by Emperor Volokop and a *demand to end this and all future wars."*

The crowd cheered while leaping in place and chanting, "Bee-Jor." Terraclon looked at Polexima. Startled by an exploding joy, she dropped her staff and grabbed his arms.

"You kept them back," she said, her eyes tearing.

"*We* kept them back," he answered. "For now."

He stood stiff before her when she gave in to a sudden urge to embrace him.

"I'm so grateful," she shouted into his ear. "Grateful to you for all you have done. And grateful to Cricket for bringing you home."

Terraclon was startled, but then tentatively she felt him place his hands on her back. The crowd went silent—shocked by the sight of their fair-skinned monarch hugging a man as dark as wet earth.

"We'll end these wars, no matter what it takes," he shouted into her ear. "I promise you that, Polly."

The two pulled apart, then raised their joined

hands, dark and light, and the crowd erupted into the loudest cheers yet. Polexima stepped up to the cone.

"Bee-Jorites," she said. "Go now and enjoy this day of well-deserved rest. But understand that we can never rest in our defense. Starting tomorrow, we must extend these higher walls, excavate deeper trenches, and rebuild watchtowers all along our border. If our neighbors will not stop warring, then we must stop their wars. If our neighbors . . ."

The crowd was murmuring, looking up as a single locust came flying from the South and circled the monument. Polexima turned to Terraclon, who looked as surprised as she was. A banner of Bee-Jor unfurled from the rider's hand before the locust made a sudden drop. "Look out!" Terraclon shouted, and those atop the pyramid scrambled to get out of the locust's landing.

The locust missed the platform but landed on its edge, clutching the structure's side for a vertical halt. The riders detached themselves from the saddle, clumsily pulling themselves up to the platform with the help of the priestesses. Polexima gasped when she saw the pilot's face. "Nuvao!" she shouted, her knees buckling with relief. "You're all right!"

"I am, Mother," said her son, alarm in his voice. "But I must speak with you and Terraclon at once."

"Bee-Jorites—go to your rest and prepare your evening feasts," Polexima shouted to the crowd. "May Cricket bless your night."

As the crowd dispersed, Polexima looked at her son's companion, a stout eunuch with a shaved head in traveling robes of brown silk. The man looked ill with flight sickness or panic or both. "Your Majesty," said the man, stumbling as he bowed. "We are not acquainted. I am Brother Moonsinger."

"What's wrong?" Polexima asked her son.

Nuvao looked in his mother's eyes and tried to speak but the words were caught in his chest.

"Speak, son," said Polexima. "What's happened?"

He shook his head, cleared his throat, then banged a fist on his sternum. But still no words would come.

Brother Moonsinger winced, then met the eyes of the queen. "Majesty, we have . . . we have lost Palzhad."

"Lost Palzhad? What?"

"It has been overwhelmed with refugees from Hulkren."

"How?" Polexima asked, but a moment later she had answered her own question. "Trellana!" she whispered through gritted teeth.

"How did they get in?" Terraclon asked Nuvao.

"The Yellow Mold has taken over Palzhad. While we were at war with Volokop, there was no one but children riding on some sickly ants to defend the southern border. Trellana failed in her duties. I want to say it was neglect but . . ."

"It was more likely malice," said Polexima.

"Where is she now?" Terraclon asked.

"She should be on her way back to Palzhad from

Venaris," said Nuvao. "Now that the battle is over, all royal woman should be on their way home. And Pious Dolgeeno will be on his way here."

"I should never have approved of Trellana attending this rite for the Nun Queen," said Polexima.

"You did the right thing, Mother," said Nuvao. "It got all the sorceress queens to the West, safe from the Seed Eaters if their invasion had succeeded. The important thing is, what do we do now?"

"I suppose the first thing is to find Trellana's sled and inform her that she can't return to Palzhad," said Polexima as she slumped with grief and fatigue. "I am sorry. I must have some sleep. I cannot think until I have."

CHAPTER 4

BED SHARING

"How many days has it been, Pious?" Trellana asked Dolgeeno. They had stopped again and were savoring a rest on the floor in the tunnel leading west.

"Only three," said Dolgeeno, "though it feels like many more."

Trellana sat on the rough floor and fidgeted with the stacks of bracelets that irritated her arms and then readjusted the cumbersome necklaces that chafed her chest. She was tired of carrying a torch, tired of her burden, tired of the darkness.

Tired.

"How much farther have we got to go?" she asked as she readjusted the rings on her toes that made them sweat and itch. The priest lifted his fungus torch and squinted to read the figures scratched into a wall marker.

"Thirty thousand human steps. At least a day's journey," he said. "But in twenty-two thousand steps, we should reach a tunnel connected to one of Mound Fecklebretz. And there we should find some lovely, sturdy riding ants to carry us the rest of the way."

"Did you hear that?" Trellana shouted to the hundreds of women and girls behind her as they moaned from their aches and blisters. "Daughters of Ant Queen, soon we shall have some saddled ants to ride to Fecklebretz, a gracious mound free of offensive heresies, a place where we will commence our holy war on the traitorous East! Arise, queens and princesses! Focus on your duties to the gods, and soon your feet will *fly* us there."

Trellana sucked some kwondle tea from her pouch and struggled to her feet. "Onward," said Dolgeeno as he stood and took a step. The women behind him followed, clattering with jewelry as they resumed their slog. Trellana looked at the first of five rings under the knuckle of her pinky and smiled; it was a betrothal present sent by Maleps before he had arrived for their wedding. *Maleps, my husband. Soon I shall see your handsomest face, and soon I will feel your warm body over mine, crushing me with your desire.*

Farther along, Trellana smelled the odor of leaf-cutter ants. She heard the faint scuttle of their claws as well as the distant murmuring and steps of humans. At last, they had reached the junction of an active tunnel to Mound Fecklebretz. In the cross tunnel, she saw bobbing torches as clusters of laborers from deep below the mound walked their way up and to home. Strangely, most of them were women, but sprinkled among them were a few old men as well as children. All of them paused in shock when the noblewomen of Bee-Jor crowded into their tunnel wearing jewelry in such a profusion that it concealed their bodies. The laborers lowered their heads, not daring to look openly on their superiors, and waited for them to pass. Trellana smiled at that.

These good laborers know their place!

From the left, they heard men making the hissing sounds of a mantis and turned to see a procession led by the mound's high priest. Twelve lower priests were dressed in the deep green evening robes of Mantis worship. Acolytes walked at their sides, holding up a lamp of a hollowed mantis head stuffed with glow-fungus. The priests stopped before Dolgeeno and made the sign of the war goddess with a twitch of their heads and an outward clawing.

"Pious Dolgeeno," said the high priest, and nodded.

"Pious Tellenteeno," said Dolgeeno. "You are very kind to meet us."

"Why have you not arrived on antback?" blurted Trellana, immediately regretting her rudeness. She looked over at a short parade of small, low ants heading downward with leaf shards for the mushroom farms as they avoided the clog by crawling across the ceiling.

"Queen Trellana, I presume," said Tellenteeno with a short bow and a cock of his head. Under the lamp, Trellana saw that Fecklebretz's highest priest was a typical-looking cleric with a fleshy body and face, but he had a strangely long and pointy chin that curved upward like the end of a crescent moon.

"Forgive me, Pious Tellenteeno. You presume correctly," she said with a curtsy. "Why have you walked here? We are most exhausted and would appreciate to ride on some carrying ants."

"We are at war again, Majesty, with the Carpenter people. All our ridable ants have gone to the frontier as well as most of our men—men from every caste including the laborers."

Trellana and Dolgeeno looked at each other.

"Laborers as soldiers. Very interesting, Pious," said Trellana. "That sounds like a . . . like a *Dranverish* way."

"It is a Slopeish way now."

"I see. And. . . . King Maleps. Have you any news of him?"

Tellenteeno was silent and then sniffed and blinked.

"His Majesty Maleps is here."

Trellana's jaw dropped and the weight of her burden vanished.

"Maleps is here?" she said, her breathing getting rapid. "Does he know I am coming?"

"Of course, Majesty. He is quite aware. However . . ." He paused again and it made Trellana hate him.

"Yes?"

"He is . . . he is not completely well. Injured in a recent battle where he fought, most bravely, near Teffelan, at the border. He is convalescing with the other wounded in the queen's palace. We shall take you to him, but first, Queen Fewlenray is eager to welcome you and the other royal women of the Lost Country."

"We are eager to see Her Majesty as well."

Trellana's heart fluttered inside her. *Maleps is injured? How?* She shuddered as she imagined the handsomest face on all the Sand being crushed to a bloody pulp with a Carpenter battle mace.

The walk up to the queen's palace seemed longer than the trek from Venaris. When the tunnel reached the base of the mound's central spiral, Trellana looked up at the bright opening between the four palaces. The climb upward, bearing loads of gold, was going to be a grueling challenge without an ant to ride—but at last she was near her husband!

As the royals ascended upward, a stream of laborers leaving work for the day filled the spiral and slowed them even as the laborers backed against the walls to let the royals pass. The laborers seemed frightened by the clatter of the jewelry, a noise similar to the screeching of summer cicadas as it reverberated in the dome. When Trellana and Dolgeeno finally reached the portal to the queen's palace, they were welcomed by over a hundred priests and servant women. The servants offered them cones of watered-down sap wine and then helped the royals to shed their burdens. The priests collected and cataloged the jewelry, then wrapped and boxed it before packing it into sled-bins. Once the jewelry was accounted for, the senior chambermaid curtsied to Trellana, then pulled back the diaphragm of the portal that led to the Great Reception Hall.

After the heavy gold and cumbersome gems were taken from her, Trellana had the mild sensation that her shoulders were floating away like a fluffy thistle seed on a summer day. She looked around the high-ceilinged hall as servants set torches in their sconces. This hall was more beautiful than her own in Cajoria. The lights slowly revealed walls covered with intricate scratch murals of green slate that depicted the gods and their pastimes. Between the murals she saw Fecklebretz's fabled and ancient tapestries of spider silk. These illustrated the victory of the Chosen Fathers over the cricket-herding savages who had dwelled in The Ignorance.

Too exhausted to do what was proper, the royal women disregarded the chairs and divans and fell to the carpets to lie down and sleep. Only Trellana was wide-awake and standing, her excitement turned to anxiety as the words "Maleps is injured" ricocheted in her head like a flea caught in a box trap. Dolgeeno looked at her, tilting his head and exaggerating a pout. "I am praying for him," he said.

"As am I," said Trellana, then gritted her teeth to stop her chin from trembling.

Atop of the thrones' platform, a sad and single thorn trumpet sounded some weak notes as it announced Queen Fewlenray. Trellana remembered her as the most alluring of all the princesses at the spring cotillions, a girl she both admired and envied so many seasons ago. At the moment Fewlenray was little more than a shadow rising from her throne at the top of the 127 stairs. As the queen made a slow, noiseless descent, Trellana wondered why she was making such a drawn-out entrance. As she came closer, Trellana saw she was wearing a simple chamber robe of flowing yellow gauze with a girdle that cinched her tiny waist. She wore a jacket of purple silk tied as a shawl over her shoulders—very informal—and her shining hair was not lacquered into an upright sculpture but was left to fall across her back and over her shoulders. When she reached the bottom step, she raised up her chin to expose and extend a long and elegant neck.

Fewlenray had become an astonishingly beautiful woman and somehow her lack of adornments made her more so. Trellana was shocked into wordlessness as she acknowledged an envy that was becoming a torture. A moment later, Trellana felt a growing annoyance. *She knew I was coming. This lack of effort in her appearance is disrespectful!*

Pious Dolgeeno tapped his staff on the quartz floor and the exhausted women roused each other from a deep sleep to stand and greet their fellow royal with waves of wobbly curtsies.

"Sisters, cousins, and aunts, welcome to Mound Fecklebretz," Fewlenray said in her clear and lovely voice. "I had not expected so many of you but I . . . I am overjoyed that you have all arrived safely." Her last words seemed brittle with sadness or regret or dread . . . Trellana wasn't sure. The queen looked over at Trellana and sensed the judgment on her clothing and hair. "Please, noblewomen," she said as she ran her fingers through the glossy fall of her golden tresses. "Forgive my informal appearance at your welcoming, but even our hairdressers and dressmakers have gone to war."

Hairdressers and dressmakers at war? Ridiculous! What would they fight with? Hair shears and sewing needles?

"Please, Cousin Fewlenray. You have no need to apologize," Trellana said through a forced smile as she fingered the simple pocket-covered shift she had worn to carry jewelry. "Consider *our* appearance, after a long journey on foot through the filthiest of tunnels. We apologize that we have arrived with so little."

"Not at all, Cousin Trellana. You have arrived with everything. We are most indebted to you for rescuing the National Treasury."

The servant women returned and lined up along the walls with trays of sleeping garments and other service items.

"Highnesses and Majesties, our good servants will lead you to a bedchamber where you will find some simple food and drink, as well as a little holy water and a bit of soap root for a quick scrub. I understand that you are all quite exhausted so I will bid you good night and the blessings of the gods."

As the servants led Bee-Jor's royal women to the eastern hall and the guest chambers, Dolgeeno and Trellana stepped closer to Fewlenray. She stood on the bottom stair and looked lost in thought, her head dipping, as if it were too heavy for the delicate stalk of her neck. Her entrancing eyes were so big and beautiful that when she blinked, her lids were like the slow flapping of a butterfly. Trellana envied the woman's full mouth even as it pouted.

"I am sorry," said Fewlenray, meeting their eyes again. "One is so easily distracted these days."

"Yes," said Trellana. "But these days will come to an end. The Slope will be reunited and renewed. I have seen it."

Fewlenray looked doubtful as she met Trellana's eyes and then turned to Dolgeeno. "Your Holiness, our Good Queen Trellana has led the other royals here because she has received a message from the gods. This is . . . unusual for a woman."

"Yes, but she is a *royal* woman and, like you, a

direct descendant of Ant Queen," said Dolgeeno. "It would not be the first time a goddess has chosen to speak through a prophetess."

"Ant Queen came to me in the company of Mantis," Trellana said, "in a vision that was as clear and real as you are before me."

Fewlenray's head gently bobbed from side to side, politely suggesting her doubts about Trellana's prophecies. "I pray it is so," she said. She was quiet for a moment and then sadly smiled. "Forgive me. You must be eager to see Maleps."

She hesitates! What's happened to him?

"Well, yes, cousin. I suppose I would like to see him."

Fewlenray's eyebrow lifted before she cocked her head and looked at Trellana with an expression both condescending and pitying.

"Fewlenray. Please. Tell me what's wrong."

"Everything is wrong. This way, please, you will see," Fewlenray said, leading them to the western hall. "I am afraid we are without men to carry us in litters so we shall all have to walk."

A hundred questions crowded Trellana's head but none could find their way to her mouth as they walked the long curve of the western corridor towards the ballroom. She was about to speak when she heard the sounds of men moaning in pain or crying for help or drink. Some shouted nonsense or the worst obscenities. When they reached the ballroom's open portal, Fewlenray stopped and looked in.

Trellana and Dolgeeno stood with her and looked down the flight of steps to the floor covered with thousands of wounded. Most were officers whose armor and weapons were piled beside them in a barely lit darkness.

"Is . . . is Maleps down there? Left on that floor?"

Fewlenray shook her head and gave Trellana a dismissive look. Fewlenray was muttering to herself when she made the sign of Grasshopper by setting thumbs to her cheeks and pointing out fingers. Trellana realized she was praying for the wounded.

"Mercies of Grasshopper upon these men," Dolgeeno said, following Fewlenray's lead and making the sign of the invoked god. Trellana joined them in their prayer but was impatient and broke away in hopes that they would hurry down the corridor after her.

Fewlenray left the ballroom portal and led them with short and delicate steps—*so irritating!*—to the antechamber of a grand, multiroom apartment. The servants sat in chairs weaving and knitting around a cluster of shriveling glow-fungus while others made repairs to gowns or scraped and scrubbed at stains on boots. When the servants caught sight of Trellana and Fewlenray, they stood and bowed to the queens and then knelt to Dolgeeno for his blessing. Once he had muttered a few words, they opened the shutters to reveal a spacious, well-lit bedchamber with rich furnishings. Trellana saw the backs of soldiers standing at the bedside of a man whose voice she recognized all too well, a voice that filled her with a thrilling warmth.

"Maleps," Fewlenray called quietly. "Pardon the interruption, but she is here. Queen Trellana of Palzhad, with His Ultimate Pious Dolgeeno, bravely escaped from the Lost Country."

The soldiers stepped aside. At last, Trellana saw him. Maleps was alert and sitting up in bed with a map on his lap. He was still her perfect Maleps, as bright and handsome as the rising moon. Trellana restrained herself from running to him but opened her arms to fall on his chest when he put up a hand to stop her.

"Trellana! Please! I'm afraid you can't hug me."

He lifted up his simple garment of egg-cloth to show her the stitched wound in his side. It looked to be healing. She was so relieved, having expected much worse, that joyful tears filled her eyes. "Just what's happened to you?" she asked with a tremble in her voice as she brushed his hair with her fingers.

"I was gored by one of their awful tridents," Maleps said. "But I was only pierced with one tine. It did break a rib, I'm afraid, but it could have been worse. I thank the gods that I am not dead yet."

Trellana caught herself shaking and gripped her own hands to steady herself. "Oh, Maleps. It is so *very* good to see you."

"And you as well, Trellana," he said, smoothing his hair back into place.

She turned to Fewlenray and Dolgeeno, hoping that they would give her some privacy, but they stood nearby, intent on witnessing their conversation. When Trellana looked back at Maleps, she caught him eyeing her belly and her breasts.

"Trellana, the rumors are true. You are . . ."

"With child. Yes. With children actually."

"I am so terribly sorry," he said, and looked away. As he grimaced and pinched his nose, Trellana was sure he was more disgusted than sorrowful.

"As am I, darling," said Trellana. "But now that I am back on holy ground there are ways of taking care of it."

"Yes, I suppose there are."

"Maleps," she said, smiling through her tears. "They have all come here, every queen and princess of the Lost Country—every sorceress with the power."

"All of them?" he asked, astonished. He quickly sat up, but then grabbed his side in pain.

"Not a royal woman or girl is left who can stop the Yellow Mold. Well, just one—my ridiculous mother, who will be overwhelmed if she attempts to protect even more than one mound. And when the Bee-Jorites' mounds implode and all their ants are dead, then we will strike."

Maleps shook his head as sweat burst on his upper lip.

"Trellana, once the East is weakened, what's to stop the Seed Eaters from taking it?"

"Nothing. The Seed Eaters are already on the march, doing just that while the Lost Country recovers from its war with Hulkren. As far as I know, Volokop has already conquered Cajoria and exterminated its inhabitants. When we're ready, we'll chase the Seed Eaters back to the Barley Lands and then reclaim every last mound of the Slope."

Maleps dropped his head in his palm.

"My dear Trellana . . ."

"What?"

"You *are* aware that we are at war with the Carpenter Nation."

"Of course I am."

"Perhaps you are not aware that it is *not* going well."

Trellana jerked her head up. "We have heard it was going *quite* well. We've been told the Slope is well armed and using Hulkrish missiles to destroy the war beetles and their riders."

"No, Trellana. It is the Carpenters who have gathered up Hulkrish weapons and launched them at us. These missiles have targeted every war ant and sent them flying onto their backs as corpses. They're using arrows with black-glass heads that pierce through our shields and armor."

Trellana blinked. "But we have heard you are fighting in the Dranverish way. With the same methods they used to defeat the Hulkrites."

"We are fighting on foot, yes, since most of our ants are dead or unridable. But we are not fighting the Hulkrites. The Dranverite and his army repelled the ghost ants with some roach potion on their shields, but the Carpenters ride on *beetles* and both are only emboldened now. At a certain point, our war ants were able to overwhelm the beetles and chew off their antennae to immobilize them. The ants we have now are so young and small they're useless— they're just a morsel for the beetles, who puncture their heads and then suck out their brains. After the beetles are done with our ants, they trample over them to attack *us*."

"But the Beetle Riders have never won a war against us! The Carpenters are primitives!"

"They *have* won battles if not wars and they have already absorbed Gagumji and several of our border mounds. For one thing, *their* army wasn't wiped out by a war with Hulkren. And their army has increased somehow—they've enlisted some bizarre-looking mercenaries with dingy skin and fuzz-covered armor who attack us day and night . . . and eat our dead!"

Maleps threw off the blanket and sat at the edge of the bed, energized and irritated.

"This is a different kind of conflict, Trellana. Now we fight in trenches, we ambush, and we hide at the tops of shrubs to shoot down arrows—things we would have thought cowardly. Sometimes, at night, we attack them in their camps before they can do it to us. Once we outnumbered them. Now, they overwhelm us."

"But you *will* defeat them," Trellana said. "I have seen it."

Maleps was silent and looked at her with scorn before he turned to Dolgeeno.

"Pious Dolgeeno, are you encouraging this?"

"I beg your pardon, Majesty," Dolgeeno shouted. "Just what would I be encouraging?"

"Trellana's aspiration—to prophecy."

Dolgeeno raised up his chin. "Trellana has not aspired to prophecy. Ant Queen and Mantis selected her to reveal Their word. I have confirmed this in my own conversations with the gods."

"Really," said Maleps, his voice sharpening. "And did not his Ultimate Pious Dolgeeno receive the prophecy that we would defeat the Hulkrites?"

Dolgeeno was silent. Trellana looked at him as his eyes shifted left and right before they settled on Maleps's face.

"If I may correct you, King Maleps," Dolgeeno said, his voice loudening with each word. "The words of the gods I related proved true. They predicted the defeat of the Hulkrites. What they did *not* predict was a *Slopeish* victory."

Silence crashed in the chamber. Maleps eyed the priest with open contempt, then stood as if to strike him. Fewlenray stepped in front of Maleps and clasped his arm. "Please sit, Maleps, we don't want you breaking your stitches again," she warned him. "I am sure Pious Dolgeeno meant no offense."

Maleps fumed as he sat, staring under hooded lids at the priest.

"Very well. I am not inclined to blaspheme or to challenge my priest even as he just resided in *Bee-Jor*," mocked Maleps. He looked at Trellana in a way she had never seen—was that contempt, a sneer, on his face?

"Trellana, it suddenly occurred to me that when the Dranverite learns of your whereabouts he may attack this mound to retrieve you."

He glared at her in a hateful silence. She could find no words. "We will talk in the morning, before I leave," he said.

"Leave? Where are you going?" Trellana asked, trying to hide the alarm in her voice.

"Back to the war, of course. We've rustled some speed ants from your *Bee-Jor* to take us to the front."

"But you are still recovering!"

"This war will not wait for my full recovery—this war that your prophecy says we will win."

In dismay, Fewlenray shook her head and then clapped her hands for the servants, who reopened the shutters. They had been all too quiet and looked in shame at the floor; it betrayed that they had been eavesdropping. "Sametta," she said to the eldest servant. "Please show Queen Trellana to the chamber you prepared for her."

"I would rather sleep here," said Trellana. "With my husband."

Fewlenray and Maleps were quiet after they looked briefly at each other. Maleps turned to Trellana to speak but then drew back his breath. "Trellana, darling," he finally said. "I hesitate to say this in such bold terms, but . . . you are pregnant with the children of a Dranverite."

"Yes?"

"Then our marriage must be annulled. It *is* annulled. Isn't it, Pious?"

"No!" Trellana said, and felt like a hornet had flown down her throat to choke her. "I am here, escaped from the disgrace of the Lost Country," she gasped. "We can rip these half-breeds out of my womb before they get any larger."

"Your womb is polluted, Trellana," said Maleps. "It is forever desecrated by the seeds and spawn of a Dranverite. And there are rumors that this Vof Quegdoth is worse than that. Some say he is a mongrel raised in Cajoria's midden, the son of a roach-woman and some toothless outcaste. They say he is a boy that was captured from your Fission Trek and converted to the Dranverites' cause. Is this true? If you entered into this willingly with him, then the punishment is death by bathing."

The hornet in Trellana had stung her heart and was pumping a venomous stream of anger, then shame, as she acknowledged that everything Maleps had said was true. The hornet was eating her from the inside out when she realized just how stupid she had been. She looked in Maleps's eyes and then those of Fewlenray when she realized the most painful thing yet.

"Fewlenray. I believe you are sharing my husband's bed."

"No, Trellana," she said. "He is sharing *my* bed."

"How could you?" Trellana shouted.

"How could I not? I had to, cousin. Like nearly all our kings and princes, my husband fell to the Hulkrites' ghost ants. Maleps is one of the few kings to survive who is still able to . . . to pass on the seeds of royal lineage. It is only happenstance that we love each other. That is unusual in a royal marriage."

"Happenstance . . . unusual," whispered Trellana as the two of them seemed so far away, as if their bed were floating downstream.

"We know that in time you will come to accept this," said Maleps. "And you will be happy to attend our wedding. And my coronation as king of Fecklebretz—if this war ever ends."

"Happy? To attend?" Trellana whispered.

"Yes. If you really love me you will be happy for us. For however long we have."

Trellana felt as if her insides had been pushed off the edge of the world to fall forever.

I am ruined for all time by Anand the Roach Boy, she thought as she fought the urge to run away and twist a dagger into her heart. A moment later she scolded herself.

Not the dagger yet, Trellana. Not until you have ruined Anand.

CHAPTER 5

THAT STUPID NAME AGAIN

Anand worried as he paced in the cage—had Daveena died of starvation or torture? Had Bee-Jor fallen? Walking made him tired, which made him sleep more, and sleep was that place where he could dream—and it was in dreams where he could see again. Often enough, the dreams were nightmares. Sometimes he dreamt of flying over Cajoria to see it taken over by Seed Eaters whose harvester ants carried out the corpses of his father and Terraclon and then Polexima along with thousands of others. With each passing day in the cell, his dread increased that he would never regain his sight.

"Give me back my eyes!" he shouted at Madricanth

while crawling on his knees. He worried that Hulkro, the blind Termite God, had taken His revenge and cursed him forever.

Once, when the Stink Ant people gathered outside the cage and noisily discussed him, he ran to the bars and spat at them. "Yes, I'm a caged, blind freak!" he shouted. "And it's contagious! Get away!" He heard their laughter and retreated when he felt them spitting back.

Blindness had always been one of Anand's fears and whenever he saw the blind it induced a crippling pity. At Cajoria, there were no blind ones; anyone who lost his sight was considered cursed and useless and was stripped of kin-scent. Among the Britasytes, the blind were taken care of. Those who had been born without sight were often good musicians and had cheery dispositions. Those who had once had sight seemed haunted to him and full of longing. He remembered, all too well, his great-aunt Wabiba and the white centers over her pupils that she said "had turned everything to blurry shadows." She spent her old age grating grains as she sang to herself, always grateful when anyone would sit nearby to fill her ears with words. Anand recollected his great-aunt's fingers probing his face to feel how much he had grown and changed. "You are quite handsome," she would say as she gauged the shape of his nose and cheeks, the height of his forehead, and the shape of his hairline. Anand was always fascinated by Wabiba's own nose, which quivered as she identified odors that were imperceptible to most. "You have eaten a fruit fly," she told him once, "about two days ago, one that gorged on a rotting prickle fruit."

"Yes," he said. "You can smell that?"

"It's coming from your skin. And there's a bit of it on your tunic. Oh . . . and you've discovered the pleasures of your man stalk."

Now Anand had become like her, sniffing the air to identify vague scents and desperate for breezes that brought a whiff of lake water, or some sprouting grass, or a shoot of green onion. Eastern breezes brought the smells of slaughtered insects and fishes from the villagers' kitchen. Often enough, there was the odor of Stink Ants, responding to predators in the distance. The best time of his captivity was before, during, and after a rain. As the water level rose on the cage's floor, Anand had to climb on the wooden table where his food was set to use it as a raft. The best smell was of the sharp perfume that followed lightning and thunder, and after that, the smell of rain as it dampened the earth—a scent both fresh and musky, one that made him feel like a nursing baby. After the rain there was the sweet scent of fresh mud, odors that triggered erotic memories and longings for Daveena. Later there were a variety of stenches—rots, molds, slimes, and then the musty smell of burgeoning mushrooms, which brought him back to the misery of the midden. The smell of death cap mushrooms would fill the air, a slightly unpleasant odor that reminded him of the Dranverites' cleaning solutions and their immaculate and comfortable homes.

Today was a blander, odorless day of little wind and the boredom was a torment. As he marched in a circle, he saw the dark blur of the bars alternating with bright blurs of sunlight when he heard the murmur of the villagers' voices as they came near. They were louder this day, seemed more excited, and as they walked towards him, he saw blurs of redness. As the redness got closer, he heard unfamiliar voices and a snippet of what might have been Dranverish. Some people were arguing, maybe haggling, and something of a shoving match broke out before a woman, shouting with all her force, led the red blurs away.

A moment later, after some softer shouting, the red blurs returned. Anand heard the soft clink of mineral chips as they were counted or perused for flaws and then dropped into a basket. Soon after, he heard the swish of ropes being untied and the gate being opened. The red blurs were coming inside the cage and he smelled what might have been roach-scent.

A woman was talking to him, in the tongue of the Stink Ant people. Anand shook his head as his heart pounded in excitement.

"Are you roach people?" he asked them, but

they were quiet. "Are you Dranverites?" he asked in Dranverish.

"We are," said the woman. "And we have come here to buy your freedom. What is your name? Where are you from?"

Anand hesitated. "My name is Anand, son of Yormu and Corra. I am a son of the Slope and a son of the wandering Britasyte tribe as well as a citizen and defender of the Collective Nations of Dranveria."

The Dranverites were silent.

"You also go by some other names," said the woman. "One of them is Lick-My-Testicles."

Anand was quiet.

Shit.

"As well as Commander General Vof Quegdoth of Dranveria," she continued. "But that is a rank you did not achieve in your short time as a defender in our collective. I believe you may also be known as the Son of Locust. And lately, as the God-King of Bee-Jor."

Anand felt a mix of relief and dread. "I know nothing of you, Good Citizen. Yet you know so much about me."

"We all know about *you*, young man. Your adventures are famous—or infamous recently. I am Captain Kessenloo, an officer in the Humanitarian Water Force. We assumed you were a refugee of some southern conflict or an escaped slave and we bartered for your release. We have gotten far more than we bargained for."

"Why have the Stink Ant people kept me alive?"

"They learned long ago that we pay nothing for human meat. They learned that we pay a great deal for living human beings."

"I will repay you when I have the chance. Thank you."

"Don't thank me. You are under arrest, Anand-shmi. Will you come peaceably or do we need to cuff you?"

"I am blind, Captain," Anand assured. "And fairly helpless. Please send a message to the City of Peace. Tell the People's Voice that I need her help, that millions of lives are threatened."

"Tell her yourself when you get there," said Kessenloo. "But we've heard it was you, Commander General Quegdoth, who threatened the lives of millions."

"Please. Return me to Bee-Jor. I swear that if I don't return home we will be crushed by Emperor Volokop and the warriors of the Barley Empire."

"You should be worried for yourself, Anand-shmi, and not so much for them."

"Is there something you know?"

"From what we can gather, it appears your new nation of Bee-Jor has survived an attack. Or at least its ants and people are thriving."

Anand shook with relief as his breath caught in his throat. Someone, a man from the smell of him, took his arm, firmly, and led him out of the cage.

"Where are you taking me?" he asked

"To a bathtub. As quickly as possible. You reek!"

"And after that?"

"No more questions. Get walking, prisoner."

They beat back the Seed Eaters! But how? Was it you, Terraclon?

CHAPTER 6

THE FORGOTTEN GUEST

Terraclon was flying above Mound Shishto when he spotted the royal sand-sled heading south towards Cajoria with Polexima and Nuvao in its cabin. Against Polexima's wishes, Terraclon had insisted she travel in the sled to rest and recover as opposed to riding on a saddled insect. He was relieved to see she had listened as he veered west under the beaming sunlight to see the aftermath of the battle.

All along the border, the Bee-Jorites were gathering and butchering an unimaginable bounty of harvester ants that they could feast on for moons—if they could find enough vinegar for pickling. The stench rising up to Terraclon's nose was even more problematic as it was the smell of thousands of human corpses. As he had ordered, all dead Seed Eaters were to be removed from Bee-Jor's middens and hauled to the top of the border wall to be dumped in the neutral strip. "In hopes of peace, we must give back the bodies," Terraclon had ordered. He remembered the confused looks on the people's faces but, nevertheless, they listened.

He wondered if the stories of the Barley people's burial rituals were true, that they bury their dead with a seed set on their chests as a payment for entry to their underworld—seeds whose roots would pierce their corpses to use them as nourishment. At the moment, all the corpses lay on the neutral strip where their stink had drawn a mass of hungry blowflies, flesh-flies, and winter gnats, which in turn had attracted the insects that preyed upon them, the rove and carrion beetles.

When Terraclon landed at the airfield in Cajoria, he nodded politely and gave cursory blessings to the locust breeders and groundskeepers who were cheering him. Pilots from all over Bee-Jor, too exhausted to fly home, were leaving makeshift lean-tos to join in an applause of grateful admiration. As his pilot led the locust they had been flying to food and water, Terraclon forced himself to smile, even as his mind was muddled with worries.

Yormu! he thought. *Anand would want me to check on his father.*

But after I first check on Pleckoo. Pleckoo!

And then what about Anand himself? Anand!

And Daveena!

Just how am I to get Anand and Daveena out of the Barley Lands?

Terraclon ran towards the parade of leaf-cutter ants as they made their way up the main artery when suddenly he realized he was something of a spectacle: a man dressed as a warrior-priest running to ride on an unsaddled ant. All around him were returning defenders from the People's Army on foot or on antback, lugging home battle trophies, which included the fresh corpses of harvester ants. Most defenders were headed up to their new homes in the higher rings, the ones they had been awarded, but he saw a smaller group of thickset men walking towards him on their way back to the midden. Terraclon held his breath and felt his blood turn to mud when he realized it was Keel and all of his unsightly sons. They were dragging travoises full of foreign swords, bows, and daggers as well as some abdomens of harvester ants full of their sweet, rich seed-pudding. In the last travois was Tal, either asleep or drunk, being hauled by his brother Dumbree. The right side of Tal's face was a bloody mess tied with a rag—had he lost an eye?

"Well, hello, little sugar moth," said Keel. "You did well for yourself in this little war. But don't the Seed Eaters always lose?"

"Not always, Keel. From now on you will address me as Pious Terraclon."

"Well, certainly," said Keel, and curtsied. "But it's

Defender Keel. We helped you win this war, Your Sacredness, and earned ourselves a comfy house up the mound. I mean, you being our cousin from the midden and all, you wouldn't forgets us now . . . right?"

Terraclon stared at Keel as he batted his eyelashes and stuck out his rump. For the first time in his life, Terraclon walked towards Keel without deference, without fear, and got into his face.

"Keel, if you ever curtsy to me again, I will rip something from between your legs and crush it under my boot. You'll spend the rest of your life squatting when you piss."

Keel was silent a moment, startled, and stepped back. He looked around and saw that other defenders had stopped to watch, were anticipating a spectacle. His sons looked at him with sideways glares, awaiting his response.

"Aww, Pious Terraclon," Keel finally said, feigning astonishment as he clutched his age chits. "How touching of you to think of my prick. Of course, I'm sure it's not the first time. But you'd never do any bodily harm to me or my sons, now would you? You'd be violating at least one of the Eight Laws."

"Get back to the midden and leave my sight."

"Of course. We always follow orders, Your Divinity," said Keel, turning away. "Oh, and Pious Terraclon," he called, looking back at Terraclon, his lips disappearing as he grinned. "Could we get your blessing before we head home?"

Terraclon glared at Keel. "Blessings of all the gods—upon you and yours," said Terraclon through a tightened mouth. "May they make you wise and decent and . . . inoffensive." He walked away from Keel to antennate a leaf-cutter on the trunk trail going up. As Terraclon climbed up its mandible and crawled over its head to seat himself, he realized he was wide-awake again.

Anger is much better than a chaw of kwondle as a means of staying alert.

Terraclon counted nine circles of dwelling rings before he slipped off the ant and walked to the weedy dew station of the grout worker caste where Pleckoo waited in a cage. Before the battle, Terraclon had ordered the cage, which had disgusted him and Polexima with its thick and stinking crust, to be cleaned. He saw his directions had been followed, but a gathering of boys was around the cage with crude, homemade spears that they were thrusting, downward, as they shrieked in excitement. Why were they stabbing at Pleckoo? He should have been wrapped in ropes, bound to the insides of the cage's bars, not fallen on the floor.

"Stand back," Terraclon shouted. "Drop those spears! No one is to harm the prisoner, by order of Vof Quegdoth!"

The boys pulled aside to reveal a limp, heaving man curled into a ball on the cage's floor. Terraclon's heart stopped when he saw that it wasn't Pleckoo, and the shock of it made him stagger.

"Good gods!" he shouted. "What's happened here?" He grabbed the closest of the boys near him, a tall one with a fuzzy mustache, and shook him by the shoulders. "Where's Pleckoo? Where is he?"

Stunned, the boy's mouth quivered and his legs fell out from under him. Terraclon pulled the boy up from the front of his tunic and slapped him, back and forth, until his nose and lips were bleeding. "That is not Pleckoo in the cage!" Terraclon shouted, his rage exploding with a heat that scorched his face from the inside.

"Please, Pious Terraclon," said a younger boy, coming up from behind. "Don't hurt my brother! He did what he thought was right."

Terraclon dropped the boy in his hands and turned to the younger one.

"What's happened here? Speak!"

"That man in the cage, he . . ."

"That man is Honored Defender Yormu, a veteran of the Hulkrish war, and you will address him as such!"

"But he can't be, Pious. That man freed Pleckoo!"

Terraclon glared at the boys before speaking.

"Did you *see* him free Pleckoo?"

"No, Pious. But before we got here, he killed the last guard, the little gimpy one, who couldn't go to the war. Pleckoo was gone and the cage was open.

We captured this traitor . . . this . . . Defender Yormu, who was nearby."

Terraclon looked down at Yormu and saw bloody punctures all over his body and blood-soaked cloth-ing. He seemed to be breathing but his face was a knot of pain.

"We did what we thought was right, Pious," said the older boy, finally gaining enough courage to speak. "We put him in this cage to await his judgment."

"Run home, as if the lives of your mothers depend on it, then run back here with a travois, a mattress, and some blankets. All of you are going to port De-fender Yormu up to the queen's palace as quickly and as smoothly as you can," Terraclon ordered.

Terraclon took out his dagger and stabbed with fury at the knots that locked the cage's gate. Once inside, he fell on his knees before Yormu and swept back the hair that covered his face—a face with scars that had been scarred again.

"I'm so sorry, Yormu," Terraclon whispered as he looked at Yormu's scattered belongings outside the cage, including his battle gear. "So very, very sorry. I see what you wanted to do—you left your bed to fight the Seed Eaters. We won the battle, Yormu. We're all right for now. I'll get you back to where you're safe and summon the best healers in Bee-Jor."

The moon was high and white by the time Yormu was returned to Anand's chamber. Terraclon picked Yormu up from the travois and gingerly set him on the bed with its view down the mound's main artery through the quartz window. Teas and potions had already arrived as well as Cajoria's healing priest, Pious Uppacharo, who wore the robe of a molting grasshopper instar. His sub-priests mumbled prayers to Grasshopper and Butterfly as they spread a fragrant powder of pine resin to lure the interest of the gods. Next was Mulga, the freckle-faced chambermaid, with a tray of prechewed foods. The sub-priests got to work painting Yormu's wounds with a styptic as the healer scraped lotion from a clay jar with an etching of a moon flower. Terraclon gasped.

"That's a moon flower—the blossom of the datura!" he said to Uppacharo, who went from looking irritated to deeply annoyed.

"It is, and there's just a tincture of it in some bee fat. It's a topical that will lessen his pain."

"I . . . I see. Proceed, then."

"No, Pious Terraclon. I will not."

"Why not?"

"I know this is the New Way. But I am not comfortable working salve into the open wounds of an untouchable from the midden."

"Give it to me," Terraclon said, scooping it up with his fingers.

"That's way too much! Wipe your hands, immediately!"

Terraclon felt a numbing of his fingers as a cloth was thrown at him to clean his hands.

"Now," said the healer. "With a light coating on a cloth, rub it gently over his wounds, keeping it away from his mouth, nose, and eyes."

Terraclon looked at Yormu's face as its features began to pull away from each other. His brow unwrinkled and his face was calmer, and within it, Terraclon saw the same handsome features of his son. Yormu's head fell to the side and he shut his eyes.

"The sleeping potion has taken effect," said the healer. "He should sleep through the night."

"Will he be all right?"

"I do not know. He is in the graces of the gods now."

Terraclon felt relief and then assaulted by his own need for sleep. He yawned and thought about his mattress in his chamber at the rectory, but that seemed too far away and he wanted to be near Yormu when he woke in the morning. As everyone was leaving, Terraclon shed his armor to sleep on the carpet of the floor when he heard a muffled sobbing. Blinking himself alert, Terraclon looked down at Yormu.

"He's crying, Uppacharo! Come back! He's in pain!"

"He is not," said the healing priest as he exited with the sub-priests lugging their chest of potions. "But your *guest* may be."

Terraclon looked to a darkened wall near the end of the chamber. Taking a torch from its sconce, he walked towards a cage that had been set against the wall. He lifted the light to see its inhabitant: the handsome young Seed Eater he had brought back from the battle. He was seated on the floor, looking up to meet Terraclon's eyes. Beside him, in a pile, was his elaborate armor made from a mix of beetle chitins. The chest plate had an inlay of gold that rendered the tendrils of the birthwort vine. The man looked at Terraclon and stopped his sniffling and backed away.

"My apologies," Terraclon said, knowing his words could not be understood. "I'd forgotten all about you—you who is hopefully kin to Volokop."

The man was startled to hear "Volokop." Terraclon looked around the cage and saw the prisoner had food, drink, a mat, and some blankets.

"And with any luck, Good Emperor Volokop wants you back and will trade you for the ones that we need."

Terraclon's eyes watered and he gave in to sobbing. He let his prisoner see his tears.

"Whoever you are," Terraclon said. "I hope you don't feel so alone."

CHAPTER 7

A GUSH OF GORY MEMORIES

Anand woke up to the sun shining softly on his skin and to the pleasant chatter of crowds promenading on a nearby street. A window was open, letting in a mix of aromas including the scent of red hunter ants as well as the sweets and savories of sidewalk snack vendors. Some other strangely familiar aromas were in the room: hair oil crushed from mustard primrose and blue skin paint made from the flowers of the black sage. Anand ached to see where the smells and sounds were coming from but his head was wrapped tight with an oiled cloth that kept his lids shut. As he probed the head covering, he heard the rustling of a scroll.

"Hello, Anand-shmi," said a male voice. "You're awake."

"How long have I been sleeping?" He raised himself up and immediately collapsed with weakness. His stomach was all too empty.

"Two days."

"Where am I?"

"In a recovery room in the Healing Center of the Second Quadrant. You were moved here while you were anesthetized. I will get the healer," said the man, and his chair scraped and the sound of his footsteps faded.

Anand was puzzled. This mysterious man spoke to him like a Dranverite with a Slopeish accent—was he being mocked? A moment later, the doctor came in and took Anand's hand in her own.

"Good afternoon, Anand-shmi," she said. "It is Healer Plinz. I am going to remove the cloth to do a quick examination. We've peeled away the scar tissue of some minor ulcerations. I'm afraid your eyes are going to hurt for a while."

"I'm used to pain," said Anand as the cloth was snipped, then peeled off. "I will never get used to blindness."

"Let us hope you don't have to. Now . . . open your eyes *slowly*."

Anand panicked when he raised his lids to see a blaring chaos of light and colors.

"It's failed!" he cried. "Everything's blurry!"

"Give it a moment," said the doctor. "Your eyes are remembering how to focus."

As Anand looked at where the voice came from, the blur became a face that was painted a bright, grassy green. The doctor was wearing her healer's uniform—a red jacket and epaulets of pink bee fuzz with a third eye painted on her forehead to designate her specialty. As she raised a magnifying quartz to look at his eyes, Anand felt them tearing from both a stinging pain and relief. Her own eye looked tiny and distorted through the lens.

"How many fingers am I holding up?" said the male in the room, mocking Anand's accent again. He turned to see a middle finger, something that meant "up your ass" in every nation on the Sand. The voice, the smells, and now the face of someone he knew came all together sharp: a face with naturally pink eyes and skin that had been painted a pale violet.

"Dwan," Anand said with a laugh as he leaked more tears. "It's good to see you. More like . . . a miracle to see you."

"There are no such things as miracles," said Dwan. "Miracles come from gods, and we are fresh out of those in Dranveria."

The look on Dwan's face was a mix of scolding and delight. He bent down to Anand and kissed each cheek in the Dranverish style. Anand was relieved to know that he was still considered family.

"I am glad to see you too, Anand. But your fame . . . or rather your infamy . . . grows like death caps after the rain. You do know you're in a shit pile of trouble."

"I was born in a shit pile of trouble. What can you tell me that I don't know?"

"That you have been . . . *invited* . . . to the Hall of Peace. When you're ready."

"A trial?"

"Not exactly—a hearing, so you can testify and add to our knowledge. We'd like to know more about your war with the Hulkrites."

"It was not *my* war. They attacked us. It was a defensive measure."

"You can explain that yourself to the People's Agent, the Council of the Five Regions, and the representatives of every district in the collective . . . as well as to the hundreds of millions of Dranverites who are just ravenous for the lurid details."

Dwan lifted a scroll from the chair and handed it to Anand. It was a news sheet and its top story was about Anand's capture and his return to the City of Peace. Below the headline was an engraving of some stranger's face who looked bitter and menacing. The caption read "The God-King of Bee-Jor." Anand sighed.

"Dwan, all of that would have been very intimidating to me at one time. Now, it's about as frightening as eating breakfast."

"**C**orrect. I slit their throats," said Anand matter-of-factly.

The People's Agent stared at Anand. Since their last meeting, she had also had a procedure, one that had peeled the cataracts from her own eyes. She blinked in silence as the murmurs and whispers of thousands swirled in the Hall of Peace.

"Just how many throats did you slit?" she asked.

"Over fifty, I believe—the captain-rulers of every revived mound in Hulkren. It was a gruesome but efficient means of execution. Stabbing them through the rib cage or the skull would have required greater effort and been far too time-consuming. It might have compromised or even broken my knife. Slicing through the soft tissue of the throat with a single stroke was a quick and merciful death."

"How very humane of you," said the agent, triggering a low wave of laughter.

The councilman from the Purple Region rotated the amplifying-cone to his chair behind the dais. "You speak about this calmly, Anand-shmi, as if you were a fly monger discussing his meats at the moist market. But these were men that you killed—men who had but one life. Have you no regrets?"

"I have *no* regrets about killing any of those men. I would do it all over again. I . . ."

The crowd was noisy once more and their shrieks of disgust drowned Anand's words. His hands trembled and he clenched them into fists, which he pulled inside the sleeves of his jacket.

"Silence!" shouted the People's Agent. "Let the citizen speak!"

Anand looked into the audience, left and right, making eye contact as he steadied his nerve.

"What I regret is that I could not save these men from *lives of sanctioned violence.* I slit the throats of the throat slitters. Every man I killed that night was guilty of murder, of enslavement, of rape and plunder. If I had not slit their throats, the Hulkrites would have massacred the Slopeites and then conquered the nations beyond—including an attempt on this one—and forced millions to convert to Termitism. Any man who refused their religion had his throat slit. Those who converted became *throat slitters.*"

Anand felt a strange and sudden paralysis as a gush of gory memories swept him back to Hulkren and the night he had freed his Britasytes. He saw and felt his blade drag though the necks of the paralyzed Hulkrites—helpless men bleeding to death on the floor. A cold, black wave of remorse washed over him, and in the rose-colored beauty of the hall, he was plummeting into inner darkness and wondering if he was dying. As he waited for the blackness to pass, Dwan ran to him, crouched, and then looked into his eyes.

"Now of all times," he said to Dwan.

"You don't have to continue, Anand."

"I must continue," Anand said. "I need to. Could you get me some water? I've only fainted—nothing more."

Dwan took Anand's hand and pulled him off the floor. Anand wiped cold sweat from his face and returned to the cone to address the assembly. "I am not unfeeling about what I did," he said as Dwan handed him a scoop of water. "Next question," he said, and sucked up the drop.

The councilwoman with a yellow beard strapped to her chin took the cone. "Citizen Anand," she shouted, raising the scroll of Anand's written testimony. "You have admitted to the use of fire in your war against the Hulkrites."

"In my *defense* against the Hulkrites," Anand corrected. "They attacked *my* country."

"From your account, you raised a burning effigy of your roach deity, Madricanth, to taunt the Termite worshippers. The citizens of the Yellow Region have so many objections to this, the greatest of which was the risk of igniting a holocaust. A wildfire could have destroyed your nation and then threatened ours and so many others. How could you risk this?"

"I was desperate. I was sure to lose against a ruthless army with hundreds of thousands of trained soldiers who were preceded by a swarm of millions of ghost ants. The ghosts are the most powerful and terrifying ant on the Sand, able to swallow other ants whole. The raising of a tree-tall effigy, lit with glow eggs, filled the Hulkrites with fear; it shattered their confidence. When the effigy burst into flames, it convinced them that a rival god had come to destroy the only deity they worship. The fire released enemy kin-scents that maddened the ghost ants and made them uncontrollable. It sent the Hulkrites into retreat."

"But your effigy was not confined to a pit," said the councilwoman. "It was dropped on the Hulkrites to burn and blind them. It could have ignited a fire."

"The risk of igniting a grass fire was very slight to nonexistent. My defenders had cleared every flammable plant or object on the battlefield. By the time the Hulkrites reached our border, the night's cooling had fallen well past the dew point. Everything, including the sand, was damp with condensation."

Anand saw Dwan looking at him with a grudging admiration and an amused skepticism. The councilman of the Red District was swinging the cone to his chair and clutching the report in his hand as if it were a thief he had caught.

"Commander General Vof Quegdoth," began the

councilman to much laughter as his ceremonial beard wiggled with his words. "There are now a number of people in your nation of Bee-Jor who know how to start a blaze. Is this not a great danger?"

"Those people are my Britasytes, my first tribe," said Anand. "Admittedly, we are secretive and clannish. We do not share our wisdom and have indulged in some necessary deceptions. That is how we have survived as wanderers for centuries and why we have never been absorbed or completely destroyed. It is not a great danger."

"But, Citizen Anand," said the People's Agent. "That does not guarantee that your tribe will not fight with fire again. And that they will not misuse it."

"They will not," said Anand.

"Are you quite sure? We are not. Perhaps this is one of *your* necessary deceptions."

"Then that is all the more reason to send missionary scholars of the Collective Nations into Bee-Jor to prepare it for its acceptance into Dranveria," said Anand. "So that all of us who live there, including my Britasytes, will obey the laws of *this* land. I request your immediate help as we face threats from our East, our South, our West, and within."

"So what you are really asking for is not our teachers, but our military—to help defend your Bee-Jor."

"Correct," said Anand. "As the leader of the Free State, I invite your defenders to join us, as invited guests, and then stay to protect the scholars who would follow to establish schools. On my return to Bee-Jor, I will commission the building of a kin-scent exchange station and a Diplomacy Dome on our northernmost border."

The agent looked from Anand to the council as the hall got noisy again, filled with grumblings and mutterings. She struck the floor with her Staff of Five Colors. "Young man, as usual you are getting way ahead of yourself. Do you know the punishment for the misuse of fire in war?"

"I do, Madame Agent. It is the only crime in Dranveria that is punishable by death. But I submit that I was not in Dranveria when I raised this effigy. And the fire I made was not a misuse. It did not burn millions to death. It did save millions of lives."

"Death!" someone shouted from the back.

"Death to Anand!" chanted others.

Anand turned to look out at the thousands of representatives. His hands were trembling again but he opened and raised them as he searched the faces of the crowd before he resumed the cone.

"Do you think, Good Dranverites, after what I have lived through that death would be a punishment? Death would be a gift! But I am a father—a father of a movement to bring an ignorant and suffering nation into enlightenment. I am also a father of children I wish to raise in that nation, children I want to raise as Dranverites. I stay alive to fight for them."

A strange silence filled the hall. All Anand could hear was the shifting of bottoms in their seats.

"I will discuss this with the council in private," the agent said. "You are returned to the custody of Citizen Dwan."

"May I urge your urgency," said Anand. "Catastrophes await me that I must resolve."

CHAPTER 8

THE FAILURES OF ARMOR

Every move Polexima made while dressing agitated her scabbing wounds, and for a moment she was tempted to let her maidservants do it for her, as they did in the old days, while they clustered around her in her old bedchambers. It was still difficult to eat and drink and she was still breathing through her mouth as her nasal passages were clogged with dried blood. She wanted more sleep but knew she must be awake and alert when Terraclon arrived for their conference in the two days since the battle.

Terraclon arrived early, wearing a startling new outfit that was tightly fitted for flying and looked like armor. It was covered with fine interlocking scales made from the blue chitin of a speckled locust. Around his neck was a blowgun and a fresh magazine. He nodded, then walked towards her with a different bearing, no longer keeping his head down and glancing left and right in fear of being bullied. Now he stood straight with an outthrust chin and a sense of authority.

This victory over the Seed Eaters has brought him certitude—and a sense of ownership.

"Blessed morning, Terraclon," Polexima said, pointing him to a chair. "How are we faring after the battle?"

"We're fine here in Cajoria and the other northern mounds," he said. "No news from the South . . . yet. For this afternoon we've planned a flight to check on the refugee crisis at Palzhad."

"We?"

"Your son and I. King Nuvao."

"I see."

She couldn't help but smile. It amused her that Terraclon and her son were on a mission together. "That is quite an astonishing garment. Is that armor or a pilot's clothing?"

"Thank you. It is both. The blue scales are lacquered and lined with spider silk from some of your daughter's old gowns. And the blue scales work as a camouflage, so that we won't be sighted. Polly, I must say your garment makers work quickly and their work is just exceptional."

Polexima smiled. With each passing day, Terraclon was losing his working caste accent and using a finer vocabulary such as "exceptional."

"The seamstresses and tailors have been less busy since Trellana left for Palzhad," confirmed Polexima. "I am certain they rather enjoy taking up your challenges instead of hers. Any word from Dolgeeno?"

"I sent a message to His Piety and to the royal women at Venaris assuring them it's safe to return to their mounds in Bee-Jor. And I sent two messengers to Trellana, one as a backup, to let her know she cannot return to Palzhad. I advised her to come straight here."

"As soon as she arrives, I should like to hang her with a noose made with ribbons of her own stripped skin."

Terraclon failed to suppress a grin.

"An understandable request, Polly. But I believe Anand would say she should be allowed to defend herself in a hearing before carrying out any extreme punishments."

Polexima shook her head. "That girl," she said. "I love my daughter. But I have never liked her."

Terraclon's face dropped. "I know what that's like."

"You do?"

"From your daughter's side."

"I . . . I am sorry, Terraclon. What I always wanted in a child was someone like you."

She set her hand atop his own. He nodded, looked

away, and she saw that he was touched. She sliced a drop of kwondle tea from a bowl and offered it to him. "Speaking of the unwanted," she said. "I haven't a scant notion as to what to do about these refugees at Palzhad."

"I don't either," said Terraclon.

"We cannot just push them back into the Dustlands."

"No, we can't. The Weedlands they occupied are now a wasteland. Soon Palzhad will be one too—once the refugees eat their way through it."

A servant led in a young messenger who looked tired from a long night ride.

"Your Majesty, Your Ultimate Pious," he said, and then prostrated himself before raising up.

"No need for that," said Terraclon. "That's the old way. A simple nod of the head will suffice."

"Forgive me," he said. "I bring a message from Venaris."

"Finally," said Polexima.

"Majesty, it is not one you will want to hear," he said, stepping back, as if she might stab him with a pike.

"Speak. You will only be thanked for whatever message you deliver."

"It is from the Matron Drageesa, the senior chambermaid of the Holy Mound. She apologizes in advance."

"Please . . . the message!"

The man took several breaths and shifted on his feet.

"The matron regrets to tell you that your daughter, Her Royal Majesty Queen Trellana of Palzhad, as well as Her Immaculacy the Nun Queen of Venaris, did not return from the Grand Cathedral following the latter's commitment ceremony to Lord Grasshopper, Hallowed Be His Hatchlings. All of the royal women, all queens and princesses of the mounds of the eastern nation, have . . . have disappeared."

"Disappeared?" said Terraclon. "All queens and princesses of Bee-Jor?"

"When were they last seen?" asked Polexima.

"On their descent to the cathedral. They never returned from the ceremony to attend the celebration in the feast hall. Guests were left waiting as well as the servants and the sled masters. The priests of Venaris are quite alarmed and are conducting a thorough search of the mound and its environ."

Polexima was shocked into silence. Terraclon's leg was bouncing as he stared straightforward.

"One more thing," said the messenger. "His Ultimate Pious Dolgeeno . . . he . . . he has disappeared as well."

Polexima felt her heart racing in fear. "Just what are they up to?" she whispered. A guard called, "Creet-creet," at the entry.

"Enter," said Polexima, anger in her voice.

The guard stepped in and bowed. "Your Majesty, Your Piety, we have brought the prisoner."

"Bring him in," said Terraclon. "He must be hungry."

Four guards escorted in the mysterious Seed Eater, bathed and perfumed for the queen. His hands were bound behind his back and his ankles were shackled with ropes. Polexima looked him over and sensed he was a royal. He had an upward tilt of his head and a firmly set mouth. He looked in her eyes as her equal. His own eyes were pointy ovals that were strangely beautiful. She was taken with the intricate braiding of his dark orange hair and the tawny undertone of his fair skin.

"I have never seen a Seed Eater so close," she whispered to Terraclon.

"Nor have I," said Terraclon, whispering back. "Not a living one."

"The fold over his eyes is enchanting. He is strangely handsome."

"You think so? I hadn't noticed," Terraclon said, looking away from her.

"It would be all right if you had," she said. "Who do you think he might be in his own country?"

"Judging from his armor and his weapons, he is someone very important. He was with Volokop—at the head of their parade as they retreated."

"Perhaps the Britasyte's two-tongued can unravel the mystery."

A platter arrived, carried in by four kitchen servants. Piled up in the abdominal shell of a harvester ant was a pudding of its curdled lymph with a sprinkling of barley sugar. It was a meal for thirty.

"I don't know what they eat for breakfast in the Barley Lands," said Polexima, "but this is our chef's best guess."

The prisoner was not pleased but turned away from the offering, a nauseous look on his face.

The Pleps were busy decorating some recently molted roaches when Polexima and Terraclon arrived at their camp with the prisoner from the Barley Lands. Guards helped him down from the saddle of a riding ant. As he looked at the roaches being adorned with paints and mica chips, he wrinkled his nose and his eyes turned to slits. Chieftain Zedral and a two-tongued woman with somewhat Slopeish features approached Polexima. They touched heads, their hearts, and then opened their palms to show their hands were free of weapons before bowing.

"Majesty, our apologies," said Zedral through a woman that Polexima assumed was his third or fourth wife. "But we have no one here at the moment who understands the Seed Eater's tongue."

"How do you speak with *him*?" Polexima asked, pointing at one of two boys returning to the camp. Atop their shoulders was a barley stem bulging with cricket eggs. One boy had his back to them while the other was light-skinned with reddish hair.

"Oh, that one. The ginger is Odwaznee," said Zedral. "He's Daveena's pet that she brought back from Halk-Oktish."

"Halk-Oktish. He is . . . a Hulkrite," said Polexima as she failed not to grimace with a sudden hatred.

"He was when we found him. He was born a Seed Eater. Now he wants to be a Britasyte."

"Then there is hope for him," she said. "Come here!" Polexima shouted in Hulkrish, regretting that there was no word for "please" in that dreadful tongue. Odwaznee was startled and dropped his end of the stem.

The boy he walked with turned to face Polexima, then smiled to reveal a gap between his teeth. "Polexima!" he shouted.

"Punshu! Good travels!" she said in the bit of Britasyte she knew, laughing to see him. He ran to Polexima and made a graceful bow and signaled that Odwaznee should do the same.

"You are the Slopeish queen captured by Tahn," Odwaznee said in Hulkrish, looking at her with a suspicious awe. She waited for him to bow before she spoke. Punshu prodded him to bend at the waist and lower his head.

"I am. You should not be eating cricket eggs," she said. "Eat a cricket egg and you are fed for the morning. Let it grow to an adult and your family can feast."

"I heard you defeated Volokop," said Odwaznee, a grin on his face. "That you turned his men into corpses and his ants into pickles."

"*We* defeated them," said Polexima. "We did not want to kill your countrymen. We offered them friendship but they answered with arrows."

"I wish you'd killed them all," said Odwaznee. "The soldiers anyway."

"Do you now. Why?"

"Why do you think I left for Hulkren? All Volokop ever offered me was the chance to die for him."

"I see. Do you recognize the prisoner with us?"

Odwaznee stared at the prisoner and winced. The prisoner gave Odwaznee a sideways glare.

"No."

"We wish to know his name and his relationship to the emperor."

Odwaznee spoke to the prisoner, who looked as if the boy's words were wet and stinky licks to his face. When the prisoner spoke, he pursed his lips and seemed to be forcing his words through a tight hole with his tongue.

"He doesn't want to talk to me," Odwaznee said to the queen.

"Because you were a Hulkrite?"

"No. Because I am a round-eye."

"A round-eye?"

"A weeds pauper, a lowly villager, a pebble dweller. He finds me disgusting and resents that I looked him in the face when speaking."

"Very well," said Polexima. "So, he is royal?"

"Yes, and like all of them, he stands like he's got a spear up his butt. Look at his mouth when he talks! It's like a wrinkled asshole, which is why his words all sound like shit."

"A very colorful description," said Polexima, raising her eyebrows.

"What's the matter?" Terraclon asked her, frustrated that he couldn't understand them.

"It appears that they are not social equals," said the queen.

"I could have told you that," said Terraclon.

"Ask his name, his rank, and what title he holds," Polexima said to Odwaznee. "And look away from him if necessary. It is important we know."

Odwaznee obeyed. The prisoner responded with an ejection of words that smacked the ear with their harshness. When he finished speaking, he put his nose up in the air. Odwaznee was shocked.

"Well?" Polexima asked.

"He's expecting me to fall on my knees to worship him."

"Worship?"

"He says he is a direct descendant of Lumm Korol,

the moon god, the Lord of Creation and the Ruler of the Night Sky."

"So that would make his father the emperor!"

"He is Treti Korolsyn. He is not the crown prince but the third in line."

Polexima turned to Terraclon. "Volokop's third son!"

"Is he now!" said Terraclon, smiling. "But how could Volokop have fathered children? I saw him naked between the legs—he has no manhood! Or it was swallowed up by the mass of his deformities."

"Perhaps he was not always like that."

Terraclon paused before speaking and turned to Zedral and his translating wife. "How do we let Volokop know that we'd like to trade his son for Anand and Daveena?"

"We cannot pass messages now . . . perhaps never again," said Zedral's wife, the both of them looking grieved. "We Britasytes would be welcomed in the Barley Lands for one reason only . . . the chance to rip our heads off."

Polexima heard a buzzing and looked up to see a squadron of locust flyers circling over them.

"Good morning, Mother," said Nuvao as he landed before her. Behind him on another locust was Terraclon's pilot, Mikexa, who slapped her chest to salute him. All the pilots were wearing their new flying kits of sky blue.

"We're off to Palzhad, Polly," said Terraclon as he climbed up the locust's leg to join his pilot.

"Or what is left of it," said Nuvao. "I am so very sorry, Mother."

Polexima was irritated by the buzzing of the locusts' wings, but once the insects had leapt into the sky, the sudden silence was hauntingly empty. She looked at Volokop's son, determined but failing to look fierce, and knew he must feel as fragile and lonely as she did and just as uncertain of his future.

You are Queen Polexima, she reminded herself. *Act like her!*

"Guards, return the prisoner to his cell," she commanded. "Make sure he has all he needs. The future of our nation depends on it."

She turned to Odwaznee. "Young man," she said in Hulkrish. "You and I should get to know each other. Will you join me in my palace for luncheon?"

It was noon when the squadron flew over Smax to see a mound that looked orderly, peaceful, and prosperous from up above. Terraclon saw that its outer flats were sparsely populated, but they had trimmed or uprooted their autumn weeds. Up the main artery, a vigorous parade of leaf-cutter ants was returning with a rich harvest of green and yellow clippings. All along the lower, middle, and upper rings, tradesmen made repairs and merchants hawked wares from shelter to shelter. From high above, Terraclon could hear the caste of ring cleaners singing as they scrubbed the grime from the paving grains that encircled the crystal palaces. On Smax's east side, the stadium's arena was active with a market and a wealth of products that spilled from its stalls.

As they flew farther south, Nuvao signaled the squadron to circle lower for an observation. As the locusts went into a spiral, Terraclon saw what had caught Nuvao's attention. Patrol ants from Smax were running east and west with their abdomens lowered to leave trails of border-scents. Other ants were hauling their dung to drop along this border as the beginnings of an ant wall: the new border of northern Bee-Jor. *The ants know we've lost Palzhad too! And if we can't save Palzhad, we'll have to reinforce the ants' wall with one that we build.*

As the squadron resumed their flight south, Terraclon felt a gnawing from within as a familiar smell filled his nose from the southern border, the same scent from the War of One Night. The acrid stench of tar filled the air along with the dank smell of marsh mud. But now another stink was getting stronger, one he knew too well yet had always detested—human waste. It was the first sign that they were approaching what had been Mound Palzhad . . . and was now someplace else.

Palzhad's lush grass, herbs, and wildflowers were thinning, and the shelters that had been abandoned for centuries were active with new occupants. The refugees from Hulkren had segregated into camps of different shapes and sizes, just as they had in the southern Weedlands. All these camps were in the process of either making walls out of sand grains or fences out of twigs, stems, or leaves tied into cylinders or bound into bales. Not a leaf-cutter ant was in sight.

Terraclon looked over at Nuvao and saw him slump behind his pilot in what had to be horror and disgust or perhaps just dismay. The squadron veered up when they reached the incline of the mound. From there, Terraclon saw that the Palzhanites had constructed their own hasty defense: a circular wall of loose sand, pebbles, household junk, and dead ants that divided their upper rings from the aliens in the lower ones. Atop these walls were Palzhanites who patrolled on foot to defend their homes, their families, and their food with readied arrows, swords, and pikes. Nuvao's locust dropped down to the peak of the mound, at the dew station near the palaces, to relay a message to his Palzhanite subjects. Terraclon joined him a moment later as the rest of the pilots spiraled above them.

"Palzhanites!" Nuvao shouted to the gathering crowd. "You have been abandoned by my sister, Queen Trellana. But you have not been abandoned by Bee-Jor. The strangers who surround us are hungry and desperate, the victims of Hulkrish crimes. We will not let any of you starve and we *will* relocate these refugees. You have my promise as your king." As rehearsed, he nodded to Terraclon.

"Blessings and protections of the gods upon you, Palzhanites," said Terraclon. "The gods are kindest to those who are kind and the gods help those that help others."

Nuvao left for the sky and Terraclon followed after him to rejoin their squadron. Nuvao signaled that they were to continue south, over what had been the Place Where Priestly Magic Ends towards the southern Weedlands. As they flew over the trash-strewn Petiole, another smell rose, one that reminded Terraclon of Anand: the musty stink of cockroaches. The roach-scent grew stronger after they flew over a barrier of blackened sand grains that Dneepish men and women were constructing. It was a scented wall with a shallow trench behind it. Just beyond this wall, Terraclon saw that the Weedlands were empty of vegetation but filled with an uncountable herd of roaches.

This is a roach land!

Masses of Dneepers from the Grasslands were building foundation platforms for a new city made from sand grains and pebbles bound with tar stolen from Bee-Jor's marsh.

Now we know why the refugees from Hulkren overran Palzhad! The Dneepers pushed them out of the Weedlands.

The grass people of Dneep had noticed the locusts and started pointing up at them, some running to their sleds for weapons. Terraclon was alarmed, fearing they should go no farther south when Nuvao signaled to ascend, veer around, and fly north.

It's just what we need—a new enemy in the South! Terraclon thought as Palzhad came back into view. He felt a strong southern wind on his face when Mikexa looked over her shoulder at him, concern on her face. The locust took a series of dips, then fell out of formation. "She's thirsty!" Mikexa shouted. "I'm losing control of her!" Terraclon looked below at a dark patch of bur clover with juicy leaves that the locust could not resist.

Terraclon clutched his pilot tightly as the locust stopped rotating its wings and dropped into the clover's thickness. He pushed his feet deep into the stirrups and grabbed the pilot's waist as they were jerked on the saddle in a hard landing. They clung to the locust's back when they heard shouting and then saw a rush of men and women coming towards them with twig spears.

"They want the locust," he said to Mikexa. "They're hungry for meat!"

Men of the tribe advanced with their spears, threatening Terraclon and his pilot, urging them to abandon their locust. He stood atop of the saddle as he lifted and mouthed his dart gun. As the horde came forward, he targeted them, one by one; they fell and twitched as others pushed in. Mikexa aimed her blowgun towards the attackers as the locust was bucking. She grabbed its antennae and attempted to still it by clutching its middle segments when suddenly her cheek was jabbed with a spear. Terraclon shot at a man aiming a javelin at his face when he heard a piercing voice. A long-necked beauty had pushed into the chaos, halting the attack.

The crowd pulled aside, and Terraclon noticed the woman had skin as dark as an ink berry and startling green eyes. She wore a filthy garment that had once been bright and colorful and he could see she was clutching something underneath it. She looked at the fallen men who were twitching from the darts' poisons and looked hurt for them. She was shouting something between her sobbing, an apology or plea. "They aren't dead!" Terraclon shouted, but knew his words were lost on her. As she walked towards him, she bowed her head, then gently reached to touch his boots. When she looked into his eyes, she seemed to be apologizing as she spoke in Hulkrish. Inside her garment was a baby at her breast—a shriveled, starving baby. Terraclon lowered his dart gun as the locust calmed.

Coming up on the woman's right was a handsome youth with a richness of battle scars on his chest and face. He was followed by another woman with a baby in a sling around her neck. More and more of their tribe were coming closer to stare at Terraclon and Mikexa and their speckled blue locust . . . admiring with an unmasked reverence. In this quieter exchange, the locust began eating.

As the beauty spoke to him, both proud and needful, she made her appeal. Terraclon pointed to his ear and shrugged. "I cannot understand you," he said as he lowered to the saddle. He watched as thin and starving children from her tribe chewed on the clover's stems and roots for their meager water and nourishment. Mikexa, using the bloodied mouth prod over the locust's head sensors, was able to get the insect back into a sudden flight. As Terraclon was jerked into the sky, he looked back at these people with their faces full of fear and uncertainty. His pity for them was a punch to the stomach as he imagined their hardships in Hulkren, their struggles in the Weedlands, and now their fear in this new place.

Refugees.

His armor had protected him from their weapons, but not from the sorrow that overwhelmed him. He could no longer think of them as a faceless horde fleeing from one land to another. They were families with babies and children, his fellow humans with warm, red blood. He knew all too well what it was like to be sick with starving and worries.

But what can I do for them—when we need to rescue Bee-Jor?

CHAPTER 9

THE MEAT ANT PEOPLE IN BEE-JOR

"I don't know *who* he was," shouted Princess Jakhuma as they watched the locust soar up to rejoin the others above them. "But we should not have attacked his insect!"

"But his locust was *food*," said Kula Priya, forgetting she was a servant as she rocked the snub-nosed baby, Chance, in her arms.

"The man was a king or a captain—a man of ranking!" said Sebetay as his soldiers gathered behind him. "We couldn't just keep him here after eating his locust!"

"Why not? Someone would come look for him . . .

and then we could have traded him—for food," said Kula.

"Food," muttered Jakhuma. "We are always thinking about food."

"Did you hear that?" asked Sebetay.

"What?"

"Someone screamed for help!"

"Shh!"

In the silence, Jakhuma heard the screaming. Immediately Sebetay and his men ran east. Jakhuma handed baby Hopeful to Kula, then trotted after them. The cries for help got louder, then turned to screams of pain and panic. The Ledackis scuttled between the brittle ruins of sand and tar shelters and then through a labyrinth of dead weeds. They quickly reached the barrier they had built between themselves and the next camp, a rough wall of burs with prickles that hooked into each other. An older Ledacki woman had been caught in a rope snare. As she was being dragged up and over the burs, they tore up her clothing and gouged her skin.

"Green-skins!" Sebetay shouted, running towards the woman as she screamed. "They're going to kill and eat her!" The men cleared the burs, scraping themselves, then leapt up to grab the woman by her ankles and pull her back. She lost her breath and went silent when the loop of the snare cinched tight around her waist. Jakhuma looked up at the trappers in the next camp. They were from a tribe that covered themselves with a green stain and had white domes of hair, like the clocks of dandelion seeds. They tugged the woman up to them from the top of an old lookout tower and managed to yank her from the Ledackis' grip.

"Spears!" Sebetay shouted. His men hurled weapons with heads of sand shards towards the green-skinned men. On the platform, one of them was hit in his throat and dropped dead and fell. Another was pierced between the eyes and screamed as he stumbled, then fell. The rest of the green-skins dropped their ropes, and screamed in a bizarre language of hums and whistles as they retreated to their side. The Ledacki woman fell to the ground, then crawled out from under the burs as a punctured and bloody mess. The men ran to her and plucked out the prickles that had pierced her skin as the rest of the tribe rebuilt the fence.

Jakhuma and the other women retrieved the shreds of the woman's garment that had caught in the burs. They were retying their loose fibers into something she could wear when they heard a pleasant music, something like the wooden tube drums of their homeland that accompanied the story-singers. All the Ledackis went still, drawn to the music, and starting walking towards it.

"Beware!" Sebetay shouted. "That is the lure of another trap!"

"Let us go together, Ledackis, weapons at the

ready," said Jakhuma to the few hundred people that remained of her crippled nation. It was a short walk before they reached the upper end of the place they had fenced off for themselves. They looked up through leafless mallow stems at the encircling wall the Palzhanites had pieced together of scraps and sand glued with ant dung. On top of the wall were Palzhanite guards pacing on foot. A few of them seemed to be trained soldiers in armored uniforms, and they threatened with the same dart weapon that the locust flyer had used. The sound of the music grew louder as a player banged at the wooden pipes of a carillon coming closer.

Jakhuma looked up as a platform was pushed towards the edge of the wall. Atop the platform was an amplifying-cone. A fair-skinned woman in rich dress with layered skirts stood behind the cone, preparing to speak. At her sides were guards with grass shields and weapons at the ready.

"Invaders from Hulkren!" the woman said in broken Hulkrish. "I am Durelma of Palzhad. We know you was captives of Hulkrites as I were too. Does not mean you belong here. King Nuvao of this mound warns you while here you will obey the Eight Laws. Those who do not will be in punishment or removed or worse."

A man in strange and elaborate robes joined the woman. He was wearing a tall hat that was shaped and painted like a field cricket. *Is he a priest of some kind, a Cricket worshipper?* He unrolled a sheet of something similar to bark paper, looked upon it, then spoke in another tongue as Durelma translated it into Hulkrish.

"Law One," she shouted. "No human shall ever kill other human unless defending self. No human can sacrifice other human, even those of other nations, to gods."

When the woman finished reciting the laws, Jakhuma felt some comfort but much uncertainty. The Eight Laws were similar to the Nine Commandments of Father Sun, but how could they be enforced?

"Who speaks for you?" Durelma shouted to the crowd as the priest unrolled a second scroll.

"I speak for them," shouted Jakhuma, stepping forward.

"Who are you? Who are your people?"

"I am Princ . . . *Queen* Jakhuma of Ledack," she said painfully, acknowledging that her father and brothers were dead and so likely was her mother. "We have no wish to stay here. We wish to return to what's left of our homeland, deep in the south of what was Hulkren."

As Jakhuma spoke, the cricket-hatted man scratched with a stick into the top of his second sheet, perhaps drawing little pictures.

"It has been *recorded*," said the Palzhanite woman, using a foreign word. "Turned into a paper memory."

"We are starving," said Jakhuma. "We have eaten what we found here and have little left but a stand of bur clover that fills our stomachs but leaves us weak and hungrier. We ask for food."

"That is recorded too," said the woman as the scratching continued. "We leaving to bring the message to other camps. Spread words to camps below you. Warn them that battles and stealing not allowed."

The platform was withdrawing, being moved to the next camp, when Jakhuma heard someone running up from behind her.

"Your Highness!" shouted a young man, breathless. "From below us—some invader is in our camp and stealing our clover!"

Sebetay raised his spear and glanced briefly at the wilting queen. "Ledackis! Mother Meat Ant is with us!" he shouted, praising their goddess. His men shouted their battle chant as they ran to confront their latest enemy at the lower end of their containment. Queen Jakhuma felt a sudden exhaustion and crouched to the ground.

"How are we to obey these Eight Laws *and* defend ourselves?" she screamed at the rough sand grains. As she turned to her left, she saw the green-skins were back atop their tower in their hunt for human flesh.

CHAPTER 10

SLOUCHING TOWARDS ABAVOON

"But it's inappropriate to walk in the open!" said Trellana. She already felt tired after walking from the palace to the riding course.

"Trellana, we don't have any drawing ants for sledding," said Maleps. He pointed to a few of the rustled ants that were being saddled and watered. "We have those few over there to take me and my men to the front. The rest are for the guards accompanying you, and later, for the eldest and infirm among you."

"But it is undignified! I am pregnant!"

"For the last time, my good queen, we are at war. We have *been* at war. We are going to *be* at war. The best I can do for you now is to get you to safety at Abavoon."

"I want to stay here! I hate Abavoon. King Flatzep is a disgusting old letch with the worst breath on the Slope, and Queen Fetsha is an ugly old slattern who never bathes. Everything about that mound is shabby."

Maleps tightened his mouth and then his fists. When he unclenched them, he looked as if he wanted to rip her tongue out. Instead, he rubbed his wound, as if his anger had burst the stitches.

"Perhaps you will inspire them to do better," he said, his pain obvious. "You cannot stay here. None of you. Your traitorous mother has likely figured out where you are and is gathering an army of darklings to pounce and drag you back. Is that what you want?"

He looked over at all the royal women that Trellana had gathered and who pretended not to listen to their argument while arranging items in the pockets of their dresses. "Is that what *all* of you want, all hundred of you queens and princesses of *Bee-Jor*?" he shouted. "Those Cricket-lovers will put you in cages, strap you to their bars, then collect your essence when it runs down your legs. Is that how you want to spend your days?"

Trellana quietly fumed as a groom brought Maleps his riding ant. As he strapped on a dented helmet with a broken antenna, she saw a sadness in his face, a resignation, and somehow it made him child-like and more sweetly handsome. "Gods be with you," he said as he prepared to extend the scent lure. "Be well."

Trellana watched him ride off, offended by his sudden departure, when he turned the ant around and rode back to her. "Listen to me, Trellana," he said, loud enough so that all could hear. "I've been thinking about this. You should go back to the East and look after our children . . . just in case there *is* a future." His mouth quivered and his face dropped, ashamed to reveal his fears and worries. She wanted to climb up the ant's legs to hug him, to kiss him good-bye, but that would be most unseemly.

And he might just push me away.

"Be well," she said. "I know my purpose here. There is going to be a future."

He nodded to her—a single, stingy nod. As his ant sped off, she watched it grow smaller and wondered if she could endure the agony of attending his wedding to Fewlenray and then witness his coronation as king of Fecklebretz. *Even if he does not survive, he is no longer mine,* she thought as she felt the heaviness of her pregnancy, of her new mission, and of losing Maleps . . . again. She realized her fellow royals were looking at her with pity or doubt and the quiet was all too heavy. Omathaza came to her, touched her arm, and smiled warmly. Trellana saw kindness in her aunt's face as well as her belief in their mission.

"Have you prayed today, my dear?" Omathaza asked, looking up to the sky. Trellana looked to Sun for a blessing and saw his thousand radiant arms, and within the center of His brilliance there was an approving smile that hurt her eyes. She turned to address the women.

"Gentle women. The lives of royals are not always easy. We have no sleds nor ants to ride today. What we do have is a duty to our gods, a duty to our subjects, and that does not always mean our own comfort. Let us go to Abavoon with expectations of a warm welcome from our fellow royals. As we walk, let us make each breath a plea to Sun to protect and guide us. And before we depart, let us offer a bit of blood to Mantis so that She can make our Slope great and holy again."

Trellana produced a small clay vessel from one pocket of her skirt and a little carving of Mantis from another. She was the first to prick her finger and scrape it on the bowl's edge. As each of her fellow royals filled the bowl, she felt a growing strength, a sense that her reward was distant but waiting.

After the rite, the royal women were muttering and moaning and some even crying as they imagined the days ahead. Instead of jewels, their pockets were stuffed with food, dew scrapers, and water bladders. Over their shoulders, each of them had a rolled blan-

ket to sleep with outside, apparently a common practice among certain working castes. *Sleeping outside!*
Trellana thought as she felt the rough fibers of the
blanket on her neck. *What are we, black flies? It's utterly
vulgar!*

The few guards mounted on antback were approaching Trellana, awaiting her orders to proceed.
She looked at them, with their fair, beardless faces,
and wondered how these *boys* could protect them
when she heard a thorn horn from above them on the
main artery. She turned to see some of Tellenteeno's
acolytes dragging a simple cargo-sled down the main
artery with a canvas tent atop it. When they reached
the docks of the riding course, they dropped their
poles and bowed to the royals. A man was helped
out of the back of the tent; he looked slovenly in his
baggy traveling garment and appeared unstable as he
walked towards Trellana.

"Pious Dolgeeno! This is rather surprising. Have
you come to say good-bye?"

"No, Majesty. I have come to join you."

"I thought you were staying here."

"It is not advisable. Some of our informants at Venaris have sent us a message. They have sighted some
activity on the eastern side. I am afraid it is not safe
for me here at Fecklebretz."

Trellana fumed. *Maleps was right—they are coming
for us.*

"Let us make haste for Abavoon," she said to her

followers. "The sooner we leave, the sooner we get there."

"Queen Trellana," said one of the acolytes holding up what looked like a battle-axe he had pulled from the sled's tent. "You are going to need these."

"What? Weapons?"

"No, Majesty. Weed cleavers, saws, and root trenchers. All of us in the Still Holy West have been busy defending ourselves—even the weeding castes are fighting at the western front. They have had no time to clear weeds on the routes between the mounds."

And now we are to work like common laborers? she thought. *Ant Queen in the Heavenly Mound, when will this trial be over?*

"Thank you, Young Pious. Won't all of you young priests come with us and show us how to use these tools?"

The acolyte looked surprised, then forced himself to smile as the others shifted and looked at their feet.

"We would be honored, Majesty, but we . . . we have our duties here at Fecklebretz . . . and our seminars."

"Ultimate Pious Dolgeeno, can you relieve these aspiring young holy men from their duties at Fecklebretz and reassign them to come with us?"

Dolgeeno took a moment to consider. Trellana

was sure he was equally uninterested in clearing weeds.

"Acolytes, you are relieved of your duties at Fecklebretz and will join us on our journey. Gather what you need, inform Pious Tellenteeno, and then return here quickly."

The acolytes froze and looked at each other in disbelief.

"Hurry it along, please," said Trellana. "Your Ultimate has commanded you."

"All guest chambers have been cleaned and restored, Majesty," said Matron Vematta to Fewlenray as she drew curtains to block the piercing afternoon sun. "It took us all of yesterday and most of this morning."

"It is always a pleasure to host, but a greater pleasure to be hosted," said Fewlenray as she collapsed, then sprawled, on her empty bed. It had been a full morning that included a visit to the Ant Queen for a Sacred Wetting. "I am exhausted, Vematta. Do we have any word of the easterners' progress?"

"We received the message late this morning that the royal party reached the end of our western hunting weeds where they spent the night. They resumed their trek at sunrise."

"I can just imagine Trellana's misery today. Everyone else's as well, but hers especially, after sleeping outside and waking up under a wet blanket. I imagine she may be running back here in order to avoid it."

"Yes, Majesty. If you don't need anything, I'll leave you to your nap."

"Thank you. As soon as I wake, I would like a little something to eat and some tea. And then we should visit the wounded before dinner. Have you noticed that just a smile and a clasping of the men's hands seems to provide them with so much comfort?"

"Well, yes, Majesty. When it comes from a young and beautiful queen like you."

"Any news from Maleps?"

"No messages since yesterday when they stopped for water at Abavoon. As far as we know he has not reached the front yet."

Vematta bowed, then excused herself. As her footsteps got softer, they left behind a startling silence. The morning's activities had distracted from the sadness of Maleps's parting, but now, as Fewlenray listened to the sound of her own breathing, she was tortured with worry for his safety. The drowsiness that had made her bed so inviting a moment ago had been replaced by dread and jitters.

"No nap today," she said to herself. "If I am awake, it is better to be up and attending to soldiers." She was reaching for her jacket when she heard a *"Creet-creet"* from the antechamber.

"Come quickly," said Tellenteeno, entering without permission.

"What's wrong, Pious?"

"We have . . . visitors. They insist on speaking to you."

"Visitors?"

"They have warned of serious consequences if you do not appear. You might know at least one of them."

"Will I be safe?"

"Yes, I believe you will be."

Fewlenray followed the priest out the portal to the topmost walking ring. She saw the reflections of flying blue locusts on the lacquered walls of her palace before she looked skyward. A locust was plummeting towards her. She ran, tripping over her skirts as the locust landed, then jerked left and right as it scissored its mandibles wet with brown slime. Tellenteeno lifted the queen up on her feet, and she saw a pilot in speckled blue armor leaning forward and patting the locust's head to still it. Behind the pilot was a man in the same strangely beautiful armor with a face as yellow as her own.

"Cousin Fewlenray," he said in the most refined Slopeish.

"We are cousins?" she said as she caught her breath.

"I am your cousin Nuvao, three or four times removed—I am not quite sure. Son of Polexima. Brother to Trellana."

She stared at him and he stared back, his face stern and still as a whorl of locusts buzzed above them.

"So it is true," she said. "You have become one of them. Why have you not stained your face with some muddy shade yet?"

"When I find the time. Where is she?"

"Where is who?"

"Do not pretend like you do not know. And where are the rest of Bee-Jor's royal females? Bring them out now and we will escort them home. This folly ends now."

"And if we do not?"

"You might want to take a look below you."

Fewlenray looked down the mound and saw an army of leaf-cutter ants crawling towards the palaces. As the ants got closer, she could see their darkskinned riders in an ugly array of homespun armor splashed with red paint. The tristriped banner of Bee-Jor was on top of their helmets or flapping from pikes attached to the back plates of their armor.

"Your men are at war in the West, Queen Fewlenray. And you are quite undefended here as our ants and your ants are all kin and they are welcomed here even though we Bee-Jorites are not. We have no wish to violate our truce with the Slope but you are sheltering some women and girls that we must have returned to us."

"I see how this goes. This was all part of your Dranverite's plan. Split our nation into two, then throw our half to the Beetle Riders. And once they have destroyed us, you finish them to take over *all* the Slope."

"I believe you have just explained my sister's plan for us in Bee-Jor, but she would throw us to the Seed Eaters before some miraculous reconquest by the Slope. As a strategy goes, it's a poor one, completely reliant on an intervention from the gods. And the gods have been so stingy lately."

The queen was silent, looked away.

"Listen to me," Nuvao said. "Commander Quegdoth, the Dranverite, saved us *all* from the Hulkrites. You cannot blame him for this attack from the Carpenters."

"Quegdoth colluded with the Hulkrites! He planned our destruction with them!"

"That is ridiculous and you know it. The Hulkrites were *destroyed*. The Slope has invited an attack from the Carpenters for the last few centuries."

"That is absurd. How?"

"By this contemptible demand for tributes of sacrificial humans—for innocent lives that are wasted in pointless rituals and cruel entertainments."

"The Carpenters have already taken Mound Gagumji," interjected Tellenteeno. "Are you saying they won't take the rest of our country to plant their pine seeds, propagate their black ants and war beetles, and then replace our race with their own?"

"Perhaps. Perhaps they might keep to themselves." Nuvao turned his gaze back to Fewlenray. "Please, Fewls. Summon my sister and the other women. As we need them, we have no desire to harm them."

"Just what will you do with them?"

"Return them to their mounds and to their duties . . . and to the comforts of their palaces."

"They will kill themselves rather than live as the prisoners of infidels."

"If they kill themselves, then Worm will condemn them to eternal punishment. Isn't that right, Pious?" Nuvao turned to his elder with a smug expression.

Tellenteeno lifted up the pointy edge of his chin as the tiny hole of his mouth unwrinkled. "Do not speak to me as your priest, *Bee-Jorite*," he said.

"I do not," said Nuvao. "But speak to Fewlenray as *her* priest. Killing one's self is a violation of the Holy Order, is it not? One of the worst of all transgressions?"

Nuvao looked at Fewlenray as if he was looking into her. She cast down her eyes and felt her shoulders slumping. Tellenteeno remained silent but she could hear him fuming through his quivering nostrils.

"Listen to me, Fewls. We were friends once, as children. I was drawn to your tenderness, your sympathy for others—for me, once, when I was beaten and disgraced for my own . . . sensitivity. You see the Dranverite as an alien, an interloper with dangerous ideas. Ideas are one thing he does have, tens of thousands of them, which he wants to bring here in something called *books*. Among those ideas is an important one—that war is wrong, whether it is for territory, or amusement, or the procuring of sacrificial humans. Should we really worship gods that drink blood and thrive on the suffering of others? Quegdoth wants to end all that."

Fewlenray looked up at him and into his eyes; only then did she realize he was serious. His words were having a strange effect and she felt surges of sadness, then waves of relief that alternated with a kind of awe. She felt herself shaking in a waking dream and all around her was bright and vivid even as she was nauseated.

"Trellana is not here," she said, "nor any other royal woman from . . . Bee-Jor. You are welcome to look for them, but you will not find them at Fecklebretz."

"Where did they go?" Nuvao asked.

"You don't have to tell him!" Tellenteeno shouted, his face gone pale as beeswax.

The queen looked down through the mound she ruled as if seeing it for the first time and, somehow, it looked ugly, filthy, and rough. *What is the best thing to do here?* she asked herself. *What would avoid another cataclysm in this cataclysmic year?*

"Tell me, Fewlenray. Please," said Nuvao. "Are they going north to Mound Kobacynth? Or to Delogock? Are they doing something as stupid as going all the way to Teffelan to aid your soldiers?"

She wiped tears from her face.

"Or are they going directly west . . . to Abavoon? Towards the conflict?"

She nodded, then burst into more tears, feeling a strange relief from problems she had never identified.

A moment later, she felt a dread of something more darkly mysterious—some great change to her life, something that threatened her very existence.

It was a cool afternoon but Trellana was sweating, something completely disgraceful of her, and she wondered when they could rest again. The patrol guards were already off their ants, having lent them to those who could no longer walk, those exhausted or with broken boots. The plumpest of the women were straggling in the back and behind them were the acolytes who had been given the secondary task of hauling the eldest women on the tool-sled, some of which were dying or dead. Everyone was going through their water so quickly they would have none left by evening. The sand grains of the route were getting larger and rougher the farther out they trekked, and the thickening weeds were alive with insects that could be heard but not seen. Dolgeeno, sucking on some kwondle candy he refused to acknowledge, much less share, had managed to stay just ahead of Trellana to lead the parade. He halted when they reached a rough and upended rock on their right and a thicket of dangerous thorn parsley on their left that forced them into a narrow path.

"Why are we stopping?" Trellana asked.

"Look," he said, pointing to an anchor strand of

a spider's web. Trellana's eyes followed the strand up to the orb stretched between drying stalks. She could see the spider that waited in the center of its web. With its legs pulled tight together, it looked like a striped pebble.

"I like spiders when they have been baked and seasoned for eating," said Trellana. "Otherwise I'd prefer to avoid them."

"The spider will not leave its web to attack us," said Dolgeeno to all the women behind him. "But as we pass this way, stick close to the rock and avoid its web."

The women walked slowly through the channel, avoiding the web's lower strands until they reached some open sand. Trellana saw some neglected hunting blinds and farther in the distance was a charmingly rough, two-story shelter of resin-glued sand where hunters might spend the night. "It looks very comfortable in there," she said to Dolgeeno. "Shouldn't we rest in there a bit?"

Dolgeeno frowned. "Another rest so soon, Trelly? That shelter couldn't fit all of us—it would fall off its poles."

"I could use a rest," said Omathaza, who was out of breath and coming up behind them. Her face was pale with exhaustion.

Dolgeeno looked at the sun's position, which was in the south-southeast. "We should keep going. The days are shorter now. We can rest after nightfall, at the next hunting preserve on the outskirts of Abavoon. It's just another thirty thousand steps or so."

"Oh. Only thirty thousand," said Trellana as she crossed her arms and rolled her eyes.

"Yes, and if our messenger has reached King Flatzep, he may be sending out a greeting party and some coach-sleds to bring us the rest of the way."

"Let us pray for that," said Trellana, but she doubted it was true. She was looking at some dying barley weeds in the distance and what might be weevils resting in the emptied florets. *Don't they look snug and comfortable,* she thought when she suddenly heard a distant hum in back of her followed by the gasps of the women. She turned to see a swarm of blue locusts coming from the East. As they circled, then lowered to the ground, she saw the riders behind the pilots were threatening their blow-darts. The women were shrieking as they were herded into a panicked mass in the circle's middle. Trellana and Dolgeeno struggled to stay at the edge of the mass when a locust landed and crawled towards them. She was furious to see it was her brother, Nuvao, in a beautiful suit of turquoise armor.

That has to be the handiwork of that mincing Terraclon.

Nuvao stared at her with a condescending smirk as the women's shrieks turned to sobbing. "Trelly. You have become quite the adventuress," he shouted at her. "For your own safety, it is time to put an end to this."

"Little brother Nuvao. It is almost time for you to die," Trellana shouted back.

"Come back to Bee-Jor and you *won't* die. This is all a terribly silly mistake. The sooner you come home, the sooner we can forget about this. Some ants will be arriving shortly to . . ."

"The goddesses have commanded me!" Trellana screeched. "This is what we must do to save our Slope!"

"Trellana, you must not mistake what you experienced after ingesting the mildew as a revelation."

"Why? Because I am a woman?"

"No, dear thing. Anyone who eats it—commoners, priests, or royalty—feels the same way you did. They have conversations with the gods, or with the dead! Some report having sexual intercourse with weed and sand demons, and apparently these encounters can be quite fulfilling."

Nuvao laughed, revealing himself.

"Nuvao, are you truly a priest?" Dolgeeno asked, cocking his head as he shouted. "Of *our* gods?"

"It is because I was trained as priest that I know my sister is no prophetess."

"You are a disbeliever," bellowed Dolgeeno. "And a disbeliever cannot be a priest!"

"I believe in the New Way, in the rise of the better gods," shouted Nuvao.

"When the Slope is restored," Trellana screamed, "all the disbelievers will be pierced by arrows, shot from the bows of the very gods themselves—arrows that will hurl them down to the Bowels of Eternal Punishments!"

"Oh, come now," said Nuvao, smiling, when his locust was jerked off its claws, turned upside down, and scraped over the heads of the screaming women to crash and die in the distance. All the locusts had been targeted with monstrous arrows—missiles!— that sent them tumbling over the sand or sliced them in half or beheaded their riders.

Trellana gasped, then laughed in astonishment. *The gods are fulfilling my prophecy!* she thought, but she screamed and then collapsed when a missile that had skewered a locust rider smashed his chest into her face and knocked her to the ground. As the women cried and ran from unseen attackers, the rest of the locusts escaped to the sky.

Dolgeeno pulled Trellana up. "Look!" he shouted, pointing towards a dreadful sight.

The barley weeds in the distance were falling in panels, a trick of some kind, a collapsing fence. Men in bright, fuzzy armor were marching towards them, pushing Hulkrish missile launchers as they were re-loaded. In back of these men, the largest insects Trellana had ever seen were crawling forward. They had large, knotty antennae that sprang from low heads that made a terrifying rattle as they vibrated.

At first, Trellana thought the giants were from the soldier caste of carpenter ants, but as they got closer she could see the elytra that opened on their backs and then the fluttering of wings that had been clipped.

The Carpenters' dreaded war beetles!

As the beetles got closer, she saw the turrets glued atop their thoraxes. Soldiers, in groups of six, were inside these turrets and aiming tridents from above their walls. The Slopeish guards fumbled for their bows and arrows but the tridents ripped through the weak Slopeish armor and then were yanked out with leashes to leave a gory trail of blood, flesh, and broken bones.

"Run!" Dolgeeno shouted to the women, but when Trellana turned, she saw beetles pressing in from the East. The beetles encircled Trellana and her followers, making a spinning wall that got tighter and pushed them into a heap of panic and wailing. The Beetle Riders shouted threats in a wispy tongue that sounded like leaves whipped around on a windy day.

Trellana was panicked and dizzy as she looked for an opening to run through when the beetles came to a stop. Soldiers climbed out of the turrets and used the steering ropes attached to the antennae to slide to the ground. Hundreds of men strutted towards Dolgeeno while shaking their three-pronged javelins. A few of the men, leading at the front, wore sleek armor of black chitin and had pale faces with a vaguely greenish undertone. Others, wearing the strange fuzz armor, were shorter in stature and stocky with dark brown skin.

They look as if they have been recruited from the Slopeish working castes!

As the attackers came closer, Trellana could see that the brown-skinned soldiers wore a short cape and had a number of blades clipped to a belt. Some larger weapon dangled at their sides, obscured by the capes.

The captain in charge of them, a tall and stately man with a green helmet and chest plate, swaggered up to Dolgeeno. The captain's furrowed eyebrows showed his contempt. He had skin with pink flushes across his cheeks and in his right hand was an elegant rapier of a lacquered mosquito's needle. Trellana looked at his long mustache that draped over a square chin as his eyes glanced back and forth over what had to be a strange sight to him: a party of defenseless Slopeish royal women who were lost in the weeds.

The captain conferred with the other white-skinned men next to him—his lieutenants, it appeared—and then he shouted a series of commands to the dark-skinned soldiers in a different tongue. These men placed their javelins in holsters on their backs and then reached under their capes for a different weapon: pinkish mallets of feldspar. Trellana heard screaming and looked behind her when she felt a thwack on her head. A mallet had sent her falling to the ground in an agony of pain and confusion. Her skin burned as her wrists and ankles were tied with ropes.

Beneath the dead locust, Mikexa was all too still, but Nuvao managed to get his hand under her nose and felt her breathing. The screams and sobbing of the royal women yielded to the gleeful chatter of the invading soldiers. Their voices got louder and he realized they were coming towards the locust corpse, but for what? They were pushing it and he felt the corpse rubbing over his face, scraping it, and he panicked. Lying as still as possible, he prepared to play dead when he heard the crack of chitin and the ooze of lymph—the soldiers were yanking out their precious arrow. *It has to be an obsidian-headed missile from Hulkren, of the type that killed the roaches,* Nuvao thought. When the soldiers succeeded in plucking the arrow out, he heard the sounds of licking and then laughter as they cleaned the arrow with their tongues before they carried it away.

As the locust corpse sank heavier on his chest, his head ached from the stuffy air. Taking his knife from his ankle holster, he worked, carefully, in the darkness to cut the saddle ropes that trapped his legs in their tangles. When he wriggled out, he felt the abrasion of a rough sand grain under his neck. As he turned over and peered up, he saw no sight of the Carpenters' army or their beetles. He pushed back under the locust to cut the ropes that bound Mikexa's ankles, then pulled her out to the light and air. When he lifted her up, her head rolled and her eyes blinked from the brightness of the sun.

"Thank Cricket," he said as he unclipped her water bladder, then got her to drink from it. "I'll be right back," he said, unsure if she could hear him. "Our army should be here soon—on ants. We'll be all right." Nuvao thanked Cricket that he wouldn't have to tell Terraclon that his best pilot had died.

With an increasing dread, Nuvao walked through the site of the attack. He felt as if his bones had dissolved when his body shook like a jelly. He could not find a single woman except some old and dead ones atop a tool-sled. "What complete idiots!" he said aloud. "Dead idiots, and none more idiotic than my sister!" He heard a rip of flesh as the faces of these corpses were eaten by carrion beetles that raised their abdomens to spray their poison to keep Nuvao from stealing their meal. He cupped his face with his hands after choking on the spray, then walked until he found the corpses of young men wearing the bloodied and shredded robes of seminarians. Their limbs had been cut from them, brutally hacked by swords, then piled up in a cone to sicken whoever discovered them. *And sickened I am,* thought Nuvao as his mouth flooded and he knelt to vomit. His body was wracked with convulsions and then a moment of relief as he spat out the last acrid bits. Fear and disgust were being supplanted by rage as he felt his body grow strong again.

Farther over, he saw the destroyed leaf-cutter ants, severed into pieces, and strewn around these were more dead in the remains of Slopeish armor. He trudged towards them to see they were very young men, boys, really, who were unable to protect the women or themselves. Their armor had been bashed into tiny little pieces and their swords had been sunk, upended, into their chests as a final humiliation. Nuvao's skull burned with fury and his hand shook as he plucked a sword from one boy's chest and slashed the air with it, imagining the beheadings of a thousand Carpenters. Exhausted and out of breath, he heard a moaning and then a prayer-chant to Grasshopper in the sacred tongue. He walked towards some shriveled fringe weeds to find Pious Dolgeeno on his back. The old priest seemed blind and deaf as one of his arms swatted at nothing. His other arm was lifeless, bent at an unnatural angle, and cut off from blood by an arrow embedded in his shoulder socket.

"You *would* be the one to survive," Nuvao said. "And just what do I do with you?"

CHAPTER 11

THE CARPENTER PEOPLE

It was another cold night and Trellana was shivering with the others who were awake again as they prayed to different gods for warmth, for food, and for safety. As she looked up at the sky, at the numbing clusters of stars, she felt the dampness of the dew as it soaked her garment and made her even colder. "Please, Ant Queen," she prayed aloud. "Send me a signal that all is well, and that Your Divine Plan is proceeding." This was, perhaps, the hundredth time she had recited this prayer, but at last she saw stars falling out of place to streak across the sky. *The tears of the goddesses, weeping for me in pity!* she thought as she started to cry. A new fit of shivers racked her so hard she felt like her teeth might shake out of her mouth. When the shivering ended, she succumbed to a shallow sleep where she dreamed of worry-monsters that hunted and ate each other in a poisonous maze of broomrape weeds.

When she woke again, Sun had climbed high enough to send warmth through the crisp winds of autumn. Trellana relished the feel of the sun on her hands and feet, but already it was hurting her eyes and she would have to spend the day clenching them shut. She looked left, then right, to see how her fellow royals were enduring. All of them were tied to pegs on the planks of low, flat sleds heading west to pine country. For now, it seemed, they were still on the Slope for she had yet to see those mysterious trees that provided the nuts she liked as well as the hard, green berries she detested.

But how has this happened? she asked herself again as she suffered from rope burns on her wrists and ankles and bedsores on her backside. *How did these Carpenter soldiers penetrate the Slope as far as Abavoon?* She worried that every mound in the West had been lost already, then wondered if it was a short matter of time before they annexed Fecklebretz, then Venaris, and then the rest of the mounds of Bee-Jor. Raising her head, she looked at the eight other women in rows of three tied on the sled with herself at their middle. At least one of them was dead, she knew, from an increasing stench. Surrounding her were the rest of the royals in the same confines, all of them treated as if they were little more than stunned grubs on their way to a meat market.

And how much longer is this journey? And to where and why?

Trellana hated the foul, musty odor of the beetle that hauled the sled, but whenever it was probed by wasps or blowflies, the stink got stronger from under its thorax and it drove the predators away. The same stink caused her eyes to water and her throat to burn, and it was very strong this morning as dreaded blood-flies grazed the beetle's antennae, then hovered over the helpless women. Below her feet, she heard Omathaza coughing from the beetle's exudation.

"I am glad to hear you cough, Auntie Oma," Trellana shouted.

"Why, dear girl? It is not exactly music."

"Because it means you are still alive."

"Not because I wish to be."

"This trial will end," Trellana said as she looked up at the dark, hairy flies with a green band across their compound eyes. "Stay alert, Auntie. Those are blood-flies above us."

The blood-flies swirled, then scattered. Finally, Trellana exhaled in relief when abruptly she heard the high-pitched sound of wings behind her. She screamed when she felt insect claws through the cloth on her shoulders. Tilting her head back, she saw a black mass of eyes, and below them, two pairs of cutting stylets that waved like fingers from the blood-fly's mouth. "Help! Help me," she screamed, but her words were muffled by the fly. She shook her head but the stylets jabbed into her neck as the insect lowered and smothered her. Her body jerked as jolts of pain ran through her chest and limbs and then sent her into spasms. Claws gripped her chin as the lapping part of the fly's mouth sucked on the incisions. She saw a sled attendant was running towards her, a lance before him, when she fainted from blood loss or fear or both.

Over the next uncountable days as the procession continued west, Trellana's existence was a tortuous fever as she was ravaged by the blood-fly's poisons. She could not mouth her words, could not complete thoughts, and felt submerged in a current of heated sludge. Her skin was one giant itch while her insides churned and threatened to burst. The light of day was long and knife-sharp, but the nights were longer when she drowned in an oily darkness, as if her mouth and nose were sucking in tar. She heard and felt the babies inside her as they attempted to strangle and devour each other and screamed in frustration from their lack of teeth.

One morning Trellana awoke and she was better. The attendant climbed onto the sled with the day's only meal. The boy looked around fifteen years old, perhaps, with fuzz above the lips on his dark brown face and a thick yellow fuzz on the panels of his armor. His face, shockingly, reminded her of the Dranverite whose infants kicked in her womb. He used a paddle to scoop into a nutshell container, then slapped a tasteless goo next to her face on the plank. The food, whatever it was, was just close enough that she could mouth some of it up. She knew she needed to eat, but she was in a new agony, suffering a pain she had never felt before that made her stomach quiver and her head ache. It did not feel like hunger, but perhaps this was *starving*—something her hateful brother had described to her. Though she had no appetite, she strained to eat all she could, and when the goop filled her stomach, the pain subsided. A short time later, she needed more—much more. This was *true* hunger.

She looked around the sled at the other women and heard them licking at their own food. "Omathaza!" she called. "Auntie Omathaza! Can you hear me?"

The other women were all too quiet.

"She cannot," said the woman next to her, Princess Vanka of Smax.

"We are glad you have returned to us, Trellana," said Queen Lania of Mound Sloveck. "But we are sorry to tell you that tonight when your aunt looks down upon you, she will be shining as the newest star."

Trellana stopped breathing.

I have no room for this sadness, no place inside me for another grieving.

She was looking into the bright blue of the sky

when shade edged over the sled. Finally, she saw the underside of what had to be a pine tree with its long thin leaves and their pointy ends. Higher on its branches hung the cones that dropped the hard seeds that took a kitchen worker an afternoon to shell just one. The bright and pleasant aroma of pine was getting stronger, a smell she remembered in her mother's apartments during the winter months when the windows were closed against cold and rain. Her servants from Palzhad, arrived from the Britasyte markets, had broken the leaves into bits to release their fragrance, then glued them together in the shape of Cricket as they sang an ancient prayer-song.

How did that song go?

> *Cricket, we honor Thee,*
> *Cricket we thank Thee,*
> *Knowing on coldest, darkest nights*
> *You have left millions*
> *Of two-eyed eggs*
> *To hatch and grow as feasts for all,*
> *When the days are longer*
> *And warm and bright*
> *And Your thrilling singing*
> *Will bless the night.*

How long ago that seems! I thought Mother was ridiculous for worshipping such a stupid and helpless goddess—a perpetual victim who hid from day and shrieked all night. But perhaps if I had worshipped Cricket, I would not be here now.

"Forgive me, Mother Cricket, for calling on You in daylight," Trellana mouthed when she heard a gasp from Vanka.

"My dear Trellana!" said Vanka in a raspy whisper as her chin quivered with shock and disgust. "Let us not go to some deity of the dark-skinned no matter how dark it gets!"

"No. Of course not, Vanka," Trellana said.

The sleds were stopping more and more frequently to clear their rudders of dried and broken needles. When the procession passed under an ancient but dying pine, it dropped its twigs, one of which fell on the sled and splattered Trellana's face with a sticky gunk. Up this pine's trunk, she saw her first carpenter ant nest. The ants had hollowed out enormous holes in the trunk and at their bottoms was a mushy dust of chewed wood. Quietly resting among the ants in the wood dust were the giant war beetles who had deceived their hosts into accepting them as kin. One of the beetles openly ate an ant, holding it down with forelegs as it chewed off the head. Some ants were crawling from their main nest in the trunk's center to second and third sub-nests with larvae in their mandibles to relocate.

After they passed the dead tree, Trellana saw the first pine saplings. The slender trunks of these were covered with glossy brown aphids bearing a single stripe of red across their abdomens. The aphids were impassive as the carpenter ants crawled over and through them. Some ants were chewing off the wings of newly hatched aphids to keep them from flying away, while others used their antennae to probe them until they secreted a drop of honeydew, which the ants promptly drank. On the next sapling, Trellana saw what she realized were Carpenter women, disguised as ants, as they tended the aphids from nets stretched between ladders. Some of these women held false antennae in their hands to rub the aphids while others collected the emerging honey- dew with a paddle that they scraped over the rim of a squat barrel.

It was late in the afternoon when the procession reached an immaculate clearing and Trellana heard the hubbub of a human settlement. Had they entered Eth or Gemurfa, these bizarre wooden cities suppos- edly built around ancient tree stumps? The black ants were increasing in number and some crawled onto the sleds, slowing them down as they sniffed the prisoners with long, bent antennae that were like a fourth pair of legs. One ant crawled over Trellana, who stiffened as the antennae probed her. The ant had found carpenter kin-scent and did not attack; she figured her captors must have bathed her with their colony odor while she was lost in the fever.

As she looked at the ant, Trellana realized she

had only ever seen shaved and roasted carpenter ants at celebration feasts, when the soldiers would return from victories in the West. Carpenter ants had scraggly chin beards, like harvesters, and they had stubby hairs around their stingers. Their chitin was beautifully, deeply black and the even proportion of head, thorax, and abdomen gave them an elegant appearance. When they crawled and lashed their antennae, it seemed refined, almost mannered, with a dignified raising of the head.

The sled tilted when they reached an incline. Trellana saw the first of thousands of houses neatly constructed with wood. They were stilted on a scaffolding of thick and sturdy poles and their walls were made of interlocking planks. Within the walls were inset windows, not made of random quartz slices, but from something poured into molds to dry in the sun. On top of the structures were sharp, steep roofs with eaves that curved into channels for guiding away rainwater. The roofs were thatched with a thickness of pine needles that were secured by a glossy adhesive. *I am hungry,* Trellana thought as she admired the structures. *Every part of these houses looks shiny and candied, as if they had been dipped in honey.*

Families slid open doors of their houses to step out to platforms so they could look down on the sleds. The Carpenter men wore loose over-shirts and pants made from the kind of pine fiber cloth that Britasytes sold to the crafting and trades castes on the Slope.

The women wore a loosely fitting single piece that showed their necks and was sashed at the waist. All the Carpenters had whitish complexions with a vaguely green undertone and the cheeks of their youngsters had splashes of pink. They were neat and clean but unadorned, and only married women, it appeared, wore a simple pendant of some small jewel—amber, perhaps—across their foreheads. Their immaculate appearance assured Trellana that she must look as awful as she felt.

The incline grew steeper as the procession twisted its way through the sprawling, sinuous surface roots of a massive stump of what once might have been the largest tree on Mother Sand. The bark on the roots had been chipped away to reveal a polished wood with intricate graining, and carved out of it were relief sculptures that had been stained with different pigments. The style of the carvings was simple and precise while the images included pine trees and their cones, ferns, meadow plants, and flowers, as well as beetles, ants, and other forest insects. These images gave way to carvings of men and women mounted on lightning flies and on war beetles: the gods of the Carpenter people. One goddess had what looked like a spray of ear mushrooms for her hair and another had a towering coiffure that was like a pine cone dropping seeds.

The false idols of a benighted people!

The procession continued up a smooth spiral that

she realized had been cut into the sides of the fabled
Tree Stump of Gemurfa. The sleds slowed when they
reached a level plane with a startlingly striking building at its center. This had to be the palace of Emperor
Sinsora, ruler of the Carpenter people, and it was as
large as the four of those combined atop Mound Cajoria. The walls had abundant windows that were
neatly and evenly placed, and indicated the structure had at least ten stories. Men were working on
platforms while hanging from ropes to apply fresh
varnish to the palace's surfaces, which were etched
with delicate, barely perceptible designs. The varnish
heightened the pattern of grains within the wood to
make it glisten and likely protect it from rain and dry
rot. Sun was ending his journey and the last of His
light dappled the varnish with glimmers of pink.

The procession halted at a great rectangular barrier before the palace. Trellana and the other women
strained their heads to look up at a sliding wooden
gate. Carved into the gates' four corners were subtle
depictions of fat-cheeked gods blowing wind. The
gate slid open to reveal a formation of soldiers, standing three-deep and armed with a short sword on the
right, a long one on the left, and a long bow over one
shoulder with quivers of arrows on their backs.

The formation parted in a silent and orderly way to
reveal hundreds of men in wraps of pure white cloth
cinched at the waist with a moss green girdle. These
were priests, most likely, and each was standing in a

designated place, evenly spaced. Every fourth priest carried a staff with a clear globe at its top that contained some glowing bark fungus to light the night. All of them had from two to five pairs of eyebrows stacked atop each other, some rising up over shaved pates. At the sound of two claps, the priests parted, almost floating in unison, to create a channel that allowed the sleds to move closer to the palace.

A chill filled the evening air when Trellana's sled was positioned with the ones ahead of her and then the ones arriving. At the command of the captain, the sleds were raised up with ropes and then supported by a beam on their undersides to stand like the panels of a wall. The women moaned in pain as their bodies dangled from the ropes around their wrists.

Trellana was in a new agony as her arms were stretched, but she was able to see a large and stylized carving of a war beetle, big enough to serve as a house, at the center of a platform before the palace. The carving was wrapped in true gold and its antennae intertwined in an ingenious spiral. Scattered across the carving's surfaces were black ants fashioned from chiseled obsidian. On the right side of this carving was a man with the same brown skin as the other captors, but the fuzz of this man's armor was a bright blue. His helmet was also different, topped with what looked like a cluster of seven gold-wrapped wasp stingers. He stood with his hands clasped behind him, shifting uncomfortably, looking as much like an alien as Trellana felt.

On the left was Sinsora's highest priest. He had six pairs of eyebrows and a green eye patch. Beside the priest was an older man with a long, white mustache who wore armor of black beetle chitin and a helmet with a striking brush of fluttering moth antennae—likely the supreme commander of the Carpenters' army. The priest and the commander bowed to each other and then to the brown-skinned leader, before they opened panels on the carving's belly to reveal Emperor Sinsora. This mysterious figure wore a severe gown of the roughest black silk and he was seated on an austere but elegant throne atop a short flight of stairs. A partial screen hid his face but not his hands, which were so white they looked as if they had molded each other out of the purest beeswax. When the emperor raised his left hand to shake a rattle, his priest clapped his hands three times.

To Trellana's surprise, a small party of Britasytes rode out from behind the carving on one of their awful roaches. The insect looked especially garish with its embroidered draperies, its dizzying swirls of paint, and its encrustations of the cheapest jewels on its carapace. The sight enraged Trellana—seeing the roach people was another painful reminder of Anand. The three descended from their saddle on a rope ladder to stand near Sinsora and his priest and commanders.

One of the Britasytes was a man with a grotesque, knotted mustache that curved up to his ears, perhaps the chieftain of one of their clans. He tied the roach's tethers to a post and bowed to the emperor. The other two Britastyes were women wearing gem-studded turbans and an exorbitance of jewelry. Their loudly colored, shiny gowns were tailored to accentuate their full bosoms, thin waists, and wide hips. The youngest of the women stepped towards an amplifying-cone that was tilted up to Trellana and the other captives. She looked unhappy, under duress, as did the other two Britasytes. Trellana sensed they had been pressed into service. The emperor spoke to the older of the Britasyte women in the Carpenters' tongue and she passed his words to the younger to translate into Slopeish.

"Yellow-skinned women of the leaf-cutter ants," said the younger Britasyte in crude, workingman's Slopeish that was bereft of the proper honorifics for queens and princesses. "My name is Ulatha, a Britasyte tribeswoman, and my cousin is Queestra, who speaks the Carpenters' tongue. The Heavenly Sovereign of the People of the Pure Pine Lands demands to know who you are and why you have left your queendoms in the Land of Acorn Trees. Who speaks for you?"

"I do!" Trellana tried to shout, her words catching in her uncleared throat. "But it is impossible to speak when my arms are about to be ripped from my sockets!"

After these words were passed, the emperor nodded and the sled was lowered, freeing Trellana from her ropes. She wobbled as she stood and then fell over the sled's edge. No one would help her up. Everyone stared in silence as she got to her knees, then struggled to stand in what she knew was a disgracefully filthy garment.

"Announce yourself," Ulatha commanded through the cone.

"I am Trellana, a direct descendant of Goddess Ant Queen, Queen of Palzhad, former Queen of Cajoria, rightful Queen to all Dranveria, and future Queen of Venaris and the Reunited Holy Slope."

The translation sent a murmur of chuckling through the priests. Sinsora's next words were an angry mumble in the distance. He shook his rattle when he finished speaking.

"'Palzhad, we are told,'" said Ulatha, pausing for a moment. "'Is a human-inhabited ant mound in this supposed new nation of Bee-Jor. Who are these other women and girls with you? And where are they from?'"

"Behold the sorceress queens and princesses of the Lost Country, of what is now the Unholy Slope of the East, from nearly fifty different mounds," Trellana shouted as the sled was returned to its vertical position and her fellow royals moaned in agony. "We do not use that other . . . *name* for our country, which *will* be reunited with the western and Still Holy Slope. These are my kin, the direct descendants of the Ruling Goddess, and all will be treated as such by *you*. I demand that all of us are freed from our ropes. We will each of us be properly fed and clothed and given a mattress for the night in a private chamber. We must then be returned immediately to the Sacred Land at the Center of the Sand, the Great and Holy Slope."

Laughter came again, louder this time, and the priests struggled to maintain their composure.

"'And what are the consequences if we do not?'" said Ulatha, passing along the emperor's sneering tone. "'You are the fabled urine sorceresses, the ones whose magical essence allows you to cohabitate with leaf-cutter ants. What other sorcery do you practice? Are we in danger from your magic if we don't comply with your demands?'"

Trellana knew the questions were an insult and saw the smirks of the emperor's men.

"I do not know what punishments our gods have in store for you," she shouted, her voice firm and assured. "Or when they would unleash them. But I warn you that these are the True Gods and tempting them to prove themselves will be most deadly to you."

When the translation was completed, all was silent but for the sobs and moans of Trellana's suffering kinswomen. The commander lowered his head to the emperor, conferring with him, and then stepped forward to look over the captives as the next message was passed.

"'Very well, Queen Trellana, *of so very many places*,'"

shouted the translating Britasyte. "'We invite your gods to this gathering. If they prove themselves true and powerful, we will turn out our gods from our shrines and temples and replace them with yours.'"

The commander raised up his rapier and shouted as he pointed to a soldier at the front of the formation. The soldier nodded his head and loaded his bow. Princess Vanka gasped when an arrow pierced her chest and blood soaked her garment. Trellana heard the sickening crunch of her skull as a second arrow crashed through her forehead.

The emperor spoke as he raised up his right hand to display an empty palm.

"'Where are your gods?'" Ulatha translated for the emperor.

"The gods command us—not the other way around!" Trellana screamed as she heaved with grief. The emperor nodded and the commander pointed to a different bowman. Queen Lania's chest was filled with arrows. Trellana fell to the ground and screamed as panic and grief collided. Everything went black when she fainted. When she came to, she felt blood on her forehead and feared she had been targeted, but it was blood that had sprayed from the slain women behind her.

"'Where is your goddess?'" shouted Ulatha in a voice that trembled with fear and disgust. The roachwoman was looking away from the carnage, her sobs amplified through the cone. "'Where are any of your gods?'" she asked again. "'Pray to them to appear and rescue you. Pray to them to punish us, we 'primitives of the pines' as you call us. Ask your gods to grab us with their powerful claws, to chew us to pieces to fill their stomachs, and then shit out our bones atop my palace.'"

More bowmen were commanded to step forward, one for each of the dangling queens and princesses. They loaded their bowstrings.

"No! No! Please!" Trellana shrieked. "Ant Queen, protect us!"

The emperor looked up to sky's left, and then its right, and shouted but a single word. Hundreds of arrows flew. Screams of agony were followed by wailing and then the last gasps of dying. Trellana was frozen with shock. Her suffering deepened as she witnessed the end of her nation, the end of her people, the end of all she was. The wall of upturned sleds was splattered with the blood and flesh of slaughtered royals. The sudden silence was monstrous.

"'You are all that's left,'" shouted Ulatha, her voice breaking with pity, even as roach people had no love for Slopeish royals and they had a special contempt for Trellana. "'If we kill you, the last of you, Queen Trellana, will your gods finally appear? Is that what it would take to get their divine attention?'"

All Trellana could do was shake her head in

shock. "Shoot me," she said faintly. "Kill me! I beg you!" she shouted.

It was silent again, but then Trellana heard the slow and distant chirping of autumn crickets.

"Please, Goddess Cricket," Trellana whispered to the ground as she prayed to her mother's deity. "I have been neglectful with my sacrifices at Your altars. I have disdained You as foolish and weak. Forgive me, Night Singer. I beg for Your mercy."

Trellana looked up to see a bowman aiming at her, awaiting his orders. She opened her arms to welcome his arrows and pointed to her heart.

"'Queen Trellana,'" the emperor spoke, "'you celebrated the arrival of your firstborns with a ritual that sacrificed hundreds of my subjects to flesh-eating plants.'"

Trellana was quiet—she remembered that day: the Dranverites had invaded and disrupted the celebration for her newborns to plant the seeds of an insurgency.

"'For hundreds of years we have defended our nation from your vicious raids. Your warriors stole our goods, poached our ants, and worst of all, abducted our people, whose blood and flesh they fed to your vicious gods. For hundreds of years, you thought you were greater than us with your multitudes of soldiers and your millions of ants. And for hundreds of years, we have waited for our vengeance, to be rid of you. Now that time has dropped before us, like a windfall of ripened pine nuts. You, Trellana, have brought us an unimaginable gift: the urine sorceresses whose absence will weaken the eastern Slope just as we finish punishing its West.'"

Trellana could say nothing. In the silence, all she could ponder at the moment was that all her beliefs were false, that her entire life was a lie. She was nothing, no one, merely a common human who reeked of her own filth.

"What do you want from me?" she shouted.

"'We should be asking that of you,'" Ulatha shouted back. "'Why did you leave Bee-Jor?'"

She hesitated. "I . . . I . . ."

"'Speak!'" shouted Ulatha as the emperor stood and raised his rattle up like a mace. "'Answer my question!'"

"We came because we were commanded. It is the gods' plan. You will have to ask them what they have in mind."

The emperor conferred with his high priest and two commanders. The brown-skinned commander of the velvet ant people grew animated, stomping his feet and throwing out his arms as he shouted his words. All of them nodded their heads—they had reached an agreement. The emperor spoke again.

"'Queen Trellana. I am told you are pregnant,'" said Ulatha for the emperor, drenching his words with some apprehension of her own.

"Yes . . . Yes, I am."

"'With more than one infant, as is usual for Mushroom Eaters.'"

"It feels to be so."

"'And the father of these children is this Commander Vof Quegdoth of Bee-Jor, a man from the land of red hunter ants.'"

"That is . . . mostly true."

The emperor spoke briefly, then shook his rattle. The commander of the league was grinning as he ran his hand over the blue velvet of his armor to smooth it. The Carpenters' commander shouted an order, and the bowman aiming at Trellana lowered his arrow. She collapsed to the ground and was overwhelmed with fatigue . . . or dying.

Dying, I hope. Please, Death Beetle, take me now.

CHAPTER 12

A CRASHING ENTRY

Anand's new suit of armor did not fit him well. It was a hand-me-down that rode high in the crotch and the under-liner was tight in the shoulders, but he was still grateful to have it on this day. It was a gray afternoon with cool breezes, but before the day had ended, his locust was drifting lower, resisting his prods, and sweeping her wings back to glide. The locust landed on a thistle plant as the sun turned into a white disc and then was smothered by a creeping blanket of rain clouds. Anand looked down at the thistle's leaves, which were more likely to snap off rather than support him. The best approach was to climb down the spikes themselves, stepping on some while gripping others, and avoiding their dangerous ends.

As Anand made his way down, the locust crawled up to the dried flower and gripped its underside in anticipation of rain. Anand ran out of spikes to climb down as he neared the bottom of the plant, but then saw a pile of its dried leaves that looked thick enough to jump in, despite their dangerous prickles. He took a leap, feetfirst, while covering his face with his hands. Thankfully, his beautiful Dranverish armor saved him from any punctures. Guarding his face, he pushed out of the leaves to a clearing of silt-sprinkled sand and looked up. Flashing tendrils of lightning burst, then faded in the darkening sky and were followed by blasts of thunder that assaulted his ears and shook his insides. A drop of rain fell before him and another splattered, then sprayed, from the helmet on his head.

He chuckled.

It was better to laugh than to indulge in the disappointment of an unheard prayer. Ahead of him he saw a clump of heavy sedge grass, green and dense at its center, where he could burrow until the rain stopped or even spend the night.

After he crawled under the broad, fibrous blades of the grass, he found a space of clean sand. He heard the stirrings of a wood louse who promptly curled up into a ball that Anand rolled away. Using the serrated side of his knife, he cut some grass blades and wove them into a mat he could sleep on and a rough blanket to cover himself with. Sprinkles turned to a gentle shower and he savored the sweet sound of soft splashes and the music of dripping leaves.

Within him was that strange tranquility that came with a gentle rain. It was the peace and security of a womb, when life was nothing more than suspension in a warm, dark liquid. As his thoughts turned to the womb, he thought of his mother, the woman who had dedicated her entire life to protecting, nourishing, and encouraging him—something she knew would be a difficult duty since she chose to raise a child with an outcaste Slopeite. He imagined Corra in the Britasytes' afterworld, where during the day she rode in a sled-mansion through the Sunny Fields of Plenty and at night through the Realm of Stars.

As the night grew colder and the shower turned to a downpour, Anand's thoughts turned to Daveena. He ached for her, wanted to reach out with his arms to clasp her, and pull her inside the curve of his body where she fit so perfectly. What a wondrous, comforting thing it was to feel the warm fall of her breasts over his arms and tuck the end of his finger just inside her navel. How he loved it when she would press her hand against his own, then backed into his sex with her smooth and naked bottom.

The longing for her took its usual turn into worries—where was she? Was she safe? Was she even alive? As the night stretched on, Anand repeated her name in his mind as an incantation, hoping that the long chain of his words would stretch to the palace in Worxict and end as a whispering kiss in her ear. *I am coming for you, my goddess, and I'll build a palace worthy of you, a place to keep you and our little ones safe forever.*

Dranverish armor was refined and comfortable but it was still a problem to sleep in. Anand woke, for the fifth time, and was relieved to hear that the rain had stopped and see the sun was out. When he peered out from the sedge weed, beads of water fell on his head and arms, and he licked them to quench his thirst. The sand was moist and slippery but walkable since the soles of his Dranverish boots were textured to keep their grip. After taking a few hundreds steps, he reached a climbable rock and hiked to its top. From there he could see the black mass of a tree trunk and its spreading branches thick with leaves. He was heartened to realize he was closer to Cajoria's border wall than he had thought, as he recognized this tree as the one that the Bulkokans had selected for their new home. If he kept up his pace, he might be there by midafternoon.

As he got closer, anticipating leaf-cutter ants, he opened his backsack to prepare for his entry. He checked the bottom of the sack to make sure that the scrolls were still there. The largest tube contained a replacement copy of *The Loose Doctrine of Dranveria*, a present from the People's Agent. He looked at another tube, shining and red, and within it was a scroll that was even more precious, a gift from the scholar Babwott that he couldn't wait to share with his father and Terraclon. He picked up the third tube and shook his head before he stuffed it back in.

This one might get me in trouble.

He took out some garments and folded antennae from a wax-sealed package that were infused with leaf-cutter kin-scent. The odor was mild, faintly vinegarish, but it filled him with a vast melancholy to smell it again. The noisy squalor and stench of life in Cajoria's outer rings came screaming back in vividly ugly memories. In an instant, he could feel the rough rods of a shit-cart in his hands as he returned in exhaustion to the dreaded midden, to that place where his fellow outcastes screamed at each other in endless anger, that deep pit of woundedness where anyone who attempted to crawl out was dragged back in and beaten for trying to better themselves.

As he made his way through a patch of purple sanicles with their dried globes of spiky flowers, his sight became cloudy and his throat got itchy. Suddenly he had stomach cramps. Without seeing them, he knew he was close to the sagebrush plants that bloomed in the autumn and spread their poisonous pollen on the wind. He was choking and coughing as he reached into his sack for a cloth to tie around his face as a filter. The pollen reaction amplified the painful memories of midden life, and they piled up before him like sudden tumbles of rocks he had to fight his way out of. The beatings, the whippings, the public executions, and worst of all, the delight that others took in it were fresh in his mind and feeding his rage. He wondered if he could ever forget the cruelties he had suffered or seen or be free of the urge for justice.

"No, I don't think I ever can," he said aloud, admitting it to himself for the first time. *I will always be that man*, he thought, and then laughed at himself. When he walked out from under the last of the sanicles, he saw the sagebrush in the near distance.

I can walk around those.

It was some time before his eyes stopped watering and he could finally remove the cloth. He saw the Cajorian border wall of fitted sand grains needed repairs and the ants' parallel barrier of rain-moistened dung pellets was messy and meager. Daunted by the rain, the sentry ants had yet to appear as Anand made an easy climb over the wall into Bee-Jor.

And where are the human sentries?

In the near distance, he could see the Bulkokans' oak tree glimmering as the sun dipped west, but a feeling in his stomach was drawing him to it. As he got closer to the tree, he saw what looked like a few men wandering in its shade. His gut feeling turned from a pang to a pulsing.

Something isn't right.

Anand got close enough to see the caged roaches

that ringed the tree's roots to repel ants from climbing it to shear its leaves. The vague stink of death was in the air, like rotting onions mixed with shit. He veered around a stalk of autumn panicum with seed heads turning purple to find a woman facedown in one of the leaves attached to its lowest stalk. She was a plump woman, and as he got closer, he saw she wore a bee fuzz jacket. He turned her over and saw that she was alive— her fall had been broken by the leaf. As she gasped for air, her eyes blinked in the sudden sunlight and she rolled out of the plant to the ground. He knew her spine had been broken as her limbs sagged in limpness. Her face was turning a blueish-brown as her breathing grew shallow. She would not be alive for long.

Anand trotted towards the massive tree trunk and stepped over one corpse, and then passed a few more. All of the dead were bee people. His heart was pounding in panic and rage when confusion set in and his chest tightened with pain. He forced himself to take deep breaths until he felt blood returning to his head. He stomped towards some thickset men near the roach cages. "Citizens!" he shouted at them, but they froze and kept their backs to him. They were scavengers with baskets and travoises, working through the corpses. From high in the trees, he heard the vague sounds of woodwork.

"What's happened here?" Anand shouted. The men slowly turned to face him. "What's happened to the Bulkokans?"

"Why, hello, Anand," said Keel with a mock bow. "Back from the Barley Lands, are you? Did you make us a nice treaty with Emperor Vollycup?"

"What are you doing here, Keel?" Anand shouted at him as he identified the other males to be Keel's sons. All of them had swords at their sides either of Hulkrish or Seed Eater making. Around their necks were blowguns and strapped over their chests were crisscrossed magazines of darts. With only a knife at his side, the sight of these weapons made Anand feel both naked and vulnerable.

"We're just doing our jobs," said Keel. "These are corpses. We've come to salvage what we can before the carrion eaters gets 'em. It's our right . . . according to what you say."

"Where's Tal?"

"Nice of you to ask about him, Commander Quegdoth. He's at home, with the women, being looked after. Lost an eye, you know, in the battle with the Seed Eaters."

Anand was stunned. *The battle with the Seed Eaters! So that is what happened in my absence!*

"You all right, Anand?"

Anand said nothing. He called on his training as a Dranverish defender and went inward and past his shock to find the Core of Resolve. From behind the core, he took his rage and readied it like an arrow to shoot.

"No," said Anand. "I'm not all right. Nothing's right here." He stared into Keel's eyes until he shifted and looked away.

"When you're feeling up to it," said Keel, his eyes to the ground. "We'll talk to you about moving up the mound for a nice house, or two, of our own. Now that all my sons is heroes, they're getting lots of attention from some proper girls."

Keel's sons looked at Anand with their curled lips and furrowed brows—that ever-constant sneer—as they made that low *heh heh heh* of annoying laughter.

"Who killed them?" Anand asked. "Who threw the bee people out of this tree?"

"Now why would I know?" said Keel as he bent to pluck amber bangles and a neck ring from a woman's corpse before tossing them into his basket. "But I suspects whoever it was, that they are still up there and making themselves at home." Keel looked up in the tree and then at Anand before he checked each of his sides to see that he lacked a sword. Keel turned and looked at his sons to see if they had noticed the same thing.

"Where's your blade, Anand? Your fine Dranverish sword?" Keel asked. "Did they take it from you in the Barley Lands?"

Keel's smirk turned to a venomous snarl. His sons looked at each other—conspiring, perhaps. Anand saw their hands were poised near their weapons and he reached for his Dranverish knife and unsheathed it. It was no match for a family armed with Hulkrish swords. He heard them snigger.

"Why, Anand," said Keel. "Do you really think that because we're all alone out here that we'd slice you up and leave you as dinner for the moon roaches?"

Anand was unsure of whether to attack or run when he heard the faint swish of a falling object. He turned to see a Bulkokan woman, her feet and hands tied behind her, crash to the ground, dead in an instant. Stout and short, she had landed on her head and snapped her neck.

"Oh, no," said Keel with mock surprise. "It's raining people again."

Keel's sons sniggered as Anand rushed to the woman while men in the same bindings were falling to the ground. One of them landed on his back and screamed in pain as his legs and arms snapped under him. His face turned a dark yellow before he paled, then died. Anand heard screeching and turned to see a man had fallen on Keel and laid him flat on the ground. More men plummeted and were instantly dead, having landed on their heads, breaking their necks, or shattering their skulls. Anand glimpsed the faces of the fallen and recognized Queen Ladeekuz and her six kings. The queen still had her scepter of amber, which had punctured her chest and was stained with her blood. The king who landed on his back was the one with strange teeth that were so long they extended over his lips. Now those teeth had gouged into his own chin.

The sound of woodworking grew louder, a fury of chopping and chiseling. Anand looked up in the shadows of the tree when he heard a loud scraping sound and then the voices of men shouting in excitement. He panicked when he saw something large and rectangular tilt over a branch, just above him. "Look out!" Keel's sons shouted to each other as they dragged their father away. As Anand turned and ran, he heard the crash and the splintering of wood and then the angry buzzing of thousands of wings. When he got some distance, he glanced over his shoulder to see the wreck of the Bulkokans' bee palace. Its walls had blown apart and its bees took wing over its broken honeycombs to hover and protect their queen. Anand ran towards a patch of low-growing weeds as the bees searched in pivoting swarms to find and destroy their attackers.

CHAPTER 13

THE WINTER RAINS COME EARLY

When Anand could no longer hear the buzzing of
bees, he made his way back to the well-trod paths of
humans and ants, the ones he had been forbidden to
use on his way from and to the dumping weeds when
he was just an outcaste. He heard the light steps of a
six-clawed crawler and turned to see a scouting ant
with a bit of leaf in her mandibles. He turned towards
her, lowered his head, and wagged his antennae,
which she probed with her own. She identified him
neither as kin nor as an enemy, and when Anand tried
to climb up her legs to ride her back to the mound,
she sidestepped him and scampered home with her
gaster lowered to mark the trail with *leaf-find* scent.

Anand sighed and kept walking—the Dranverites leaf-cutter *kin-scent* had changed or faded or the ant was as exhausted and distracted as he was.

Night slithered in, as cold and damp as an earthworm, when he reached the outskirts of Cajoria's midden. He looked over at the crude, crooked huts atop their stilts and noticed that only half or so seemed occupied. A man was crawling up the ladder of one dwelling and Anand recognized him as Pleckoo's stepfather. He had rebuilt his hut and gone as far as reinforcing its walls and rooftop with tar and sand grains. It looked sound and proper, and the steeped roof included an extravagance of glittering bits of mica.

Pleckoo, you might have been proud.

Pleckoo . . .

Anand's thoughts turned to tortures for the man who had inflicted so much violence on so many. What would it be like to open his skin and cut all his tendons to leave him as a living blob? A moment later, Anand felt ashamed. "I'm a Dranverite," he said aloud.

Dranverites do not torture. When the time is right, there will be a trial, witnesses, and then a discreet execution. The Dranverites may not believe in capital punishment, but this is Bee-Jor—and a man who has taken so many lives does not deserve to keep his own.

As Anand continued his ascent up the rings, he realized no one recognized him in the plain, colorless garb that covered his armor. All were busy with their last tasks or thinking of the evening meal and their sleeping sack on the walk home. A few took notice of Anand's Dranverish helmet and handsome antennae but they paid no attention to his dark face without its stripes of red, brown, and yellow. As he got closer to the dew station of the scrapers' caste, he felt excited, anxious, and a touch of fear, but not *of* Pleckoo, rather of how he might react on seeing him. Would he give in to a sudden rage and decapitate the man who justified his crimes as the prophet of a Termite God? Or would he be overwhelmed with pity and forgive the *boy* who had protected and inspired him, the Pleckoo who would have been so different if only he had been allowed to keep his nose.

Anand walked through some stinky tar weeds that grew next to the dew station and was alarmed to see that the cage had fallen on its side and no guards were near. *I ordered a band of guards who were never to leave him!* Nearby were some women scraping water from the dew barrels for their evening needs. Anand ran to the cage, his head pounding when he saw that it was empty except for a pile of filthy ropes that were cut into shreds.

"Where is he?" Anand shouted at the women. "Where's Pleckoo?"

The women looked over at Anand and then away. A stout mother with a baby on her hip came closer, cocking her head. "Who are you, citizen?" she asked. "To be shouting at us like that?"

"I am Quegdoth," Anand said.

The woman gasped and so did the others near her. "Commander Quegdoth! You're back!"

"Where is Pleckoo . . . Good Citizen?"

The woman lowered her head and shook it. "He was . . . he was freed. Queen Polexima has ordered a search. He likely slipped past the Place Where Priestly Magic Ends."

The world grew small and distant around Anand as his fingers and toes went numb.

"Who freed him?"

"No one knows, Commander. It happened during the battle with the Seed Eaters, when all the guards left to fight. Pleckoo was all tied up to the bars inside that cage, watched over by the last of the guards, just a poor boy with a gimpy arm . . . a boy who had his teeth kicked out of his mouth before he was killed."

Anand felt his nostrils quiver as rage coursed through his veins and pounded in his head. He felt as if the lid of his skull was bursting through his scalp.

"Commander," said the woman. "Drink some water, please. Yours is bursting through your skin."

Though the evening was cool, Anand realized he was wet with sweat. It was drenching the lining of his armor and stinging his eyes as it dampened his beard.

"Please," he said, and took the scraper and licked the bead of water on it.

A crowd had gathered, and they were shouting his name. "Quegdoth! Commander Quegdoth has returned!" was ricocheting around him. The Cajorites were coming closer, wanting to touch him, and they stared in an adoration that Anand found unbearable.

A train of carrying ants had stopped to unload its passengers when Anand hailed it. "Wait up," he shouted, and ran towards the last ant at the back and then climbed up its rope ladder. He was helped to his seat by the other riders as they continued to shout his name.

"Quegdoth! Quegdoth is back!"

Crowds of people were leaving their houses and the dew stations and outdoor altars and running to the edge of the artery to see Anand. They were bewildered to see him riding atop the last ant of a train as if he were the most common of workers, but soon they were cheering, pumping fists, and bowing to him with palms pressed together. The crowd multiplied and followed the passenger train to the top of the mound as the chants of "Quegdoth" grew louder. All of it seemed obscene to Anand, who could think of one thing only: *Pleckoo has escaped!*

A sudden loneliness crushed Anand from within. He forced himself to wave and acknowledge the crowd even as he felt hollowed by their cheers and smothered by their numbers. The frozen expression on his face became a mask as heavy as any boulder. More than anything, he needed to see his friends and family and it irked him when the train was slowed by the adoring crowd, who got tangled in the ants' legs. When he reached the royal dew station, thousands filled its plaza, and expected him to speak. Defenders in armor helped him down from the ant, then carried him on their shoulders up to the platform of a Monument to the Eight Laws. An amplifying-cone was waiting for him and looked absolutely enormous, like a giant sieve that could never be filled.

What should I tell them? That I was in Dranveria where they considered executing me? That on my return here my life was threatened by my old foreman and his sons?

As Anand looked out at the crowd, he felt the weight of his responsibilities in a way he never had before. *I'm utterly depleted—and they expect to be inspired.* He clasped his hands behind him, forced a smile.

"Bee-Jorites!" he began, and the crowd cheered for a thousand breaths or longer.

They don't know yet that our Bee-Jor no longer has bees to make honey.

"Bee-Jorites, thank you for your welcome. My journey has been difficult, but not as hard as the challenges that tower before us, before each of you. While I was gone, you met one of these challenges, for *you* turned back an invasion led by Emperor Volokop!"

The crowd cheered again, their thousands of

voices reverberating through the palaces as the wind whipped the tricolor banners of Bee-Jor.

"We offered Volokop a peaceful truce," Anand shouted. "We offered him the return of mounds stolen by Slopeish royals and a chance at friendship with our new nation. Instead, he held to his hatreds, held to vengeance. He held for the chance to steal from *us* and slaughter *our* people."

The crowd hissed.

"But someday we must attempt to secure that peace again, to offer our friendship at a time when it might be accepted. We can hate Volokop, but we cannot hate the Barley people who are our neighbors. They are our fellow humans, with warm, red blood, who have children they love and want to protect. They, too, are victims of Volokop."

The crowd was quieting.

"Bee-Jorites, I have not just come from the Barley Lands. I have returned from Dranveria."

Waves of murmurs rolled through the crowd but Anand felt a warm rush inside him—feelings that had been smothered by months of fear and uncertainty.

"The Dranverites are not one nation, but a collective of thousands," he shouted, his voice growing strong. "In order to benefit from their wealth and knowledge, we must transform our nation into one as fine as their own, into a place where the weaknesses and evils of humans are expected, but where the chance to rise above our darkest natures is *demanded*.

We must, all of us, commit not just to our own welfare and our families, but to the welfare of all, even the enemy Seed Eaters—for one day, we hope, they will not be our foes."

Anand paused. In his head, he imagined what he really wanted for Keel and his family. It was not forgiveness, a fine house, or a peaceful existence—it was a long and protracted public execution where each of them would be subjected to at least ten of the most painful and humiliating tortures.

"At this moment, I am struggling to rise above my own dark nature, my yearning for revenge," he continued. "But I am asking all of you to do something, even as it may seem impossible. I ask you to love your enemies . . . to forgive them . . . to see yourselves in them and have compassion. Most of us have been *slaves*," Anand said, using the Dranverish word. "This is a new word in our language, meaning a human who does not own himself, but is owned by another and forced to work for a master or mistress . . . or worse, forced into acts that violate that person's body. Sadly, from what I know about the history of humanity, most slaves do not want freedom. What they want most is to have a slave of their own. Humans are more interested in war than in peace, in vengeance than in justice, and in the gathering and hoarding of riches than in sharing them. We are more inclined to hate than we are to love."

Anand paused and looked into the faces of those

closest to him and then to those in the darkness beyond.

"It is not always possible to forgive those who have harmed us. I would be lying if I said I could. I have met Emperor Volokop and have no love for him, but he is trapped in a massively deformed body, a prisoner of his own flesh, something that was imposed on him by nature. He dwells in ignorance and inflicts his pain on his subjects and, if he could, on all the rest of the world, including Bee-Jorites. I do not excuse his attempt to destroy us, but Volokop has my pity. We must remain wary of our neighbors, but just as we have been transformed from Slopeites to Bee-Jorites, so can the Seed Eaters be transformed. That change begins by setting an example. I ask all of you to be your kindest selves, to love your enemies even as they might hate you."

The crowd was in a confused silence but considering Anand's words. He knew the ideas were not his own, that they were cribbed from a long line of Dranverish philosophers. But he was surprised at the depth of his feelings as he spoke in what was no longer a performance but a heartfelt plea.

"And now, forgive me, Bee-Jorites, for I have urgent matters. Know that soon I will be asking you—*again*—for your sacrifice, for your bravery, as our nation faces more challenges to its very existence. Someday we will have peace and prosperity and leisure time, but those days are very, *very* far away."

The crowd applauded, quietly at first, but then in a sustained way that was somber and respectful. Anand turned behind him to find the same men and women he had assigned as his personal guards so long ago. They were standing by, ready to resume their duties—they had been waiting for him and had been sure of his return. They nodded quietly, smiled, and encircled him as a living barrier as he walked to the closest entry of the queen's palace and squeezed through its portal's diaphragm.

"*Creet-creet*," Anand called through the portal of his bedchamber. Mulga, the freckle-faced, took a wall sconce and scurried towards him, her eyes popping when they met his.

"So it *is* you," she said. "You might have sent some notice."

"It's good to see you too, Mulga."

"Worried sick, we were, having to face those Seed Eaters without you! And your father's been nearly dead with concern."

"Please," he said. "My circumstances were somewhat . . . extenuating. I'm hungry and exhausted—the last thing I need from you or anyone else is a scolding. I'll appreciate whatever meal you might find for me."

Mulga frowned and left for the kitchen. Anand stepped into the chamber to hear the rustle of scrolls and the breathy sounds his father made when he was excited. "Ah-huh! Ah-huh!" he managed to get out as his son's name. The sight of his father with his teary eyes and spindly arms reaching to hug him sent clashing waves of joy and pity through Anand. Yormu tried to rise on his elbows and Anand saw that his body was covered with dressings that needed changing.

"Don't even try to get up, Dad," Anand said, and took his father's hand as he bent to kiss his cheek. "I know you missed me. I missed you too."

Yormu nodded as sobbing wracked his body. His tears were bulging, and he turned away.

"Don't hide your tears, Dad," Anand said. "I'm not hiding mine." He brushed his father's hair back behind his ears, hair that needed washing.

Yormu smiled and revealed his missing teeth and the stub of his tongue, something he usually hid behind his hand. Anand found it both beautiful and saddening and he smiled back as he felt the warmth between them, that quiet bond he never doubted. On the nightstand, he saw a scratching tool as well as the page with the Dranverish alphabet he had written out. Scattered on the mattress were pages of Yormu's scrawlings.

"You've been practicing," Anand said. Yormu nodded and handed his son a sheet. Anand looked at it and saw uneven rows of ill-formed letters and all of them were crammed together.

"You've written something down."

Yormu nodded and Anand searched through it, looking for something that might make sense. "Dad, if these are words, you have to separate them, give them some room." Anand took the scratching pen and wrote in a space on the sheet's bottom. "Yormu is my father," he read aloud, and showed Yormu his lettering. "We'll practice, all right?"

Anand watched as Yormu copied what he had written. His father was agitated, tortured by some message he had to relay, wishing for the millionth time for the return of his tongue and teeth. "I understand, Dad. You have something you need to tell me, right?"

"*We* have something we need to tell you," said Terraclon as he pushed through the portal and held its diaphragm open for Polexima. She squeezed through, gripping her staff and using it to pull herself in. Both of them were dressed in their loose sleeping clothes, something very royal but comfortable looking. Anand rose, overwhelmed with relief.

They're alive!

He attempted to step towards them, mouthing their names, when he doubled over and cradled his face in his hands. When he stood, he attempted to look tall and strong, but he could not stop weeping. "This is embarrassing," he said.

Polexima hobbled towards him with moist eyes and a warm smile as she reached to embrace him. "I am just as relieved to see you," she said. "My tears are little splashes of joy."

Anand looked over at Terraclon as he pursed his lips, looked up at the ceiling, and rolled his eyes in impatience. "Well, well. The winter rains have come a little early this year and this room is getting rather wet. If everyone's done with all of their blubbering, we have some urgent issues to discuss."

"It is very good to see you, Ter," Anand said. "So very, very good."

Terraclon lowered his head. "Yes, Anand. We . . . we had some mild fear that you were lost forever," he said, not meeting Anand's eyes. "And we are . . . *relieved* to have you back. Chew on this, Anand. It may take all night to catch you up."

Terraclon handed Anand a plug of sweetened kwondle gum. Anand reached for the plug and clasped Terraclon's hand and did not let go. He watched Terraclon close his eyes, his mouth trembling before he turned away to hide his own tears.

"Come here," Anand said, and then jerked Terraclon into his arms. "I missed you too, brother. I worried about you every day that I was gone."

Terraclon fell against Anand and let himself be hugged.

"Your armor is too hard," Terraclon said, and pulled away, wiping at his eyes. "Where's Daveena?"

Anand gulped in the quiet.

"She is a hostage in Worxict. Hopefully still a hostage. Volokop expects my return. He sent me to Dranveria to issue a warning."

"Dranveria! You have been in Dranveria?"

"And other places in between."

"We have our own hostage from Worxict," Terraclon said, his voice returning to its natural pitch and the tuneless accent of their caste. "Someone the emperor might want back."

"Do we now? I'd heard you'd been rather busy in my absence."

"We have been," said Polexima. "And Terraclon has been brilliant. But for now, you must know that we have lost Palzhad."

"Yes," said Terraclon. "And are on the verge of losing every mound in Bee-Jor."

"To whom? The Seed Eaters?"

"No, Anand," said Polexima. "To the Yellow Mold. And to refugees. And to some strange, new threat from the West."

Anand was stunned again in a day of endless shocks. He looked over at Yormu, who had taken a fresh page of scratching paper and was attempting another message. He was drawing crude objects and combining them with letters and other scrawls and doing it with a fury.

What has Dad got to tell me?

CHAPTER 14

A FULL SACK AND AN EMPTY SACK

Trellana awoke inside a small room with a sweet, woody smell that emanated from its walls. A golden light came in through a framed window and its pane of flawless amber. Under her back, she felt a fine mattress that was perfectly rectangular, and laid over her was a soft blanket that was hemmed at its edges. She reached to lower the blanket and realized her hands and feet were tied tightly but with the softest of ropes. In a corner of the room, she saw an old woman asleep on a straight-backed chair.

"Help," Trellana said with an urgent need to urinate. "Help!"

The attendant awoke, startled, and then spoke in her wispy and whistling tongue as she rose and smoothed her simple gown.

"A chamber pot! I'm about to leak!" Trellana shouted as she struggled to stand.

The attendant sternly cocked her head, the top of which was piled high with white hair braided into a coil.

"The rain must fall . . . I must make water . . . I need to *piss!*" Trellana shouted. "Pssssssssss," she hissed, and the woman nodded her head and clapped. She pointed to a strange cube in the corner that had a lid with a quartz veneer and an ovular hole in its center. After guiding Trellana to sit on the cube, the woman lifted the back of her garment. As Trellana relieved herself, she recalled some of the details of the night before. She remembered fainting in the palace's courtyard, then being carried on a stretcher to a bathing room where she was scrubbed with a pine essence that left a tingling sensation. After she had been dried and dressed, someone passed her a chiseled bowl with a bulging drop of liquor that tasted of pine berries. The first suck of the drink had her drunk in a moment. The last thing she remembered was someone attempting to take the drink away before she could slurp up the rest.

After cleaning Trellana's bottom and wiping her own hands with a white cloth, the attendant took down a tray from some neatly built shelves. The tray was filled with attractive morsels molded into shapes of simple flowers, pine cones, and insects. Trellana ate while standing as the morsels were raised to her mouth with a pair of cunning little pincers. Sweet rainwater was set before her in a glazed bowl of green clay that she recognized as an export from Smax.

Why are they treating me well?

She was finishing the last bite of some sweetened lymph paste when she heard a strange sound at the door, a gentle rapping with knuckles. Using a handle, the attendant slid open the door to reveal palace servants with a litter. The servants wore loose trousers of a deep green cloth and tight blouses that were sun-bleached to a bright white. Their hair was closely cropped but had designs shaved into it of spirals, mazes, and tree branches. Trellana was ported down the long, straight hall and passed innumerable doors until she reached a screen decorated with the wings of a checkerspot butterfly. The screen was moved aside and the litter was set in the emperor's reception hall. By Slopeish standards, the hall was small and modest with a low ceiling. Its walls were unadorned, and its corners had no carvings of deities nor amber furniture, but the walls' wooden panels were beautiful and selected for the complexity of their grain. Trellana was helped to a hard and simple bench that faced the royal party.

Emperor Sinsora wore a mask carved from cloudy amber that featured a stylized beard and a large, looping mustache. *Why doesn't he show his face?* she wondered. He was seated on the Pine Cone Throne and in back of him stood his high priest with his six pairs of eyebrows, the lowest of which were lifted as he stared at Trellana. Next to the emperor's throne sat the Eldest Empress, whose fabled beauty was visible behind the sheerest of veils. To the emperor's left was his military chief in a severe black jacket and a stole of green caterpillar fuzz.

On Sinsora's right side was the dark-skinned chieftain of the League of Velvet Ant Peoples. Up close, Trellana thought his face was repulsive—it was far too much like that of a Slopeish worker. *Of one Slopeish worker in particular*, she thought as she was reminded of Anand. The chieftain looked uncomfortable and awkward in the royal setting, and instead of his velvety armor, he was wearing a bizarre tube-like garment of multicolored fuzzes that was held up by shoulder straps. The tube was short and revealed his legs, which were covered in curly black hair. Next to him, on the floor, were two strange-looking sacks. One sack was full and its top was tied with a scarlet rope while the other was flat and empty.

The Britasyte women arrived, without their chieftain, to serve as interpreters. They looked even less happy as they stepped off of litters. Trellana wondered if their chieftain had been killed or imprisoned. The women had been given modest shifts of pine bark cloth that hid their obscene curves and their gaudy garments and muffled the sound of their ridiculous jewelry as they walked. Sunlight from a broad window in the back of the hall gave this royal tableau a harsh outline.

The Britasytes bowed to the emperor, who spoke to them through the hole in his mask.

"Emperor Sinsora invites you to ask him questions," said Ulatha in Slopeish. Trellana was surprised.

"Why does the emperor want *me* to ask *him* questions? I thought I was not permitted."

"The questions you ask may inform the emperor of what *he* would like to know," came the answer.

"I do have a question," said Trellana. "But it is not for him. It is for you, *roach*-woman. How do I know that what I say will be accurately interpreted?"

The emperor cocked his head as he received the translation.

"You cannot know," said Ulatha speaking directly to Trellana as her thick, sensual mouth shaped the words. "But there are no other two-tongued in the Pine Country at this time. So you see, Your Majesty, *you* are at *our* mercy."

"But Britasytes are infamously unreliable," said Trellana. "Among themselves, they celebrate their lies. They boast about their deceptions and ridicule those outside their tribe as gullible for having believed them. Am I incorrect?"

Trellana saw anger on the Britasytes' faces as the chain of words was passed to the emperor.

"How do I know," Trellana continued, "that you will not insult the emperor on my behalf, or fashion falsehoods that will infuriate him to the point of his wanting me executed?"

The emperor was silent. The two roach-women spoke to each other, briefly.

"We Britasytes are a persecuted tribe," the young woman said, addressing Trellana. "Sometimes we are forced by our persecutors to tell untruths in order to protect ourselves. Often, when we are asked to pass messages between your nations' leaders, they are lies—lies that are attributed to *us* instead of to the leaders who mouthed them. We do not see the Slopeites or Seed Eaters or Carpenters as any more or less truthful than we are. All of us, we Britasytes too, are liars."

Ulatha paused a moment, blinking with her long and spidery lashes as she cocked her head and looked imperious. "I have something I need to tell you . . . *Majesty*," she said, seeming to spit the words. "Something which I will *not* interpret for the rest here. Our lives and those of our Roach Clan are in as much danger as you, *Trellana*. The Carpenters have detained us and ended our freedom to roam the Pine Lands, perhaps forever. We all must be very careful."

Trellana watched as the older woman, Queestra, spoke to the emperor, interpreting Ulatha's words. Trellana wondered what lie Queestra had fabricated in place of the warning Ulatha had just made. Trellana then wondered if this was all some trick between the three of them, a scheme between Carpenters and Britasytes to deceive her. The emperor's next words sounded angry as they were shouted through the hole in his mask.

"The emperor has taken offense at my calling him and his subjects untruthful. He demands the truth from *you* when you speak and warns of painful consequences if you lie. He invites your next question."

"Why are my hands and feet bound?"

"'So you do not kill yourself. Your words have suggested you are inclined to do so.'"

Trellana cocked her head and squinted at the man in his fuzz wrapper. "Who is this man at your right side who is so . . . interestingly garbed?"

"'He is the Great Leader of the United Tribes of Velvet Ant Peoples, or Greeyas as they call themselves, their commander-king. In the tongue of the League of Velvet Ant Peoples, he is the *Setcha* Greeya, or Great Greeya.'"

"The Velvet Ant peoples," said Trellana. "They were your enemies, were they not, Emperor Sinsora? You mixed in hundreds of them, captives, with your own people as part of the human tribute we demanded."

The emperor nodded.

"But now they are fighting beside you. Why?" Trellana asked.

"'We have a common enemy.'"

"Do you? Why would this league wage war on the Slope?"

"'It was the Slopeites who waged war on them.'"

"That's absurd. How could we? No Slopeite has ever been that far west."

Sinsora's military commander conversed with the Setcha Greeya in his own language for a clarification. As they conversed, Trellana could see and hear their tongues fluttering in their mouths. Some of their words climbed into their noses from their throats and were expelled with a little sneeze. It was some time before the translation was given.

"'Tens of thousands of moons ago,'" said Ulatha, singing it like a Britasyte song-poem. "'The people of jaundiced skin and dead blue eyes invaded the glorious country of acorn trees that shade the slope known in our tongue as Greeya-Tepic.'"

Trellana bristled.

"'The Jaundiced chased the original inhabitants, the Greeya people, from their ancestral lands, forcing them into the Great Dispersal. Some of the Greeyas were *enslaved*, forced to remain on what you call the

Holy Slope. Their cricket ranches were replaced with leaf-cutter mounds.'"

"Enslaved," Trellana said. "A Dranverish word."

"'*Enslaved*,'" Ulatha repeated, louder, as her features clenched together in an anger that reflected the Setcha Greeya's words. "'Defined as the ownership and exploitation of one human being by another.'"

Trellana fumed. "I do believe you mean the protection, salvation, and guidance of another by his natural superior in exchange for the inferior's labors."

After these words were translated, a tense silence filled the room. The Setcha seethed, his limbs trembling, before he began shouting in a voice that filled the hall and made its walls vibrate. As he blasted his words, he stomped with his hairy feet in sandals that slapped the floor. His outburst startled the emperor, who stiffened in his chair while his empress trembled behind her veil.

"What has he said?" Trellana shouted. "I demand to know."

"You should demand nothing, piss-sorceress," said Ulatha to Trellana directly. "You are hardly in charge here."

Trellana stared at the Setcha as he ranted, her contempt building to a disgusted rage. *So he is just some outcaste laborer descended from ancestors who dwelled in The Ignorance, from the ones who fled from The Taming.*

Ulatha cleared her throat and could not hold back a smile. "'The Setcha Greeya wishes you to know that your *naturally superior countrymen* are losing the war to his captains and his warriors. The future of your yellow-stained race has yet to be decided. Some in the league want the complete elimination of your people from the Sand with no chance to procreate. Others are for the hobbling and enslavement of the Jaundiced, to do unto you what you have done to others for so many centuries.'"

Trellana stiffened and resolved to show no expression as she asked her next question. "Emperor Sinsora. What is your aim in fighting with . . . these Greeya peoples against the Slope?"

"'We wish, for all time, to be rid of you Mushroom Eaters and your abominable leaf-cutter ants who have plagued us in our East,'" came the words of the emperor. "'We also wish to be rid of the League of Velvet Ant Peoples to our west. We have made the league aware that your Slope is weak from its war with the Hulkrites. Carpenters and Greeyas have agreed to the terms of a truce. Soon enough, the Greeyas and their insects will abandon the disputed lands of our western frontier to occupy what has been your Slope.'"

Trellana was scared into silence. She forced herself to find her words and speak them.

"This is unwise, Emperor! Foolish!" Trellana shouted. "This will bring nothing but endless war!

What if everyone decided to go back to where they thought they came from?"

"'We already have endless war,'" the emperor responded. "'We believe the league's claim to the Slope is true. We do not care if it is false. The League of Velvet Ant Peoples will reestablish their lost nation of Greeya-Tepic and we will have back our Lost Western Fields.'"

"Greeya-Tepic," Trellana repeated.

Somehow this name is familiar.

"Emperor, since I am encouraged to ask questions . . . what use do you have for me?"

The emperor laughed before speaking, a high-pitched giggle that struck Trellana as both undignified and unmanly.

"'I don't know that I have any use for you, Queen Trellana,'" he replied. "'But the Setcha does.'"

The Setcha spoke haltingly in the Carpenters' tongue. His words were not immediately translated.

"What did he say?" Trellana asked, annoyed that the man was looking her over as if she were a trollop he was considering.

The Britasyte woman cleared her throat. "The Setcha says that although your womb has been used and polluted by men of an inferior race, you are still a queen of the Slope."

Trellana blinked. "Yes, I . . . I certainly am."

"The Setcha says, 'You will remain a queen when you are returned to your home.'"

Trellana gasped. "Home?" she said, and the anger, the fear, and the frustration that had been building in her skull started to subside. "He is going to send me home?"

"He says, 'I will be taking you to *my* home. The one I am reclaiming from the Slope. You will give birth to my children with your fruitful womb, and live as my slave-queen. You, Queen Trellana, will be a living testament to the submission of your yellow race to my Greeya people. After thousands of years, we will have our revenge.'"

It took a moment before Trellana could absorb these words. She felt crushed, then numb as the Setcha Greeya was speaking again, leering at her as he did. Ulatha hesitated before giving the translation. Trellana could see that the Setcha's words had offended Ulatha.

"What did he say?" Trellana begged, betraying her desperation.

"The Setcha says, 'In order to make you my wife, you can have no other husband. In order to marry you, I will need to stand with you on top of a sack that contains the bones of Commander Quegdoth of Dranveria.'"

The Setcha grinned as he picked up the sacks next to him and spoke again.

Ulatha and Queestra were staring in disgust at the Setcha, barely able to continue their translations. The emperor, his wife, and his general were all looking away from the Setcha, ashamed, it seemed, of the cruelty and coarseness of this ally.

"I am so sorry, Trellana," said Ulatha through her sobbing. "I am speaking for myself at the moment. The Setcha says, 'The bones and the skull in the bag I hold up are an engagement present for you. They belonged to a man who said his name was King Maleps of Cajoria of the Great and Holy Slope. The empty sack I hold up . . . is for Commander Vof Quegdoth.'"

CHAPTER 15

A NEW ANT FOR BEE-JOR?

Anand finished his drawing of a triple dome structure and wondered if the Bee-Jorites could build something so intricate. It had to be constructed with sand-bricks of the clearest quartz to allow the Seed Eaters to see inside its space. It needed to be large and impressive but not imposing, not a threat, and it should not in any way resemble the crystal palaces atop the Slopeish mounds. Mulga called, *"Creet-creet,"* and entered the chamber with food.

"Commander Quegdoth, the Pious King Nuvao has returned from Mound Fecklebretz," she said after setting down a bowl of tea and a grated screw-bean in its own syrup. "He has urgent news."

"What news?" Anand asked.

"He did not impart it to me. I am, after all, born to be a servant. His Piety-Majesty will be joining Queen Polexima shortly."

Anand shoveled in his breakfast when he heard Yormu calling, faintly, from his bed with a weak smile. "Good morning to you, Dad! I've got to leave soon but I've got something to show you!"

Anand picked up some sheets and a stylus from his bed-desk and brought them to Yormu. "Here," Anand said, presenting his father with a diagram he had worked on during the night when he couldn't sleep. "One thing you know well is all the parts of a dead harvester ant: what to cut up, what to discard, and what to salvage for parts and food."

Yormu looked at Anand's drawing of a harvester ant with its massive head and he smiled in admiration of its rendering and then at Anand. With his finger, Anand traced one of the curving arrows that pointed from the insect's claw and then to the word for it.

"Claw," Anand said, and then announced each of its letters. "The words for these parts of a harvester ant start with each of the twenty-four *consonants*. Five other parts are words that start with *vowels*—those are the soft sounds. Vowels are like the glue between consonants that keep a word together. Your name has these three consonants and these two vowels." Anand pointed to letters and then to their corresponding words on the diagram.

Yormu looked at the sheet, his eyes protruding, and his mouth dropped. It was making sense! "Yormu," he tried to say as his finger ran over the letters.

"That's right, Dad!" Anand said gleefully. "You're reading . . . and aloud! For vowels you don't need teeth or a tongue. Let's try the dust-box."

Anand pulled over the box and wrote his name with the stylus in the finest of powders. Yormu looked at the letters and then referenced each of them on the diagram. It took a while, but finally he pointed at Anand. "Yes! It's my name! Anand!"

Yormu nodded as Anand gave into a tearful laugh. *Dad is reading!*

"Can you write what this is?" Anand pointed to his hand.

Yormu consulted the diagram and pointed to the different parts of the slaughtered ant as he worked out the letters. When he finished, he mirrored Anand's smile as he shone with pride.

"That's it, hand! But this is the right vowel," Anand said with what was both a laugh and a cry. "The vowels are tricky because working people say them differently than the soldiers and royalty. And some sounds differ from mound to mound."

Terraclon entered the room and walked towards

them with a look of surprise followed by resentment. Yormu grinned at Terraclon and then went to work in the dust-box.

"Good morning, Ter."

"It must be a good morning as the both of you are beaming like sun rays. Has Yormu learned to read before I have?"

"He has just spelled out your name."

"I can see that. And I'm not at all jealous."

"You shouldn't be. It's not like you haven't been busy."

Anand handed Yormu a sheet. It was an early draft of the Eight Laws written in the Slopeish way with pictures and symbols in its top half. On its bottom half was the Dranverish way in letters.

"The priests of the Slope have this way of writing," Anand said, pointing to the mysterious drawings. "But here's our way, below, with letters. It's better, meant for all people to learn and understand. Today when you hear the priests reading the Eight Laws, you can follow along."

"Polexima and Nuvao are expecting us," said Terraclon.

"Right, but first I've got something to show the both of you."

Anand pushed at his bed, then lifted up a floor tile where he had hidden his scrolls in a secret compartment. He brought one to Yormu, a bright red tube that featured stripes that spiraled up its sides in the five colors of the Dranveria Collective.

"This is a *book*, Dad. A book is a collection of pages that tells a story or teaches a lesson. This one is a true treasure, a first of its kind, and we must all take very good care of it."

"I thought you said they had millions of books in Dranveria," said Terraclon. "What's so special about this one? Are its pages made of gold?"

"This is far rarer than gold," remarked Anand as he uncapped the tube. He pulled out a scroll with colored drawings and words written at the bottom of each page. "This is the first book ever written and printed in the Slopeish language. It uses Dranverish letters."

Yormu looked through the pages of the scroll that were fastened to a thin spool.

"I'll read it to you when I get back," said Anand. "It's the story of how Brother Sun and Sister Moon came to share the sky."

Anand bent to kiss his father's cheeks. Yormu's eyes were moist when he pointed to his heart.

"I love you too, Dad."

Before he went out the portal, Anand looked over his shoulder to see his father, wide-eyed, as he continued to look at the book's first page and began, perhaps, to make sense of the writing in it.

"So what took you so long?" Terraclon asked as

they walked the corridor to Polexima's apartments. Anand was lost in thought, worrying about Daveena and the lost clan of Entrevean Britasytes when he realized he had been ignoring Terraclon.

"I'm sorry, Ter. What?"

"Why were you in Dranveria for so long? Once they dragged you out of Stink Ant country?"

"It's hard to explain, but they are a nation with a long and established *democracy* with a balance of different powers. No one person can make an instant decision. My situation was documented in what's called a *deposition* and then *debated* and . . ."

"*Democracy. Deposition. Debated.* All these Dranverish words!"

"Yes, my *testimony*, my story as it were, was recorded on paper. As I was out of Dranveria when I raised a fire effigy, I could not be accused of breaking Dranverish laws and I could not be put on *trial*. I agreed to participate in a public hearing. When all the facts were presented, a *debate* followed. People of differing viewpoints who were experts on the law argued over whether I should be punished or released or . . . put to death. The People's Agent *presided* to make sure my hearing was fair and then a vote was taken."

"And in the meantime, we had to defend ourselves from the Seed Eaters without you."

"I explained that to them."

"Then why didn't they release you immediately?"

"It's one of the hazards of rule by all. It takes time. It's imperfect."

"But Volokop could have destroyed us! It might have been the murder of millions!"

"I know, Ter. But the Dranverites worried that the greater threat to the Sand's million-millions was *me*."

"*You?*"

"They had a point."

Terraclon was silenced and came to a complete stop. Anand took him by the arm and prodded him towards the queen's portal.

Polexima and her priestesses were completing a prayer-dance at her shrine to Cricket around an offering of the morning's food and drink. Most of the priestesses were women of yellowish complexions, but a few were novices with brown skin. They were still learning the steps and the proper way to pluck a chirp harp. The ritual concluded with the recitation of all of Cricket's names. After that, the Cricket idol was picked up and set on a bed at the back of the curtained shrine. A perfumed blanket, shaped like an oak leaf, was pulled over Her face so She could sleep during the day. As the ritual was completed, Anand summoned the first of the messengers waiting by the portal.

"Good Messenger, take a speed ant to the Britasyte camp near the border and tell Chieftain Zedral I will meet him shortly. Ask him to prepare a *badaboo pradakash*."

"A *badaboo pradakash?*"

"Yes. He will know exactly what that is."

"Yes, Commander," said the boy, trembling with pleasure to be addressed by Vof Quegdoth. He slapped his chest and ran off.

"Cricketites," Polexima said as the priestesses picked up the offered trays to the goddess to eat as their own breakfasts. "Take your meals with you to enjoy outdoors while I confer with Commander Quegdoth and Pious Terraclon."

Polexima looked with concern at Anand and Terraclon as the priestesses departed with the false legs of their Cricket vestments rising and falling. Once they had left, Nuvao appeared in the chamber after pulling open a curtain from one of its recesses. He was still dressed in loose sleeping clothes and had allowed his hair and beard to sprout. He had been hiding, lying on a cot in a garment room. Anand saw that he was stooping and had lost weight. From the paleness of his complexion, he looked to be ill or grieving.

"You are not well, Nuvao," said Anand.

"I am not."

The four seated themselves on the floor around a low table. No one was interested in the food.

"Every urine sorceress in Bee-Jor has been lost," said Nuvao. "Every last female who could provide the essence." Nuvao looked over at Polexima. "All of them but you, Mother."

"But there must be other women who can provide this essence—if they eat roach eggs," said Anand.

"No," said Nuvao.

"But plenty of women are the offspring of royal males and women from other castes. Every war trollop must have a daughter who inherited this trait from a king or prince who seeded her."

"I am afraid you are wrong," said Nuvao. "On rare occasions, a Slopeish queen has given birth to a false princess: a daughter whose father is not a royal but a lower caste lover she secreted into her bed. In order for a girl to be born as a true and potent urine sorceress, both her mother and father must be of royal blood."

Anand realized Nuvao was right as he remembered that the members of the Leaf-Cutter Guilds in Dranveria only married their own kind. Anand had thought they were clannish racists, but now he realized that their guild was just practical.

"What's happened to these royals? Where are they?" Anand asked.

"They're dead or captured. My stupid sister led them into the Slope for the sole reason of sabotaging Bee-Jor. Unknown to her, much of the Old Slope is already lost to the Carpenters."

"But the Carpenters have never been aggressors," said Polexima. "Why are they taking territory?"

"They're not. Not exactly. Emperor Sinsora has allied with the League of Velvet Ant Peoples."

"With who?" Terraclon asked.

"The Greeya tribes, as they call themselves," Anand said. "Known to us as the Velvet Ant people. The Britasytes know of them but have never traded their goods—they don't have any, or none that they didn't steal. The Dranverites have attempted contact but all their envoys have been killed. We have never entered the Greeyas' countries, which are dangerous and undefined. They raid and plunder and feud with each other."

"They do not feud anymore," Nuvao said. "They are united now, and being aided and advised by the Carpenters. I got the sense that the party that stumbled into Trellana's herd of imbecilic women were scouts—they were there to survey their next conquest."

"Where is their country?" Terraclon asked.

"They've mostly been confined to the Scrublands, west of the pine country," said Anand. "*Mostly* confined. The Scrublands are a waste area of rocks and hard-packed clay where little grows and where there is little game. The velvet ants are actually wingless wasps, solitary insects that don't live in colonies. They have the deadliest poison in their stings, and their shells are the hardest chitin on the sand."

Anand pulled up the sleeve of his pilot's garment to reveal his armor. "The best, most desirable Dranverish armor is made from velvet ant chitin. Once it's lacquered from the inside and lined with spider silk, there's little that can penetrate it. Spiders who capture velvet ants can't suck their blood, and their velvet prevents them from being eaten by larger insects. They have only one enemy who can challenge them."

"What . . . or who?" asked Terraclon.

"Ghost ants," Anand said.

Anand realized his words were like a sudden haunting of ghosts that seeped into the chamber and chilled it. Terraclon involuntarily shuddered.

"How do the Carpenters keep back these Greeyas?" Polexima asked.

"I'm not sure that they do. It's constant warfare, from what Dranverites and Britasytes know of it. I'm both astonished and alarmed that the two nations are allied now as you couldn't imagine more opposite peoples. I imagine this is an attempt of the Carpenters to relocate the Greeyas to someplace that's weak and crippled in return for a treaty that ends their conflict—that finally gets rid of the plague of velvet ant riders."

"Someplace like the Old Slope," said Terraclon.

"Or like Bee-Jor," said Nuvao.

In the startling quiet, Anand saw his own worries in his friends' faces. He cleared his throat just to make a noise.

"Polexima," he said, and she took his arm. "Terraclon and I must go on a reconnaissance today, to see what's coming from the West. But before we go, I . . . I want to bring up . . . an *idea*."

"Yes, Anand?"

Anand was quiet for a moment, unsure if he should continue.

"Please, Anand," insisted the queen. "This is just a discussion."

"Thank you, Polly," Anand said after a sharp intake of breath. "You know that someday I hope our nation of Bee-Jor will be invited to join the Dranveria collective."

"It is my hope as well," she said. "My greatest desire is to see Dranveria before I die."

"In order to join the collective," said Anand, looking into each of their faces before he continued. "We would have to . . . have to replace the leaf-cutter ant with the red hunter. The hunters would become our beasts of burden, our border protectors, and our mounts in hunting and in defensive wars."

"Yes, Anand, People of One Red Blood and One Red Ant."

"So you will not take offense when I suggest that instead of trying to save the leaf-cutter ants from the Yellow Mold that we may be . . . may be better off with a different kind of ant for Bee-Jor."

Polexima was quiet and then looked thunderstruck as she leaned back, then forward.

"Anand," she finally said. "I must admit that the thought of this land without leaf-cutter ants is a jarring notion. It is one that completely eliminates my purposes as a queen. And I don't believe red hunter ants are available to us until we are invited to join the collective. What other ant did you have in mind?"

"Bitter ants," Anand said. "The exploding ants of the Silk Moth people."

Polexima folded her arms. Nuvao looked sicker. Terraclon's mouth was agape.

"Anand, those are very dangerous ants," said Nuvao. "How would we tame and domesticate them?"

"There could be some Silk Moth people at the mound of Jatal-dozh," said Anand. "And there might be some among the refugees in Palzhad."

"This is all highly speculative," said Polexima.

"It is," said Nuvao. "We shouldn't abandon the leaf-cutter ants so soon. Not before we have to."

"What do you suggest?" asked Anand.

"We will need some Slopeish queens back in Bee-Jor, some viable urine sorceresses," said Nuvao. "There are still a few left in the Slopeish mounds just beside our border. We should offer them something."

"Offer them what?" asked Polexima.

"The chance to survive and flourish in Bee-Jor."

"Or succumb to a coming massacre," said Anand.

The four nodded their heads in the silence.

"I have someone I need to speak with," said Polexima. "What's the best way to get me to Fecklebretz?"

"I shouldn't accompany you," said Anand.

"Why not?" asked Terraclon.

"Because the Slopeites hate me and will never trust me. And if we fail at this, I want to have a backup plan. After the reconnaissance, I'm flying into the Dustlands, to see what's become of the bitter ants."

"To live among explosive ants," said Terraclon, affecting the royal accent. "It does sound terribly lively."

CHAPTER 16

AN UNENDING PARADE

Anand woke up tired and felt even more exhausted after breakfast. All the kwondle tea he consumed had done nothing except irritate his bladder and send him to the bowl for one more piss before getting in his armor. He sensed what was at the root of his exhaustion—a dread of the day ahead. He was unsure of what he would discover, but his gut, that most reliable of indicators, was letting him know there wouldn't be good news.

It's just a matter of how bad it will be.

His armor wasn't going on easily and he was having to figure out its parts and resnap them. It wasn't the armor's fault, which was beautifully designed. His head was just too full of worries to concentrate.

"Someone didn't sleep well," said Terraclon as Anand joined him and Nuvao at a hitching post.

"I slept like the dead," said Anand with a smile that was more of a mocking grimace. All of them were wearing plain cloaks of eggshell cloth as they descended on their speed ants to a weedy area south of Cajoria's airfield. Anand sighted a Britasyte banner flapping atop a collapsible pole in a thicket of autumn daisies to signal their whereabouts. The three tied their ants to milkweed stems when the ants halted in resistance to roach odor.

As they walked, Anand looked up at the daisies and their sunny color brightened his mood . . . for a moment. "Zedral!" Anand shouted when they found the chieftain with Grillaga and his other wives, who were wearing breathing masks and goggles. The masks were colorful, multilayered, and had intricate patchwork; they looked like little quilts. They were fastened with strands of stretchy spider silk to knobs on the temples of the goggles, the frames of which were studded with tiny bits of gold and silver pyrite. *Britasytes must decorate everything,* Anand thought. He saw that they were harvesting the autumn daisies. Piles of the flowers' seedy centers were drying in the sun while their petals had been given to some tethered roaches as a treat to munch.

"Good travels," said Anand, surprised to find that

he *could* smile. He was comforted to see some roach people and happy to speak some Britasyte.

"Good travels, Anand," said Zedral. "We are praying for Daveena each day. Mercies of Madricanth upon her."

"It will take more than prayer," sighed Anand. "And she is not the only missing Britasyte."

"Yes." Zedral hung his head. He glanced at Terraclon and the young Slopeish priest with his yellow skin. "I wasn't aware you were coming with others, Anand."

"Apologies. I should have let you know, Chieftain," said Anand. He looked over at Terraclon and Nuvao, both of whom were watching the roaches eat. They were fascinated or disgusted by the flapping, goo-covered lids of the insects' mouths and the pulsing yellow palpi beneath them that grew brighter as they were stained by the flower petals.

"Have we any news of the Entreveans that went west?" Anand asked.

"None, I'm afraid."

Anand was silent. "No Britasytes should travel west until further notice," he said. "Not to the Slope. Not to the Pine Lands. Perhaps never again."

"Never?" The chieftain was confused.

"The Old Slope is under attack," Anand said. "Parts of it may be lost. My fear is that the Entreveans who went west are prisoners of the Carpenters. Or worse."

"What will you do? What can *we* do?"

"I don't know," Anand said, aware that despair had entered his voice. He reminded himself to sit up straight in his saddle. "For now, I need to see if we can at least find them. Where might they be?"

"Hiding if there is a war. But the usual route is to Gagumji, then north towards Teffelan. From there, they'd cross into the Pine Lands to trade at the Carpenters' outposts. Britasytes are not allowed to travel as far as Gemurfa, but they are allowed at Brignakoo."

"Brignakoo?"

"Yes, it's a pond settlement, just east of Gemurfa, where minnow hunters and scum collectors are easily parted from their money. If the Entreveans are there, you'll see their sleds on a sand clearing on the southern side of the pond."

"Commander Anand!" shouted Punshu as he ran out of the daisies. He lowered his breathing mask to reveal his face and the gap between his teeth as he smiled. He handed Anand a plain brown backsack that was waterproofed with beeswax and tightly cinched at its top.

"Punshu! Thank you," Anand said as he pulled the sack over his back while coughing from the irritant in the flowers. "I've heard the most amazing things about your bravery in the Barley Lands."

"It's all true," Punshu said as he thrust at the air with his pole-saw. "I want to go with you, wherever you're going. I'm the best warrior you've got!"

"You mean *defender*. And first you'll have to learn to fly. Who's that behind you?"

Arriving behind Punshu was a Seed Eater boy and a muscular young woman from an unknown people. Her thick hair was a yellowish white and so tightly curled that it was like a ball around her head.

"You knows me and so is your wife. I'm Odwaznee," said the young, ginger-haired Seed Eater after he lowered his breathing filter. "And I now is speaks the roach tongue."

"You most certainly do. I'm glad to see you're all better," said Anand, trying not to laugh. It was strange to hear the roach tongue spoken by a Seed Eater. "I have a need for you at some point, Odwaznee—something important."

Odwaznee cocked his head, delighted. "As you wishes, Commander."

Anand nodded to the female stranger. "And this lovely guest—who are you?"

The woman stepped closer to Anand and nodded before lowering her breathing mask to reveal an expression both fierce and sad. She had the palest brown skin, like the sun-bleached shell of an acorn. Her eyes were widely spaced with purple irises that glistened like amethysts in a squarish face. "Good morning," she said in Britasyte. She held her cutting tool like an upright spear, and looked to Anand like a warrior princess.

"This is Putree," said Zedral. "She was one of the

few to survive the fall when her people were thrown out of their tree by the . . . bee people." Zedral winced as he referred to the Bulkokans.

"We are teaching Putree our tongue," said Grillaga through her breathing mask. "It goes well, Anand. She wants to learn."

"Good," said Anand as he heard Terraclon sneeze and Nuvao cough—the processing of the autumn daisies was irritating their lungs. "Perhaps, someday, Putree can tell us who threw the bee people to *their* deaths. Maybe it was her own tribe."

Anand frowned as he considered his greatest mistake. *I should never have brought the Bulkokans here. But I won't take responsibility for their murder.*

He looked up at the sun. "We have to leave now if we're to get back to Bee-Jor before sunset."

"Yes, let's go," said Terraclon. "These flowers are making me sick."

"Protections of Madricanth," Zedral said.

"Yes," said Anand with a kind smirk. "Thanks for your . . . blessing." Zedral waited for Anand to return his blessing and looked offended when it was not.

As the three walked back to their ants, Terraclon gave Anand the sideways glare.

"If you have a question, you should ask it," Anand said.

"All right," said Terraclon. "What were you talking about with the chieftain?"

"About our lost Entreveans, the clan that divided

to take separate journeys. I'm hoping we sight them today—that they haven't been killed or enslaved."

"What else? He didn't like that you brought us with you."

"He would have liked a warning, yes, that I was bringing strangers. He does not know King Nuvao."

"I was surprised to see roaches eating autumn daisies," said Nuvao. "That would kill most insects."

"Not all," said Anand. "Roaches are immune. They thrive on them."

"What do Britasytes do with the daisy seeds?" Terraclon asked.

Anand frowned and stayed quiet.

"They are a powerful poison against insects," said Nuvao. "And when mixed with other essences are even more deadly to humans."

"Nuvao's right," said Anand.

"Which is why their collection and propagation is strictly prohibited on the Slope," Nuvao continued. "A concentrate from the seeds would endanger any ant mound. Those seeds are so toxic that they have never been collected or stored by the Slopeish priesthood."

"The weeding caste usually destroys them before they can appear," said Anand. "But when they do appear, well . . . the Britasytes have had their uses for them."

"What uses?" said Terraclon, cocking an eyebrow. "Why would the roach people need poisons?"

"No more questions this morning," said Anand,

shutting down the conversation. "Let's hurry," he said, running back to the ants and forcing the other two to keep up.

At the airfield, a squadron of thirty pilots was waiting beside saddled locusts that had been gorged for the long and risky flight. Standing next to each of the pilots were archers with full quivers on their backs, loaded blowguns around their necks, and dart magazines bulging from under their cloaks. Anand, Terraclon, and Nuvao removed their own cloaks to reveal their speckled blue armor. The other pilots did the same and onlookers murmured in admiration to see a squadron fitted out in turquoise blue. Anand thought the armor was too beautiful—envy making—but it did allow for the freest movement. Terraclon could not stop staring at his own creation. He was proud and in awe of its collective impact.

"Pious Terraclon, to your locust, please!" Anand whispered.

"Just checking up on my work," said Ter. "It all looks to be in order . . . except for what you're wearing on your back."

"This is the backsack I need," said Anand, tapping at the one he had been given by Punshu.

"But I ordered you a blue one!"

"I *have* to wear this one."

"You're ruining my color scheme."

Anand looked at the locust selected for him as it

was led from a water trough. All the locusts were plump and their wings were thick and glossy. He felt assured they could take the squadron as far as the Pine Lands and later bring them to Palzhad. After he climbed up to the saddle, Anand was handed some weapons by his pilot, a smiling young man with a light brown face and hair in ringlets that escaped from his helmet. He brimmed with the honor of serving Quegdoth.

"Commander," he said, and bowed his head.

"Good morning, Good Defender. What's your name?"

"Pilot Viparee," said the man, confirming Anand's guess that he was a son from a crafting caste.

"Pilot," Anand said. "You mean *Defender* Viparee."

"I am *Pilot* Viperee," the man corrected him, and Anand winced. The differentiation of military status on Bee-Jor had already begun; locust riders were setting themselves above those who fought on the ground. The weapons Viperee handed to Anand were well made, lacquered and decorated. Terraclon and Nuvao were looking over their own weapons, and after admiring them, they linked the hooks on their belts to those of their pilots to strap themselves in. Anand did the same and then looked up at the midmorning sun as it burned yellow-white in the East. "Up, Bee-Jorites," he shouted, and no one moved. Terraclon shrugged and bobbed his head in expectation. Anand then remembered that all flying directions were to be indicated with standardized hand signals.

And hopefully I have all these signals memorized. He searched through the fog of his head and remembered—a rising fist for takeoff and then pointing three times in the proper direction.

The locusts leapt into the air and quickly soared to heights beyond the reach of human weapons. The blue of the sky was bright and deep, but its western end was filled with thousands of dark little clouds that looked, for a moment, as if they were crawling towards Anand.

Crawling like an army of fuzz-covered wasps.

It was near noon when the squadron reached Venaris. From above, Anand saw the ongoing construction of the watchtowers and barriers that Terraclon had designed to great success on the eastern border. He looked over and saw that, again, Terraclon was inspecting his work from above. Anand smiled in admiration and felt a touch of envy. Ter was an *innovator* in the Dranverish tongue, an *ingenious* man. How many other geniuses were hidden among the Slopeish outcastes, men and women with something to contribute if they had just been allowed? And then Anand realized something that made him frown: velvet ants had chitin that was nearly impenetrable. The warriors riding the velvets would be wearing armor made of the same material. Both might likely crawl through the pikes that thrust from Terraclon's barriers.

Anand realized that they were just to the left of Mound Fecklebretz, that the locusts had drifted with the south-blowing breeze. He circled with his fist to guide the squadron directly over the mound, which was located in the center of a rough circle of flat-topped boulders near a grove of ancient and ant-ravaged oaks.

That all looks normal, Anand thought as he looked down at the mound. Healthy processions of leaf-cutter ants were going up and down its main artery. The human activity was meager—it was, after all, a Slopeish mound, so its obedient masses were sticking to the confines permitted to their castes. Anand signaled the squadron to follow him west.

He felt the sun burning on the exposed part of his neck, just below his helmet, when the squadron neared Mound Abavoon. From high above, it looked like a typical Slopeish mound except for the masses of neglected death cap mushrooms that overwhelmed its environ—the death caps were everywhere along the Slope, clustered around the roots of the oak trees.

Since the rain, I've seen enough death caps to poison both our nations!

Anand raised his fist and made a semicircle and pointed slightly south, expecting that the next mound they would fly over would be Ospetsek, the mound that was midway between Fecklebretz and

Teffelan. He was assured they were traveling in the right direction when he sighted the legendary sycamore trees with their tipsy trunks that slouched around Ospetsek's fabled spring. From above, the spring was just a muddy water hole where diseased and aging nobles made pilgrimages to worship Damselfly and bathe in Her restorative waters.

If only cures were as easy as bathing.

As they flew lower, he saw a multitude of pilgrims, surprised that so many were making the journey in such a dangerous time. A moment later, he realized that the travelers below were not walking to the spring, but past it. As the squadron veered between the sycamores, Anand signaled that they were to fly lower for surveillance. As they neared the ground, he saw that these walkers were finely clothed with light complexions. The adults were female, and the rest were children.

Those aren't pilgrims! Those are Slopeish refugees! And they're headed east!

Anand was heaving with worry as he looked to Terraclon on his right and to Nuvao on his left. Both shook their heads, as concerned as he was. They continued their flight over the sparse parade of refugees until, finally, they reached the outskirts of what had to be Mound Teffelan. Anand was dreading the sight of it, but something stranger was making its appearance: a tall fence of crimson-colored ropes that stretched between posts. Behind this fence, Anand saw a hundred, then a thousand, and then a hundred thousand velvet ants. Some were as orange as spring poppies and others were as yellow as dandelions. Most had fuzzy coats that were as bright and red as human blood.

Anand felt like he was looking at his own blood, as if it had been drained and poured before him as his last sight before dying. The velvets were tethered to each other with ropes to keep them from climbing out of this stupendous pen. Most of them were rubbing their legs over their striped hindquarters and making a chattering noise that was disturbingly loud and disorienting. He looked over to see that Terraclon and Nuvao as well as their pilots had their mouths open in horror.

As the flight continued, the mass of velvets only grew thicker with ever larger insects. The Carpenters' war beetles were mixed among them and hauling massive sleds that bore great squeeze tubes of liquid food. Weaving through the velvets were women and children with long-handled scoops or scrapers. As the women scraped at mites hidden in the fuzz, the children ran from the ends of the squeeze tubes to bring drops of nectar to the velvets' mouths.

So war beetles have no quarrel with velvet ants, Anand thought. *And roaches won't repel them either, because the velvets are not real ants. I'd wager that food is aphid milk, courtesy of the Carpenters!*

Anand guided the squadron upward when he

thought he saw Teffelan's mound coming into view. But the mound before him was not Teffelan—it was an enormous pile of dead leaf-cutter ants. As the squadron got closer to the pile, Anand could see thousands of men were at work around it, butchering and preserving the edible parts. Around the central pile of corpses were smaller ones of inedible claws, antennae, and emptied shells. As some butchers snipped, severed, and sawed, others scraped lymph out of the carcasses that they spread on leaves, then rolled into tubes and tied at the ends with twine.

As the squadron continued west, they reached a lushness of autumn weeds that had taken over Teffelan's lowest habitation rings. Anand saw that the mound's environ had been neglected for some time, that its inhabitants had been too occupied with war to deal with encroaching plant growth. The stilted shelters in the workers' rings were occupied by new human inhabitants—the Greeyas, as they called themselves, the herders and riders of velvet ants. The sand and tar dwellings of the next rings were also occupied by them. Not a living leaf-cutter ant was in sight, but the velvets were everywhere on the mound. They were rigged and saddled and tied to the stilts of the lower shelters or they were tethered to the hitching rails outside the houses.

As the squadron flew closer to the mound, Anand saw some striking blue velvets. These were the bright, deep color of malachite, and they were saddled and hitched to posts in the uppermost rings. Some had been unhitched and were most likely mounted by high-ranking officers gathering for a ride. The fuzzy armor these men wore was made from their insects' blue chitin.

Something tells me they want more than just this mound.

Anand, Nuvao, and Terraclon flew over Teffelan's western side to see its stadium. As Anand had expected, there were cages on the stadium's arena, and through the cages' bars he could see the male velvets, which were smaller and winged. He remembered when he had toured the ranches of the Armorers Guild in Dranveria. The armorers used the scents of male velvets to subdue and control the females, an insect that was raised for its hardest of all chitins.

From the south, he saw a short train of Greeyas on foot. They were lugging blue and red sand-sleds, which were bulging with the translucent black eggs of burrowing beetles, out of the weeds. The sleds were headed to the deep chambers of Teffelan's emptied mound where the black eggs would hatch into larvae to serve as the living hosts for the velvet ants' eggs that would hatch in spring.

The squadron continued over Teffelan's hunting weeds on its western end, but within them, Anand saw a continuing parade of mounted velvets marching east. And then, disturbingly, he saw a junction where the parade branched off, to mounds in the North and the South.

Just how many are they in this league? Millions?

Anand's heart was beating so fast it felt like its four chambers were chasing each other in a circle. All he could hear was its pounding, and when he went deaf, he worried that his eardrums had burst.

CHAPTER 17

BRIGNAKOO

Anand looked behind him to make sure the squadron was still with him, that they hadn't panicked and abandoned him.

They were still there. Nuvao looked sick again, pale and in pain. Terraclon, with his teeth clenched, had that blank look he got when he was being beaten—a look that refused to give his tormentor any pleasure. While practicing his deep breathing, Anand repeated in Dranverish, "Nothing overwhelms me unless I let it."

A few moments later, the buzzing of the locusts returned to his ears. His heartbeat slowed and the fear that throbbed inside him was reduced to a dull pang. Ahead, in the distance, he saw the first pine trees with their rough, ruddy trunks and their short upward branches. When he looked down, they were still there: the unending parade of velvet ants, and their riders crawling over a path strewn with dried and scattered pine needles. As Anand absorbed the coming challenge, he fought a deepening exhaustion, one that was pulling him off the saddle. Pilot Vipa-ree looked over his shoulder, his brow creased with worry. Anand sat up, thrust out his chin; he would look brave until he felt brave.

"Onward, Viparee," he said flatly, as if dealing with some minor annoyance.

War. That is a war crawling towards Bee-Jor. And all I really want to do is rescue Britasytes. One Britasyte in particular . . .

An image of Daveena shimmered before him like a haloed goddess, an image so vivid he thought he could pull her towards him and kiss her. He shook his head sharply and banished all distractions. *Pay attention, Anand!* he scolded himself. *You're flying over dangerous territory.*

The Carpenters' border barricades came into view. They were masses of pine needles, held together by nets, then piled atop each other as great sacks to make a tall, thick wall. Protruding from the sacks were sharp twigs and thorns that would be dangerous for men and ants to climb between. Atop this barrier were the Carpenters' sentries, who were perched in wooden shelters. The sentries had their tethered tridents at the ready, poised inside the long, cupped shafts that increased their speed and accuracy when flung. Also at the ready were the massive crossbows laid on their sides: the missile launchers that had been salvaged from the Hulkrites' invasion. Through an opening in the barricade, the parade of velvet ants were continuing their eastbound crawl, unmolested by Carpenters, and as Anand flew farther west, he still could not see their end. A mix of war beetles was within their parade to haul sand-sleds full of supplies. The beetle drivers were not Carpenter men, but Greeya warriors, easily identified by their fuzz-covered armor.

Anand knew that the Pine Lands had only two large cities, both of which were built around some ancient and massive tree stumps, but they had many villages, some of which he could see below him. Most of these were built atop smaller tree stumps where they could avoid floodwater. Some villages were built into the trunks of the trees, which they shared with the wood-chewing ants that were a source of food and materials.

The squadron was nearing a sudden thickness of young, shorter pines, which forced Anand to lead the locusts into a nearly vertical ascent. As he held tight to Viparee's waist, the sudden heights confused him and he blacked out. When he came to, he forgot for a moment where he was and what he was doing. He looked down at the thickness of pine saplings and his heart flopped in his chest like a fish plucked from water. *I must remember the point of this mission,* he thought, and he was relieved when the details came back. A moment later, he smelled the dank scent of mud and algae. They were nearing a pond and this place called Brignakoo.

The pines got older and taller and thicker, forcing the squadron to fly even higher until they saw an expanse of brown water and, near it, a large settlement of wooden houses on stilts near its edge. Anand looked down at deep, wide boats and a series of floating structures tethered to posts on the shore where men were at work dredging up algae, gathering mosquitoes' eggs and checking their fish nets. A moment later, an expanse of dried sand came into view. Anand's heart beat with excitement and he gasped in relief when he saw the Entreveans' sand-sleds, glinting in the sun near a cluster of sword ferns. But where were their roaches?

And where were the Entreveans?

Anand gave the signal for landing and then a second signal for readied weapons. The archers loaded their bows as the squadron flew in a tightening spiral, then landed near the sleds. The locusts were positioned to make a living fortress of themselves as the bowmen faced outward, arrows poised.

Anand felt like an axe had been embedded in his chest. The Entreveans' sleds were abandoned and had been plundered. They were stripped of their jewels and decorations and vandalized in a vicious way that destroyed everything about them that was beautiful. The sliced quartz and amber of their windows had been shattered or stolen. Surely, their interiors had been emptied of every useful and sacred item, including the gold-leafed idols of Madricanth. Anand felt violated and then shattered. He knew what feelings would come after that.

"Commander," Nuvao shouted from his locust. "Look, under that fern."

Anand focused on the darkness under the sword fern to see the clan's cockroaches. They were on their backs, their legs in the air, dried into husks that rocked in the breeze.

"I'm going in there," Anand said. "Protect me."

Pilot Viparee guided their locust into the shade where Anand could see the rest of the Entreveans' roaches, easily identifiable by remnants of their decorative paint. Some roaches had been severed in two and some were shells whose insides had been eaten by carrion beetles. All had been stripped of their decorative jewels. After Anand examined the deep breaks in their chitin, he was certain they had been killed with Hulkrish missiles that had pierced them through to their other side.

And surely these precious missiles with their obsidian heads were retrieved to shoot again.

Rage was burning through Anand, a feeling he

never welcomed, but one that was like an attached twin brother. But rage had its uses. With rage came a new determination, a new urge for justice.

"Pivot," Anand ordered his pilot, who guided their locust to crawl back to the squadron. Anand could see the Carpenter water workers, some of them in their round boats, as they stared at the invading locust riders in fear and fascination. And just to the north, he heard the sound of an ant parade and saw the first of the carpenter ants up close, as black and glossy as beads of obsidian. The ants were crawling towards them on the pale sand from a hole in a tree trunk. Their antennae had sensed the kin-scent of leaf-cutter invaders and black gasters were raised and mandibles scissored as the carpenter ants marched into battle. Anand looked up at the sun to check its position.

"To Palzhad," he said. "Up!"

As the locusts leapt into the air and safety, Anand wondered if Palzhad would be any less dangerous.

CHAPTER 18

ATROCITIES MUST SERVE A PURPOSE

Anand was certain that to the South, Mound Gagumji had fallen to the Greeyas, but his worries deepened when he saw refugees fleeing Mound Bentilimak for Mound Caladeck . . . and Caladeck could not be safe for long. It was late in the afternoon when he sighted the crescent-shaped grove of dead or dying oaks that clustered outside of Caladeck, the second oldest mound on the Slope, which, like Palzhad, had been on the verge of falling into the Dustlands for decades.

And I can see why.

Anand frowned to see so many oaks turned into ugly, black skeletons surrounded by their fallen and crumbling limbs. Here and there he saw oak saplings that had attempted to grow but their leaves had been sheared by leaf-cutter ants, which left nothing but drying stalks. A few of the largest oaks were sickly but alive and had dropped acorns that would neither grow into trees nor could they be eaten by Slopeites as they were surrounded by death cap mushrooms that contaminated them.

All that rotting food down there. The weeds workers have neglected those death caps!

Anand was startled when Mound Palzhad came into view in the yellow light of late afternoon. From above and below, it had always been lush and inviting with its wealth of flowering, fragrant, and seed-bearing weeds. For the Britasytes, it had provided a wealth of game, as well as wild mushrooms, garlic, and onion shoots along with cilantro and epazote. Now, nearly all the vegetation in its vicinity had been eaten or uprooted, which left only the bitter dwarf-prickles, the sour stench-worts, and the spiny witch-tits that leaked a poisonous milk when their stems were cut. Farther away from the mound was another wealth of autumn daisies, something else neglected by the weeding caste or too difficult for them to get to—and avoided by ants and other insects.

As they got closer and circled the mound, Anand saw that most of the weeds had been dried and bound into cubes or logs and these were piled up as barriers between the different camps of refugees. Some of these camps were positioned higher, almost midway up the mound, in what had once been the homes of craftsmen and traders. The refugees were prevented from rising farther up by the rough barrier ring that the Palzhanites had improvised and were patrolling on foot. The lower camps on the mound were sectioned off in a way that imprisoned the refugees in tight, little pens since there were no corridors between them. The people in these camps had access to nothing. They had to be both hungry and thirsty since there was little vegetation in their confines to collect dew.

How can we bring them food and water when they have boxed each other in?

The refugees who were the last to arrive at Palzhad were more fortunate. These camps on the outermost ring were open on one end, which allowed them some space to roam and meagerly forage. But the free spaces just beyond the ring had already been desolated and all that was left behind were stubs, sand, trash, and shit. From above, Anand saw what looked like one ragged clan who were mixing their morning dew with dust to have something to fill their stomachs. Terraclon glanced over at Anand and winced—it was a reminder of the famines. Nuvao was looking at this process and seemed both mystified and disturbed.

As the squadron flew into a spiral for a landing, crude and feeble arrows struggled upward towards the locusts' undersides in hopes of bringing one down. The squadron pulled into a tighter formation, then landed, one by one, on the clearing of the royal dew station where facilities had been hastily erected to cage and care for the locusts. Anand landed to find the Palzhanites bowing or curtsying and was about to reprimand them for treating him like a royal when he realized they were doing it for Nuvao, the man who was still their king.

"Thank you for your welcome," Nuvao said, and nodded his head. Anand was relieved some color had come back into Nuvao's face. A cadre of bodyguards went immediately to Anand and slapped their chests in respect before encircling him as he dismounted. Over the guards' heads, Anand turned to see Terraclon was still sitting on his locust, miffed that he had yet to attract some attention.

"Blessings of all gods upon Mound Palzhad," Terraclon shouted to the attendants and guards. "And on its oh-so-lovely people."

"Thank you, Pious Terraclon," Anand shouted, trying not to smirk. All in the squadron were brought beads of water in cones made of mushrooms, which was a simple, all too familiar meal that Anand had not eaten in ages. The dampened mushroom was chewy and acrid, and the water tasted like sweat, but he savored every bit of it as he thought of the plights of the refugees. "Good Defenders," he said to the squadron and the Palzhanite guards. "Let us meet these refugees while there is still some light. We'll need

our blowguns, our bows, and quivers full of arrows."
More than anything, Anand wanted a nap, and when
he yawned so hard and long that he stumbled, a guard
offered him a plug of kwondle with a glittery dusting
of crushed honey crystals.

The descending sun was as bright and orange
as a marigold flower when Anand, Terraclon, and
Nuvao reached the barrier ring that divided Palzhanites from the masses of hungry and homeless below
them. Anand's bodyguards hung shields of bound
grass over their backs, then climbed up ladders to join
the foot sentries who paced atop the crude barrier,
their arrows or darts at the ready. The bodyguards
made a wall of themselves as the commander, the
king, and Bee-Jor's highest priest climbed up to stand
behind them. All three were still wearing their striking armor of speckled blue, which the refugees could
glimpse from behind the guards.

Anand's face fell when he looked down on the
first camp, which seemed more like a pen for insects
than a camp for humans. The grounds contained
the dusty remnants of some ancient sand and resin
houses, but all Anand could see was a sprawl of
emaciated women in filthy gowns of a violet gossamer. The women were lying on flat surfaces, hands
over their eyes, and looked to be sleeping. But soon
Anand realized they were just too weak to shoo
the blowflies that hovered above them. They were
women of different complexions and nations but

most of them appeared to be of Hulkrish stock with yellow-white skin and fair hair. Among them were some children, a few girls and some boys, the latter of which were weakly standing guard at the far ends of the pen with flimsy spears of sharpened straws.

Anand was wondering why there were no men when he realized, from their dress, that these were Termite Harlots: women whose devotion to Hulkro was in the maintenance of His altars and the servicing of His warriors. They were wearing the violet robes of the New Moon ceremony, when a hidden Hulkro had to be lured by their beauty to return to the sky and light the night.

And now that there are no more Hulkrites, they are women without a future.

Some of the women were rousing now, alerting each other to the arrival of some men in spectacular blue armor who stood atop the wall.

"Vof Quegdoth," shouted one of the women, gasping with excitement. "Send us our honey! Quench our thirst with berry punch! Fill our stomachs with locust roasts stuffed with pine nuts and sauced with grub foam! We are in Bee-Jor, are we not?"

Anand wondered how to address them.

"Good . . . Women and Children," he finally shouted. "We will find you *something* to eat . . . just as soon as we can."

The women were walking towards him, pleading with their eyes. Anand saw their wispy bodies through their gauzy dresses. The sight grieved him as they clasped their hands and fell on their knees, as if pleading to a god. He looked at Nuvao and Terraclon, who looked both saddened and bewildered. The three men were all too silent as they walked to view the next camp.

The next people were familiar to Anand. They wore garments made from a felt of matted punk weed seeds. Their hats and boots were of fish leather and some of them were attempting to eat these, grinding them with their molars until they might tear a piece away and swallow. They were the Kweshkites, the southern shore people, who tamed and rode the water striders. Anand remembered their massive, unsinkable boats that were crafted from the stalks of punk weeds and held the bounty of the Great Brackish Lake including its fathead minnows, its back-swimming beetles, its water fleas, and lace weeds, which were dried and eaten as a treatment for constipation. Anand wondered why they were among the refugees. Many of them were older women and they were at least a few thousand where the previous camp was just a few hundred.

An elder of Kweshkin, gray-haired but sturdy, rose and looked at Anand with her pale blue eyes. Her skin was the same color as the pale yellow marsh grass her people used to make their boats.

"Good Kweshkite," Anand said to her in Hulkrish. "I am surprised to find your people here."

"We were surprised to find ourselves here too," she said. "But we had no choice. I am Elga, the regent of Kweshkin—since my husband was killed."

"Why aren't you on your shores? Where you have always been?"

"We had no love for Tahn or Hulkrites, but they left us to our ways. They traded, fairly, for our products, and left us to run our own affairs as long as we worshiped the lump of wood they set on our altars. After the War of One Night, men who had been Hulkrites, the deserters, hid in our city, then took it over. They threatened us with their weapons and stole our boats and killed many of our men. They captured and enslaved our women and children and forced the rest of us to flee. We came here to appeal to Vof Quegdoth."

Anand could see that the woman was doing her best not to break down in tears.

"I promise I will get your land back," Anand said. "And please . . . before your people consume their boots, we will find you something to eat."

The three proceeded to the next camp where Anand saw the pen's barriers were made from piles of the prickly seedpods of bur clover. He looked down on a tribe of people with skin and hair as dark as the night sky and eyes of a piercing green. They were mostly women who were seated on the ground and all of them were wailing in distress. Anand felt a deepening pity. He wanted to look away but would not.

"I know these people," Terraclon said after gulping. His face looked as if it was sliding off of his skull.

"Who are they?" Anand asked.

"I don't know their name . . . but I'm not afraid of them."

"Why do you think they are weeping?" Nuvao asked in a trembling voice.

"I'll ask them," Anand said.

Once again, the people below were looking up at him with hope, muttering, "Quegdoth!" as they roused.

"Good People," Anand shouted as he stepped through the guards. "I have come here to help you."

A tall, all too slender woman wobbled as she stood to address Anand. Although she was frail and thin, her face was intensely beautiful with eyes the color of new grass. "I am Queen Jakhuma of the Ledacki people," she shouted in her weak voice. "We need your help. Now."

Ledackis, Anand thought. The southern people who live among the meat ants.

"Why are you weeping?" he asked.

"We weep because our men have been captured while trying to defend us—caught with net traps. They are being killed and eaten by those cannibals over there!" shrieked Jakhuma, pointing to the next camp.

"What? Cannibals?" Anand shouted, startled into outrage. The word "cannibal" was the same in

Hulkrish as in Slopeish, and Nuvao and Terraclon stiffened with alarm. "Has no one here tried to stop them?" Anand asked Jakhuma. "No soldiers?"

"No one," said the queen. "The Palzhanites are too busy defending themselves."

"Have the Eight Laws been read to you and to your neighbors each morning? In the Hulkrish tongue?" Anand asked.

"Each morning to each camp," said Jakhuma. "As if laws ever mattered to *green-skins*. They're more spiders than human."

Green-skinned cannibals, Anand thought, and then he remembered. *The spider people of Vundjeloo! Those faithless Hulkrites who had been imprisoned at Halk-Tritzel! Even Tahn and Pleckoo detested them.*

Anand felt his head clear and his limbs grow strong. *Pity is weakening but rage brings strength.*

"Follow me," he commanded, and led the guards and sentries to the next camp. He slung his bow over his back and dropped to his stomach to squirm like a worm until he reached the center of the barrier of the green-skins' pen. Anand did not see any Palzhanite sentries along this part of the wall and was wondering why when he heard excited voices in a foreign tongue and then the sounds of ripping flesh and feasting.

When Anand squirmed up to the edge of the barrier and looked down, he spied a noisy group of men with loose, fluffy hair who crouched in a circle. Their skin was stained with a green pigment and their jaws were painted with designs of spider fangs.

"Vundjeloos," Anand whispered, and remembered Tahn's exasperation with them—they were disobedient soldiers who ate the dead after battles, and even worse, killed and ate the prisoners and their children. At the moment, the Vundjeloos were butchering a human corpse and distributing cuts of it to their tribespeople. A woman was arguing over her share, resentful that she had gotten an arm when she wanted a leg. The man offering the arm yanked it from her hand and then used it to beat her. Anand saw that next to this circle was a cluster of net-traps that contained living captives with black skin—the men of the Ledacki tribe! The nets were cinched so tight that the Ledackis only had room to breathe. Some of the Vundjeloo men were brazen enough to be wearing the cl othing and armor of a Palzhanite sentry they had captured, killed, and likely eaten.

Anand quietly rose up and loaded an arrow. He shot one green-skin through his throat and another between the eyes. A third man was shot in the back of his neck as he ran, which sent his head tumbling under him before his body fell on top of it in a crooked heap.

"Shoot to kill, no women or children!" Anand commanded as the Vundjeloos ran for cover and their own weapons. Terraclon and Nuvao hesitated before they began shooting at the green-skins, most of which were easy targets. A few Vundjeloos were shooting up at Anand's men with stolen weapons, but these men attracted a barrage of arrows that shredded their chests and faces. Other green-skins, their women and children, were fleeing to the lower end of their pen, climbing over its walls and igniting a conflict with the inhabitants of the next camp.

"Release those men in the nets!" Anand commanded the guards. "We'll cover you."

The guards dropped over the wall, then ran to the nets, cutting them with knives to release the men. A ladder from the Palzhanite side was lowered, but many of the Ledacki captives were too weak to climb or their limbs had been broken. Guards and sentries dropped to the ground and hoisted these men over their shoulders to take them over the wall.

"You, Vundjeloo people, have violated the first of the Eight Laws," Anand bellowed in unfiltered rage at the green-skins in Hulkrish, knowing that some were hiding in the ruins of the shelters. "No human shall ever kill another human unless in self-defense."

Or unless in the defense of others, Anand thought, realizing that this would be the first of his amendments to the Eight Laws.

"If any of you who have survived chooses to kill again," Anand shouted, "you . . . will . . . be . . . punished."

Anand heard the distant panting of a man and

searched through the rubble and stubs of weeds to sight a crouching green-skin, poorly hidden behind the broken stalks of a white sage plant. His mouth was smeared with human blood. Anand felt near to exploding with hatred for this complete stranger as he nocked his arrow. Steadying himself, Anand felt that enchanted moment when an arrow locked on its target. He pulled the string and released. The arrow shattered the man's skull and sent bloody bits of flesh spraying over the white stalks as his body slumped in death. Anand felt relieved as he reloaded his bow and searched for others, sure that only the death of more Vundjeloos could leach the hatred that poisoned his mind.

Nuvao and Terraclon stared at Anand in silence, worried and in shock. A few moments later, Mother Sand had eaten Sun and would slurp up the sauce of His bloodied light.

"Anand," said Terraclon. "It's night now. Come on—you've done what you can."

Anand lowered his bow, turning to the men and women awaiting his next command. He thought a moment. *This atrocity must serve some purpose.*

"Good Defenders," Anand shouted. "Gather eight bodies of these green-skinned flesh eaters and bring them up to the royal mews."

When they reached the barrier above the Ledacki camp, the rescued men fell to their knees before Anand. "Deepest obligations, Commander Quegdoth," said one of them in Hulkrish, a scarred young man who had seen much battle.

"Stand, please," said Anand. "No man kneels to another in Bee-Jor. What is your name?"

"I am Sebetay, subject of Queen Jakhuma, a soldier of the Ledacki tribe," said the young man, out of breath and overwhelmed with relief as he rubbed his shoulder sockets.

"Sebetay, I am asking my guards to lend you and your men their weapons. You will use them only to defend yourselves against the Vundjeloos—or other attackers. Is that understood?"

"Yes, Commander," said Sebetay as Anand handed him his own bow and his quiver and realized he had no remaining arrows but the one he held in his hand.

"**W**e must bring these refugees something to eat," Anand said as he stood with Nuvao and Terraclon in the royal reception room at the foot of the stairs that led to the thrones. Gathered just below them were the selected representatives of each of the mound's *trades*—the new word that was being used instead of "caste."

"Commander, we should be thinking of our own people first," said a richly dressed merchant whose belly stretched the lavender felt of his tunic. "These refugees will be nothing but a drain on us."

"No, Good Merchant," said Anand. "The refugees

may be an advantage in the coming conflicts—an asset to Bee-Jor. We can offer them refuge in return for their service."

"Commander," said a man wearing the green, leaf-shaped cloak of what had been the foragers' caste. "We have no food to share with these strangers. The stores of dried meats, eggs, and pickles have already been distributed to Palzhanites."

"Then they can keep and eat them," said Anand. "I know we have mushrooms we can share—an excess of mushrooms that might have been exported to the Seed Eaters."

"Commander," said a man wearing a cap in the shape of a mushroom head. "We will have just enough dried mushrooms to get the lower castes . . ."

"The working trades," corrected Anand.

". . . the working trades through the winter hibernation. We can't share them with Hulkrites."

"They are *not Hulkrites*," shouted Anand. "They were the *captives* of Hulkrites, their slaves."

"Commander, the presence of the refugees has made it impossible for us to hunt," said a light-skinned man wearing a gold-wrapped arrowhead that had been his caste's medallion. "Even if we could get past their camps, they've destroyed all the weeds that feed and hide our prey. And likely they've pulled every burrowing creature out of the ground."

Anand was silent a moment. He turned to some darker-skinned Palzhanites who had clustered under a wall torch, still too diffident to mix with those of once higher status. One wore a scraper around his neck, and another wore the messy garb of the blinders' caste. A third was wearing a papery tunic of eggshells.

"What remains of the ants here?" Anand asked, his accent slipping into low Slopeish.

"Very little," said the scraper. "The foraging and scouting ants were all slaughtered by refugees on their return. The sleeping giants were roused long ago to fight the ghost ants of Hulkren. The last of the giants were summoned, before reaching full size, to face the recent battle with the Seed Eaters' harvester ants."

"So far," said the blinder, "the nurseries are still free of the mold as those chambers are very deep. But the larvae are starving and most are dead. They crane for food but there are no nursing ants to feed them. All we can give them is water."

"The blinders' foreman is correct," said the egg gatherer. "The queen ant laid tens of thousands of eggs before she expired. They are living eggs, free of the mold for now, but once they hatch, they will die without immediate attention."

Anand looked at Terraclon and Nuvao, searching their eyes. He hesitated before speaking. "Bee-Jorites. At this moment, leaf-cutter ants have no future at Palzhad. King Nuvao, my suggestion is the immediate distribution of all living larvae and uncontaminated eggs to Palzhanites. To the refugees, I recommend the distribution of three mushrooms per person per day until we can commission the delivery of acorns from the West and preserved harvester ants, which are in abundance at our eastern mounds."

Nuvao nodded. "I will supervise the distribution," he said. "With what remains of the men in the priestly . . . vocation."

"Good. I suggest taking a flight above the mound after sunrise to count, as best as you can, the number of camps."

Anand pointed to the foremen of the building and sand-bricking castes. "Foremen, tomorrow after the Eight Laws are read, your *guilds* must supervise the clearing and reinforcement of spaces between each camp. They must be corridors wide enough to allow for the passage of cargo-sleds. I will instruct the refugees in each camp on how to assist you."

"Yes, Commander," said each of the foremen.

"That is all for now," Anand said, turning away from them.

"Commander Quegdoth," shouted the stout trader in his lavender felt, startling Anand with his commanding tone. He bowed in apology when Anand turned to him with an angry stare. "If we are to defend this mound and feed its people, we must have ants," said the trader.

"Agreed," said Anand. "I will not let Palzhad fall into chaos or surrender it to what is now the Dneepers' country. If you will forgive me, I have a lot to accomplish before my flight tomorrow."

"Commander," shouted the trader again. Anand stared at him.

"If I may ask, Commander Quegdoth . . . just where is it you are going?"

"You may ask," Anand said. "But that does not mean I will answer."

The following morning, just before sunrise, Nuvao and Terraclon met each other under fading torch-lights at the movable speaking platform. They were approached by Durelma, their interpreter, a young Palzhanite woman who had been a captive in Hulkren. She curtsied to Nuvao, who wore his jewel-studded antennae-crown and the cleanest royal garment he could find: a simple morning robe of white silk. Terraclon removed his wrapper to reveal the gaudiest of the priests' cassocks. It was strips of green and yellow silk sewn together, then spangled with curlicues of crushed amethyst and silver pyrite. Nuvao tried not to stare at him but could not.

"What?" said Terraclon as he adjusted the cassock's fasteners to wrap it tighter around his trim waist.

"Pious Terraclon. You are . . . just a bit overdressed this morning."

"*That* is a matter of opinion."

"*That* is the ceremonial garb for the Celebration of the First Ant Eggs," said Nuvao. "And this is autumn, not spring."

"Everything else was filthy and threadbare," said Terraclon. In his gloved hands he unrolled the scroll that contained the words of Anand's speech as they were written in the Dranverish script as well as in the Slopeish form. "Can you read this . . . Your Majesty?" he asked as he lighted the page with his torch.

"Not in the Dranverish way of writing. Not yet. But perhaps by the end of the day I just might have more of an idea of it."

Nuvao wrinkled his nose when it caught a whiff of flesh going bad. He looked over to the place where the platform had been modified. Instead of the carillon to summon the people, there was a different, gruesome structure in its place. He sat with Durelma and Terraclon on the platform's straddling bench as guards with grass shields arrived to surround and protect the king and priest.

Without hauling ants, the platform was dragged by men of the building and sand-bricking trades to the first of the camps on the western side. The sled was positioned to face the refugees just as Sun slipped from the vulva of Mother Sand. Nuvao and Terraclon walked towards the front of the platform and stood on a rostrum near its edge where they were just a head higher than the bodyguards.

Nuvao looked down at a pen of refugees who were

frantically sucking up or scraping every bit of dew from every place where moisture beaded. The refugees, a tribe of hairless men and women wearing rough clothing of cheatgrass straw, were startled when the platform appeared above them. Instead of the carillon that called them to hear the morning recitation of the Eight Laws, they saw the strange sight of dangling corpses with green skin and heads of fluffy white hair. Terraclon made a short ceremony of unrolling the scroll and holding it up so that Nuvao could read from it as Durelma shouted the translation.

"Good Men and Women," Nuvao began. "I am King Nuvao of Palzhad, the southernmost mound in the Free State of Bee-Jor. No one at Palzhad or at any mound in Bee-Jor will go unpunished for violating the Eight Laws. Behold the corpses of these eight men from the Vundjeloo tribe who were guilty of violating Law One. They were humans, like all of us, but they killed and then ate other humans. As a result, they have forfeited their lives. Do not do as they have done or you, too, will be a corpse that hangs from a rope."

As the words were translated into Hulkrish, men climbing up the back of the platform brought forth a bale of dried mushrooms bound with straw-string.

"These mushrooms are an offering from the Palzhanite people of Bee-Jor even as they face their own food shortage," said Nuvao. "But together, all of us can work to feed each other, and to make the Sand we share a place that is safe and prosperous for all. As we have shared this food with you, we ask that you share it with each other. Make sure that all in your camp receive the same portion. Do not run to the food just yet."

The bale of mushrooms was tossed to the people below who froze and stared at it.

"Before you come forward," said Nuvao. "Look to the sides of your walls, to the barrier you have built. You will see men and women of Bee-Jor who have come to build corridors between your camps—passageways—so that all refugees of Hulkren can be serviced and connected to each other *in peace*. These corridors must be respected and must stay open in order for you to receive your rations. You may reconstruct your walls once the corridors are set."

Nuvao nodded to the laborers behind him who set a wide multirunged ladder over the ring barrier and then descended into the pen of the refugees. They began pulling the crude walls of weeds deeper into the camp until there was a sizable swath between their camp and the next one.

"It will take days before we've reached each camp," whispered Terraclon as the sunlight grew stronger and the sled was moved to repeat the message at the next camp.

"Yes," said Nuvao as he looked down over the sprawling, tangled mess of fenced-in camps. "It looks like a nest constructed by drunken wasps."

He heard a faint buzzing overhead and saw a blue

locust was circling above them. Nuvao and Terraclon looked up at Anand, flying east by himself on some mission, and then the two looked at each other.

Nuvao could see from Terraclon's expression that he was not the only one who thought Anand's mission was foolish.

CHAPTER 19

NECESSARY DECEPTIONS

Queen Fewlenray kissed the cheek of a soldier who had died just a moment after she had reached him. The man had blinked a few times and there was a hint of a smile when she took his hand but then he went all too still. She closed his eyelids, but they popped back open.

"I'm afraid we've lost another one," she said to a funerary attendant who nodded to her and signaled to his fellow caste members. They were out of silken shrouds, so they wrapped the body in a square of common mallow leaf, set him on the sled with the other dead, and then took him to the Pit of Heroes at the edge of Fecklebretz to offer to the carrion eaters.

The queen realized she had visited all who had been convalescing on the floor of the ballroom, but from the cast of the sun, it was only noon and it used to take her until sunset. No more wounded were arriving from the western front and the ones that had arrived were not recovering. They were dying, she suspected, from some slow poison mixed with an agonizing wasp venom that coated the enemies' arrowheads. "Oh, Maleps," she said aloud, as if he might hear her. "Come home now." Her hands were trembling and she grew light-headed when she accepted that no more soldiers might be coming home—including her own.

"Your Majesty," said a voice behind her, and she turned to see Pious Tellenteeno and his sub-priests dressed in their mourning whites for another mass funeral. That was something which had been a daily ritual for far too long now.

"Pious. You are early today."

"We may need to delay today's rites," he said. "We have visitors!"

"More war widows fleeing the West?"

"No, from the East—the Lost Country! We are graced with a visit from Pious Dolgeeno!"

"*Dolgeeno?* Are you sure? I thought he'd been returned as a prisoner to the Dranverite."

"He was, but he has arrived in the Venarian Sled of the Ultimate Pious with a large and somewhat official-looking retinue."

"Somewhat? You are sure it is him?"

"Yes. Pious Fuppelo saw him through the sled's window. Oh, Majesty, it is a strangely beautiful reminder of the old days."

"Why would His Ultimate be visiting?"

"You will have to ask him. He did request to see you."

Fewlenray was stunned. "This is all very unexpected. How soon before he reaches the palace?"

"His spokesperson said he is still recovering from his wounds. He would prefer not to make the climb up the mound. He requests that you come to where he has stationed himself near the riding course. You are to bring whoever you think is appropriate."

It was midafternoon when Fewlenray and a modest entourage reached the riding course. With the queen were Tellenteeno and twelve of his priests, each of whom had dressed for the occasion in bejeweled robes that represented the constellations that rotated through the year. Tellenteeno explained his sartorial choice as, "A trust in the gods that all will pass, that everything has its season, that all that is good and right will renew." Following after them were some female palace servants who carried some impressive vessels of glazed and painted clay, but most of these were empty. The ones that were filled contained little more than mushroom porridge mixed with chopped midges or the cheap liquor of some fermenting greens.

Since they were out of proper riding ants, Fewlenray and her entourage had to ride on the speed ants used by the intermound messengers. The ants were hobbled with heavy bangles above their claws and weighted with heavy saddles to slow their gait for a more royal comportment. Fewlenray had dressed her own hair by combing it out, then gathering it within a simple snood of spider silk. Her only garments were some tight leggings under a clean and practical riding gown that was split up its middle to allow her to straddle the saddle. The lone piece of jewelry she wore was a small devotional medallion of amber around her neck; it was carved in the image of Ant Queen.

To puff up the queen's arrival, a few of the dwindling border sentries joined her retinue in the rear just before she reached Dolgeeno's massive, three-story sand-sled. It was a mansion on rudders with gilded carvings of Mantis, Grasshopper, Bortshu, and Ant Queen as its support pillars and its exterior was covered with an abundance of fine scratch murals. When Fewlenray neared it, she saw that the forty hauling ants that had drawn the coach were being watered and fed with a slop of predigested mushrooms. All the ants had been beautifully draped but with the rainbow silks of springtime instead of the browns and yellows of autumn—this was strangely inappropriate and a careless mistake.

As Fewlenray got closer to the sled, she saw that the Ultimate Holy's entourage was dressed in the frenzied pomp of the old and glorious way, but the men in polished silks were people of darker complexions. Some of them, she suspected, were *women* dressed as men. They brought an inelegant swagger and a haste to the ritual of accompanying her to the sled's entry, and the footmen selected to help her down from her ant had a questionable skin color, one, she suspected, that had been lightened with an oily cosmetic.

I don't know that these men should be touching me!

As the footmen escorted her over an unspooling carpet of bee fuzz, the bowing of the attendants was short and jerky. Jilting all protocol, they whispered among themselves and some looked directly in Fewlenray's eyes. Through the crystal window of the sled, she searched for Dolgeeno when she saw that indeed he was seated on the Mantis Throne. *What a relief!* He was dressed correctly, in his purple traveling costume, but he looked drunk or half-asleep and did not seem to notice her. She stepped into the sled's vestibule, glanced briefly at a wall mirror, but then hesitated to enter what looked like a dark reception chamber—or was that just how she was feeling? For some reason, she was afraid.

Behind her, she heard the sounds of rustling skirts and turned to see Tellenteeno was joining her. He had left his sub-priests behind and his face was calm as he urged her forward with an opening palm. When she entered the ornate chamber, His Ultimate Pious Dolgeeno did not rise to greet Queen Fewlenray, but remained slouching on his throne. A moment later, he looked at the queen in surprise, as if she were a fish that had fallen from the sky and was swimming in his tea bowl.

Fewlenray curtsied. "Your Ultimate Holiness," she said as he looked to be scoffing at her. She worried she had underdressed or appeared immodest. A moment later, he started chuckling in a low way before he returned to staring out the window. She noticed that one side of his garment was loose and flapping from his shoulder—had his dressers forgotten to pull his arm through the sleeve? Or was his arm missing? She cleared her throat.

"Pious Dolgeeno, it is very kind of you to visit. I do hope you are well," she said. His low chuckling turned to loud cackling before he fell silent and then shook his head as if he hated her. A strange mewling sound escaped his throat as he opened his mouth and stared at the ceiling mural: a depiction of the wedding of Mantis to Grasshopper. As he stared, a long strand of spittle fell and anchored itself to his lap, like the first strand of a spider building its web.

"No, I am afraid that Dolgeeno is not well," came a voice from behind her. Fewlenray turned to see a woman with a startling appearance step out from behind a dressing screen. She had a shaved head and a pair of cricket antennae clipped to her head. Within the loose confines of her dark and spattered garment, the woman made an awkward, almost crippled curtsy. "He has not been well since the attack near

Abavoon," said the woman in her musical, southern accent.

Today is a day of startling surprises.

"And with whom do I have the pleasure of speaking?" asked Fewlenray as she looked at the staff in the woman's hand, an elegant thing that was topped with the carving of a cricket head.

"My apologies, Fewls. Poleximaof Cajoria, your distant cousin, who you used to call Auntie, and now . . ."

Fewlenray was numb with confusion. Something between laughter and weeping shot from her throat as she realized she had been deceived.

"Polexima . . . Polexima of the Free State of Bee-Jor. Polexima . . . the traitor."

"Traitor to the Slope, yes," said Polexima. She cocked her head, like a mantis, in the stark and sudden silence between them. Fewlenray felt heat in her face and her jaw tightening as her hands made fists and her nails dug into her palms.

"How dare you come here! Why? To gloat?"

"We do not have time for gloating," said Polexima. "Do not be stupid."

"Stupid? Who was stupid enough to come here? Guards!" she called. "Kill this traitorous whore!"

Fewlenray pushed past Tellenteeno, who was stiff with shock, to leap out of the sled. She saw that the attendants from Bee-Jor were facing her, blowguns at the ready. Some in Fewlenray's retinue had fallen to the ground with their swords partially drawn and were twitching from darts in their necks and faces.

"Queen Fewlenray," shouted Tellenteeno, his face changing from a fearful white to an angry red. "Step back inside . . . please! I don't want them shooting at you!"

"Listen to him," Polexima said.

The two women stared at each other and heard each other breathe. "I have something to offer you, Fewlenray—something you dare not turn down."

"What could you possibly offer me?" asked Fewlenray, spitting the words as she took a step inside.

"Your life and that of your subjects."

Fewlenray lifted her chin and slit her eyes. Whatever fear she had felt had been burned away by her outrage. "My life and those of my subjects are threatened because of *you*, you bloodsucking she-tick, because *you* betrayed us to that half-breed outcaste posing as a Dranverite—that roach-riding *dung worker* whose only aim was to destroy our world and take it for himself."

"That is a lie you tell yourself."

"Was it a lie that you were a whore to this Tahn in Hulkren? And later, to his successor, Pleckoo of Cajoria? This other *dung worker* who stuffed his seeds in you, this blasphemous Hulkrite, whose abominable offspring are being fattened and spoiled in Cajoria's nursery? Tell me, Polexima, just how many Hulkrish warriors enjoyed your royal vulva?"

Polexima stiffened herself as she gripped her staff and stepped closer. Her free arm snapped out and slapped Fewlenray across her cheek, then swung back the other way to smack her under her chin. Fewlenray's face was stinging and she heard a ringing in her ears as she turned to escape the sled.

"Come back here! You will listen to me!" shouted Polexima, raising up her staff and bringing it down on the young queen's shoulder. Fewlenray heard the crack of her own clavicle, then felt an intense pain that emptied her head of blood. When her head fell forward, she knew she was fainting. She came out of the blackness with a pain in her shoulder that was sharp and pulsing. As she lay on the floor and cried, she looked up to see Polexima threatening her face with the sharp end of her staff.

"I was a prisoner in Hulkren. And I was *raped*!" shouted Polexima. "And I will not have you or anyone else trivialize that crime or my suffering. I never gave myself to *anyone* other than my husband. Do you understand me?"

Fewlenray would not speak. The sharp end of the staff was under her chin and tilting it up to face Polexima. She was clenching her teeth and raising up her boot as if she might step on Fewlenray's throat to choke her.

"Can you understand my words?" Polexima asked. "Are you alert?"

"I . . . I am," said Fewlenray.

"Good. I don't want to hear a word from you until I have told you why I am here. We both know that what is left of the Slope is falling quickly to the League of Velvet Ant Peoples. They have been enabled by the Carpenter Nation, have been *encouraged* by them to make this conquest. We both know that Slopeites of yellow skin are fleeing the fallen mounds in the Slope's west—some of them are already here."

Polexima paused a moment and looked grieved. "And we both know," she continued, "that you and your people *have no future at Fecklebretz*. At this moment, there are five to ten mounds near the borders of Bee-Jor that have yet to fall to the league. I have come here, as the last queen of Bee-Jor, to save you and the people of those mounds, before you are stung to death by velvet ants and thrown as food to the war beetles."

Fewlenray was heaving when Polexima pulled back her boot, then set it on the floor. Her eyes had been stabbing into Fewlenray's own, but now she started to see a softness, some maternal concern from the Traitor Queen.

"Why save me, Polexima?" Fewlenray asked. "Why save any of us on the Slope?"

Polexima sighed. "I would like to tell you that it is because it is the right thing to do . . . that in my superior, Dranverish morality I am able to love my enemies even as they wish for my painful death. But that would be lying, my loveliest princess. The truth is, we need you and your essence in Bee-Jor—you and the remaining sorceress queens. Palzhad has been lost to the Yellow Mold and soon we will lose the rest of our mounds. I am approaching you instead of Queen Elgotha or Billotzy or the other surviving queens because you . . . you have always shown some intelligence, a little compassion, and some sense of life beyond the Slope."

Polexima's face softened and for a moment it betrayed her own fear. "You, Little Queen Fewlenray," she continued with a tremble in her voice. "You might be able to persuade the others."

Fewlenray sat up from the human hair carpet that depicted Sun strutting under the arch of Locust the Sky God.

"So you want us to join you," Fewlenray spat. "To cleave our queendoms to Bee-Jor as your first defense against this western horde on their wingless wasps."

"Yes," said Polexima as she positioned herself in front of the exit.

"In return for what?"

"In return for your *lives*," shouted Polexima. "Which you can continue in palaces atop the mounds."

Polexima suddenly looked older and she wobbled on her damaged legs as her tone turned from imperial to pleading. "We need each other, Fewls," she said. "You must send messengers—right away—to the mounds of Caladeck, Bentilimak, Escarte, Zilpot, Tathorek, Shamorda, Dobsahn, and Fwumbry. You will ask their queens and their people to make an alliance with Bee-Jor. We must all fight together. Or we can all die alone."

Fewlenray stood and looked into Polexima's eyes. "I will speak with Tellenteeno about this, Your Majesty Queen Polexima. And I will send you my answer tomorrow, after sundown."

"I will need it sooner than that."

"May I remind you, Polexima, you are at my mound, where I rule. You will have my answer tomorrow *after sundown*. Now, will it be safe for me to leave you?"

"I am very interested in your safety," said Polexima.

"Then I am asking you to step aside."

CHAPTER 20

AN EXPLOSIVE DISCOVERY

The drone of locust wings was a pleasing sound and the sight of Mother Sand from above was a heady pleasure. But Anand could not give in to distractions of any kind, especially when flying alone. He had made sure his stomach was full and his bladder was empty before his locust flew south over New Dneep or the Promised Clearing or whatever its racist inhabitants were calling it. He wondered if their new home could possibly meet their expectations, this place they had mythologized over the centuries. Anand imagined they might enjoy its sunny openness and its variety of greens and insect game, but Britasytes knew that roaches did not fare well in the Weedlands south of the Slope.

And that was going to be trouble.

It was just beyond Bee-Jor's borders when Anand saw the first of the new pebble buildings of the Dneepers, most of which were as small and tight as the ones they had left in their Grasslands. At the center of what was becoming their capitol, he saw a platform with a structure that was a cluster of expansive, curving shapes that resembled ant chambers. Its walls were being built of transparent grains of quartz adhered with marsh tar. Anand chuckled when he recognized what the building was.

It's an imitation of a Slopeish crystal palace!

He shook his head in derision to see the Dneepers' aspirations to the Slopeites' ways and wondered what was next—an artificial ant mound but teeming with roaches? A moment later he was surprised by the enormous number of humans that had crowded onto this land. A moment after that, he was shocked when he saw all their roaches—hundreds of thousands of them were packed into pens, tethered to posts, or were in stacked cages. Some were roaming free.

Grass roaches feed on almost anything but mostly grass, Anand thought as he circled over this sudden city. *They've brought too many insects and too many humans. And it's not like they've got anything to trade . . . or anyone to trade with.*

That's even more trouble.

Anand readjusted his hand on the left flagellum of the locust's antenna to turn it south again. He sighed in dread as he considered his next destination and then felt a return of the sickness and fatigue that had plagued him for days. Even as it reminded him of his worst defeat, he had to fly next to Jatal-dozh.

Yes, you have to fly there, Vof Quegdoth, he scolded himself. *Bee-Jor's fate may depend on it.*

It was somewhat of a guess as to where Jatal-dozh actually was—a guess, Anand suspected, that was clouded by his apprehension in having to go there. He remembered it was just under a southwest pocket of the Great Brackish Lake, an area the Hulkrites called the Water Chin. When the lake came into view, he followed its shoreline that nuzzled patches of yellow-ray goldfields and then flew over a dark tract of helleborine orchids in somber bloom. When he saw the first of some prickled orb cacti, he knew to veer south. The cacti gave way to weedy fields and then a grove of ghostly oak trees falling into rot.

Anand veered lower when he sighted what he was looking for: bitter ants, as black and shiny as drops of tar. Looking at them, he felt nothing. He tried to imagine riding one and felt stupid.

He circled above the ants and watched as they scoured the fallen, gray branches for termites. He could see the bitters enter into the termites' galleries to pluck their soft bodies from the powdery darkness. The sight of plump oak termites was more interesting than the ants and made Anand hungry—he imagined them leaving a sun kiln with a sizzling chitin made crispy from a coating of chili oil. He saw that the termites were defenseless against the ants, the latter of which had long, serrated mandibles that pierced their victims' heads. Before they could attempt a counterattack with their puny mouth blades, the termites were sucked dry.

Bitter ants don't bring solid food back to the mounds like red hunters—they just drink blood. And the ants and their eggs themselves are impossible to eat, bitter and poisonous.

Anand sighed. The trunk trail of bitter ants was crawling south over a meandering channel of sand that would lead him directly to Jatal-dozh—or whatever it had become since the demise of Hulkren. Some clouds smothering the sun broke away from it to release all its rays, and there, pushing up from a lushness of greenery, was Jatal-dozh, bright and gleaming in the light.

As he got closer, Anand saw a frantic whirl of bitter ants as they scurried widdershins around the mound, speeding through its outer arteries and over its human structures, which were in various states of repair. The lowest of the shelters were disintegrating, but the barracks of black sand and the rose-colored rectory were sound and perhaps even occupied. At least one of the four palaces looked rebuilt and had been freed from the crusty grime of abandonment. The rain shield was intact and functioning and from the patches on its top he saw it had been recently repaired.

"Who's down there?" he asked himself, but dared not land. Were they the Mummy people, enslaved by the Hulkrites and forced to tend the bitter ants? Or perhaps they were an enclave of Hulkrish warriors awaiting Pleckoo's return. Maybe they were just Hulkrish deserters, hiding from the world.

As the bitter ants crawled atop the rain shield to sniff his locust, Anand reconsidered them. They were good predators of other insects, but their greatest defense was in the suicidal act of exploding when attacked. Tahn had easily defeated entire mounds of them by drawing them out until they all had detonated. And as war mounts, bitter ants were dangerous to their riders—soldiers risked explosions that could tear off limbs and heads or kill a man with a blanket of flesh-eating gunk.

No, bitter ants would be a disaster.

If only the Dranverites would send us some fertile hunter queens!

Anand's head was aching when he sighted a second parade of bitter ants returning to Jatal-dozh from deeper south with a different food find. Something about these ants smelled familiar yet frightening. He looked up at the sun, lowering in the west, and knew he should spin around and race to Palzhad—but the scent from below had roused his feelings. A whirlwind was whipping within him as a nervous excitement gave way to rage and then to hatred—what was stirring up these emotions? Anand knew he should resist his curiosity, that he had sniffed danger, but his hands stayed clamped between the scape and the pedicel of the locust's antennae. The locust was resisting him, drifting lower and gliding, but he forced her to take him deeper south.

They remained above the vigorous ant parade crawling north when at last they reached the place of the food find: a low boulder nudging just above some sand. On the edges of the boulder were some sparse milk-vetch plants with their fine, downy leaves and large, pink seed pods. As he circled lower, Anand saw scattered black ant fragments spattered with goo and then thousands of pieces from a different insect.

Going lower still, he saw that there had been an ant war. The bitter ants had engaged the scouts of an invading enemy, which had been blown apart and were splattered with a poisonous gunk. The invaders were much larger ants with a clear and vaguely greenish chitin. Their blood was being scavenged by the bitters who had not come to sacrifice themselves, but to bring home nourishment. Several bitter ants were crawling over the massive skull of one of these invaders. As Anand flew lower, his heart bounced between his throat and stomach.

He was looking at the fresh corpses of ghost ants.

Ghost ants!

The locust resisted his prods and Anand realized she was responding to the fresh, juicy shoots of some blue grama that had sprouted after the rains.

She dropped to the grama and consumed the tender blades. He was scared and excited as he decided his next move and slung his backsack around to his chest. He reached his left hand in to search for a capsule-husk full of Hulkrish white paint that he crushed with his fingers and then smeared over his face and neck. The smell of the paint was like some drug he had loved and then loathed and swore he would never take again.

Something made him sneeze and then sneeze again as his eyes watered. Farther off, he saw them again—dreaded clusters of sagebrush at the peak of their autumn bloom. Where he was going, there would be plenty more sagebrush, so he pulled his neck rag over his mouth and nose, which made him feel, once again, like he was assuming a guise in a dangerous land.

And perhaps I am assuming a guise.

CHAPTER 21

TWO SISTERS OF FADTHA-DOZH

"**G**host ants!" Anand repeated to himself, still unsure of why he was steering the locust farther into the dangerous South instead of turning her around for Bee-Jor. He was shifting his eyes left and right in search of something he wasn't likely to see: scouting ghosts that would not be on the hunt until well after nightfall. Part of him felt shamed by his recklessness, but part of him was intrigued as he pondered a gambit with an outcome that was far from certain.

In any case, I have to know what poses a threat to Bee-Jor.

Hope was surging over shame when he sighted a long, worm-shaped grove of dead and dying oak trees and then, farther south and east, a low, broad seep where sycamores were tall and thriving and had dropped a mass of their giant leaves with ends that curled as they decomposed.

Leaf-cutter ants have not been in this land for decades. If I am right, Fadtha-dozh should be just beyond that seep and up the incline.

Anand checked the sun and saw it had gone from white to yellow as it lumbered towards the horizon. Coming on the sun's right were some gray clouds that looked predatory, as if they wanted to jump it from the rear, drag it to the ground, and steal all its gold. When the sky darkened for a moment, the locust's wings stilled into gliding and then sputtered again when the sun reemerged. Anand knew his locust was both thirsty, hungry, and fatigued; he would have to satisfy her needs before night fell. "Just a little farther please, madam locust," he mouthed to her and then, out of habit, he looked up to Madricanth and repeated the same words as a prayer.

Will I ever break myself of this prayer habit? he asked himself a moment later.

A distant, conical shape was coming into view. Below him was an open field of weeds and grasses with spatters of rocks and smooth, round boulders. In a web of clearings, Anand saw the first of some harvesting sleds and some hauling ants, which was an indication that Fadtha-dozh was both populated and functioning. One sled was loaded with glow-fungus scraped from the bark of fallen tree branches and a second sled was loaded with honey grass. He sighted one crew who were using rope-loops to pull down new spurts of leafy weeds that were covered in sugar aphids. The crewmen were scraping the aphids off the stems and leaves and then yanking out their legs before tossing them into piles on the sleds. Farther up, he saw a band of men on raised platforms in the twiggier weeds. This crew was harvesting an abundance of white fuzzy aphids to shear their fibers, which would be shredded and spun into yarn for finer, gauzy fabrics.

Fine fabrics! This mound is thriving!

When he reached the first of the mound's habitation rings, he saw little human activity. A few slaves, mostly males, were concluding their tasks and returning to modest sand huts bound with ant dung and built in the bulky, Hulkrish style. Farther up he saw ghost ant sentries scattered through the neglected dwellings of the middle rings where they kept a quiet vigil. As it was still day, the ants were largely motionless or cleaning their massive eyes with brushes of their claws or were licking their antennae down their lengths. Other ghosts slowly pivoted, left, then right, with their antennae gently shifting as breezes teased them with distant scents. A few ghosts were activated when they caught either Anand's aroma or that of his locust, and they raced under him and up to the top of the mound in pursuit. He realized that Fadtha-dozh was completely lacking in human sentries—at least a few cadets and some old men should have been riding on ghost sentries to patrol the mound's perimeters.

But perhaps there are no Hulkrites here, neither warriors waiting for Pleckoo's return nor deserters or survivors.

As he flew above the middle rings of the mound, he took in an increasing human presence. From their oversized dresses, the inhabitants looked to be Hulkrish wives. As they walked, they were trailed by their hamstrung slaves, most of which appeared to be men! At a dew station, Anand spiraled above to observe the strange sight of a male slave stretched across a whipping pebble as he was lashed by a female mistress before a crowd of spectators. Anand felt a shocked surprise as well as the urge to stop and free the man—but now was not the time for rescues. His right hand clamped his locust's antenna to get her into a spiral while the other plunged into his backsack. He grabbed a pod and smashed it hard into the chest plate of his armor and then smeared its contents over its scales. After that, he reached deep into the bottom of the sack to scrape up something else.

Above the uppermost dew station, Anand could see, even from a distance, that the women were wearing their usual overload of jewelry as they waited in a queue with their slaves to collect their evening water. But at their sides was something he had never seen on a woman in Hulkren—a black obsidian sword that was straight and tapering. And it appeared they also carried an obsidian dagger on the other side. Foot peddlers—women, it appeared—were working the queue, hawking jewels and dainty little sweets, when one of them looked up and noticed Anand's circling locust just as he threw out a mass of pyrite flakes that fell in a glistening flutter. He had everyone's attention as the ghost ants that had raced up from below crowded onto the dew station with their antennae lashing upward to sniff/touch him and his flying insect. The ghosts' mandibles scissored and their abdomens raised up in the attack position, but just as the locust swooped down and came to a crawling stop, the ants scattered in a sudden, noisy retreat as if repelled by a powerful magic. Only Anand knew they were responding to roach-scent.

Anand looked around him, in search of assassins, and then turned his eyes back on the grossly bejeweled women and the swords they had reached for and were now letting go. All of them were getting to their knees and dropping their heads to mutter prayers. This was a relief but it was also disturbing. Their slaves, most of them men, were falling to their knees as well but Anand could see it pained them to do so. *They must all be hamstrung!*

"Who rules here?" he shouted.

The women were quiet.

"You, madam!" he said, pointing to the closest of

them, a woman wearing a gown of pleated silk and jewelry in the forty different styles of the nations conquered by Tahn. "Who is your ruler?" Anand asked again as she looked at the ground. "Look at me."

The woman whose eyes met his was of Seed Eater stock with reddish hair, celadon eyes, and light skin with an orange tinge. "She still rule here," said the woman in fractured Hulkrish. "And she is expect you. She is expect you for some time now."

Just who do they think I am? Anand asked himself just as he was about to remove the neckcloth from his face and then decided to leave it on. As he saw hundreds of people kneeling to him in worship, he knew that whoever they thought he was he had complete authority.

"Do you have cage makers at this mound?" he asked.

"Of course do."

"Have them come here immediately with panels large enough to contain my locust."

The women did not flinch as Anand made his demand but nodded their heads. "I need a cage that will not constrict my mount nor damage her wings," he continued, pushing his demands to see if they would resist. "And bring me a sled-load of your freshest honey grass—lots of it. My locust is hungry and thirsty."

Anand waited atop the locust as the woman and some others who might have been her sisters or cousins bowed quickly, then excitedly scurried in different directions to carry out his orders with their slaves limping after them. Other wives and their slaves were just arriving, approaching slowly, in awe of the locust and its rider's astonishing armor. The Fadthans—if they still called themselves that—were falling to their knees, quietly weeping, it seemed, in both relief and worship.

A short time later, the panels of a twig cage were making their way up on the shoulders of men who limped as they walked. At their rear were women with taloned whips clipped to their sides; they prodded the men with the bloodied points of black-glass rapiers to quicken their pace. Quietly, the slaves lashed together a roomy cage around the locust. While everyone was distracted, Anand freed his cape from the inside of his armor's collar and arranged it around his body. He held his chin up to look dignified and then carefully ended the torture of a very full bladder. Afterwards, he reached into his backsack and ended a day-long fast with some satisfying slices of dried marsh-fly meat set between mushroom slices that had been moistened with some whipped mustard oil.

After the cage was completed, a sled arrived with a cargo of freshly cut honey grass. The ants hauling it would not come close to Anand so men wearing grass-stained rags pulled it the rest of the way. The sled was too large to fit through the cage's gate so the men used pitchforks to stuff the grass between the bars.

"Stop," Anand shouted in Hulkrish. "The locust can't bend its neck to reach its food. You need to raise the cage off the ground and then slide the sled in."

After Anand spoke, he watched as the women chastised the slaves in what sounded like the Seed Eaters' tongue, screaming at them as if they were the worst of all children, stupid and lazy, and threatening to whip them. The slaves set themselves at the corners of the cage and along its sides and then strained to raise it up. As it wobbled on the men's shoulders, others pushed the sled in close enough so that the locust could feed at mouth level. It was almost dusk when Anand saw two young and voluptuous women who looked to be floating towards him in the sheerest of clothing. Instead of shoes, they were wearing cloth-covered box-stilts. Their blouses were baggy and white, rippling behind them, and as they got closer, they revealed full, upturned breasts. Their pink nipples were tipped with crimson buds that beckoned like bits of berry candy. It was a few moments later when he noticed their swords and daggers.

Anand was surprised to find that at this strangely tense moment he was deeply aroused. He had the impulse to reach out to both pairs of breasts and feel their radiating warmth and rub their nipples to make them harder before inserting them into his mouth to lick. Resuming his good Dranverish manners, he averted his eyes from their bosoms but made the mistake of looking down at their skirts. These were just as sheer but they had been dyed the faintest green. As he caught a glimpse through the transparent material he saw bejeweled navels, like little god's eyes, that gazed from above wasp-like waists that flared, then rounded into the curviest of hips. Farther down he noticed dark, reddish patches of silky curls concealing that place where he wanted to sink his fingers and then bury his face before one more part of him followed. The painful confines of his armor tamped down his excitement. "I am a married man," he muttered to himself in Britasyte, and then felt a sudden painful longing for Daveena.

Daveena! I am coming for you, little goddess!

Anand cleared his throat and then nodded his head, uncertain of how to address them. "Good evening, Good Women of Fadtha-dozh," he shouted in Hulkrish.

"Good evening," said the first of the two women. "My name Soblazni. My sister she is Nimfa."

The two bowed in unison, deeply dipping their heads. Anand had been so distracted by the rest of them that he had barely noticed their faces until they raised them up. Their heads, typical of Seed Eaters, were pleasingly squarish and the pale orange of their perfect skin made their blue-green eyes a pleasant shock.

"Blessings of Lord Termite upon you," said Nimfa, and Anand knew he was still on a Hulkrish mound. When either of them finished speaking, they licked their lips, then tilted their heads, which was not just provocative but brazenly seductive. Soblazni was taller and the older of the two and had seen perhaps twenty-four summers. Nimfa was deferential to her sister but no less beautiful if a bit shorter. Both of them had the ginger hair of Seed Eater women, but the color of it was redder, as if it had been rinsed in the juice of hymen berries. In the Seed Eater fashion, their hair was braided into hundreds of beaded plaits that were braided again into lustrous cables that fell across their shoulders like ten tailed whips. Their antennae were plain and functional—simply woven grass fibers that were stiffened with orchid glue.

"If you like," said Soblazni as she blinked her long-lashed eyes thickened with a dark red paint. "Come down from locust and we will accompany you to Priestess Muti."

Priestess Muti! Anand thought. *There are no priestesses in Hulkren!*

"Obliged," said Anand. "But I need to leave some magic to protect my locust."

"But locust is in cage."

"Yes, but she will be harassed and frightened by ghost ants outside her bars if I don't leave her an amulet."

Anand reached into his backsack and unwound the long string of a medallion for the locust, which he tied around the back of her head. Once the necklace was secured, he smashed the pod on its medallion to release a concentrate of roach-scent and then jumped down to smear some of it on all six femurs of her legs before he opened the cage's gate to exit. He retied the gate's lock ropes in the Britasyte manner and then leapt to the ground, slowly rising from a crouch to meet the sisters' eyes.

"Follow us," said Soblazni. The two walked just ahead of Anand as the hems of their gossamer skirts flickered up to his body and face. The sight of their backsides was a torture of temptation as the women's legs and bottoms were a bounty of sweet, smooth flesh with the subtle jiggle of some syrupy sweet. As they walked on their noiseless box-stilts, Anand realized, to some small shock, that the women were wearing the robes of a Termite preacher: the ceremonial clothing that revealed a warrior-cleric's weapons to his congregation as he led them into submission to Lord Termite. The shock subsided and Anand was soon lost within these women's legs and wanting to lick his way out. He was relieved when it grew too dark to see them as other than flickering shadows as they guided him up to the ring outside the palaces. When they reached the sloping steps up to an entrance of the western palace, the women stopped before a platform with a hitching post where a saddled ghost ant strained at its tether.

"End magic if willing," said Soblazni. "So we can ride on ant up to palace."

"I . . . no. It's a short walk," said Anand. "I have been sitting all day and would rather not ride."

The two women bowed and then continued up the terraced incline that led to an entry of a restored crystal palace. From outside the palace's translucent building grains, Anand saw an abundance of the bluish light that came from the bark fungus torches of autumn. He followed the women through a wall diaphragm that had been parted by a male slave who bore a pained expression and had little hair on his face.

A eunuch at a Hulkrish mound? Anand wondered.

The three walked up a short corridor to what Anand expected would be a typical Slopeish throne room modified by Hulkrites into the austere quarters of a Hulkrish captain and consecrated to his termite deity.

It was not what Anand expected.

Not at all.

CHAPTER 22

PRIESTESS MUTI

Anand looked up at the reception chamber's ceiling to see the blackness of the night pressing itself in, yearning to flood the place with its tarry darkness. On the southern side of the ceiling, he saw the diffracted light of the moon. What had once been a glorious chamber for Slopeish royals was now a gaudy and chaotic blend of a Seed Eaters' palace, a Britasyte market, and the treasure-stuffed home of a greedy Hulkrite. Riches pillaged from far-flung lands were mixed with ancient furniture chiseled from amber, the tapestries of the Seed Eaters, and the sleek wood carvings of the people of the Pine Lands. Britasyte carpets slathered the floors and Anand recognized one of them and knew its maker, Tareena of the Fallogeths, and her skillful depiction of a black widow spider devouring her mate.

His eyes were drawn to the parade of blue fungus torches making their way up the 127 stairs of what had been the platform of Slopeish thrones. At the top of the stairs he expected to see the usual lump hewn from termite-infested wood. Instead, he saw two tall objects that were draped with embroidered cloths. Slaves arranged the bark fungus in lighting kettles to shine on these cloaked objects and it both intrigued and disturbed Anand as he pondered their mystery.

Soblazni pointed Anand to a massive carving at the back of the wall that directly faced the bottom steps of the staircase. When he first looked at the carving, it seemed like something made for royal children to play in: a miniature of a Seed Eaters' palace with renderings of insects and humans and walls encrusted with semiprecious jewels. It had two recesses in it that were dark and purplish, which he assumed were its doors or windows, but above these were domes shaped like insect skulls and sprouting pairs of gilded antennae. As he stepped closer, he saw that the recesses were not portals, but that they were richly upholstered chairs with high backs and thick cushions that were covered in a dark fuzz-cloth.

Are they offering me a chair?

"Have seat," said Soblazni when she saw him hesitating. Anand walked to the chair closest to him. He was about to sit in it when she shouted at him. "Not that one. Other chair!"

Anand looked up at the dome above the first chair and its antennae, which were longer and bent into two at the scape—like an ant's. He looked up at the dome over the other chair, which had antennae that were shorter and curly, like those of a termite. When he reseated himself on this chair, he realized he was sitting on a throne—on one side of a double throne. His heart was beating hard in his chest as he wondered what came next. Soblazni and Nimfa bowed to him, then drifted away into the darkness of the eastern hall.

Just as the women disappeared, Anand heard a strangely beautiful sound: a clear, ringing pitch that faded and then was sounded again. Girls of nine or ten summers were coming out of the hallway dressed in star-shaped garments of pink gossamer. They were hauling a massive sled-gong behind them whose height nearly reached the ceiling, but instead of a wooden sound-plate, there was a dangling tube of that rarest of all treasures: lightning glass. The tube was cleanly round and filed into an even length at its end even as its surface was spattered with an erratic lace of fused, gray crystals. A woman who could have been Soblazni's third beautiful sister was atop the sled-gong banging the tube with a cloth-covered mallet. She counted to six in the Seed Eaters' tongue before striking the tube again.

Following the sled-gong were thirteen adult beauties in that diaphanous garb of white and green with the strange contrast of a deadly dagger tucked into their sashes. *Likely one priestess for each of the year's full moons*, Anand thought as he remembered his studies of comparative religions. As the priestesses walked, they swung moist balls of white sage fibers that reeked of nightshade, evening primrose, penstemon, and cannabis oil. The latter became the dominant smell, and it was rendered from toasted and crushed seeds. The perfumes were pleasant and then dizzying and then they made Anand's lungs ache and his ears ring. As the women whirled the balls overhead, the first priestess danced up to him and offered him one to sniff. When he did so, to be polite, she smashed it into his face and soaked his face cloth with its oil. Time slowed and the whole world began to wobble. Anand prodded himself to keep calm as he accepted that he had just been drugged.

It's better to submit to its influence and save my strength than to try and fight it off and lose.

The twelfth and thirteenth priestesses were Nimfa and Soblazni, who had joined the others at the ends of two lines, facing each other, as if for some courtly dance. *But someone is missing in the left line . . . perhaps this Priestess Muti.*

Anand expected Muti to arrive on a shoulder-palanquin if not on the throne of a palace sled. He expected her to be wearing masses of jewels, a crown with gilded antennae, and a voluminous gown of knitted spider silk. Something fluttered out of the darkness, like some drunk and lovely moth, but the woman arriving was dressed more like her sub-priestesses. Instead of a blouse and skirt, she wore a gauzy cloak with a tall and roomy hood that fell down the sides of her intricate coiffure. The small braids of hair that were braided into larger ones were studded with beads of white and green moonstones and all of these were piled up into a swirling tower of coils. Everything else about her appointments was very simple; her antennae were short and plain, her feet were bare, and her long dagger was simple and elegant with finger grooves in its amber handle.

As Muti came closer to Anand, he stood in respect. In the blue light of the fungus torches, he could not discern the color of her eyes but he saw that they had the enchanting fold of a Seed Eater royal. She was a woman, not a girl, and judging from her broader hips, she was likely a mother. Her skin was smooth and glistening in the blue light and her legs and arms were long and firm.

Making the most discreet of all glances, Anand saw that Muti's breasts were plump and tempting, but it was her face that dazzled him. This was the face of a goddess. It was a kind of drug ingested through the eyes and beautiful to the point of maddening. Her widely spaced eyes had long, dark lashes that flapped above the tops of her cheekbones when she blinked.

As for those cheekbones, they were not just high and broad, but they had a dramatic curvature that arched out into a kind of flight before they receded. Her lips were full and moist and they were suggestively open to reveal the rows of her flawless teeth. An enchanting hollow was at the center of her neck, which was strong yet slender. She lifted her cunning little chin up and took a moment before she spoke.

"Honored and happy for your return," she said in Hulkrish, and then dipped on one knee before slowly rising.

My return! Just who do they think I am? They know from my color that I can't be one of Tahn's sons.

"It is good to be here," Anand said, speaking the truth, for he did want to be there. He had the dissonant feeling that cannabis always gave him of being two people at once: one who said and did things without thinking, and another who was like a scolding parent who stood nearby and was ready to correct him.

"You have returned just in time," said Muti. "To defend us. Join us, if you like, for evening prayers and meal."

To defend us? Are they under attack?

"Obliged," said Anand, reminding himself that in Hulkren it was better to offer reciprocation than to express gratitude.

But is this mound truly Hulkrish?

"You will notice changes since you were here

last," she said. "Much has been revealed to me. As I am sure, much has been revealed to you too."

Roach Lord, no! Anand thought, determined to make no response and glad that his face cloth hid his mouth. *Another one with revelations from above!*

His armor felt more uncomfortable than it had all day; he was suddenly hot within it as his undergarments went moist and sticky. Muti signaled to the gong player. She nodded her head, made a graceful sweep of her arms, and then struck the dangling tube of crystals. As its sound rang out, Muti took her side of the double throne. The girls in pink, starry finery left the sled-gong to arrange the queen's cloak so that it fell neatly around her feet. The first of the thirteen priestesses approached Anand to personally greet him. Each priestess kneeled and then slowly rose, meeting Anand's eyes. He could not help but be dazzled by the beauty of each of them, but he also felt startled—this presentation was openly sexual in its intentions. The women made another corridor of themselves as Muti rose and extended her palm towards the stairs.

"Join us now, will you?" she asked. "Blessed are we, finally, so eager for your return."

Anand nodded and stood. He was exhausted from a long and extraordinary day, and though everything around him was frighteningly gorgeous, it was difficult to see straight—the whole world was on a spinning disc and its objects were flying away. *These sensations will pass,* he told himself. *I am Anand, and I choose to see the reality beyond this cannabis spirit who will not hold me hostage!*

Muti took Anand's hand in hers and for a moment he felt like a little child, as if his mother, his beloved Corra, was helping him to climb over a pebble in their path. He looked up the vertiginous flight of stairs and it seemed to be growing taller and steeper, like a wave of stormy lake water that would break over him. The lights at the stairs' peak grew brighter and harsh as the priestesses surrounded the mysterious draped objects and then sat around them in a semicircle. Soblazni and Nimfa handed each of the women some carved shards of twigs. One shard was smooth and the other was larger and rough with serrations that grew bigger up its length.

Muti was handed her own shards and began a chant in something like the Seed Eaters' tongue. Under the influence of cannabis, Anand heard her words like they were the language of another race, of orange-blooded beings that lived and breathed in lake water. Likely, Muti was just speaking some dead language that the Seed Eaters used in their religious rituals, something that was the privilege of their priests. She entered into what looked like an ecstatic trance as she ran her smooth stick over the rough one to replicate the sounds of termites banging their heads on wood. She began the recitation of Termite's names in Hulkrish: Blind One, Wood Eater, Tunnel

Dweller, Dust Lord, Great Provider, Father of All, and then . . . she repeated them in some other tongue than Hulkrish!

Tahn would rip her tongue out for that sacrilege!

Soblazni and Nimfa rose and went to the first draped figure and together the two of them untied its covering. Anand gasped when he saw a statue of a termite with a human face. The idol was pieced together with molded clay, carvings of wood, and it had been painted with a fine, bright white. In five of its six hands were different weapons but in the sixth hand was a tiny figure that had to be Tahn, clad in Hulkrish armor, and seated at the edge of Termite's fingers.

An idol! An idol of Termite! If Tahn could see this, he would punish these women by ripping their scalps off!

Muti and the other priestesses set down their shards and got to their hands and knees. From below, the lightning glass sounded again and Muti looked up, a crazed look on her most beautiful of faces as she shook her shapely rump until it rippled. She screamed out a sound that was something like one Anand had only heard twice in his life: the ear-piercing screech of a ghost ant queen demanding attendance from her daughters—a sound that was unbearable to human ears. The other priestesses joined Muti, lost in a trance, to add their raucous and throbbing shrieks. The noise was unbearable and it jolted Anand back to that time in Hulkren when he had seen his first ghost ant queen, and to the last time, when he had killed one by shooting her skull full of darts. Through the mad screeching of the priestesses, Anand heard the ring of the tube again. Nimfa and Soblazni untied the covering on the second idol.

Anand looked at an idol that had been assembled from clear bits of lightning glass and had been stained with a green tint. He knew it was a female deity because under her human head was a pair of stylized breasts with nipples. At her feet were bits of lightning glass polished into eggs with etchings of what looked like larvae inside them.

It's a ghost ant goddess! he realized. Anand reminded himself that he was just looking at a statue, at a lifeless object, but its appearance and intentions were dangerous and disturbing. Nimfa and Soblazni opened a nutshell chest and unrolled a gossamer sash between them, then they wrapped it around the waists of the idols to bind them.

Married! Anand realized. *They have married Hulkro to Goddess Ghost Ant and pushed Hulkra-tash aside. For this, Tahn would have stomped on these women until they were puddles of blood and bones!*

The shrieking subsided when servants arrived to set down a drinking-bowl of grain spirits. Anand sniffed to detect if the liquor was mixed with turpentine and he was relieved it was not, as surely he would be expected to drink. The bowl was set before the two idols as an offering as Muti mumbled a blessing over it.

Nimfa and Soblazni raised the bowl up so that the two gods could take the first sips. After the bowl was set down, Muti signaled Anand to take a swallow, something he needed to do to counter the anxiety of the cannabis. He walked towards the bowl, lifted his face cloth just high enough, and scooped up a drop with his palm to suck down. The effect of the spirit was calming, almost right away, and he relaxed and felt safe as he stood with his feet apart and felt stable. As he watched the women drink, he hoped they would consume it all and then, like Hulkrish warriors at a Strategy Dinner, they would pass into sleep.

But the night was all too young.

Muti dipped both her palms into the bowl and pulled up a sizable drop that took her three sucks to consume. She stood and signaled to sound the gong. This time the sound was so long and clear that Anand felt almost at peace, at one with a sound, which he imagined was Madricanth as He/She exhaled before falling into Cosmic Sleep.

Muti's eyes were closed now, in a silent prayer, and when she opened them she looked at Anand. Her face was peaceful with a charming little smile on her lips as she lowered the hood on her head, released the sash that held her dagger, then dropped the cloak from her shoulders to stand completely naked, as an offering to him and their mutual gods. The other priestesses dropped their own garments and then looked at Anand as if he were a sweet and precious babe that needed to drink their milk.

Anand staggered when Muti stepped closer and lifted up the bottom of his face cloth to kiss his mouth.

No, no! he wanted to shout but could not.

"I . . . I . . ." he muttered. *I am a married man who loves his wife!* he wanted to say when he felt a transfer of warmth as her lips met his and then . . .

There was that sudden, inner pull, that irresistible draw between a man and woman when they had no choice but to join their bodies. This inconceivably beautiful woman was playful now, pushing him lightly to the floor where he was caught in the arms of the other women. They splayed him across a carpet of the softest moth fluff.

Quietly, the women's hands were exploring Anand's armor as they figured out its fastenings and how to get him out of it. His flight boots were removed and then they unsnapped the leg casings and took them off. His long undergarment was easily removed to free his sex, which had a sweet ache that came from its fullest arousal and throbbed in time with the beat of his heart. He gasped when he felt hot moisture from a skilled tongue that licked up the underside of his sac to the base of his stalk. He moaned when Muti took his glans in her mouth. She was tender at first and then vigorous as she took him down to the back of her throat before she released him to look in his eyes. She had tasted the beginning of his seed but he knew she would be angry if it was planted in her mouth.

Muti arched above him, her breasts bobbing as she kneeled over his hips, then took him inside her before rocking atop him. The warmth and sensation was intense as she bent to kiss his mouth and slid her tongue atop his own. When his face cloth got in the way, she gingerly pulled it off of him as he grinned in bliss.

She gasped when she saw his exposed face. She rolled off of him, recoiling and then grasping at her dagger.

"You are not Pleckoo!" she shouted.

CHAPTER 23

SIMPLE GIFTS

Pleckoo! Anand thought. *They thought I was Pleckoo! He was here!*

Anand knew he should be more frightened than he felt. He was surrounded by thirteen naked women who had been anxious for his seed, but now they looked like they wanted to slice off his testicles with the daggers they clutched. As he thought about it, it seemed like all the men at this mound were missing their testicles. He reached for his own to cup and protect as he stood, backing away, but meeting their eyes. The women stood in place, staring at him, and in the long silence he felt a weird calmness, some of it coming from the spirit he had drunk as it vanquished the anxiety of the cannabis. Within him, he felt a growing ball of light, a warm and radiating joy, and it grew bigger when he grinned. His nakedness was no longer a vulnerability but a strength. Holding up his hands in a kind of mock surrender, he smiled to reveal his teeth. As he had admired these women, he saw that all of them were admiring him—all of them but Muti.

"Who are you? And why you here?" she asked, her face tense with suspicion.

Anand hesitated before speaking. *How much do I tell them? As much of the truth as is possible.*

"I am Pleckoo's cousin."

Muti was disbelieving. She looked at the other women, who shrugged or shook their heads.

"Cousin to Pleckoo? How we know this true?" Muti asked.

"You would not know. But he is my cousin. I was with Pleckoo in Hulkren."

"So like him you are Mushroom Eater who became Hulkrite?"

"I was a never a Hulkrite."

She stiffened.

"But I lived as one and I trained in the Hulkrish army. I knew Tahn and served as his interpreter. And I knew of your husband, Captain Fadtha. He was one of Tahn's favorites, a good fighter and a better recruiter who converted many Seed Eaters into Termite worship. Like you, Fadtha was from the Barley

Lands, but he was a round-eye, a weeds worker. He had ink punctures on his cheeks, which was a punishment that marked him as a thief. That made him unfit for marriage to a Barley girl and unable to enlist in Volokop's army. So he joined with Tahn and worshipped Hulkro."

He saw her relax.

"So you are from Pleckoo-dozh, sent to me by Pleckoo."

"No," he said, shaking his head and frowning. "There is no Pleckoo-dozh."

Her face went still.

"Pleckoo does not rule Slope?"

"He does not."

"Who does?"

"I do. With Polexima, the queen of Cajoria. She is queen of . . ."

Anand hesitated to use the name "Bee-Jor," either in Hulkrish or in the Slopeish tongue.

"Polexima is queen of all in our new country— one that broke away from the Slope."

"Polexima is in Hulkren! She is in Zarren-dozh, to piss for Tahn."

"She is not. There is no more Hulkren."

Anand heard her gasp, as if she had been knifed. Her eyes were darting back and forth when she began to heave. "No, no!" Muti muttered when her legs went out from under her. Soblazni and Nimfa caught her fall and held her up as she trembled and screamed—a sharp, ear-puncturing scream that gently rang the gong tube with its reverberation.

Anand watched and waited, glancing down at the floor as the screaming turned into a prolonged sobbing, which was even more difficult to witness. Her priestesses were turning inwards and quietly chanting as their thumbs tapped over their fingers instead of prayer beads.

They're used to this! Anand thought. *Used to her outbursts!*

Muti's sobbing turned into sniffles and then she looked up, as if her strength and resolve were high on a shelf, something she could take down to drink and feel better. A moment later she was calm again and made eye contact with Anand.

"So it is true," she said in a quiet voice. "What deserters and cowards who came here said. That Hulkren has lost war."

"They lost it in a single night and quite a few moons ago. This mound has been isolated."

Her feelings were shifting again. She was staring at Anand with tight lips and squinting eyes when her chin thrust up and she bared her teeth. "All men are liars!" she shouted. "All men are shit! Worse than shit!"

"Not all men," Anand said.

"Why you come here?" she shouted as her anger edged towards a new round of sobbing. Anand's face went from a polite mask of concern and sorrow to an honest expression of anger at his being drugged and dragged into some ritual without his permission.

"Because I need your help," he shouted as something of a reprimand.

Muti was not offended by his outburst, but impressed and intrigued. She cocked her head, shifted her hips. "You need *my* help?" she said, her voice growing husky. "You who says he rules the country that defeated Pleckoo and Hulkren?"

"Yes. And soon after, we defeated the Barley Lands. Volokop attempted an invasion when he thought we were vulnerable. But it is our people who feasted on the blood of harvester ants."

Muti's eyes were darting again as she sorted through pictures in her mind. What Anand had said had pleased her. She arched her neck and looked upward at an angle that was almost unnatural, as if it might snap. He watched as she engaged in what looked like a private conversation between herself and some ghost that floated just under the ceiling. Her lips were quietly mouthing words in the Seed Eaters' tongue, and then she seemed to be listening as she nodded her head.

Oh, no. She is another prophet!

A moment later, Muti looked resolute, in control of herself. She wiped at her tears with the backs of her hands and smiled. A slight laugh came from her as she looked into Anand's eyes. "Forgive me, please," she said to him. Her face was even more beautiful as it glowed with a sudden joy. "Priestesses," she said, her grace returned as she raised up her hands with her fingers splayed. "We have . . . guest from afar. Your name is?"

"I am best known as . . . *Commander* Vof Quegdoth," Anand said. "Here, I was just Lieutenant."

"Vof Quegdoth," she whispered as she looked at him with awe. The other women were staring at him again, not in admiration but with the deepest hatred as their hands clenched their daggers' handles. "Killer of Tahn . . . and my husband, Fadtha."

"Yes."

"Priestesses," she said after a long silence all the while staring at Anand. "Commander Quegdoth, leader of new nation, is sleeping in our palace this night. Prepare bed for him in apartments was for . . ." She dipped her head, sadness overwhelming her again. "Apartments set aside for Pleckoo, Second Prophet of Termite. Quegdoth is tired from long journey. See to comforts. Goddess Ghost Ant had reason to bring him here."

Anand watched as each of the beauties picked up his belongings. None of them had bothered to redress but had set their clothing over their arms. He looked over at Muti, still in her own nakedness, to see she was studying him and still musing about his purpose for her. She squinted and frowned as her joy turned back to suspicion and disdain.

Something I've said pleases her, but part of her hates me . . . maybe just for being a man.

The women grabbed some wall torches and accompanied Anand down the long flight of stairs. He felt a giddiness that had come from drinking the pure spirit, but his pleasure was as much from walking in the company of so many nude and beautiful women. They led him into a dark suite of rooms that lit up with their torches and then guided him through paths that wound through sacks and chests and barrels of treasure until they reached a vast bedchamber. It was more of a walk until they reached a great bed with a mattress made of polished silk pods that were stitched together and stuffed. The mattress was topped with a quilt that was thick yet puffy and visible under it were thin, shiny sheets of polished silk. Nimfa left a torch in the wall sconce near the bed stand as the women crawled over the mattress to arrange its pillows and turn down its coverings, all while showing Anand the soles of their feet and their smooth and rosy backsides.

Soblazni pointed to a tray on a table where they had left Anand a squeeze bag of water as well as one of grain spirits. Next to these was a platter with a chunky wedge of finely powdered seeds that had been sunbaked and then soaked in a perfumed syrup. The food looked and smelled delicious, but the bed was far more inviting. After the women exited, Anand set a dimming cloth over the torch and then slid between sheets that felt cool and smooth on his naked skin and he shivered a little before the quilt warmed him. He looked up at the translucent ceiling and to the broken bits of moonlight that glinted within its crystal grains. Overwhelmed with fatigue, he was desperate for sleep, but his mind was alive with fresh, hot memories of the naked women and especially of . . . Muti.

That one is difficult but oh-so-beautiful!

He was stiff again—achingly stiff and wondering what he might clean up with when he heard the marching of insects and then felt a vibration in the room. The marching grew louder. He remembered this noise—these were ghost ants in a nocturnal eruption from deep in the mound. They were racing towards a conflict, a territorial encroachment from other ants, or they had been alerted to a massive food find. As he looked up at the ceiling, he saw the spectral flicker of the ants as they crawled over the clear grains of the roof, scattering the diffracted light into something finer, a kind of glimmering dust.

These ghost ants are thriving!

Hundreds of thousands of them continued their crawl with their claws clattering and their mandibles softly squeaking as they scissored. Anand was in a frightful awe again, remembering that first time he had experienced a roof march in his chamber at Zarren-dozh.

And if there are a hundred thousand ghost ants out on a night raid, then there are hundreds of thousands more below who are tending their egg-layer and her larvae in the nurseries.

Anand was wide-awake as he listened to the march grow even louder until it sounded like a rain of sand. He wondered when the parade would finally end when he sensed something or someone within the chamber. Sitting up, he reached to yank the dimming cloth from the torch when he saw the quilt fly up. Someone had slipped under it and had crawled on top of him. He grabbed at wrists and pushed up to see that intensely beautiful face again. Before Anand could say anything, Muti had slammed herself onto his manhood and jammed it inside her. When Anand opened his mouth to speak, to tell her to stop, she dropped her head and clamped her lips on his. She pushed her tongue inside his mouth as her hands pressed down to grab at the muscles of his chest to ride him as he squirmed.

Anand felt violated, and at the same time intensely excited. He was trapped yet exhilarated by this sudden turmoil as the marching of the ants grew to its loudest. He wanted to pull away and knew that he should, but it had already gone too far. Reaching for her shoulders, he was soft at first, but then he gripped them tight to throw her back and force her under him. He lay on top of her, bearing down with all his weight as he yanked up her arms and stretched them tight. "Be still!" he shouted as she bucked. She was silent as he stared into her eyes, but then he felt her thrust upward to grip him with her walls of wet fire. She clenched tight, released, and then clenched again. She laughed in triumph when he closed his eyes and succumbed to the extreme sensation.

"Show me the man you are," she said as her fingernails scraped up the sides of his thighs and then scratched into his buttocks. He felt the need to punish her with his thrusts, to make her pleasure so extreme it would be an ecstasy that broke into agony. Soon her gasps of pleasure turned into soft screams and then to weeping as she closed her eyes and rocked her head.

"Stop?" Anand asked.

"No!" she said, and then slapped him hard across his cheek. It hurt him and he wanted to slap her back, but he sensed it would only deepen her excitement and make her more uncontrollable. Her face with its bright, perfect skin was something he wanted to taste, so he licked her lips, her nose, her cheeks, and even the tops of her eyelids before he licked inside her ears to make the sounds of a soft, wet thunder. She spluttered and gasped, stunned by this strange act. "Stop it!" she screamed at him. "Stop licking me or I will tear your tongue out!"

They stared at each other, heaving, their eyes locked, and neither of them feeling safe enough to let the other go. He watched as her eyes turned to slits and her mouth shrank into something coiled.

"Fuck me, you dingy, low-caste bastard," she whispered.

Rage, that most common of Anand's emotions, was at the ready and it burst. His thrusts sent explosions of pain and pleasure through her and she screamed until the moment she succumbed to waves of bliss that left her shaken, limp, then silent. Anand would not stop when at last she whispered, "Enough, enough."

Anand achieved his own release, which was as much of an ache as it was a bliss. He stayed atop her, looking down at her face, when she touched his lips with the ends of her fingers. Looking up at him in complete adoration, she gingerly probed through his beard with her fingers.

"What you want from me . . . Quegdoth who is really roach boy Anand?"

He smirked.

"What do *you* want from *me*?"

CHAPTER 24

A GIFT OF SHARPNESS

"**A**nd were you able to reach the deities?" Fewlenray asked Pious Tellenteeno, who was bleary-eyed and morose as they rode back from a Sacred Wetting. The tea in the squeeze bladders was weak and unsweetened but they drank it because neither of them had slept well. They had brought breakfast with them but the priest had just picked at the ugly clump of dried mushrooms at the bottom of a basket while Fewlenray held a consecrated wafer in her hand that had yet to meet her mouth.

"Our contact with the gods was brief," the priest said after coughing on some tea that had gone the wrong way. "In starving them of blood, we have crippled them, crazed them, made them blind and defenseless. They are going early into the Winter Rest and are weary, having to hide in shame. They will rouse again when their mortal chosen are strong and able to renew the blood offerings."

Fewlenray was wordless as the riding ant reached the palace entry and was docked by just one attendant, a boy who struggled with the task. The strange quiet in the dimness of the central spiral was so complete that she heard the sound of her own blood as it pumped to her head. "Pious," she said, and then hesitated. "Would you be so kind as to join me in my chamber devotionals this morning? I have some special prayers to make . . . a . . . a *circumstance* I need to address."

"Perhaps later, Majesty," said the priest as he helped himself down, dropping awkwardly without anyone to assist him. "If you will excuse me, I must join with my other priests. We have so many more of our brave soldiers to say good-bye to today . . . so many prayers to complete."

"Yes, of course, Pious."

"Majesty, you have not eaten your wafer."

Fewlenray looked at the stale, oily disc that she had forgotten was still between her fingers.

"No, and I cannot. I am not very hungry this morning . . . I . . ."

"What, dear? What is wrong?"

She sniffled and cried silently as she fought to maintain her composure.

"I believe that I am pregnant."

The priest gave her the most artificial of smiles. "With child! What a lovely surprise, Your Majesty! Congratulations are in order. I will add the Gestation Blessing to our prayer-chants this morning. And I will ask Goddess Butterfly to bestow Her gifts if it is a girl and Lord Grasshopper to do the same if it is a boy."

"Thank you," she said, dropping her head to hide her face and the beginnings of tears.

"Not at all. It will be a . . . a joy."

The priest was quiet a moment as he stood and considered his next words.

"Majesty, might I suggest something," he whispered. "I think we should keep this between us for now. We should certainly wait to make an announcement of a royal birth. This would be a bit complicated even in these complicated times without . . . without . . ."

"Yes," she said. "Without the completed sacraments of marriage."

"Well, yes. Do not worry, Fewlenray. We will find a way. And as for that bitter, little wafer, why don't you try it again at noon when you might have more of an appetite."

Fewlenray stood and nodded to the priest before he lumbered off to join some other clerics who looked as if they were at the end of their day, not at its beginning. When she returned to her bedchamber, she stood and stared at her bed, which had somehow become a strange object. It was both inviting and terrible to look it. She had never noticed just how large it seemed and how empty. Lately when she lay in it at night and was unable to sleep, she stared into the blackness and saw what she thought might be Maleps's ghost, but the entity was something faceless and made of a weak blue light. Sometimes the entity reached out to her with phantom arms that fell to the ground and twitched before they rose up and reattached.

The queen yawned. The stuffed quilt on the bed looked both warm and thick enough to bring her darkness if she pulled it over her head on this all too sunny morning. And once she did, she could imagine Maleps under the quilt with her, where he slid his thick, warm hands up her waist and over her breasts to cup them before he pulled himself atop her. She longed for his body, something which had been as warm and firm as a sun-kissed stone. *Something I will never feel again.*

"No, no, no, Little Fewls," she said to herself. "You are a queen. And you have your royal duties this morning—most important duties. You will not be captive to a quilt."

She walked to the next chamber, the vast royal closet, with its room for shoes, room for frocks, room for antennae, and room for jackets and jewelry. In the center of the closet was the mirrored and furnished dressing area where her servants were at work on the eight boxes Fewlenray had been preparing in secret. The servants were just completing the sealing of the boxes with beeswax that they had warmed between their thighs and under their armpits to make it pliable. Fewlenray looked over the seven boxes that were reflected on the surface of her cosmetics table with its inlay of black obsidian. The eighth box was unsealed, the one she had set aside for herself, and it sat atop the chest that stored her coronation gown. She thought of that happiest day, when her future was a sunny series of feasts, elaborate entertainments, and the attentions of her first love, Prince Jubf of Mound Abridor. He had never had enough of her either and took their every private moment to ravish her again and again . . . once, even, between courses at the funerary feast for her wicked old stepmother!

"Majesty," said her chambermaid as she pulled some wax out from under her skirt. "You did not want us to seal that one, correct?"

The servant pointed to the open box.

"That is correct, Sametta," said Fewlenray, hesitant to leave her memories. "I will prepare that one myself and finish it with a very beautiful wrapping. Now, ladies. Just how shall we wrap the rest of these?"

"If they are for other queens, perhaps a square of some garlic skin paper," said the youngest of her servants with a sweet and sincere smile that made

Fewlenray sad. "Perhaps, Majesty, it should be tinted bright yellow with some lily pollen and then tied up with a shiny violet ribbon!"

"Hmm. Sounds lovely, but I am not so sure."

Fewlenray worried that if the boxes were too pretty that they might attract the interest of a thief. "Ladies, let us just use some barley husk paper to cover these up and then tie them with some packing twine. None of the usual perfume either . . . just my royal stamp, but on the inside of the wrapping, so that the recipients are sure about who it came from."

"Yes, Majesty," said the young servant as she unpeeled the lid of a wide-mouthed jar of ink. She coated the carved cylinder of Fecklebretz's royal stamp with the black liquid and then rolled it across eight sheets of the kind of paper that was usually used for the wrapping of meat or boots that needed mending. Another servant called, *"Creet-creet,"* outside the closet.

"Your Majesty, they are here."

Fewlenray returned to the antechamber where she found sixteen messengers lying facedown on the floor and awaiting her orders. "Good morning, Good Slopeites," she said. "You may stand."

The men stood, eyes to the ground as she addressed them.

"I have summoned you this morning to bring an urgent message to the queens of the mounds in our West, of what remains in our hands of our Holy Slope. I am sending two of you, a team, to each mound to ensure that this message and my packages are delivered. Will each of you swear to Mantis that you will dedicate your every effort to this mission?"

"I swear," said the first messenger, pressing both palms together as Fewlenray turned to him. The rest followed until she had everyone's word.

"Here is my message. Repeat after me," she said, and then paused a moment to review the words that she had been composing since the night before. "Majestic Queens of the Holy Slope. We face a threat not just from a new invader from the West, but one from our East, from the insurgents of what had been our Holy Slope, who call themselves Bee-Jorites. Polexima, the last remaining sorceress queen in the Lost Country, has insisted that we are to join her eastern nation of workers and outcastes. If we do not, we risk conquest by a barbarian horde riding from the West on the backs of velvet ants. Our gods are weak and are starved for blood and they must be fed. Please accept this gift from Fecklebretz and join me in my own decision to do what's right for our race's future. I look forward to seeing you all in that happiest of all places."

Fewlenray exacted the correct recitation of her words from each of the sixteen messengers as the packages were brought out and distributed.

"Blessings of Grasshopper upon you, Good Slopeites," she said, "and protections of Ant Queen on your journeys."

The darkest of all moods gave way to a brighter one. She was smiling, at peace, and felt a loving warmth that touched these young men, who were smiling in return. She felt a loving radiance from the Treetop Above and knew, was just certain, that the good and righteous gods had summoned a reserve of their dwindling energy to bless and protect these messengers. They bowed, then left for the royal hitching post where their speed ants had been fed, watered, and saddled for their rides to the Slopeish mounds that had yet to be attacked by this strange, new enemy.

As Fewlenray returned to her bedchamber, she felt a mix of dread and ecstasy and then a growing relief. Her maidservants were still inside the closet, tidying up and preparing the dress and shoes she would wear for her visit to the dwindling wounded.

"Thank you, Good Servants, for all your help today," she said through a bright smile. "Though it is still morning, I am just a bit tired. I would like to be alone and take the sleep that evaded me last night but is offering itself at the moment. Sametta, would you be so kind as to turn down my blankets and pull the curtains shut and then put up the muffling gate at the portal?"

"Yes, Majesty."

"And would you make sure I am not disturbed until dinnertime? Until well after sunset? Not until the crickets chirp."

"As you wish."

After the servants finished preparing the chamber and left her, Fewlenray went to her closet to retrieve the eighth box, which she brought to the altar of her chamber shrine. She set the box before her carved and bejeweled deities and suddenly marveled at the beauty of their rendering—even though she had encountered them nearly every day of her life.

Just who had made these wondrous things? I should know that.

"I fulfill your holy will," she said to the idols, and then looked at each of their little faces, some of which seemed to be coming to life with blinking eyes and smiling lips. "I offer all I have to you."

Fewlenray lifted the lid from the box and took out an amber dagger fashioned like the fangs of the brown recluse spider. She thrust it deep into her belly and sliced left to right and then deeper until her blood bulged onto her fists. She felt her blood's warmth and was satisfied with her sacrifice before she slumped and fell into total blackness.

CHAPTER 25

DEEP INSIDE

"**W**hat have you done to all these men?" Anand asked Muti as they toured the ghost ant nurseries of Fadtha-dozh while sitting on the skull of a riding ant. All the laborers he had seen were either castrated, hamstrung, or both and many had beardless faces, thin legs, and fatty bellies. Anand realized he was already speaking to Muti in the casual way of those who have seen each other naked, then shared the same chamber pot before eating breakfast together. She turned and looked at him with a fierce expression, like she might cut off his balls . . . or cup them in her mouth. He wasn't sure.

"Did what I need to make myself safe from *men*," she said with a scowl. "Made other women safe here too."

"I see," said Anand.

And I do see . . . she had to defend herself from all these drunken Termite worshippers and their prophet's permission to "seed the infidels."

"But why did you castrate them? They're mutilated!" he shouted. "You took away a part of their bodies, something that belonged to them. That's a part few men want to part with!"

"I saved these men," she hissed at him.

"What? How?"

"Men all too willing to stick their pissers into women—get us pregnant with babies we not want, then put us to work while they drink spirits. Take away their balls and their pissers shrink and lose their seeds. Men without balls and who works hard is men who can live at Fadtha-dozh."

"It doesn't have to be like that!"

"Where is different? On Slope? You think Slopeites don't stick their pissers into Barley women before slaughtering them?"

Anand gave an involuntary shudder.

Of course they did . . . and never spoke of it.

"It is different in my country—and one other I know of," he said. "Where it is a *crime* to force another into sexual union."

"What is this word 'crime'?"

"It's a Dranverish word. It means to do wrong to someone, to mistreat them. The closest word in Hulkrish is *sin* but that means 'harm against Hulkro,' not 'harm against another human.'"

"Dranveria. People of red ants? How is you know Dranverites?"

He hesitated. *If I am to keep her trust, I must tell her the truth.*

"I am a Dranverite."

"What?"

"And a Britasyte. And a . . . Bee-Jorite."

"Bee-Jorite?"

"Yes," he said. "The name of our new nation, carved out of the Slope, is Bee-Jor." He repeated the word in the Slopeish tongue and then in Britasyte.

She was stunned but smiling at him, renewed in her wonder—it was not the reaction he expected. He looked hard into her eyes.

"Muti, you know you violated *me*," he said. "Forced your way into my bed, then onto my body. You did not ask for my permission."

"It's *my* bed," she said. "Not yours. And I could not make your pisser stand on end if you not interested. Would wilt like old, rotting onion shoot if you did not want me."

I did want her . . . of course I did, but she used me! I felt like a victim, some object that was used.

"An erection does not mean consent," he said.

"And what gave you erection? Who were you thinking of?" she asked.

He was quiet for too long. She smirked in triumph.

"You should have asked me," he said, almost shouting.

"And how would you have answered?"

"I would have said no. I'm already married . . . to a Britasyte woman. And . . . to a Slopeish queen . . . but that's for political reasons."

"Grows more interesting. But if you put pisser into two, why not three?"

She was looking at him intently again, rubbing her hand over his thigh and then stroking him under his rising loincloth. He was excited yet shamed when he thought of Daveena. *My wife, my pregnant wife, is suffering in the Barley Lands, and here I am, overwhelmed with urges for this outrageously beautiful woman.* As Anand looked at Muti under the blue light of the fungus torch that swung from the hoop above them, he sensed a deeper mystery about her, something both alluring and dangerous.

"You wanted a baby with Pleckoo," he said.

She met his eyes, stayed silent. *She is not disagreeing.*

"But now you like my 'pisser.' Why, Muti?"

"Is a good one. Seen better, but . . . it can do." She was trying not to grin and failing.

"But what you really wanted was my seed last night."

Her magnificent eyes were darting again as she gathered her thoughts.

"No. You claim to rule Slope, yes? Place now called Bee-Jor?"

"*Half* of what *was* the Slope."

"Then we have use for each other . . . Commander Quegdoth. But seeds last night will not take."

"Oh. You used *satchu* pollen," he said, using the Dranverish word. "From the sticky phacelia."

"How you know of *satchu*?" she said, surprised.

"It was forbidden in Hulkren. But not in Dranveria."

They reached the voluminous chamber of the ghost ant queen, which for practical reasons was better lit than the palaces. The riding ant was resisting Muti's prods as the ant wanted to go to her great mother and feed her. Streams of ghosts ants were grooming the egg-layer, probing her for mites, but most were scampering between her jaws to leave their regurgitations on the floor of her opened mouth. Other ants were waiting in clusters at the end of her abdomen where a chain of eggs was gushing, eggs that were carried off one by one to the brood chambers. Hobbled human laborers competed with these ants to grab at the slippery eggs for themselves, eggs for the dining leaves of Fadthan women. Anand saw one man he reckoned was the chamber's foreman even as he was monitored by women bearing weapons. He limped when he

walked but he wore boots instead of sandals and he
still had a beard.

And his balls.

Like most people at Fadthá-dozh, the foreman
had ginger hair and light skin and was of round-eyed
Seed Eater stock. When he saw Muti, he bowed, but
his facial expression betrayed his fear and showed his
contempt.

"Blessings of Goddess Ghost Ant," Muti said. "And
of Lord Termite."

The foreman nodded.

"Do you speak Hulkrish?" Anand asked. The man
looked surprised and then worried.

*He's wondering who this dark-skinned stranger is that
sits on a saddle with his castrating queen. Perhaps he
wants to warn me.*

"I am Hulkrite," said the man with his low Barley
accent. He looked away from Anand in shame.
"Praise Hulkro."

*He does not know me as Vof Quegdoth. He thinks I've
come here to punish him for deserting!*

Anand looked at the masses of ghost ants streaming in and out of the chamber through multiple
tunnels. They were crawling across the tunnels'
ceilings, over their floors, and along their walls, all
of them enabling the massive ant queen to lay endless amounts of eggs. He recalled the horror, the awe,
and the shock of the first time he had seen a ghost
ant queen, something so magnificently ugly it had

haunted him for days. Now he was looking at this enormous insect with its glassy chitin and her eyes as long as the tallest man and it was only just a little strange. The creaky, clacking, chirpy noise of her thousands of daughters swarming around her faded into a near silence as he stared at her strange and eerie grandeur and at her longest of antennae sweeping slowly over her subjects like the arms of a living goddess. He watched as one of the human laborers—a eunuch, it appeared—antennated a smaller ghost that stopped and regurgitated some food. The eunuch scooped out some of this gooey mass with his hand and then licked it up as his breakfast.

These people aren't starving, Anand thought. *No one ever starved in Hulkren.*

"It's midautumn," Anand shouted to the foreman. "This egg-layer is still laying thousands of eggs a day."

"She is," said the man. "She'll lay eggs for at least another moon or until the winds blow colder."

"She is well taken care of," Anand said. "By her ants and by you. I can see that the right number of eggs and larvae are being harvested."

"Correct, sir," the man said, falling into Hulkrish military cadence. "We only take larvae to slaughter when they are in excess. Otherwise, it will disrupt the digestive process for all the ants. We do not worry about taking eggs. Those are very plentiful . . . for now."

"How many rivals have you seen?" Anand asked.

"Rivals, sir?"

"How many ants are born as females with wings—potential queens who would challenge the egg-layer if they were allowed to live?"

"Four or five a day, sir."

"Four or five!" Anand said, unable to hide his excitement.

"Yes, sir. But once the winged ones eclose, they don't last for long."

"No, they don't," said Muti. "Because they are our favorite food."

She was looking at Anand with her bright, mischievous eyes, and admiring him again. She made another attempt to prod their riding ant out of the chamber but it was still resisting. "Must let this ant regurgitate to mother ant," she said, "before she will obey again."

The riding ant pushed through and crawled over a thousand of her sisters to the queen ant's mandibles, which opened like palace gates to her mouth as big as a bedchamber. The riding ant's regurgitation bubbled from her mouth, which she scraped onto lumps on the lower inside of the queen ant's mouth. Once completed, the riding ant ran out with the other feeding ants when the queen ant's mandibles scissored as a signal that her great mouth was closing.

Anand looked at the foreman, who was watching

him in the deferential Seed Eater fashion, with his head lowered and a sideways glance.

"What's your name, foreman?" Anand asked.

"Soldier Pozlushny," he said.

"Take good care of the egg-layer, Pozlushny," Anand said. "And better days will come for you."

The man said nothing.

"Did you hear me, brother?" Anand asked. The foreman looked up briefly and gave Anand the vaguest nod. "Better days . . . I promise," said Anand.

"He is your brother?" Muti asked on the ride back. "Look nothing like you."

"All men are my brothers," said Anand. "And all women are my sisters. We are one human family."

"Sound like something Tahn would say."

"Tahn was right about a few things. Just a few."

"Why do you care about some 'brother' who was Hulkrite?"

"I think about who he used to be—about what made him run from the Barley Lands, about his treatment under Volokop. And I think about the person he might become with some *education*."

"Slopeish word?"

"No. Dranverish. Knowledge . . . and learning how to think *better*. Education."

You could use one, he wanted to say. As the ant crawled up the central spiral, they passed many other women who were both steering and riding on ghost ants, something that would have resulted in their immediate decapitation if Tahn were alive to see it. Only men and boys were walking, all of them crippled, and Anand worried for some ten- or eleven-year-old boys that they passed when a woman scolded them and threatened her dagger.

"How did you do it, Muti?" he asked.

"Do what?"

"Get all these men under your thumb."

"Ghost Ant gave me permission. She said was new way. Was big argument She had with Hulkro, who is Himself lazy and drunk. Men here always drunk and lazy when not fighting, even more after war with Slope. Not hard to control when you . . . you . . ."

"When you cut off their balls and slice through their tendons."

She shrugged.

"Who told you that you could speak to Ghost Ant and Hulkro?"

"Pleckoo. Who was told so by Hulkro."

Pleckoo! His mischief never ends!

"I see. Where did you get all these obsidian weapons? These are the deadliest blades on the Sand."

"Plenty more here. Stockpiles of arrows, missiles, daggers, swords. Brought here by my husband, Fadtha, and his men after raid on Foondatha."

Anand was both stunned and excited into silence. He felt her leg press against his.

"I know what you want from me," Muti said when

their ant neared the tunnel docks of the palace. "Now I tell you what I want."

"Speak," said Anand.

"A ride. On locust."

"That's all? A locust ride?"

"No, stupid Bee-Jorite. To show you why they are growing giants deep inside this mound."

CHAPTER 26

A THREATENING STRUCTURE

"**W**hat is it?" he asked as he looked at a bit of cloudy, gray crystal hanging from a string of spider silk braided with strands of ginger-colored hair.

"Is protective amulet," said Muti, holding up a crystal much like the one around her own neck. Even in the late-morning sun, the jewel had little brilliance.

"What's it made from?"

"Is chip from the Great Blessing, a present from Hulkro and Ghost Ant."

Anand realized it was a shard of lightning glass, likely a remnant from the honing of the gong tube.

"And just how is this little crystal a blessing?"

"Is a miracle. One day after rainstorm, we find this

holy treasure where there was only sand and weeds. I pray to Hulkro and He tells me is His gift to humans to celebrate His marriage to Goddess Ghost Ant. Is some of His semen, which fell to Sand and make this wealth of protective jewels."

"His semen," Anand said, and smiled. "Muti, the Hulkrites believe Hulkro is married to Hulkra-tash, the Great Layer of the spirit eggs, which are invested in Hulkro's human children when they are born on the Sand. But she is not a goddess—she is Hulkro's consort. His *modest* consort," he said, emphasizing the Hulkrish word.

"And point you are making?"

"If Hulkro is married to Hulkra-tash, how can He be married to your Goddess Ghost Ant?"

"You are married to two women."

"This is . . . this is not what Tahn taught his people. His prophecies . . ."

"Tahn was married to many women," she interrupted. "And he was not only prophet."

"Pleckoo, your Second Prophet . . ."

"*My* Second Prophet? Pleckoo is Second Prophet to all people."

Anand hesitated. *Now is not the time to tell her that there is no such thing as prophecy.*

"Was it Pleckoo who told you of the wedding of Ghost Ant to Hulkro?"

"No, I saw it for myself. I was guest when sky split open and revealed Great Thrones of Lapis and

Moonstone. It happened just before Great Rain of ninth moon, just after Pleckoo came to Fadtha-dozh and told me Hulkro had chosen me as His Entrusted and would advise me."

"Advise you?"

"Yes. He would speak to me."

"But, Muti," Anand said, shaking his head and squinting at her. "Tahn and Pleckoo insisted there was *no god* but Hulkro."

"I do not disagree."

"You don't?"

"No. But there is also Goddess. I know because sometimes She speaks to me."

"I am sure She does," he said. Anand sighed and looked at the amulet again and its neck string as the sky got brighter. "Is that hair mixed into this string?"

"Yes."

"Why?"

"To protect one. Is *my* hair."

"I see," Anand said. "You're a witch."

"Some in old country called me that. Those who did not like me."

"What do you call yourself?"

"In Barley people tongue, we have word *dolkunya*. Is more like queens of your Holy Slope. Magic woman."

"Sorceress," Anand said.

"Sorceress, yes, like my ancestors. Here. Put it on!" Muti extended the amulet again. "Will protect us when we fly."

Anand obliged her before he took his saddle on the locust.

"Help me up," she said.

"Not dressed like that."

She was wearing a long and elaborate coat suitable for Volokop's court with a high collar that accentuated her neck. As beautiful as it was, it was stiff and heavy with embroideries that were almost sculptural.

"You said it would be cold when we fly," she said, and flirtatiously held the fuzz-lined collar and pretended to shiver.

"Yes, but you need to sit over the saddle, legs apart, with your boots in the stirrups."

"Fine," she said, and walked out of the coat, which stood upright with its own stiffness. Anand was stunned. Except for some boots made of ghost egg leather, she was completely naked.

"You can't go like that!" he said.

"Why not?"

"Because for one thing, it will be extremely distracting!"

"Is nothing wrong with this," she said, and tapped her breasts. "Is the human body, one given to me by Ghost Ant."

Anand laughed, then sighed in exasperation before lifting Muti up to sit in back of him. Distracted by her nakedness, he fumbled with the reins and fasteners and belt hooks. When he was confident that they were both secured to the saddle, Anand shouted to the male slaves outside the cage.

"Men! Unlash the ropes. Take off the top panels first!"

The men did nothing.

"Take cage apart!" Muti shouted, and they scrambled to obey her. She continued further instructions in the Seed Eaters' tongue.

The locust was still, tentative, just twitching on her claws once she was freed from the cage. Anand could hear and smell Muti's heavy, fragrant breathing in back of him and he knew that she was excited or scared or both.

"Locust is not going," she said.

"Give me a moment. I hope you didn't eat much breakfast."

"Why?"

"Because you're very likely to lose it."

As Anand readied his mouth prod and pulled on his gloves, Muti lowered her hands from his waist to his thighs.

"What are you doing?" he scolded.

"We have time."

"Stop that right now!" he shouted. "I am not going to spend all day feeling crusty."

Muti snickered as Anand positioned his hands on the antennae for the launching position. The locust's wings flared and buzzed and she made a sudden jump into a rapid flight with a steep ascent that excited

Anand and made him smile. He felt the warmth of Muti's arms through his armor as she clung to him while making sounds like weeping or sexual ecstasy. Perhaps she was just afraid. The noises from her turned to a melodic gasping as she savored the beauty of the Sand from above.

Anand's eyes hurt when the sun grew brighter and bashed into them as he continued their flight east. He alternated opening and closing his eyes but was still flying blindly when the algal smell of the Great Brackish Lake climbed up his nose and triggered memories of his first journey into Hulkren. He looked away from the harsh sun and down at the tail end of the Borax Barrier, that strip of lifelessness, where it spread out into an empty cape in the brown-green waters of the lake. Near the cape's shore were water striders that darted after prey or drifted and spun in the wind. Farther over, he saw the broad, ovular boats of the Kweshkites, stretching in a long chain that led to the Stone Bridge where once they passed their cargo to the Britasytes to trade. And then Anand remembered—those were not Kweshkites in boats along the southern shore, those were Hulkrites who had fled the battle, banded together, and then forced the Kweshkites into exile.

Anand urged the locust into a loop to go southeast and it was sometime later when he saw humans wading on stilts at the lake's edge. They were setting out, then drawing in, thick, broad cloths to soak with water, then hang to dry to scrape for their meager salt.

Among the salt makers, he saw a couple of sentries wearing orange helmets who were mounted on the backs of harvester ants to oversee and keep peace. This meant a larger settlement of Seed Eaters was nearby.

"So it's true," he shouted over his shoulder.

"I not lie," Muti said.

"Why would the Seed Eaters colonize this place?"

"Why would they not? Grasslands good for harvester ants. Is best place for them—once Dneepers and their roaches abandon it."

"But why all the way down here and why so soon?"

"Volokop knows we are here—the defectors to Hulkren."

"How?"

"Men who escaped from Fadtha-dozh—Seed Eaters, as what you call them, who fought for Tahn but could not go back to Hulkrish mounds. So they go back home . . . to Barley Lands. Men who saved themselves by telling Volokop all about us and where we hide."

"Men who wanted to keep their testicles," said Anand. "And their hamstrings."

She was silent.

"Why would Volokop care about Seed Eaters at Fadtha?" he asked.

"He wants us back."

"Why? He has more than enough subjects already. You'd think he'd want to offload some."

"Volokop can never have enough of anything—

including subjects. He will take all of Dneep and Fadtha-dozh to extend empire . . . and multiply his people."

"He'll need a fleet of boats to do it."

"No boats. Volokop hate water. Can't swim with deformities. No boats allowed in Barley Land."

"Then he'll have to cross the Borax Barrier. And that will kill his ants."

"Won't."

"Of course it will."

"You will see when we go west," she whispered into his ear, nuzzling it with her mouth.

Anand looked down and saw the edges of a vast camp that had been cut into a great density of grass. It did not appear to be a Seed Eater garrison as there was no pit being dug for human sacrifices nor were their cages of war ants or soldiers being drilled. Instead, there were thousands of small, round shelters of twig frames pitched above the soil and covered with woven grass. Rolled up on the side of the camps were great bundles of twigs from shrubs and saplings. Some of these bundles were hitched to draw beetles and were joining a parade of cargo-sleds on their way east. In the camp's middle were a few luxurious shelters: large, ornate tents that were up high on sand-sleds and likely the dwellings of the emperor's builders. Most of the men below were laborers who were busy at their tasks but a few of them, the ones mounted on sentry ants, were looking up at Anand's locust when it dipped lower and they heard its buzzing. A moment later, they were reaching for their bows and arrows.

They're not hungry for my flyer, Anand realized. *They've figured out I'm from Bee-Jor and that I'm spying on them!*

Anand steered the locust out of the range of attack and was heading west when he saw a clearing and the beginning of some strange, zigzagging structure that looked like millipedes biting each other's ends. As he flew closer, he was astonished to see that this was some kind of man-made construction, and laborers were hard at work on its completion. Vaulting trusses of twigs were secured to foundations of barley grass stubs. The trusses were stacked on top of each other, rising higher into multiple stories as it continued to the West, and they were supporting a long deck of thickly woven grass to be used like a road. The structure continued well into the barrenness of the Borax Barrier where hundreds of men were laboring on the next leg of its construction.

"It's a bridge!" Anand said aloud. "Volokop is building a bridge over the Borax Barrier!"

"You not as stupid as I thought," said Muti. "Where you think Volokop want to travel, hmm?"

"It's astonishing, what he's done. But it won't last," Anand said. "It's made of twigs and grass—flimsy."

"His army only need to come to Fadtha once."

"Why? Why is Volokop obsessed with this mound?"

"You will have to ask him."

Anand steered the locust into a cool, south-blowing breeze. The flight back to Fadtha-dozh was uneventful, leaving him time to consider his plans, which turned to time to worry. Muti disrupted Anand's brooding to run her hands over his armor and see how much of him she could grope through its scales. Slapping her hands as they came towards his crotch, he dropped an antenna, which sent the locust into a spiral. The locust circled over itself, plummeting upside down before he righted it.

"Do that again and I'll eject you!" he shouted. When she laughed and grabbed at his testicles, he reached behind him and deftly unhooked her belt attached to his and then clamped the antennae in the drop position. As the locust plummeted, Muti swung just above the saddle, the straps keeping her barely attached when her boots fell out of the stirrups. Threatening to cut the reins with his dagger, Anand turned to her. "You wanted to fly?" he shouted, and started sawing at the reins.

"Noooo!" she screamed. "I promise to be good!"

Anand righted the locust, then veered up again. For the rest of the flight, she wept like a little girl and only quieted when the verdant outskirts of Fadtha came into view.

Anand made a wide circle around the mound to check for any dangers and then landed on the topmost dew station where the cage's panels were flat on the ground. The clearing was full of women wearing their strange combination of formal dress and heavy jewelry with whips and weapons at their sides. Anand spiraled lower.

"Landing," he shouted as a warning to them, and then brought the locust to a jerking halt. He reached behind him to unhook Muti, but she had already released herself and was dangling from the saddle's edges before she dropped to her feet and then rose in a landing that was both athletic and assured.

"Come for supper tonight," she shouted up at him as she jutted her chin and squinted in anger.

"I have to return to Bee-Jor."

"Is not request. Is command." She cocked her head and frowned. "I will give you what you want . . . Anand. But you must give me what I want."

"What's that? Another fuck?"

"No, you filthy roach-boy. More than that. Much, much more."

CHAPTER 27

AN OUTRAGEOUS REQUEST

Polexima paced inside the darkening interior of the Venarian Sled as Dolgeeno was returned to his chair by Cricket nuns who had helped him take care of his needs. He was back to babbling again, in conversations with at least two invisible entities, one of which he seemed to like and another he detested. "Why, of course you may!" he said to the one on his right. "When you are so very handsome, you may have all you need and more." Turning to the other, he shouted, "Oh, no, not at all! Not tolerating this for another moment! Do that again and we will tie you up and offer you as a meal to a hungry mantis just to watch her chew off your legs." The nuns went to a pile of freshly delivered torches and giggled quietly as they set them in the chamber's sconces.

It is well past sunset, Polexima thought. *Where is Fewlenray?*

Polexima heard the beginnings of chirps from the stout, black crickets that sang in autumn, and she chanted her prayers in time with their song. Finally, she heard a thorn horn outside the sled's door. "His High Holiness, Pious Tellenteeno of Fecklebretz," said a voice from outside.

Polexima hobbled to the door and saw that Tellenteeno had arrived in a small hunting sled that had been hauled by some miserable-looking men from a working caste instead of ants. His Holiness was in the company of only one other priest, the young man who had announced him. Both their noses were up in the air and their lips were pursed as they stared directly at her. The young priest took Tellenteeno's arm and helped him descend down the sled's unfolded staircase. In the light of the torches on their sleds, she could see that both priests were wearing simple sandals of woven grass fibers and their skull caps and robes were made from rough egg-cloth. Polexima was puzzled—they were dressed in something suitable for the Long Night of Atoning on the eve of the winter solstice.

"Good evening, Pious Tellenteeno," said Polexima. "My royal days keeper is not with me on this journey. Is it already time to make amends with the gods?"

"Yes, Polexima. It is time to make amends. The Long Night comes early this year."

She saw that he had a box in his hands. It was wrapped very prettily and she smelled the faint odor of mulberry perfume coming from its ribbon.

"Is Fewlenray joining us?"

"She is not."

"Then she has sent you with her answer."

"Not exactly. I do think she would want you to have this."

"A gift?" asked Polexima in puzzlement.

"It is a gift that was sent out to the queens of the border mounds we discussed."

"The ones I invited to take refuge in Bee-Jor?"

"Correct, Polexima. It is a gift that they would have all received and . . . *enjoyed* by now."

He calls me by my name instead of my title! How dare he!

Tellenteeno stared at her as the young priest brought Polexima the box. Reverting to her royal training, she opened the package by daintily untying its ribbon and then gently unwrapping its paper to reveal a lidded box. She lifted the lid and peered closer in the dim light to see a dagger that was coated in dried, red blood.

The box fell from her hands and bumped down the sled's steps to the sand grains between them. The dagger spilled out of the box with a clatter and landed near Tellenteeno's feet. He looked down at it and then at Polexima with a faint sneer above his long, sharp chin, which he extended as if to pierce her heart. She was crushed with an unbearable grief, as if her bones had been broken into pieces and then hammered into powder. Slumping, she fell to her knees, then felt as if she might never move again. She looked behind her, sure that Lair Spider was at her back with a boulder in Her claws to smash on her head and pound her down into Worm's Court of Judgment.

All had gone dark when Polexima felt her arms being gripped and pulled up to stand. She heard voices, words, and felt herself being sat on a chair as she was tenderly slapped on the cheeks.

"Majesty, Majesty!" said the voices of women dressed to resemble crickets. Polexima looked up into their concerned faces and tried to remember who they were and where she was. It all came back quickly when she saw the box with its bloodied dagger sitting on a table across from her.

"Send messengers!" she said. "On locusts to Palzhad, first thing in the morning. "I . . . I . . ."

"Yes, Majesty?"

Her heart was pounding now and she shook with chills as sweat burst from her skin.

"No," she said. "Arrange a flight for me to Palzhad, one I will take as soon as we can return to Venaris."

"Majesty, you are going to *fly* to Palzhad?"

"I have no choice. Send a message to Quedoth, Nuvao, and Terraclon that we must gather immediately."

Flying on a locust is not quite so frightening, even for a crippled woman of a certain age, thought Polexima as she held tight but not too tight to her young, darkskinned pilot. He had no fear of flying but he had some fear of her. When she first approached him, he had started with a low bow but then remembered he was only supposed to nod his head. He had yet to make eye contact with her. His hands had trembled as he strapped her in, and when he took hers to set around his waist, they were as cold as winter dew. "Are you ready, Majesty?" he asked, glancing over his shoulder. She was not ready, but she never would be.

"I am."

Polexima was grateful for the pilot's silence when they launched into flight and her bowels twisted with a sudden attack of gas that was beyond anyone's power of containment. If the pilot was surprised or offended, he did not show it. He looked straight ahead, steering the locust skillfully between the two other flyers that escorted them. Later, when they met some rough currents, he was kind enough to ignore her retching and pretended that nothing wet and foul smelling had ended up on his fine suit of armor.

The moment came, late in the flight, when she could stop staring at the pilot's neck and take a look at the sights below. The pleasure, she was delighted to learn, was greater than had been described to her and diverted her from her worries. To see a landscape from above was like seeing it for the first time—astonishing and unexpected. The tops of trees with their clusters of sun-dappled leaves were especially beautiful as were the grounds between them with their waving grasses, patches of plants, spatters of rocks, and thrusting boulders. All the humans, ants, and other living creatures she had spotted looked so tiny and delicate, like something she could sweep up with her hand and then pour into a bowl. It made her feel, for the first time, like she was the true descendant of a goddess and looking down on her godly ancestor's Creation.

As they flew over Smax and Shlipee, she thought each had a sprawling grandeur, and their rising mounds topped with palaces were a dignified mass at their centers. The hunting weeds on their edges were lush from the autumn rains and bright with late-blooming flowers including some lovely, golden blossom that was profuse and thriving.

Why don't I know this flower? Why didn't it grace Palzhad or Cajoria? Why weren't its yellow petals strung into wreaths to decorate our palaces in the darkening months?

It was sometime later when she looked below her and approached a mound that was strangely, bleakly ugly and which she thought might be Hulkrish. Her heart sank and she felt a moment of panic—had the pilot veered off course? This mound had little in the way of plants or even scrub and it was pocked with unsightly stubs of decapitated grass. Its environ was dry and empty with sprawling barrens of exposed sand. Near what had been a royal obstacle course turned to an airfield, she saw the crowding cages for the locusts but they were empty and unmanned. She saw the beginnings of some other man-made structures, of what looked like crude, lidless boxes from above. Blinking and wiping at the gunky dirt in her eyes, she saw that the boxes contained something within them that moved, ever so slightly, within their sides. The pilot lowered his fist as a signal to the escorts and all three locusts began a rotating descent.

"Pilot, are we . . . are we *stopping*?"

"Yes, Majesty," he shouted.

"Why? Where are we?"

"Mound Palzhad," he shouted. "We've arrived."

The gut-busting punch she had felt in her stomach upon takeoff that morning was nothing like the blow she felt now, one that rattled the base of her spine as she absorbed the transformation of her native mound. As they flew lower, she saw that the open boxes were the pens of refugees who had divided into more than a hundred little tribes. Palzhanite foot soldiers were patrolling the corridors between these pens and some were distributing food and other supplies. Polexima started believing it was Mound Palzhad only when she recognized the four massive and bulbous structures at the mound's peak as the crystal palaces that she had grown up in.

The pilot was steering the locust into a widening spiral that took them north of Palzhad and close to the border—or what had *been* the border—with the Dustlands. This had been the place of the refugees, and as she had expected, it was ravaged and lifeless, but as she looked out, she sensed something, smelled something, that brought her back to her time in Dneep.

When the locust spiraled inward, she saw what she had sensed—a triangular mass of grass roaches, some with hauling-sleds, had ventured close to the edge of what had been the border wall.

That's too few in number to be an invasion. But why are they here?

Refugees in the pens facing south were on top of their walls, keeping vigil of this possible invasion. At the head of the roach procession, Polexima noticed a rough-looking sled of woven grass with a tented top. Slotted into the sled's corners were poles topped with plain banners of white egg-cloth—a request, it appeared, for a peaceful conference.

"Hold tightly, Majesty, we are landing," shouted the pilot as the spiral grew shorter and she sighted a clearing and a landing crew near the royal dew station. The pilot grunted as he shifted hands over the locust's antennae, which raised up and seemed to stiffen, then bend in resistance—the locust seemed to be drawn to, or perhaps repelled by, some scent. The locust fell away from the escorts, then took a sudden plummet, landing atop of one of the domes of what had been Queen Clugna's palace. The locust was facing in a downward angle, clutching the dome with its claws and forcing Polexima to be more intimate with the young pilot than either of them were comfortable with. She felt a violent bounce as the locust pivoted left, then right, and then leapt into a short, erratic flight. Closing her eyes, she resisted screaming but the pilot managed to get them off the dome and to land them in the place that had been prepared.

"Apologies, Majesty. This was not a good landing for your first flight."

"Good Pilot, I will never forget this glorious experience, thank you," she said. "And I believe we should hold the locust responsible for the landing . . . not you."

Terraclon and Nuvao trotted towards her. Behind them were a cluster of Palzhanite priestesses dressed in the black garb of autumn crickets and carrying garlands of clover petals.

"Mother, are you all right?" Nuvao asked.

"I have never been better," Polexima said as they helped her down. As soon as she touched the ground, she fell on her bottom. Nuvao and Terraclon lifted her up.

"Do not let go," she said. "I cannot feel my legs."

"The feeling will come back," Nuvao said. "Let's get you on some crutches, Mother. Moving will help."

The Cricket sisters coming towards Polexima set the garlands around her neck, then handed her a pair of fine crutches that were bright, shiny, and green and made from the femurs of tree crickets. Once the crutches were under her arms, she looked up and managed a smile.

"Polly," said Terraclon. "You are aware that there are Dneepers on our outskirts."

"Yes, I smelled them first and saw them later."

"When you are up to it, they want an audience with you."

"With *me*?"

"Yes. Our scouts heard them shouting your name."

"Oh. Is Anand here?"

"He has . . . he has not returned," said Terraclon, his eyes lowering to relay his worry.

"He has not returned *yet*," said Polexima. "Until he does, I suppose we should go and see what these annoying Grass people want."

"Not dressed like that," said Terraclon. "They are expecting a queen."

Polexima pulled back her hood and rubbed the top of her head and felt the stubble that came from missing a few days of shaving. She looked down at her tightly fitting bodysuit of plain egg-cloth—one that was spattered with the morning meal.

I must look a fright.

Terraclon clapped his hands and palace servants trotted towards them carrying a long chest.

A chest? Good Cricket, Terraclon's brought me Mother's old coronation gown and the Jeweled Antennae of Palzhad!

The Cricket sisters made a circle around Polexima and Terraclon and then held up the ends of their gowns to make a screen of privacy. Terraclon opened the chest and reached into it to raise up a suit of blue turquoise armor along with a baldric that held an elegant yet deadly rapier. Within the armor she saw that there was the skillful inclusion of the braces that straightened her back and legs.

"Oh, Terraclon!" she gasped. "It is all too beautiful, I . . ."

"The credit goes to the dressmakers here. Here's the headpiece," he said, and reached into the chest again to pluck out a pair of long, cricket-like antennae of stiffened silk threads rooted in a band studded with crushed turquoise. She was admiring it when he reached in again.

"And Polexima, Queen of Bee-Jor and High Priestess of Mother Cricket, should also have this," Terraclon said as he raised up a sharp-ended staff with a cricket's head fashioned of faceted obsidian. Its deep blue eyes were made of polished lapis.

"If you'll excuse me," he said, and stepped away

to let her dress. Her strength renewed as she donned each piece. *So a warrior-queen I shall be,* she thought as she reappeared. She wished for a mirror but knew from Terraclon's face that the end effect was astounding—he was stunned.

To meet the Dneepers, Nuvao had assembled anyone who looked at all like a soldier. They dressed in whatever armor was available—Slopeish, Hulkrish, and Seed Eater styles—and all of it had been stained or painted with red. They carried whatever weapons looked threatening. All had brought their grass shields with them and had blow-darts at the ready even if their tips had been dipped in nothing other than berry dye. Terraclon and Nuvao were in their turquoise armor and marched just ahead of Polexima, carrying their own grass shields as a small but protective wall for her. They made a show of the longbows slung over their shoulders and had quivers full of arrows with bright, white fletchings that flashed above their heads. The procession marched through a wide, central corridor that cut through the pens of the curious refugees and then continued over the flattened rubble and ant dung that had been the border wall. They stopped when they could see the beards on the Dneepers' faces.

Polexima turned to a soldier just at her back. "Raise it!" she commanded, and a woman unfolded a pole to raise up the three-striped banner of Bee-Jor and waved it in friendly approach. The smell of the grass roaches was getting stronger, and Polexima heard their mouths gnashing as their antennae sniffed the kin-scent of leaf-cutter ants. From behind the Dneepers, Polexima glimpsed other hauling-sleds—were they filled with weapons? Hidden soldiers? Men were dismounting from saddles at the back of the roaches' heads to strut in a protective formation around one man at their center whose tall and impressive headgear was visible. They came to a stop when they were within hearing distance.

"Be brave," Polexima muttered to herself in case this was an ambush. Stepping ahead of Terraclon and her son, she stood with her head up and back straight, swinging her staff out to support herself. The man who stepped forward with a woven grass miter on his head was not Medinwoe, but his nephew, Crown Prince Tappenwoe. He looked angry and imperious with scrunched brows. With his long, thin nose and his close-set eyes, his face looked as if a little mantis had landed on it.

"Greetings, Queen Polexima," Tappenwoe shouted with a bow over fists pressed together. He then acknowledged Nuvao with a nod of his head. His eyes flashed at Terraclon, whose brown face was free of paint. "King Medinwoe sends his warmest greetings and his wishes for your health and longevity."

"Prince Tappenwoe. Please extend the same to King Medinwoe. And I would be remiss if I did not take this chance to thank you for the good care and return of my children from Dneep."

Tappenwoe looked over her head and took in the mound and its strange condition with its patchwork of pens that climbed up its incline. He squinted his eyes as he wrinkled his mouth.

"Where are your ants?" he shouted.

"What is the point of your visit?" asked Polexima, countering his rudeness.

"I am sorry," he said. "I was just . . . expressing my concern."

"In case you have forgotten, cockroaches repel ants."

"Yes, Majesty; however, we have been observing this mound for some time—from a respectful distance. There are no more leaf-cutter ants at Palzhad."

"You are correct," she said. "We no longer have ants at this mound. As to where they have gone, I am sure you can guess."

"Forgive me, Majesty, if I cannot."

"They were killed and eaten," Polexima shouted. "By the starving slaves of the Hulkrites—the refugees who were driven onto our land by *Dneepish riders of roaches*."

His upper lip stiffened as he raised his chin.

"We apologize," Tappenwoe said, "if that is truly what happened. But it was not our intention to drive anyone anywhere. We were simply taking what was our due."

Polexima shook her head and tried to contain her rage. Her staff trembled in her hand as she fantasized using its sharp end to slice off his smug expression.

"We might have had a discussion," she shouted through clenched teeth, her voice growing hard and sharp. "And considered some alternative instead of herding all these miserable people into a bloody panic! What you have done to them is a cruelty greater than anything they suffered under Tahn and the Hulkrites! You, Grass people, have proven yourselves to be void of sympathy for those outside your race. Perhaps, in all your isolation, you never learned that the other peoples that share this Sand are as human as you are and feel as much as you do."

Tappenwoe was cocking his head one way and then the other, as if she was a cut of worm roast that was too dry to eat. "Are you quite finished?" he said.

"For the moment."

"We fulfilled our promise, Queen, to you and your swarthy Dranverite. When Bee-Jor failed to complete its promise to us, we took responsibility for the situation and did you the favor of removing the vermin that infested our Promised Clearing."

"Vermin," said Polexima with hatred. "*Vermin* you call these men and women and *children*."

Tappenwoe sighed, looked exasperated. "You are one of us," he said. "A hallowed descendant of our ancient pioneers. I do not wish to offend you, Majesty, but I . . ."

"Too late," she said. "Now tell me why you are here?"

"In the interest of peace between our two great nations and the well-being of all our subjects . . ."

"Speak plainly!" she interrupted. "What do you want?"

He looked at her with a deadly serious face. "Speaking plainly," he said. "Your promise to us was not fulfilled."

"Of course it was!"

"Majesty, no. Our roaches do not thrive in the place south of here. Many of the hatchlings live no more than a few days. Some eggs never hatch. The older roaches die early deaths and are useless as mounts and as insects of burden. Something in the soil—perhaps the spirits of sand or weed demons—is not good for our insects."

"Polly," Terraclon whispered to her. "Anand always said that was true—this is why Britasytes avoid the Dustlands." Polexima made a discreet nod.

"I see," said Polexima, speaking to Tappenwoe. "But what is it that we can do for you?"

"We have waited a thousand summers to return to our Promised Clearing. But we know now that we have come to the wrong place."

Polexima's heart was starting to pound and in her head she heard an angry buzzing like bees.

"We will not go back to Dneep," shouted Tappenwoe. "Even if we wanted to, we would have to wage war on the Seed Eaters who are colonizing our old country, filling it with hundreds and thousands of their own."

"I am very sorry," said Polexima as her anger gave way to unease. "But I am asking one last time—how may we help you?"

Tappenwoe pointed up to the palaces. "You can surrender, peaceably, our *true* Promised Clearing— this place where Dneepers and their roaches will thrive. This place, here, that you call Palzhad."

In the brittle silence, Polexima had the urge to run at this man, and jam her staff through his forehead. She was trembling with rage, and felt as if the veins in her head might burst through her face when she heard the sound of an insect flying overhead. She looked up and saw a blue locust circling above them.

"Anand," she whispered.

CHAPTER 28

A TIME FOR MILDEW

"**W**hat's that?" Anand blurted to himself as he saw roaches on the edges of Palzhad. His heart quickened with excitement. *The Entreveans have returned from Pine Country! Thank Madricanth!*

As he spiraled lower, his heart plummeted when he saw that the dull, rough hauling-sleds were of Dneepers' make. His heart pounded with worry when he realized that Dneepers were conferencing with Bee-Jorites.

And I think I know why.

Anand clenched his mouth prod and thrust it into the sensors that were center left of the locust's head. Both of them were falling from the sky when Anand used his hands to push himself above the saddle before impact. The crowd below scampered and screamed as the locust landed with a thump. Anand slammed onto his saddle, and though the impact was painful, he raised his chest, his chin, and then straightened his back to glare at Tappenwoe.

"Majesties," he said, glancing at Polexima and Nuvao. "Is everything well here?"

"No, it is not," said the queen. "Prince Tappenwoe has made a most unusual request."

"I would assume he wants more land," said Anand, loud enough that all could hear him. "Land that is more hospitable to his roaches. Is that right . . . Your Highness?"

Tappenwoe grimaced as he looked away. "Queen Polexima," he said to her. "Please tell the Dranverite he is correct."

"You can tell him yourself," she said. "We have heard enough from Dneepers today. You will kindly return to your own land and to your own king."

"We will do you that favor," said Tappenwoe. "For now."

Tappenwoe met Anand's eyes one last time before he turned with his men to remount their roaches. Anand kept his eyes on the Dneepers, watching them as they ascended up rope ladders to their saddles. Nuvao, Terraclon, and Polexima gathered around Anand and were looking up at him, he knew, for guidance, for ideas, for hope.

"Nuvao," Anand asked, eyes still on the Dneepers. "Would you have any of the Holy Mildew?"

"I believe so," said Nuvao through a chortle. "But whatever for?"

"He wants to chat with Madricanth," said Terraclon.

"No," said Anand. "I don't actually believe in a talking Roach God—unless I'm desperate for one."

"Then why the mildew?" asked Nuvao. "This is hardly time for some giggly frolic."

"I need to figure things out," Anand answered. "If you ask the mildew, it will show you the beauty of the world. If you ask it to show you the truth, it will thrust it before you in all its harshness. Sometimes the two are one and the same."

"What truth are you seeking?" Polexima asked.

"What to do next," said Anand. "Perhaps with the mildew I can figure it out."

"If you're having this mildew, then so am I," said Terraclon.

"Are you sure, Ter?" Polexima asked. "It has its dangers. I am told it can be very unpleasant."

"Or extremely pleasant," said Nuvao with a knowing smile.

"I'm a priest, the Ultimate Holy Priest—such as it is," said Terraclon. "If this mildew lets you talk to the gods, then I've got some questions for them. For one thing I'd like to know why they did such a piss-shitty job when they created the Sand. And I want to know why I was born with such an embarrassingly huge penis."

Nuvao doubled over as he laughed. "I am sure the gods will find you terribly amusing," he said.

Terraclon was suddenly shy and quiet and, like any outcaste, he was suspicious of all compliments—he looked away as he waited for the insult that should follow, but Nuvao was still regarding him with a bemused admiration.

"Your penis aside, whoever or whatever you might encounter will be all in your head," said Anand. "And if you know that, the one person you can speak with and see most truthfully might be *you*. Not the 'you' that people tell you that you are, or the person you tell yourself you are, but the 'you' that is both unique and at one with everything else."

"And this is something you want to do on the verge of war?" asked Polexima, utterly confused by Anand's request.

"You can pick your reason," Anand said. "Mine is clarity. Whatever you might see or hear, it has to be sorted and reconsidered when the mildew's influence has passed. It may bring me nothing . . . which in itself might be everything."

"I would like if you could ask this mildew to show us where my daughter is—if she is safe," said Polexima. "As much as she disappoints me, I am worried for Trellana."

"Mother, the mildew does not have those powers,"

said Nuvao. "It does not enable remote viewing or allow us to see into the future."

"Yes," said Anand. "But it may allow us to look inside and at our pasts—and at those things we hide about ourselves from ourselves."

Nuvao and Terraclon looked at each other and then just as quickly looked away. Anand grinned at them, let out the slightest laugh, and then looked at the sun as it neared the West. "Terraclon, fly up with me," he said. "If you'll excuse us," he said to the royals. "I've got something I need to show His Ultimate Pious while we still have daylight."

"Of course," said Nuvao. "I'll meet you in the throne room later with some . . . refreshments."

"If the rest of you are having this mildew, then so am I," said Polexima.

"Mother, really! Why?"

"Because it may be my last chance."

From its flaccid antennae, Anand sensed his locust was tired and he knew it needed food and water—she would only be good for one short spiral around the mound before the sun dimmed.

As they flew around Palzhad, Anand looked with pride on the progress the Palzhanites had made in organizing the refugees. Neat, wide corridors connected the pens to make them both accessible and distinct from each other.

"You've done a good job here, Ter," Anand shouted.

"We have. No skirmishes for a while. What have you got to show me?"

"A book," said Anand. "It's in my backsack."

"Anand . . . I can't read."

"This book has pictures. You'll have to be very careful with it. I borrowed it."

"Oh, *borrowed* it, did you? What's it about?"

"It's a Book of War *Machines* and *Chemical* Tactics."

"War what?"

"Machines. A device that increases power. You've already built some."

"What are *chemicals*?"

"The closest word we have to it is 'potions.' You've used some of those as well."

The sunlight was fading in the palace's throne room as Terraclon leafed through the pages of the book. Over his shoulder, Anand read aloud the captions and explained the details of the drawings. Suddenly it was all too dark. Terraclon, much annoyed with Sun, went to a wall sconce and took its shriveling fungus torch back to the desk where he held it close to the pages and looked over images of other fungus—white death caps, blue poison clouds, tawny soft snatch, and dusted sick fudge.

Nuvao and Polexima entered, followed by some Cricket nuns who struggled with a large and heavy basin of kwondle tea. The palace chefs brought in a single long platter with a simple dinner of fermented mushrooms sprinkled with garlic powder and topped with shreds of a short-horned grasshopper. Polexima went to the food and speared some with a fork.

"Mother, it is best to eat afterwards," said Nuvao. "The mildew, like any of the visionary potions or funguses, takes fullest effect on an empty stomach."

Nuvao took out an orange box carved from carnelian from the pouch of his cloak and opened it to hand each of them a square sheet of something black and translucent. He folded his own sheet before inserting it in his mouth to chew.

Anand chewed his sheet and found it bitter and astringent and would have preferred it dissolved in some sweet punch. He scooped up some kwondle tea to chase it as his mind turned to his concerns. "How long before the Yellow Mold appears at the Slopeish mounds on our western border?" he asked Nuvao.

"Without the proper urine, it will be about two weeks before the mold makes an unmistakable appearance," replied the king. "As soon as it does, we can expect masses of anxious refugees."

"They'll be even more eager to come when they realize the threat of the League of Velvet Ant Peoples," said Terraclon.

"More refugees are the last thing we need," said Polexima. "Especially Slope loyalists who would undermine Bee-Jor."

"Undermine it in favor of what?" asked Anand. "Their complete self-destruction?"

"That is the current fashion," said Polexima.

Anand stood and walked to the viewing window and saw nothing but unending darkness on a moonless night. When he turned back to find his chair, he stumbled over the carpet.

"How many days do you think we have before the league takes the central mounds of the Slope?" Anand asked. "Before they cross our border?"

"We don't know," said Nuvao. "From our last reconnaissance, they were on their way to Mound Ospetsek and might have reached Abavoon. It could be a moon or two or it could be a fortnight before they reach Fecklebretz and take on Venaris."

"Or they may head north to Loobosh and then to Cajoria to spread from there," said Polexima.

"They might try both. Let's figure it's eight nights," said Anand as he felt that mild trembling in his gut that preceded a rush. "And we'll prepare like it were. Let's assume they'll attack any of the remaining western mounds before they cross into Bee-Jor."

"How do we fight them?" Polexima asked. "If they're as innumerable as we think they are."

"Innumerable, yes," Anand said. "But invincible? No."

"How are you so sure?" asked Nuvao.

"Because the Carpenters held them back for centuries. They never destroyed them, but they could contain them."

"How?" Terraclon asked, looking up from the book.

"I'm not sure," Anand said.

The faint chirping of crickets was filling the silence, but Anand was sure he could hear the workings of Terraclon's mind as he tapped his fingers.

"Roach Boy, let me ask you something again," Terraclon said, using his guttural accent. "Why do Britasytes secretly gather the poisons of autumn daisies?"

"Because it's illegal," said Anand. "Punishable by death."

"But they do it anyway. Why?"

Anand gasped. "To sell!" he shouted.

"And sell to who?" Terraclon said.

"To the Carpenters!" Anand replied. He felt ashamed and embarrassed that this had not occurred to him.

"Yes," said Terraclon, and then chuckled. "So when are we going to war?"

"Somebody here sounds just a bit bloodthirsty," said Anand as his thoughts came flying now. "We are not going to war. Not now, not ever."

"Then what are we doing?" asked Terraclon.

"We are taking a defensive measure."

"Anand, they're crawling towards us by the hundreds of thousands if not in the millions," said Nuvao.

"If we aren't setting a trap for them," said Polexima, "then are we throwing the first punch?"

"What we need to do first is offer them a kind

warning and then peace and friendship," answered Anand.

"Really, Anand," Polexima scolded. "What if we had offered the Hulkrites peace and friendship?"

"Our throats would have been slit," said Terraclon. "And Pleckoo's buttocks would be warming a cushion on a throne in Cajoria."

"We will warn the league," Anand said. "And there will be no battles until they cross our boundaries."

"What about the Dneepers?" asked Polexima. "While we're at war with these Greeyas, they'll take Palzhad."

"Let them have it," Anand said. He had caught a vision by its toe and was pulling it in.

"What?" shouted the other three.

"For a price. And they can have Caladeck and Rinso. We will absorb Escarte, Zilpot, Fecklebretz, Tathorek, Shamorda, Dobsahn, Fwumbry and Loobosh. We must have Loobosh . . . for now."

Anand looked into the faces of the gathered and saw their shock in the dim light. As he stared at them, their faces transformed. Their eyes grew larger and lidless and mandibles erupted from the sides of their mouths. The false antennae on their heads came to life and twitched. He chortled as he watched the three of them turn into ants.

"What's so funny?" Terraclon asked through his scissoring mandibles. Anand gasped when he saw the Yellow Mold creeping across the floor like a thousand little worms and envelop his friends turned to ants. The three imploded and sent up a last wisp of yellow dust that faded into the blackness. Anand closed his eyes and when he opened them the vision was gone. His friends stared at him, waiting.

"I know something now!" Anand shouted. "I know it!" He was quiet again, both excited and full of dread as the chirping of crickets grew louder.

"Would you care to share it with us, Anand?" said Poleximia. Fright was in her voice as she felt the first effects of the drug.

Anand was silent, but when he spoke it was with certitude.

"I don't care to. But I must, Polly. We must kill all leaf-cutter ants."

CHAPTER 29

THE END OF THE PAZOOPA DOPIDARU

"No one should live through this much pain," Trellana said to herself as a fresh secretion of beetle-scent wafted over the travois to deepen her nausea. She had been traveling for days, likely towards Bee-Jor, while tied at the wrists and ankles. She was buried neck-deep in broken pine needles with the roach-women and could think of nothing to distract her. She was without a single hope. "Please, Death Beetle . . . or whatever god there is," she prayed aloud. "Take the breath from me and end my life . . . and these hideous bastards that grow inside me."

"I will pray for your death too," said Ulatha with

a sideways glare. "But why don't you just try holding your breath?"

I will give that a try, Trellana thought. She could not pinch her nose, but she exhaled and then resisted inhaling while repeating *kill me, kill me, kill me* in her head until the moment the pressure was too great, too painful, and she had to snort up air and gasp. The roach-women laughed at her.

"Keep trying," Ulatha said. "You'll get better at it."

"That is not at all what I was doing."

"Of course not, Your Majesty. Not when so many adore and need you."

The endless army of Greeyas on their velvet ants had been crawling through a thickness of hunting and foraging weeds when at last they reached a well-trod path that led to the outermost rings of some Slopeish mound. Trellana smelled the intense stink of garbage, shit, and human and insect corpses and knew that they were near some unkempt midden. The velvet ants that rode alongside the travois were making loud clicking sounds again, which meant that they were about to enter into some insect conflict, a notion that both alarmed Trellana and gave her hope.

Let this be an all-out war, she prayed, *in which I am the first casualty.*

Ulatha and Queestra were talking over each other, gasping, the pitch of their voices getting higher and breathy. Trellana did not understand a word of their language, but she could hear that the two were frightened. When the velvet ants' clicking grew louder, the women, weirdly, started singing, and when the melody repeated, they harmonized, which led to a further variation. After an unsteady start, it turned into a pleasant song. Even the Greeyas riding at their sides were listening to them, smiling with their ears bent towards the travois. After the women stopped singing, Trellana felt removed from her suffering. Fragments of the melody were in her head. She wanted to hear it again.

"That . . . that was very pretty," she said.

"What?" said Ulatha in mild shock.

"Please. Don't make me repeat myself. I said it was pretty. If you would please . . . sing it again."

"Not right now," said Ulatha. "Madricanth welcomes our prayers, but He has others to listen to."

"You were . . . you were *praying*?"

"Yes, it was a song-prayer."

"For your rescue."

"No. We prayed for the others in our clan, for their safety—if they are safe at all."

In all her discomfort, Trellana felt something unfamiliar, a feeling that she finally identified as shame.

Here they are, suffering as much as I do, but their thoughts are on others.

Trellana cleared her throat. "I'd like to ask you something," she said. "Where do you think they are, your Roach Clan? Where is the man who was with you when I arrived at Gemurfa . . . the chieftain?"

Ulatha took a deep breath and then slowly exhaled. "We hope Thagdag and our people have escaped or been released," she said. "And returned to Bee-Jor. It is not a great hope."

"But Britasytes have always had the privilege of traveling the Pine Lands."

"We are not needed anymore," said Ulatha. "Sinsora wants no more contact with the Slope or Bee-Jor or even with the Seed Eaters, regardless of their good liquors and confections. The Carpenter people have always seen us as a 'filthy necessity' and 'corruptors of morals' and now the Setcha Greeya has banned us from the land he claims."

"Why?"

Ulatha was quiet, keeping something back. "He hates roach people," she said after a moment. "He does not want anyone other than Greeyas in what they call the Sudhi-Greeya-Tepic—the Redeemed Land."

"Why has he kept you alive?"

"When he has no more need for translators, he will kill us and feed us to his war beetles."

"For whom does he expect you to translate?"

"Whoever succeeds your dead Britasyte husband as the leader of Bee-Jor—the one who will negotiate its surrender."

Anand. This is all his fault! Trellana thought as disgust and resentment repossessed her body. She clenched her jaw and imagined tearing Anand's throat out with her teeth.

The Greeya warriors were calling to each other, passing a message that rolled in waves through their uncountable number—they had arrived somewhere and were halting. From their voices and their insects' clicking, the Greeyas seemed mildly cautious. Trellana got a whiff of what might have been alarm-scent from leaf-cutter ants. The beetle that hauled the three women was guided into a pivot by its driver, and for the first time in days Trellana could look at something other than Greeyas and velvet ants. They had reached the lowest ring of a Slopeish mound. From its tattered and dirty banners with their embroideries of Mother Damselfly, she realized they were at Mound Ospetsek.

As she had sensed, a tiny army of unmounted ants was trickling down the mound's main artery to attack the velvets, but the ants did not appear to be leaf-cutters—they looked more white than yellow. They had no roused giants to face their enemy and most of them were small and all were slow and weak. As they got closer, Trellana saw that they *were* leaf-cutters, but they were covered with bumpy crusts of whitish mites that had multiplied on their chitin. Some ants wobbled from infestations that clustered on their heads while others dragged abdomens that were weighted down with parasites. Trellana had never felt pity for insects, but the last of the ants to arrive were barely hatchlings: tiny little things with soft yellow shells that could be picked up with hands and eaten raw.

The velvet ants were barely excited. Unlike ants, they did not strain to enter battle and they were not united by war-scent into a cooperating army, even those velvets who were the same color. The drivers atop the velvets barely held their insects' antennae to keep them in control as they almost waited to be attacked. The bowmen sitting behind their drivers were relaxed and laughing when the leaf-cutters braved the velvets and attempted to use their mandibles to cut through their fuzz, completely failing at piercing their thick, hard chitin. Smaller ants that managed to crawl atop the velvets were slain by men. They used their swords to pierce them through the thorax or hacked off their heads at the joint. All of it looked ridiculously casual.

The largest of the leaf-cutters, posing some threat, managed to engage a few of the velvets. After the Greeya riders jumped from their saddles, these velvets bothered to lock mandibles and wrestled with the ants as both attempted to sting each other. The leaf-cutters' stingers broke on the velvets' chitin but the velvets' stingers easily punctured the ants, then pumped them with a venom so deadly that they died in an instant.

The velvets were uninterested in eating the dead leaf-cutters, but the Greeyas were excited by it. Men on foot peeled and scraped the mites from the ant corpses to munch right away or to stack on their rapiers for later eating. The peeled, dead ants were cut into three and then tossed into sled-bins for the evening feast.

Trellana burst into tears. She was imagining that on the eastern side of Ospetsek, the ant queen, if she were alive, was struggling out of the mound with her retinue as they pushed her to some pointless refuge. Trellana looked left and right and knew that the Greeyas' army had surrounded the entire mound, a hundred thick, and no leaf-cutter could escape the encirclement, much less the giant egg-layer.

What made Trellana weep was that no human could get out either. The velvet ants, in all their different colors and stripes and spots, were driven forward and up by their riders, and like some massive patchwork quilt, the velvets were blanketing the mound. Trellana heard ten, then a hundred, then a thousand screams as a bloody slaughter of the humans began. Whatever Ospetsites were alive at this mound had to have raced up to the main entry, then run down to hide in the mushroom farms, the cathedral, or the nursing or giants' chambers—but then what? When and where could they escape after that? The only hope was to reach a tunnel that connected to another mound—and how long before that mound was overwhelmed by these voracious Greeyas?

It was later in the afternoon when Trellana saw the blanket of velvets had reached the mound's highest rings. Some were even clustering atop the rain shield and bending it with their weight. On the ground, she could see even more velvets, even more men, and many more war beetles arriving—the next wave to overtake the next mound. *Where are they headed next?*

The beetles pushing into the mass were hauling sleds with leaf-tanks full of nectar. When the sleds came to a stop, hefty women climbed up ladders, then sat atop the tanks, pressing down on them with their weight as children with extended scoops collected the thick liquid from spigots and then weaved through the hungry velvets to feed them. For Trellana, it had been another endless day of physical and emotional tortures, and all of it was maddeningly noisy. When it couldn't get any louder, it suddenly did—the masses turned to clapping and cheering and then a chant of *"Dirgok jivana Setcha"* over and over. Something or someone was approaching from the East. A shadow was cast over the travois and Trellana strained to look up.

Passing by her were seven of the largest velvet ants yet. These were all the more startling because their color was a deep and piercing blue. Their velvet was thick and glossy and their abdomens were bright with striking white spots. Atop the tallest of the blue velvets, Trellana recognized the Setcha Greeya, that darkly ugly man who sat behind his driver. The Setcha held up a long, ceremonial sword that waved stiff banners in the seven colors of the peoples of his league. As his mount came closer to Trellana, he looked into her eyes with a smug smile before he shouted down to the roach-women in the Carpenters' tongue.

"The Setcha says welcome to Greeya-Tepic," said Ulatha after Queestra translated his words.

"Tell the Setcha he is unwelcome on the Great and Holy Slope," said Trellana.

Ulatha frowned and passed something that evoked a flat response from the Setcha.

"You told him something else!" Trellana scolded Ulatha.

"The Setcha calls you 'dear slave' and asks if there is anything you need," said Ulatha.

"Yes," said Trellana. "I would like a pond of honey-sweetened scorpion venom, enough to kill the Setcha and all his glorious people."

The Britasytes did not translate Trellana's last statement but were promptly plucked from the pine needles and taken away on the backs of velvet ants with a long white fuzz. Once they had left, Trellana savored a moment of solitude, and then, strangely, she missed the two roach-women.

Over the next two days, Trellana was left in the pool of pine needles to watch as the Greeyas transformed Ospetsek. Thousands of dark-skinned Slopeish women, some with children or babies, wept and screamed when they were removed from hiding and forced down the mound by Greeya women who were on foot and bearing weapons. Thousands of young men and older boys from the working castes were prodded down the mound by Greeya warriors. On the third day, women and girls were returned up the mound in the velvet garb of the league but in the company of Greeya men. The dark-skinned men were not returned. Late in the afternoon, Queestra and Ulatha were returned to the travois. They had been bathed, redressed, and were reinserted into the pine needles with Trellana. "Where have you been?" she asked them.

"We have been translating," said Ulatha, "instructing the Slopeites of Ospetsek in the ways of their liberators."

"Their 'liberators'? You mean their 'masters.'"

"No. The Slopeites here have been freed from their castes and invited into the league. The women have been married to Greeya men and the Slopeish men have been recruited to the Greeyas' army. The dark-skinned inhabitants here have been told that they are the proud and noble descendants of the *Vadama Greeyas*, the True Holy People, who were conquered and enslaved by a deceitful race, the *Pazoopa Dopidaru*, the "yellow degenerates" of the Grasslands. They are told that their lands and their birthright have been returned to them."

Trellana trembled with so much rage that it caused the dried pine needles to shake around her. *That's the same poisonous message that Anand spread on the Slope!* Before she could stop herself, Trellana gasped and screamed and cried with anger turning to anguish.

The next phase of the transformation of Ospet-sek began the following morning with the removal and extermination of the last leaf-cutter ants. Sleeping giants, brood ants, and farming and excavating ants deep inside the mound had all been killed and dragged out. Ant corpses with nooses around their petioles or head joints were lugged down the mound's main artery by the war beetles. When these last ant corpses reached the lowest rings, they were butchered into pieces, then passed through the Greeyas. Holy men with towering hats of tubular fuzz looked skyward atop their black velvet ants to bless the ant-flesh before the masses consumed it. Once all the leaf-cutter ants had been cleared, a process that took days, something far more gruesome followed: the removal of the human corpses.

Trellana could see from their clothing and skin that the dead had all come from the upper castes, and most of them were war widows and their children. For days, Trellana endured watching as dead Ospet-sites from the noble, priestly, and merchant castes were dragged by the Greeyas' insects to what had been the midden. It was there that the corpses were piled up like trash. Since the carrion insects could not approach to eat them, they were left to rot and stink. Their skin turned from pale yellow, then to dark blue, and after days of sun exposure, it changed again to a dark brown—the greatest humiliation of all.

And yet the Setcha wants me *alive,* Trellana thought,

as a living symbol of his triumph over the Slopeites, the last of the yellow-skinned to flaunt as his trophy. Our offspring will live as freaks that he puts on display on the insides of a cage!

For the first time in days Trellana remembered she was already pregnant with someone else's abominable offspring. What would the Setcha do with them?

When all the human corpses had been removed from the mound, Trellana witnessed the final stage of the mound's transformation. The Greeyas had been foraging in the surrounding weeds and were returning with the living larvae and pupae of the ground-nesting insects that had burrowed for winter. Tens of thousands of these had been collected and wrapped with loose, oily cloths and then set in massive containers to be hauled to the top of the mound by beetles. In her hunger, Trellana had mouthwatering memories of the autumn feasts and their sumptuous roasts of cicada grubs and the rich and tangy egg of a velvet ant that had been stuffed into its center. She realized the larvae going up the mound would be reburied inside the underground chambers where velvet ant females would exploit them as hosts for their eggs.

It was a cool gray morning when Trellana awoke from a sweet dream of being back in her bedroom in Cajoria, but soon after, she realized the travois had been rehitched to a war beetle. After a Greeya retied the reins, he set a piece of an ant's skull that was still moist under the chins of the three women.

Trellana and the roach-women bobbed their heads in the shell to lick its thickened lymph and did not care if it smeared their faces. When her stomach was soothed, Trellana felt a moment of comfort and then realized the army was finished with Ospetsek, a transformation that took but seven days, and was moving again.

"To another mound, to start all over," she muttered to herself. Once again, she had that feeling of falling off the end of the Sand, of plummeting endlessly in a cold and windy darkness. And once more, she realized she had nothing to distract her and no hope to savor, until she noticed the blue ants and their riders high above the rest of the masses. The Setcha Greeya was raising up his sword again with its seven-colored banners to lead his army west—to Bee-Jor. Trellana felt a twinge of hope and then savored a moment that was bright with joy.

I have got something to look forward to. That moment when the Setcha weds me as his wife . . . and stands on a sack of Anand's bones!

CHAPTER 30

PREPARATIONS

Queen Jakhuma savored sitting on a cushioned saddle atop a leaf-cutter ant even if the ride was rough. Baby Chance was cooing inside a soft pouch strapped over her chest and seated beside them was Kula Priya nursing little Hopeful, the snub-nosed infant foisted on them by some desperate and deceitful Hulkrite. *Just where is Khali Talavar?* Jakhuma wondered as she looked over her shoulder. *Has he survived to threaten us again?*

And what other threats are ahead at this new mound?

She looked at Sebetay's back, sitting just ahead of her on his own saddle that was set before the first of the three spikes that jutted from the leaf-cutter's thorax.

After three days of riding, he had learned how to probe a leaf-cutter's antennae with the scented gloves and had achieved a smoother and more direct ride. The knotty muscles of his back were less pronounced, and his shoulders were almost slack. Every so often he looked over his shoulder, checking on his charges, and smiling a bit as their ant kept pace with thousands of others heading north to the mound called Loobosh, a supposed center of Slopeish learning.

The other Ledackis, on their own ants, were doing their best to keep pace with Jakhuma, but their drivers were still fumbling—at times, the ants raced ahead, sometimes they slowed or strayed from the parade. Ants that drifted from the column were guided back into place by Bee-Jorite guards on war ants who prodded them back into the column.

As they proceeded north, Jakhuma took in the appearance of refugees from other tribes when their ants surged ahead or fell back. All of them were crawling alongside the edge of Bee-Jor's western border, a border, they were told, that had just been extended in the face of the coming threat. These other refugees heading to Loobosh were strangers, but they had also been slaves in Hulkren who spoke Hulkrish. None of them looked at Jakhuma or her Meat Ant people with malice or suspicion, and more importantly, like they might be something good to eat. Some of them nodded their heads and shouted, *"Sigo nya,"* the closest thing to "hello" or "good day" in Hulkrish but which meant "I see you." None of them, thankfully, used the greeting *"Mekoodge Hulkro"* to praise the Termite. The faces, clothing, and hairstyles of these others were different from the Ledackis, but she realized that all of them were blessed with skin as dark or nearly dark as her own.

Was this on purpose? Had Vof Quegdoth assigned refugees to different mounds according to their skin colors? Was this in order to discourage strife? His own face—such a handsome one—was as dark and as lustrous as beads of brown obsidian. Perhaps the commander wanted all who were blessed with black and brown complexions to join him at what was his *favorite* mound.

And as for that mound, Loobosh was at last coming into view. Just ahead was a mix of drying grasses and new plants thriving after the rains of autumn. Within these she spotted some hunters, foragers, and trappers, as well as some weeds workers who were clearing the path of beggar-prickles, snotstitches, pus-creepers, and other useless and annoying vegetation. Mound Loobosh looked smaller and less broad than Palzhad, but its crowning palaces were newer and taller and topped with jar-like spheres that stretched a sunny, yellow rain shield between them. The ants continued up the clearing and then past a density of profusely blooming autumn daisies. Strangely, these flowers were being cut and processed by men and women wearing breathing masks.

Whatever do they want with autumn daisies? Jakhuma thought, and felt frightened. *And why did they let them sprout in the first place?*

The first of Loobosh's rings came into view with its plaza and dew station. Beside the station was an outdoor shrine with shabby, little idols made of rags, pebbles, and woven grass fibers—materials that were far too humble for the rendering of gods. She looked up to see the first of the houses on the flats that were perched high on twig poles rooted deep in the sand. These dwellings were crooked and irregular, really shanties more than houses, and they were constructed of twigs, bark, and sand bound with tar for waterproofing. As places to live, Jakhuma thought they looked awful; they were nothing like her father's palace atop its clean, sun-warmed boulder. And they were grossly inferior to the apartments provided for working people and soldiers in Ledack's pebble fortresses. But after the pens of Palzhad, these rough little houses were somewhat appealing as they looked to be quiet and, most importantly . . . private.

Kula placed Hopeful over her shoulder to pat him until he burped. "Highness," she began as she looked at the scattered Looboshites. "I wanted to ask . . ."

"Kula, I am now Your Majesty," she said, "As I do believe I am queen now."

"Yes . . . Your Majesty," said Kula, giving her a brief glare. "How do we know that the people at this mound are any more welcoming than the people of Palzhad?"

"We don't know," said Jakhuma. "But supposedly the Looboshites are grateful to Quegdoth and to Bee-Jor for reclaiming this mound before this horde arrives: the League of Velvet Ant Peoples who want to destroy everything."

Hundreds of Loobosh's leaf-cutter ants were coming towards the new arrivals in a slow, unthreatening crawl. Their gasters were neither low nor high and their antennae waved in a low pulsing as they sensed kin-scent in the approaching ants. As the ants got familiar through the sniffing/touching of antennae, the first of the Looboshite humans filtered through the insects to greet the Ledackis and the other arrivals from Palzhad. They dipped their heads and opened hands at their sides as their leader stepped through. He was a man with soft, womanly features, lighter skin, and he looked very well fed. He stood with others like him who wore robes with long, draping sleeves and necklaces that held a little jar as a pendant.

In the back of these men, if one could call them that, were clusters of dark-complexioned people who were preparing a table made of a polished split-rock. They were scenting the table with wipes of fragrant leaves and then covering it with platters of ant eggs, mushrooms, and cold roasted crickets. Ant wranglers with scented turbans were taking control of the arriving ants and helped Jakhuma and her party drop down from their saddles.

"Welcome to Mound Loobosh," said the leader with the high voice of a eunuch in something like Hulkrish. He then made the same greeting in Slopeish with similar sounding words—this was their first instruction in the language of the Mushroom Eaters. The eunuch smiled warmly, opened his arms, and then bowed down to the refugees to show them his dyed hair, which was razored and pasted into the shape of a snouted pink moth. "My name is Brother Moonsinger," he said. "And I have learned just enough Hulkrish to extend the warmest greetings of Commander Vog Quegdoth and Her Majesty, Queen Polexima of Bee-Jor. They thank all of you for joining us in our *defensive measure*, our effort to defend ourselves from a western aggressor. We have prepared a supper for you as well as places to sleep. Rest and nourish yourselves, Bee-Jorites, for tomorrow we all go to work."

Jakhuma watched as the eunuch fell out of his trance—perhaps he was like the knowledge guardians of her tribe: the masters of stories, histories, and information with their capacity to remember long chains of words. She heard Kula sighing just as Hopeful was rooting for her teat again. "What's wrong, dear Kula?"

"I forgot," said her servant with pursing lips. "That we came here to fight."

"Not to fight," Jakhuma said as baby Chance roused and started crying. "To defend ourselves."

"**A**nd in return for this *cooperation*, as you call it, you are offering us thrice what we asked for," repeated King Medinwoe with one eye closed as he stood with his retinue before Polexima and her guards. Both were some distance from the packs of roaches that had carried them to the smooth top of a low boulder at the edge of the Promised Clearing.

"Yes," said the Queen. "We are offering both Palzhad and Mounds Caladeck and Rinso and their surrounding areas as outlined on this map."

Medinwoe cocked his head. "What is wrong with Caladeck and Rinso?" he asked.

"Both are failing mounds, ones that cannot sustain a colony of leaf-cutter ants for much longer," said Queen Polexima. "The area would be well suited to roach people with its abundant clearings, patches of weeds, and stands of seed grasses. Its sands are safe for roaches and other insects."

"But why would you give them to us?"

"Because we need your nation to succeed if ours is going to survive," said Queen Polexima. "We both know that new enemies are festering in what was once called Hulkren. Your people would plug up the Petiole on its north end and have the responsibility of dealing with threats from the South . . . and West."

"You speak too plainly, Queen."

"I speak honestly, King."

"It seems like a trick."

"Of course it does—a stupid, ill-conceived trick that would fool no one. But I assure you, this is *all* we are offering and will *ever offer again*. If you even *attempt* to take any more land from Bee-Jor, then we will push you back into the Dustlands where you and your roaches will die."

"And just how would you manage that with your silly little ants that run in fear of roaches?"

Polexima pointed to the Britasytes that had accompanied her in the distance.

"Do you see those people over there? The dark-skinned ones who are also roach riders?"

"What about them?" Medinwoe's eyes slitted and his mouth grew tight.

"They know how to breed roaches," said Polexima. "They also know how to kill them by the thousands."

Medinwoe was quiet, lost in thought and rapidly blinking. He looked over at Prince Tappenwoe and the rest of the men who had accompanied him. The king and prince both looked at the map they had been given with their eyes darting around its lines.

"Majesty," said Tappenwoe as he met the queen's eyes. "Are you saying that Palzhad, Rinso, and Caladeck and the surrounding areas drawn on this map would be completely evacuated by ants and Bee-Jorites before our arrival?"

"I swear it on Cricket's Antennae. Caladeckens, Rinsonians, and Palzhanites that wish to remain in Bee-Jor will be relocated to its western mounds, areas that are currently falling back into our possession."

Medinwoe, Tappenwoe, and the nobles and priests of Dneep stepped back to huddle and passed around the map. After a storm of whispers, Medinwoe turned and stepped towards Polexima to look into her eyes in a long silence. "We are in agreement," he said.

"Indeed," confirmed Polexima. "But there will be no transferral of land until the terms are complete. Is that understood?"

"It is," said Medinwoe. He watched as Polexima was brought a squat jar of ink by King Nuvao. She dipped her thumb in the ink, then pressed it to a copy of the map that Anand had drawn and that Terraclon had decorated. She handed the map to Medinwoe, who returned to her a copy of the same map after he had pressed his own inked thumb in the sheet's corner.

Polexima watched Nuvao as he scratched with urgency onto a roll of paper attached to a hardboard to document the terms of the agreement. To the Dneepers' astonishment, he read to them from the completed paper, which detailed all that had been agreed to that morning, an act that looked magical to them. As he read, Polexima looked back at the Britasytes. Punshu and the others were waiting atop their glinting roaches, their bows and arrows and dart guns at the ready if not directly aimed. Punshu was grinning as he usually did, but his smile was even brighter when he saw the exchange of documents. After Nuvao finished reading, he reached into his robe's pouch and untied the ribbon around two more sheets before handing them to his mother.

"Majesty, we have one last proposal," Polexima said as she handed this new sheet to Medinwoe, who was perplexed when he looked it over. He passed the sheet to Tappenwoe, who looked surprised by the sheet's mysterious image.

"Explain, please," Medinwoe said as his eyes ran up and down a drawing of what looked like an insect with a bulging thorax and long straight legs. "Is this an ant?"

"That is a building plan for a *Diplomacy* Dome," said the queen. "It is a structure we would like to build on the border between our two nations. This yellow dome would be built on your side, this red one would be built on ours. The larger, orange dome in the center would be shared between us as a meeting place to converse in safety. We could arrange to trade goods, unite against common foes, and aid each other in times of disaster. Most importantly, we could avoid wars with each other."

Anand felt strange and a little sickened to be back in a boat again, especially in such a precarious one that wobbled with every wave. The shore people of

Kweshkin looked confident in the crafts they had quickly improvised from the leaves and stalks of punk weeds for this single voyage. The Kweshkites were seated along the boats' sides, dipping shovels in unison to propel the crafts south, while thousands of Bee-Jorite defenders, taking their first boat ride, clung to straps on the boats' insides. The bravest defenders were at the prows where they held up sails of sycamore leaves to catch the breeze blowing south. Others were at the sterns to shift the rudders that guided the boats to the southern end of the Great Brackish Lake. Most of the Bee-Jorites looked ill at ease and others were just ill, but all were resolute in fulfilling Anand's newest mission to save their country from the new invaders, the barbarian riders of velvet ants.

Anand stood with bended knees atop the pebbles on his boat's bottom where he held the end of an amplifying-cone secured to his boat's prow. The pebbles provided just enough ballast to keep the boat from flipping over but only a few more would have made it sink. He heard the riders gasping and looked over to see what had astonished them—it was a school of red-tailed killifish swimming under the boats. They had black top-fins and the scales on their bodies glinted like flakes of silver pyrite. The killifish were chasing after water fleas, the clear, disc-like creatures that seemed to leap through the water to escape being eaten. A moment later, the Kweshkites screamed out warnings when they sighted a mass of backswimmers, the predatory water beetles who swam upside down and used oar-like legs to propel themselves. The Bee-Jorites had been warned not to fall in the water as backswimmers might kill them with their stabbing mouthparts and they shrank from the beetles, as if they might leap up from the water to snatch them from the boats. Anand saw the first of some water striders and knew they were close to shore.

The water grew choppier as they approached the docks where large and sturdy fishing boats of Kweshkite making came into view. These were elegant crafts with high curving ends, broad decks, and storage space for the catches. Anand looked at Elga, the dignified Kweshkite elder he had enlisted from a refugee pen at Palzhad, and she nodded her head. "We have come home. Commander Quegdoth. That is Kweshkin," she confirmed with a tremble in her voice. Anand raised up a banner of Bee-Jor and waved it to the locust flyer who circled above them.

"Drop sails," Anand shouted, and the men in a nearby boat released their sycamore leaves, signaling to the thousand others behind them to do the same. From the East, Anand saw the approach of water striders—he knew these were patrol striders, mounted by men who had been or were Hulkrites. When the Hulkrites saw the thousand boats and realized it was an invasion, they raced back to shore to warn their fellows. Anand could hear the banging of wooden gongs and their shouts to each other as they activated a defense. If Anand was correct, they would man their boats, which was likely where they kept some weapons. The boats did not venture out, but as Anand expected, they waited for the attackers to come closer and used that time to ready a defense.

"Shields up!" Anand commanded in both Slopeish and Hulkrish. All in the boats turned their shields of straw from their backs to their chests. The oarsmen kept their paddles in the water, steadying the crafts. "Wait for the first arrows!" Anand shouted, and his message was passed through the fleet. He stepped closer to the cone, which would not only amplify his voice but serve as a shield.

"Abandon your weapons!" Anand shouted in Hulkrish, "And save your lives! You are ordered to abandon these boats, these houses, and the land along this shore that you stole from the people of Kweshkin. Attack us with your weapons and we will destroy you with ours."

The Kweshkite boats remained in place. On the first of them, Anand could see a missile launcher being pushed up to the boat's prow as men with bows and quivers scuttled over its deck to aim their arrows through crenels.

"We should shoot now!" sputtered Elga to Anand. "Before they can fire!" Her old and veiny hands trembled as she struggled to hold back the drawstring of her bow.

"We will not attack first!" Anand said with a loud whisper. He grinned when he heard the buzzing of wings, then looked up to see hundreds of locusts had arrived and were spiraling overhead. Terraclon's white striped locust was leading the squadron into a slow descent. As they did, the bowmen on the locusts made a terrifying noise with harps of cicada wings, a sound so loud and piercing that Anand was tempted to clamp his ears. The Hulkrites on the deck were looking up, hunching in fear of the flyers. The commands of their leaders were lost in the noise and the men pointed their arrows up, then down, and even at each other. Moments later, they pulled together to aim their arrows down at the flimsy boats coming forward.

As Hulkrish arrows flew, Bee-Jorite defenders caught them with their shields. Anand raised his banner again and waved it as a signal to Terraclon. "Fire!" Anand shouted, left and right.

A Hulkrish missile flew into the amplifying-cone, tore it into pieces, and then pierced through Anand's straw shield to puncture his armor and prick his chest. He had been blown to the back of the boat, the impact cushioned by a collision with defenders, one of which fell overboard. Anand was stunned and in a breathless panic as he watched thousands of Bee-Jorite arrows fly up from their boats to pour down on the Hulkrites.

"Help me up," Anand shouted, staggering after he was raised by his arms to his feet. He saw a storm of darts and arrows rain down from the locust flyers to fell the Hulkrites. Those who were pierced screamed in pain, then screamed even louder when the poisons of wasps and spiders that coated the arrowheads spread inside them with a pain that ended in paralysis. As the locusts of the Bee-Jorite forces flew lower, they aimed their darts at the last standing Hulkrites, some of which threw themselves overboard to attempt an escape. Some Hulkrites were swimming away when they began screaming and thrashing—they had been caught, stabbed in the neck, and then dragged underwater by backswimmers who would drown them, then eat them.

Anand waved his banner once and then dipped it towards land. The defenders of Bee-Jor pushed in, skirting the docked boats and paddling for the shore. When his own boat got closer to land, Anand threw the first of the pebbles out of it and the rest of the defenders followed his lead. When the boats were emptied, they were flipped over and the defendants walked under them as a carapace that deflected the arrows of hidden or retreating Hulkrites. The Bee-Jorites walked through the mud in boots with long-toothed soles that gave them traction until they reached dry land. The Kweshkites among them were shouting to their own in the shelters ahead of them, letting them know they had been freed. Some of these Kweskhites were already running towards the defenders, women and children, to join their advance.

The defenders continued to a city of pitched buildings woven from rush leaves and set among their stalks.

The last of the Hulkrites were leaping from these buildings, some in their old armor of ghost ant chitin and with a Hulkrish sword at their sides. They disappeared in the thickness of rushes behind them where they would weave their way back to the emptiness of the Dustlands. The Kweshkites were taking aim at the last of these Hulkrites, shooting the slowest and drunkest of them as they fell from ladders or platforms. The Kweshkites laughed and cheered as they ran in with swords to finish off the fallen.

"No killing!" Anand shouted. "We don't kill unless in self-defense! We will imprison these men until further notice!"

The Bee-Jorite army went into a sudden, shamed quiet as they lowered their weapons. The Kweshkites among them went to the fallen Hulkrites and, unable to kill them, took delight in tying their wrists and then their ankles together, leaving them facedown. Kweshkite women and children appeared from the shelters crying and shaking in disbelief. Husbands, fathers, and sons who had been in exile ran to their families. The reunions were loud with sobbing as they crashed into each other's arms.

"Thank you," said Elga, who had been standing by Anand in silence. She sniffled and her eyes were red with tears.

"You are quite welcome, Elder Elga," said Anand. "And as we have no time to waste, I must ask that you complete your promise."

"Of course, Commander, we will port your cargo to Bee-Jor as quickly as you bring it to us . . . but I am an old widow," she said. "You will forgive me if I remain here in Kweshkin to restore order to our little nation."

"Of course, madam," Anand said. "We should return here in two days, once we have all we need . . . or can carry."

After the Bee-Jorite defenders rested and fulfilled their needs, the boats they had brought with them were patched and repaired and then filled with the shovels they had used as oars and the waxed leaves they had used as sails. The defenders set the boats on their shoulders, like giant baskets, and left for the next leg of their mission over land.

CHAPTER 31

DAYS OF SLAUGHTER

"Our own fucking ants? Why are we killing our own fucking ants?" asked Tal as he readjusted the eye patch that made his face itch. After days inside their shelter, the morning sun was crashing into his good eye and everything looked bleached and harsh.

"So we can eat through the winter," said Keel as he sawed open the abdomen of a freshly killed ant. "Got to get as much as we can into acorn barrels and rolled up into vinegary leaves. While it's sunny, the women can curd some of it and dry it into flakes. We'll get rich off of this."

"But kill *all* of them?"

"All we can. Most of them were killed already, others were saddled up by the People's Army to get them quick to the South. Even the queen ants got to die at every mound in . . . Bee-Jor." Keel grimaced, hating to say the name that Anand had given their nation.

"The queen ants too? Why?"

"Gotta slaughter 'em all before the Yellow Mold gets 'em and turns 'em into poison slime. That's something we can't eat . . . or sell."

"But how will we live without ants? How do we feed ourselves? Defend ourselves?"

"Why you asking me? Ask that ass-wipe Anand," said Keel. "First, he brings us the Hulkrites. Next, he incites the Seed Eaters. Now we've got some new fuzzy menace coming from the West, courtesy of the Carpenter people who sicced 'em on us. It's what happens when you let roach people take over as the governors."

"But why do we have the threat of Yellow Mold?"

"Trellana's marched all the sorceress queens out to the Old Slope. Not a royal pisser left except Polexima, and her stink-water only goes so far. Now stop asking all these stupid questions and get to work."

Just as Keel turned back to his butchering, a leaf-cutter ant appeared with a dead, black sweat bee in its mandibles to drop in the midden.

"Well, lookee here," said Keel. "This one's brung us a gift. Would you like to do the honors, Tal? Save the shell of that sweat bee for the roach people—they'll make bangles of it."

"I can't, Dad," said Tal as he looked at his brothers, who had stopped again to slurp from the ant they had just slaughtered, its fresh blood splattered on their bloated necks. "I can't do it with one eye. Couldn't Dumbree or Shimus do it?"

Keel's eyes popped open as his brows crunched. "You little moth-cunt! You've been lying on your fat ass for too long. No son of mine's gonna beg off killing a little leaf-cutter ant!"

"But I can't use my sword . . . or aim a blow-dart. I tried and I keep missing all my targets. I . . ."

"You go tell your mother to get her tit ready since her oldest son ain't weaned yet and won't be getting any ant-flesh tonight. And then tell her to wipe your ass and change your diaper before she finds you a pretty little ribbon to tie up your hair."

Tal frowned and walked towards the ant to nuzzle her with his antennae. The ant probed over the bee corpse she held in her mandibles, then dropped it to touch/sniff him. The sharp hairs of the bee punctured the skin on Tal's arms and drew blood when he fell under it. "Oww!" he screamed as he squirmed out, unsheathed his sword, and attempted to sever the ant's flickering antennae, then missed—he needed a better eye for this. The one that remained had been damaged long ago by his father's own fist.

As his brothers snickered, Tal sheathed his sword, then flailed at the ant's antennae with his hands until he caught one and climbed it like a rope. As the ant jerked, Tal was shaken back and forth. He struggled but pulled himself atop the ant's head just as the antenna was coming loose. The ant went into a spin as Tal grabbed her other antenna, then managed to raise his sword with his free hand. He hacked at the ant's skull until he broke through the chitin. The lymph splattered over his face and into his working eye when the ant stilled and fell. Tal fell with her, his feet in her brains, then tumbled facedown. He stood to whack blindly at the crushed head, his rage building and his arms aching, as goo and chitin splattered everywhere.

His brothers and the others in the midden had gathered to laugh at him, but now his father was lurching towards him. "You're wasting it!" Keel shouted, yanking Tal by his arm. "You gather up every drop of that lymph and get it into a barrel now!"

"Ow! Dad! You're tearing my arm out!"

"I'll yank 'em both out and your legs, too, if you ever tell me again that you can't work because you got one eye. Plenty of us out here are missing something."

"Hey, Dad," Tal said, staring into his father's face as his fear vanished—a hatred as hard as stone took its place. Tal's free arm shot up and his fingers gouged into the folds of his father's neck to claw at its waddles and draw blood. "How about if I rip your fucking throat out?"

Keel screamed as Tal sank his nails in deeper, dragging his father's head down. Tal used his head to bash into Keel's nose until it was crushed and bleeding. Keel grabbed Tal by his ears and proceeded to rip them off.

"What's going on here?" someone shouted. Tal and Keel released each other to see two men riding atop sentry ants. Both were wearing the old armor and helmets of Slopeish sheriffs, but their underclothes had been dyed dark red with hymen berries to show their loyalty to Anand.

"Nothing's going on . . . Good Sheriffs," said Keel. "Just a little roughhousing."

"Right," said Tal. "Just having a bit of fun with my dad."

The sheriffs looked at each other, shrugged their shoulders.

"We need volunteers," said the first sheriff, a dark-skinned man with ears that wiggled back when he finished his sentences. Tal recognized him as someone from the salvaging caste, a man he used to haggle with over the clothes and boots of enemy corpses. *That lucky bastard's found his way up. Now he gets to boss everyone around!*

"Every trade," said the sheriff, his ears shifting back when he paused, "is to send two volunteers to help with the slaughter inside the mound. You'll be permitted to bring home two full loads of larvae at the end of the day."

"I'll go," said Tal, stepping forward and not even looking for permission from his father.

"I'm going too," said Keel. Tal wondered if he could withdraw his offer.

"You're Keel, aren't you?" said the sheriff. "You're the foreman of the midden?"

"I am. So what?"

"So you're to stay here. You have enough to take care of," said the sheriff just as another ant showed up that required slaughtering.

"I'll go," said Dumbree, stepping forward before Shimus could speak. "I'm second oldest, so it's my right. I've always wanted to see the inside of the mound."

"Get on that ant that just arrived," said the sheriff. "The both of you can ride it to the top and report to the Cricket priestess who's up there under the rain shield. Someone will get you a torch helmet, take you down to the brood chambers, and show you the work. It has to be done quickly! When you're done, you'll be joining everyone else at the border."

"Which border?" asked Tal.

"Where you been? Drunk for the last fortnight? The eastern border."

"What?" said Tal. "We're at war again with the Seed Eaters?"

"The East has got to be defended when we are attacked from the West," said the other sheriff, a young man with lighter skin and hair and a royal way of speaking. "We cannot let the Barley people think we are vulnerable on this side when they realize that we do not have any ants."

After the ant dropped its pellet of dung, Tal and Dumbree ran towards her to antennate and climb on her. Without a saddle, they held tight to the spikes of her thorax as they let her take them up the mound.

"I fucking hate Dad," sighed Tal, careful to avoid the spike's point that curved towards his chest as they were rocked on the way up.

"You hate him today," said Dumbree.

"I hate him every fucking day."

"Well, someday he'll be dead, and you'll be fore-man, if you don't rip his throat out . . . and if I don't rip out yours."

"Kind of you to warn me, Dumbree. Move back already. Your fat ass is taking up all the seat."

"Oh, it's my ass that's fat? And yours is sweet and dainty? Your ass is the biggest one in the family, Tal. The reason you're back at work is because your ass got so big it threatened to bring our house down. Why, at one point it ripped right through the floor—I know because I did the repair. If we starve this winter, we can just slice off your left buttock and feast for moons. The right will get us through spring."

"Shut your lips. Your breath stinks. It's like your asshole took over for your mouth."

"Yeah, well, your shit took over for your brain."

The two bickered until they reached the upper

rings when Dumbree was stunned into silence to view the clean, white shelters of the tradespeople and merchants. His amazement expanded when they passed through the spacious black-sand barracks, the latter of which was peopled by veterans of the Hulkrish war, most of whom had skin as dark as his own. Dumbree's mouth was wide open in awe when they passed through the pink sand rectories and he had his first close view of the uncountable carvings of the gods. He snickered when he saw the panels featuring Mantis and Grasshopper engaged in an endless variety of sexual positions, counting at least twenty different ones before he ran out of fingers and toes.

"Look at that one," Dumbree said, pointing to a depiction of Mantis on her knees. Her mandibles were open and her antennae were fallen across her back as her mouth took in Grasshopper's human-shaped protuberance. Tal felt something poking against his back and looked over his shoulder.

"That better not be what I think it is," he said. "Strap it up if you want to keep it."

The ant entered a sparse parade of her sister ants as they passed under the shadow of the rain shield. Tal turned around to see Dumbree was slack-jawed, his head tilted back in astonishment as he took in the crystal palace of Queen Polexima and viewed its luxuries through its clear grains. "Don't drool," Tal said, "or you'll come off like the low-bred shit worker that you are."

"Stick this all the way up your ass," Dumbree said, pointing to his sword. "Until it cuts off your tongue."

Both brothers were looking up when they noticed a man gazing down at them from behind a broad slice of the clearest quartz.

"Dumbree, who's that looking at us through the window?"

"It looks like . . . Yormu!"

"It *is* Yormu! He's staring right at us!"

"Where'd you expect he'd be after he left the midden? He's the father of Commander Fucking Quegdoth."

"I don't know. I didn't imagine he'd be sleeping in what looks like Polexima's own bedroom."

"Probably putting it up her royal muff. I heard they take turns with her, him and Anand."

"Yormu the Mute," Tal said, as if he were slowly vomiting the name. *That toothless, tongueless turd of a man is polluting Queen Polexima's bed. He's likely stolen all of her jewels too.*

Tal's envy turned to hatred as they reached a Cricket priestess with a roll of scratching paper. Men from the riding stables halted their ant, and as soon as they jumped down someone from the lighting caste handed them helmets with a bit of glow-fungus glued to the visor.

I'd like to crush that toothless fucker's head in, thought Tal. *Yormu's no better than me . . . and neither is his son, the Roach Boy.*

Yormu's hand trembled as he dropped his stylus with its obsidian point. He stared out the window at Keel's eldest sons, wondering why they were at the top of the mound. He feared the brothers might enter the palace if the guards slacked off or were busy with the coming battle. Just the sight of Tal's face felt like an arrow in his chest, one that seeped a poison of rage. Yormu stood as they stared at him and then looked to his left and right just in case there was a spiked mace he could use to run down and crush in their faces. "My son is commander of Bee-Jor now, and when he returns, you will be executed . . . before all the mound. I will never live in fear of you, or your father, or any of his flea-spawn again!" Yormu shouted in words that only he understood and then grabbed at the bloody aches at his sides.

Mulga entered the room with two other maid servants carrying loaded baskets. She had only heard his shouting as a screeching babble. "Yormu! What are you gibbering about?" she shouted. "And I better not find out you're bleeding again! Get back in that bed, now!"

She pointed to the bed, her arm as stiff as an arrow.

Yormu stared at her, too weak and in pain to defy her. He would feel better on the mattress, especially if he could fall into a little sleep. He walked to the bed as the servants went to his table to set down their baskets. Mulga picked up his scratch paper piled up in sheets and his diagram of an ant with its Dranverish letters. "What is all this?" she asked.

Stupid woman! Asking me to explain anything.

"It's writing," he tried to say, but what emerged sounded like sobbing.

"I'll throw these out," she said as she started to crumple his scratched papers. He screamed at her, leaping up from the bed, and snatched the sheets with one hand, then pushed her with the other.

"Get away from me!" she said as he collapsed to his knees in pain and protected his sheets. All three women were staring at him, wondering why he was obsessing over a little waxed paper.

"All right, keep your stupid scratchings—whatever keeps you busy," said Mulga. "We've brought you food and water for the next eight days, per order of our queen, Her Majesty Polexima . . . the only reason I'm doing this."

He shrugged his shoulders, threw his hands up. *Why?*

"All of us who are able have to get to the border," she said. "We can ride on an ant if we can find one, have to walk if we can't."

"Why?" he tried to say. *Why are all the ants disappearing?*

"Why? Because your son ordered it. Part of his 'defensive measure' as he calls it. Looks like we'll be sleeping in some shack until this job's completed. Lucky you—you get to stay here and scratch on your paper."

After the three women left, Yormu straightened his sheets on his bed-desk and looked them over for the fiftieth time.

Please, Mite, he prayed, *let my son be able to read these when he gets back . . . and let him return safe and well.*

Tal no longer envied the castes whose work was inside the mounds. Yes, they had the pleasure of leaving their ring each day, but the walk must have been exhausting before ant rides were allowed to everyone. And then they spent most of their time inside a place that was darker than a moonless night. Every step Tal took was a careful one where he had to cast the bit of fungus on his helmet downward in order to see the ground of uneven sand grains that were covered with smears of slime and littered with slippery moltings. Within each of the multiple brood chambers was a fungus torch shedding dim light from atop its pole, but with only one eye, Tal struggled to kill the little nursing ants that clustered around the piles of larvae that craned for food. Dumbree was severing the nurses' heads and then their abdomens with a single blow before tossing their pieces into a bin, but Tal kept missing as he swung. He was out of breath and exhausted.

"And we thought we had the shit work," said Dumbree as he tossed the head of another nurse into a travois and then her thorax and abdomen. "How much fucking longer are we supposed to do this?"

Overhearing Dumbree, the foreman of the egg-gathering trade stomped over, followed by members of what had been their caste. They glared at the mid-denites, who they still saw as beneath them.

"Come on now, men," said the foreman with a forced grin. "You look like right, strong workers who are up to this task. Soon as we kill all the nurse ants, we'll go on to slaughter the larvae. They're easy, but don't chop them up—just a good puncture to the side before they go up to the palace kitchens to be jarred and pickled."

Tal was out of breath when his latest attempt at a decapitation failed him. "I can't do this," he said to the foreman. "I'm fucking blind."

"Blind? Then why did you volunteer?"

"I wanted to see the inside of the mound."

"I thought you said you were blind."

"I am. In one eye."

"Got one good eye myself," said the foreman. He reached into his skull, plucked out an orb from his eye socket, and then tossed it up and down as he spoke.

"And it ain't this one. Keep going, Good Worker—do your best for Bee-Jor."

"Yeah, right, for Bee-Jor," scoffed Tal.

"Remember, do a good job and you can haul some of them larvae home. You'll eat like Good Queen Polexima herself. Here, take a plug of kwondle," said the foreman, reaching into his crusty apron. "To keep you going."

Tal and Dumbree took the plugs of kwondle bark, and when Tal placed his in his mouth, he delighted in its thin coating of aphid syrup and a hint of mint. But the pleasure was fleeting and after a moment the plug was just bitter on his tongue.

Like everything else in life.

As Tal hacked angrily at the nursing ants, he thought of Yormu, lying on his bed with his perfumed sheets and silk blanket. An ant evaded Tal and crawled up and onto a pile of larvae before it slipped and fell and landed on its back. Raising up his sword, Tal hacked down at the ant, then screamed when he realized he had sliced through the ant's joint . . . and into his own shin. He fell on his own back and saw that his sword was lodged in his leg.

"What you done now?" Dumbree shouted at him, running over.

"I cut through the bone!" Tal shouted at him.

"Yeah, you did," said Dumbree, reaching for the sword's handle and jerking it up. Tal screamed again.

"Fuck, it hurts!"

Dumbree raised the blade to the light, then dropped it to look at Tal's shin.

"It's not cut all the way through."

"So fucking what!" Tal screamed. "I can't take it!"

"I know it hurts, but . . ."

"Punch me . . . hard in the face."

"I can't do that, I . . ."

"Knock me out, Dumbree. I can't fucking take this pain!"

"As you wish," said Dumbree as he dropped to his knees and straddled Tal's chest. Tal shut his eyes and took a blow to his face.

"Owwwwww!" he screamed.

"Sorry, I . . ."

"Harder, you fucking idiot! I'm suffering!"

Tal felt a shocking blow to his chin and then felt himself flying into a depthless blackness.

When Tal came to, he was unsure of how long he'd been sleeping—if he had been sleeping. He was looking up at a beautiful vision of the gods, all of them smiling, beautifully clothed, and glittering with jewels atop their draped and bangled ants. They had quivers on their backs and were aiming arrows, but they weren't at war—they were hunting. A cluster of shiny, green blowflies with arrows through their heads had fallen in a neat pile. Surrounding them were red-lipped, happy children with pink cheeks, bright yellow skin, and halos. They had broken into the flies' bodies and were feeding each other the lymph.

Have I died? Tal wondered. *Is this the Promised World?*

He knew he was not in the afterlife when the pains in his shin and his chin intensified with every waking moment. When he clutched his chin, he knew that two of his teeth were loose. He realized that he had not seen a vision of the gods at their pastimes but was looking at a painting on a ceiling—and what a painting it was! Around him was the soft murmur of voices as well as weeping and cries of pain.

Slowly, Tal raised his head and saw he was in a vast room of some kind and its intricately tiled floor was covered with men, women, and a few children who were lying on mats under thin blankets. They had been segregated by skin color and were being cared for by attendants of the same color. *So much for Anand's end to castes,* Tal thought. *But I'm in the palace again! Me, Tal, from the midden caste!*

A woman wearing an abundance of jewelry and a gown of shiny silk was coming towards him. Her hair was clean and combed and bound with a jewel-studded snood. When she got closer, he saw her nose had been broken at least a few times.

"Do I know you?" Tal said.

"You certainly do. Some call me Splooga, son. You call me 'Ma.'"

"Ma! I didn't recognize you! Where are we? And what are you doing here?"

"They needed someone who would look after the

dark-skinned invalids. So I volunteered. And here I am! Me, Splooga, a middenite woman, here in this place!"

Tal looked over her rich dress and a tangle of necklaces and pendants.

"Why are you dressed like that, Ma?"

"How else would I dress? They told me I was going to the ballroom in Polexima's palace."

"But where did you get all that jewelry? These clothes?"

She shrugged. "Hardly anyone's up here now—they've all left for the border."

"So you stole it," he whispered.

"It's the New Way, son—everyone shares. When you feel like you can walk again, you should have a look around, see what *you* can find."

Tal noticed the other women tending the sick were similarly dressed and bejeweled. "Maybe I will, Ma. But you might want to hide some of that jewelry before everyone gets back."

"These are just servants' jewels, no gold in it," she said. "Maybe you can find the good stuff."

It hurt to raise his head, but Tal had to have a look around. "Just who are all these people?"

"Everyone that can't get to the borders. Mothers are at home with their little children and the sick and old and wounded are here. You hungry, Tal?" she said, grinning as she whispered. "I've got half of a sugared bristletail under this dress."

"Couldn't chew if I had to," he said. "But I just might take a look around. What you got for spirits?"

Yormu sighed in bed, looking out the window at the darkness that smothered Cajoria. The few fungus lights he could see were dull and distanced from each other. The darkness in the bedchamber was almost complete since Mulga was not there to exchange the torches in their sconces. Yormu was as sad as the night was black and realized he was still clutching his stylus in his hand. He dropped it atop the night table and then pushed aside the bed-desk that held his latest scratchings.

Darkness.

No one was bringing him dinner, but he could smell the food in the baskets across from him. Slowly he set one foot and then the other on the floor and took tender steps, each one sending a sharp little pain that flashed up his sides. At the basket, he pulled out a thick berry roll with a curd of cricket blood in its center and was thankful that it was soft enough to chew with what remained of his teeth. He was reaching for something else to sample when he heard a distant shuffling in the dead silence—they were human steps, but whoever it was wanted to be quiet, as if it was already bedtime.

Yormu was startled when he heard the faint sound of cloth rubbing against cloth. He turned to the

portal. The diaphragm had been parted and someone had put one leg inside and now they were pulling
in the other, grunting in pain. Someone was in the
chamber!

"Who are you?" Yormu tried to shout, hoping his
words could be guessed. The figure was silent. Yormu
heard the sound of a filled sack being set on the floor
and then he saw the unraveling of a cloth that revealed the dim, green light of a plug of fungus atop a
work helmet.

"Anand?" Yormu tried to say, and felt foolish—his
son would have spoken to him by now. The figure
coming towards him was tall and bulky and dragging
one foot behind him. The pounding of Yormu's heart
filled the chambers as he set his legs over the bed and
tried to rise.

"Well, hello, Defender Yormu. I thought it was
you," said Tal. In the sparse light, Yormu could see
Tal was wearing an eye patch.

"Aren't you going to offer me a seat? How about
some cactus ale and a toasted treehopper or whatever little delicacies they serve up here in the queen's
palace?"

Tal pushed Yormu back on the bed. "Forget all
that," Tal said. "I've just come for the jewels. Queen
Polexima's best. Wasn't this her chamber?"

Yormu shouted, "No," shook his head, and then
shouted, "Guards, guards!" as best he could.

"Whoever you're shouting for can't hear you,"

Tal said. "Ain't nobody in these hallways. Would you mind telling me where things are, Yormu? Maybe we can split the proceeds after we sells 'em to some roachy people—they won't ask any questions, right? Oh, wait, you can't talk anyway."

Tal went around the room, opening the chests. He yanked out their blankets, their sheets, their pillows. He went to the chests of drawers, uncertain as to how to open them until he noticed their handles. He yanked out drawers and dumped them only to find nightgowns, loincloths, winter cloaks, and other simple clothing. Most of the drawers were empty.

"Where does Her Majesty keep her jewels, Yormu? I found a few things elsewhere, but I want the gold, the good stuff. Are they under this floor? Under the bed? Is there a loose tile somewhere that covers the treasure?"

"No! No!" Yormu tried to shout. "The priests have all the jewels! They took them to the rectory!"

"As ever, I can't understand a word you say."

Tal was heaving, grunting in pain as he came towards the bed. He grabbed Yormu by the front of his sleeping gown and shook him back and forth. "Where are they?" he said. "The queen's jewels. The king's jewels. Where do they keep all them crowns with their glittery antennae? Tell me and I won't smash your head against these walls."

Yormu could barely raise his arms to resist Tal. *He's going to kill me whether he finds any jewels or not.*

Yormu mumbled his prayers to Mite. "Save me, Lady Mite! Drain this man's blood until he's a husk!"

"Praying, are you?" said Tal. "To who, Madricanth, you little roach-fucker? Pray harder!"

Tal threw Yormu against the wall, cracking his head. He slumped next to the night table, then used it to pull himself up. His hand brushed over his stylus. Tal was at him again, pushing him up against the wall, his breath stinking from cheap liquor.

"Last time I'm asking, Yormu. When I let go, you're taking me to where the jewels are. Understood?"

"Uh-huh," Yormu said, and nodded. Tal released him. Yormu clenched the stylus in his hand, and before he knew it he jammed it into Tal's face, aiming for his eye. Did he get it? Tal was screaming in agony, fallen to the floor. In the glow of the fallen helmet's light, Yormu could see the bloody stylus that Tal had plucked from his face.

Tal wobbled as he raised himself up and set his helmet back on his head. The soft green light of the fungus grew brighter in Yormu's eyes, then became white and blinding as he felt thumbs gouging into his throat and fingers clamping around his neck. His head was bashed again and again.

"Anand!" Yormu cried out. "Anand!" Then, magically, Yormu heard himself pronounce Anand's name with its consonants as the stub in his mouth grew into a thick, warm tongue and touched the backs of sprouting teeth. Yormu looked up into a bright, blue sky and saw that the clouds had taken on the shapes of Dranverish letters—there, up high, he could read his own name! Ahead of him was a fragrant thickness of gold-colored grass with seed heads that held grains of sun-toasted wheat. Riding out of the grass was a beautiful woman whose dark skin reflected the blue of the sky. She was atop a sleek and gleaming roach, and as she got closer, her mouth fell open.

"Yormu!" shouted Corra before she leapt off her saddle.

"Corra!" he shouted back, saying her name for the first time. "Where's Anand?"

"He's right back there, with Daveena and the grandchildren," she said, pointing to their sand-sled in the shade.

Yormu ran to Corra, and just as he entered into her arms, the world went bright with sunshine . . . and then white . . . then utterly black.

CHAPTER 32

THE BORAX BARRIER

"This is the place," said Anand as he set down the boat he had sailed on. He looked at the hundreds of Bee-Jorites and Kweshkites behind him as they set down their own boats in a wasteland devoid of life. The sun bounced harshly off of the grainy, whitish powder that covered these barrens. Anand squinted as he set to work with his shovel and began filling the boat/basket.

"Fill it halfway," he commanded, "and then cover with the leaf-tarps."

A mild breeze was whipping up some of the powder and shifting it into low and rippling dunes. In the distance, Anand saw what seemed like men approaching from the East, a small party that came to a sudden stop as the wind-whipped powder obscured them. Their clothing was covered with the whitish powder, but from their masses of braided hair, they looked to be Seed Eaters.

Are those bridge builders carrying tools or are those the weapons of Volokop's army? Are there more behind them?

"Inveedra," Anand called to a Britasyte woman wearing the bright orange garb of the Fallogeth clan. "I will need your second tongue."

He turned to the men and women who were shoveling. "Defenders," he shouted. "I'll need all of you who were in my boat to follow me, fifty paces behind. Do not draw your weapons unless we are attacked. Let us walk towards these strangers with hands up."

"Men of the Barley Lands," Inveedra shouted for Anand as they got within hearing distance of the strangers who shifted uneasily on their feet. "We want nothing from you. We extend our wishes for peace and prosperity. We promise we will leave these lands shortly when we have what we need."

The Seed Eaters were quiet, whispering among themselves, before one of them shouted back.

"'Have you come here to burn our bridge?'" Inveedra relayed.

"Interesting idea," said Anand to himself, smiling at the thought of it.

"We have not," Anand answered. "We will never set a fire again and we will not destroy your bridge.

We will never invade your new colony in what was Upper Dneep. We make no claims to the northern Grasslands."

"'Why are you here? Why are you filling your baskets with borax? Will you use it to destroy our harvester ants?'"

"We will not. We have no wish to harm the Barley people or their ants. We will use the borax to defend our borders."

Inveedra turned to Anand, tension in her face as she translated the next question. "The stranger asks if you are Slopeites."

"Let's tell him the truth," Anand said. "Tell him we are not Slopeites, that we are a new nation made up of many united tribes. Tell him we will respect the border of the Barley Lands if our own border is honored."

The Seed Eaters looked at each other again, and then, walking backwards in fear of arrows, they left. When they had gotten some distance, they turned and ran and raised a trail of flying powder behind them.

"Defenders," Anand said, turning to the men and women who had followed him out. "Space yourselves twenty strides and stand guard. Those men may have left to alert an army . . . one that will have arrived on foot, not on ants."

Anand returned to his boat to see it had been half-filled with borax and was covered with the waxed leaves and then weighted down with a pebble. "That's one that's done," Anand said. "Now just a few hundred thousand to go."

The basket was hoisted onto the defenders' shoulders and Anand watched as they carried it north, back to shore. Hopefully, before the end of the day, the basket would be returned to fill again. He looked south, to the long, lifeless expanse of powder, and saw some distant specks that were likely insects that had wandered too far east—dead insects whose insides had been shredded by the imperceptibly small daggers of borax powder.

Anand wondered about this long, deep strip that created a barrier. It did not seem to be a natural thing, but something man-made. He wondered what tribe was defending themselves against what other tribe and how many centuries ago they had ported borax from someplace else.

And were these the same people who had poisoned the land the Dneepers were now rejecting, a poison that was faded and centuries older?

And how long and well would a strip of borax protect his own country?

And can we get it there in time?

CHAPTER 33

THE POWDERING

Jakhuma's arms and legs were aching but it was her back that was the sorest. She had never imagined spending her days in a simple garb of egg-cloth that revealed her legs and arms. And the boots she was wearing may have protected her feet, but they were as thick and ugly as they were sturdy. She was tempted to take them off because they made her feet sweat and someone in her tribe had said they were made out of cured roach eggs! She was lost in that thought when Kula turned to glare at her.

"Pay attention!" shouted Kula, annoying the queen with her bossiness as the weeding rope was passed to them again, that thick and heavy cable. The end of the rope was cinched around the base of the last and largest weed in the northernmost outskirts of Loo-bosh. The weed was a woody, wing-leafed soapberry that was on the verge of becoming a shrub. The men and women of Ledack as well as Bee-Jorites and other tribespeople were taking the rope by its loop handles, then stretching it tight. A Bee-Jorite foreman shouted, "Pull . . . pull . . . pull," through an amplifying-cone. Jakhuma dug in her heels, trudging in unison with the others until that moment the weed uprooted and fell to expose its ugly underside.

It was a moment of joy. All those who had pulled out this last, difficult growth were applauding and cheering. Women were plucking and then rolling away the large, hard berries. They would use the seeds inside to shred for fibers for durable baskets and then the pulp would be pressed for an effective cleanser and carved into scrubbing brushes.

Older boys and girls ran to the hole left in the ground and to the roots of the soapberry to search through the dark, almost blackish earth where a wealth of grubs and even a few earthworms attempted to rebury themselves. With permission from the foreman, the girls went into the dirt or climbed up the roots to push out the grubs to clean and prepare them for the midday meal. The boys attempted to impress these girls by capturing the earthworms, but these were impossible to hold on to; they squirmed away after leaving a shiny slime on their faces and hands. Some of the men who were called *defenders* in the Bee-Jorites' tongue lent the boys their swords and battle-axes to hack at the worms and turn them into manageable pieces.

"Lunch!" shouted the foreman through his cone.

"Thank Meat Ant," said Jakhuma to Kula as they picked up their weeding tools with their broad shovel head on one end and a scythe on the other.

"Kula, my hands are so blistered, and my arms are so tired. Can you carry my tool for me?"

"I can but I won't!" said Kula, her eyes popping open in irritation. "I am just as tired as you."

Jakhuma stopped and gawked at her servant. "Fine, then. But I do not like your tone!"

"Speaking of tones," said Kula. "I think it is time you adjusted yours."

Jakhuma halted, dropping her tool and her jaw. "I do hope you will explain!"

"Jakhuma, I . . ."

"Jakhuma? I am your queen!"

Kula was silent. "Are you . . . Your Majesty? Queen of what?"

"Queen of Ledack!"

"Listen. I do not like saying this . . . but there is nothing majestic left. We are not in Ledack. We are in Bee-Jor, where someone named Polexima is queen. They are going to let us live here and asked us to follow their rules . . . *good* rules. I don't know that we will ever go back to Ledack."

The two women were silent when Jakhuma felt her lip quivering and tears leaking. She dropped her head, and when she did, Kula did something strange. She placed an arm around Jakhuma's shoulders, comforting her in the way of a mother to a daughter.

"The work here is hard," said Kula. "For all of us. They tell us it will get harder before we can rest, before this attack that is coming. We will help each other, yes?"

Jakhuma nodded her head. It was not just Kula who had stopped treating her with deference. Since they had arrived, the deep bows and folded hands of her remaining tribesmen had turned into nods of the head.

As they usually did at the noon break, the two went to the thatched roof structure where the babies of the *New Settlers*, as the Bee-Jorites called them, were cared for by the elderly women of Loobosh. The old, toothless auntie who looked after Chance and Hopeful lifted them up from a rocking cradle carved of an acorn shell and handed them to their adoptive mothers. Both babies were opening their mouths, hungry, and the women lifted up their tops.

"They've both gotten so heavy," said Kula with a grin.

"The babies or our tits?" said Jakhuma. The two women laughed and the ease between them returned. As they nursed, they sat in the shade and watched the making of strange weapons: missiles of some kind, but instead of arrowheads they had blunt heads and pouches on their ends that were to be filled with something. In the other direction, the Bee-Jorites were painting designs on enormous, stretchy banners, the corners of which had rope tethers made of spider silk. Each banner had two slits at its center and they were painted with one of three images. The first image was of a stiff hand, palm out, in the gesture of halting. The second was of a skull seated atop a pile of bones. The last was of an insect, on its back, as if dead, with a dark cloud painted above it.

"Those banners are not invitations," said Jakhuma.

"Not exactly," said Kula, her eyes drawn by something else. "Look ahead, Jakhuma. You have a visitor."

Jakhuma saw the approach of a young man in the red-stained armor of a Bee-Jorite defender. Sebetay was smiling, a little embarrassed to see Queen Jakhuma nursing baby Hopeful. Sebetay bowed his head, took a knee, and presented the women with a fresh, folded grass blade. "Your lunch, Majesty," he said.

"Thank you, Sebetay," she said, failing to contain her smile. The world around her had grown brighter and colorful.

"It is nothing," he said, unfolding the blade to reveal a freshly chopped grub on a salad of shredded leaves from a garlic vine. "I should be thanking *you*—this grub came from your hard work."

"Stand, Sebetay. And do not call me 'Majesty' or 'Highness' anymore . . . I should say *please* do not."

"Then what shall I call you?"

"I am . . . Jakhuma. Please, sit next to me. And please, join us in the food you have brought us."

"I would be *pleased*," he rejoiced, and they laughed as he took a seat.

"How are your days here at Mound Loobosh?" she asked.

"The training is long but no harder than in the Ledacki army. And they are teaching us their tongue. It is easy to learn, but too much like Hulkrish."

"And they treat you well?"

"We are well fed and housed," he said. "No whips." He turned away as he recalled something painful in his past. "But I have come here to see that *your* needs are met. Is there anything I can do for you, my queen?"

"Yes," she said, surprising herself. "After the evening meal, if Kula will look after these babies, I would like it if you would meet me at our shelter. From there, we can walk a bit in the moonlight."

"Of course . . . Jakhuma," he said, and when he reached for her hand, she took it and felt its warmth. With fresh aches from holding the baby, she used her other hand to rub the small of her back.

"Or maybe," she said, "We can just *sit* in the moonlight."

"I'll bring the cushions."

A strange and sudden silence fell on the camp when what looked like an endless, white millipede approached from the South, winding up the middle of the strip the New Settlers had cleared on the fringe of Loobosh. As it got closer, they saw that it was not a millipede, but a long chain of marching Bee-Jorites and each of them had ported a lidded basket strapped to their backs. The woman at the head of the chain stopped and spoke with the banner makers, who nodded and smiled and stopped their work to welcome the marchers.

The camp turned festive as platters of food and barrels and sacks of drink appeared to refresh the porters. Jakhuma guessed that they had completed a long journey and would not go any farther than the loose wall of ant dung and piled sand grains that marked the northern border to some unknown weedlands. When the porters set down their baskets, Jakhuma looked at one, the lid of which had popped off. She saw the basket was full of nothing but a rough white powder.

As soon as the porters refreshed themselves, the foreman called everyone back to work for an altogether new task. Jakhuma heard a noisy commotion behind her and saw that ten, then thirty, then one hundred or more baskets of the white powder were lining up behind her. Farther back, she saw that the thickest, greenest twigs from the scrub they had removed were being buried as posts in the ground and the painted banners were being stretched between them.

"What is this powder about?" Kula asked.

Mulga had never been this far from the palace and never wanted to be again. After a few days of being at the extremes of the eastern border, it was just a little less strange and a lot more frightening. She had never been in any weeds and had only ever seen them from a distance. All she knew of them were scary tales told on idle afternoons and on rainy nights—tales of lusty demons, lonely spirits, and monstrous, bloodthirsty insects. The weeds were stranger than expected because they were filled with tens of thousands of people, nearly all of which were from the lowest castes—people she had only ever seen from a distance who had worshipped the royals in obedient silence at the assemblies. Here in the weeds, the darklings, who all called themselves Bee-Jorites, talked all the time, talked over each other, and talked even when no one was listening. When they spoke directly to her, she could understand them, but between themselves, it was just gibberish and all of it seemed to be shouted.

I am so, so tired, Mulga thought. The work of clearing weeds on Cajoria's fringe was much harder than keeping a bedchamber. Now that a long, wide swath had been cleared of weeds, Mulga and the other palace servants had been set to the clearing of sand to turn the strip into a long and shallow basin. Mulga's hands were raw and blistered as she loosened, then raised up, sand grains to be tossed into a bin hauled by one of those awful Britasyte roaches. Some of the sand grains were packed so tightly they seemed almost glued together by some invisible mud.

She looked at the women from her own caste, her sisters and cousins, as they kept their heads down and labored in silence. They were as uncomfortable as she was at mixing with all these coarse people who hadn't the common sense to dress for laboring. Mulga and her kin had arrived in their old, worn, and stained clothing—the garments they wore on the days they scrubbed the palace walls and tiles. But the laborers were wearing whatever used finery they had some-how gotten ahold of. Both women and men were wearing necklaces, ear pendants, and bracelets while they uprooted, sawed at weeds, slaughtered insects, or sorted through or hauled off trash. Some of them were even wearing old priestly garments as they painted and stretched these frightening warning ban-ners on their poles.

Part of why Mulga was tired was because she had barely slept in the last few days. The thought of having to sleep again in the hastily built, stilted shel-ter made out of weeds was distressing. She hated the crude bed she slept in with three other women: a sack stuffed with crumbled leaves and covered by a smelly blanket of rags stitched together. Each night, she awoke when the dew crept in and moistened the shelter, the blanket, and the frock she was wearing to leave her shivering in the cool night air. And when she stepped out at sunrise, there they were, just above her, numbers of long-legged grass spiders who had woven their sheet-like funnel webs across the roofs of the dwellings. The spiders stared down at her with their eight eyes before they were coaxed out of their webs only to return to make new ones on the following morning. The old webs were gathered for their silk, a task undertaken by both the rope-making and weaver castes who fought over the webs and shouted and screamed at each other before Sun was even up.

Sleep would be so sweet, Mulga thought as she wrestled out another sand grain, but she was too tired to lift it and toss it in the nearby bin. "How does anyone live like this?" she said aloud to her kinswomen, breaking the silence.

"I don't know," said her younger sister, Flandeek, as she struggled to raise a grain over the bin lid. Her plump face with its jowly cheeks was looking thinner and the sunshine had brought out every freckle on her skin. "But apparently hundreds of thousands always have."

"I will never complain about palace work again," said Mulga as she slumped and sat on the grain she could not lift. She looked south and to the strange structure that was nearing completion, a kind of crystal bridge with domes that stretched over the strip—a building, they had been told, where they might converse with the Seed Eaters in peace instead of passing them messages through the roach people. Mulga was entranced by it, and thought it looked like some great jeweled bracelet.

"Slowing down again, are you?" said a woman not far from them with a prominent underbite whose lower lip covered her top lip. She and her kin were dark-skinned and lowborn, from the trap-maker caste—or *trade* as they were calling it now. "Underbite," as Mulga thought of her, was wearing some old and worn ant-riding breeches with a purple hunting jacket, as if she were a royal spending a leisurely day hunting mantid flies. Her forearms were stacked with the cheapest and noisiest of Britasyte bangles.

"We are just having a rest," said Mulga. "If you have no objections."

"Oh, if we have no objections?" said Underbite, mocking Mulga's accent as she turned to her kin. "Gentle women! Do we have any objections to these fine ladies taking yet another rest?"

"Fine ladies?" said another trap-maker wife, a ridiculous-looking woman who was wearing a silk morning gown inside out. "Just because these *ladies* have some yellow spots on their faces don't make 'em any better than we are."

"We do not have yellow spots on our faces!"

shouted Mulga. "We have yellow faces with brown spots!"

This brought a howl of laughter from the lower caste. They immediately starting cooing and making curtsies. "If you would, your highness, how about sharing some of your holy piss with me?" said Underbite. "I hear that if I drink it, I might be able to get some yellow spots too."

"You are welcome to drink as much of my *piss* as you like," hissed Mulga.

The dark-skinned women laughed. "Good one!" said Underbite. "Maybe we'll take you up on that later."

Strangely, Mulga started laughing, and so did her kin. Underbite grabbed some chunks of kwondle from out of her pocket and extended them to Mulga.

"Here, this might help," she said.

Mulga was stunned, looking into the woman's eyes and feeling as if she had seen her for the first time.

"Th-thank you," said Mulga. "I don't know what to say."

"You already said it," said Underbite with that strange smile that revealed just her lower teeth.

All were returning to their labors when they were alerted to the unexpected sight of an endless line of porters trudging just to the west of them. The porters had a spattering of white dust on their clothes and faces. They looked as exhausted as Mulga felt, but they kept on walking with their baskets attached to their backs.

It was later in the afternoon when the endless parade of porters finally came to a halt. Taskmasters with identifying banners atop their helmets hauled little supply-sleds into the cleared basin and organized the next step of this mysterious process. The porters were guided into making new, shorter lines of twenty people facing east. The freckled taskmaster, once an upper-caste servant, stood before Mulga and her kin with her arms clasped behind her. She turned her head left and right to address all those in the thirty lines under her supervision through a handheld amplifying-cone.

"Bee-Jorites! Commander Vof Quegdoth sends his greetings and gratitude for this magnificent effort in protecting our nation. This is the task before you now: the treatment of this sand strip that you have so valiantly cleared of weeds. Your next task is to cover the strip with powder brought from the Dustlands."

Mulga looked north and south and gasped in awe when she realized she was in one of hundreds of thousands of lines that stretched along the border with the Seed Eaters. She looked behind her and saw thousands of baskets full of borax powder, something that had been floated over the Great Brackish Lake, then carried on the backs of humans to this very end of the Slope.

Or rather . . . Bee-Jor.

So that is where my husband has been! In the Dust-lands, digging up borax that's just arrived here! The very idea of bringing all this powder here is . . . astonishing!

As usual, I have underestimated Anand.

"First baskets!" shouted the taskmaster, pointing at Mulga and the others who were at the head of their lines. Frandeek tapped Mulga's shoulder and thrust a basket into her arms. Mulga looked under the lid and saw the whitish powder up close—it had no magic glow, no wisp of sorcery. She strapped the basket to her back, then hiked across the broad length of the clearing towards the piles of ant dung and up to the stacked sand grains that marked the border before the neutral strip with the Seed Eaters. She halted when she reached the banners with their warning signs that were stretched between posts all along the border. Following the example of the others to her left and right, she dumped her basket. Her sister dumped hers, just behind her, until they had twenty neat piles in a row. Mulga shook her head and felt even more tired when she realized this process would go well into the night and perhaps the next day.

Before returning for her next basket, Mulga peered between the banners at the Seed Eater Nation. She saw that both the Barley wretches and their harvester ants had gathered at the frontier, the latter stimulated by the kin-scent of leaf-cutter ants—although there were few remaining ants at Cajoria, the Bee-Jorites' clothing still held their odor. The strange activity in Bee-Jor had roused the curiosity of the Seed Eaters and their orange-helmeted patrolmen were pacing on their ants, cautious of an attack, struggling to keep control of their mounts.

"Next basket!" shouted the taskmaster, and Mulga and the others started the long walk back when they heard screaming. The orderly lines scattered into a panicking crowd, sending up clouds of borax dust. Climbing over the banners and crawling towards them were unmounted harvester ants with their massive, grain-grinding heads. Their abdomens were up in a defensive stance as they readied to shake and spray their poison while their mandibles scissored, slicing the air.

"Do not panic!" shouted the taskmaster as she ran to her supply-sled and reached into a lidded box. "Everyone step back!"

"Why is no one attacking those ants?" Frandeek asked Mulga as they were jostled in the crowd. They watched as the taskmasters pulled up their breathing masks and lowered their goggles and then approached the harvesters with blankets they had pulled from their sled-boxes. Red blankets were thrown over the stingers of the harvesters' abdomens to block their sprays while yellow blankets with scent lures were used to draw them back towards the neutral strip.

"They want to return the harvesters alive!" Frandeek said.

"Alive for the moment," said Mulga. "I imagine that by tomorrow those ants will be dead—and the Seed Eaters will know why we have spread this powder."

Anand was sick of white powder but not sick from it. His hands, his legs, his clothes, and his hair were all covered with it and so were those of the men who continued to shovel it. It was less heavy than soil, but they were having to travel farther and farther south to find the softer deposits instead of scraping through the harder, grayish mix of sand with its remnants of dust, dead insects, and dried soil.

People from the working castes were unlikely to complain about work—that was part of their indoctrination—but Anand could see in their faces that they were just as anxious as he was for rest. They kept looking to the sky, praying in hopes for the return of locusts with a message that enough borax had reached Bee-Jor and that, finally, they could put down their shovels and sail for home.

"I pray for their return too," Anand said, looking from the sun to the shovelers as a squeeze bag of watery lymph was passed around to quench their thirsts and stave off hunger. Just as they resumed their digging, Anand heard the faintest buzzing and turned to the western sky. The buzzing faded and he sighed. He turned to dig more powder when he heard the buzzing again.

"Thank Madricanth," he whispered when not one but two locusts came into view. The locusts could not land or even come close to the ground without risk of being poisoned, but all were watching when they went into a spiral above them, flying from left to right.

"Oh, no," Anand said. "Widdershins."

"What's it mean, Commander?" asked the man next to him who was covered with so much powder that he looked like a Hulkrite.

"Defenders, I must get back to Kweshkin so I can hear the message from these locust flyers. I'm sorry, but we're not done digging yet."

Anand dropped his shovel, weaving through the thousands of diggers as he ran back to the boats at the shoreline.

Just what was I thinking! he scolded himself. *Trying to get enough of this powder to both the eastern and western borders before an invasion. This project should have taken at least a moon . . . or three . . . or six.*

As the locusts circled above him, the Kwekshite boatmen rowed Anand across an inlet of the Great Brackish Lake to the shore of one of their marsh hamlets. He jumped in the shallows and the cool water revived him. After stripping, he used his knife to cut some rough and stringy bark from a punk weed, then scrubbed himself three times, swimming to cleaner, clearer water each time to rinse himself. Once he felt free of borax, he tied a shard of marsh leaf around his middle, then ran to the plaza of the hamlet where the locusts could land. He waved his arms.

The first locust made a somewhat awkward landing that threw its pilot forward and tossed him in his tethers. The second made a landing that was speedy yet smooth and looked like the end of a dance. Anand looked at the pilot in his turquoise armor and braced himself for ridicule when the pilot removed his face cloth.

"Oh, dear. You are completely, inappropriately dressed," said the pilot in the most irritating upper-caste accent. "And I am terribly afraid that I shan't be able to fly you back to Bee-Jor until you can make yourself decent."

"I thought this was urgent," said Anand.

"It quite is," said Terraclon. "I am afraid, Commander Quegdoth, that this League of Velvet Ant Peoples is terribly close to our recently annexed mounds. It appears that they will be at our western border within days. I am afraid, Good Commander, that you have completely mistimed your defensive measure. I do not know that we will have time to seal the western border with this rather tedious powder of yours."

"Your sarcasm is a poor mask for your fears and concerns, Pious Terraclon. Speak plainly. Where is the league likely to attack?"

"Our scouts told us they're going north," Terraclon said in his true voice. "To attack Loobosh, then Mound Imclotta before continuing to Cajoria. It makes sense: they would take our capitol and, from there, every other mound in Bee-Jor would fall."

Anand smiled. "Yes, that would appear to make sense."

"What could you possibly be grinning about?"

"Are Loobosh and the northern mounds ready?"

"Of course they are."

"And Polexima is coordinating with the Dneepers?"

"They have already assumed Palzhad and are making progress otherwise."

"Then you know what to do at Loobosh. I'll need your locust, Ter. I've got to leave *now*."

Terraclon dismounted as Anand mounted the locust.

"Anand, you can't fly naked," said Terraclon as he joined the pilot of the second locust. "You really must put some clothes on."

"I don't have any. And they won't mind where I'm going."

"Anand!" Terraclon was looking away.

"Yes, brother?

Terraclon sighed. "Nothing. I forgot what I was going to say."

"I love you too, Ter. Be careful."

"You're going to be a father—*you* be careful."

Daveena.

The thought of her and his unborn children sent Anand into a spiral of worries he could ill afford as his locust climbed up air. The second of his worries was wondering if he had enough daylight to get where he was going. Another thousand worries followed after that, buzzing behind him on noisy wings like a scourge of hungry mosquitoes.

CHAPTER 34

THE TAKING OF LOOBOSH

"I thought we were living here, at Mound Loobosh," said Kula.

"We all thought so," said Jakhuma.

They had very little to pack up in the shack—some crude toys for the babies, changing rags, and a couple of rough blankets. Jakhuma lifted up the dusty, hole-ridden wrap that was the only thing she had from Ledack. She remembered the first time she saw it, the swirls of its vivid colors, and the impudent clothing merchant who stood outside her window with it and said, "I am sorry, Your Highness, but not even a princess could afford this garment."

The wrap was what she was wearing for the spring festival of the First Larvae, when she had just been installed as the Crown Princess Jakhuma. But it was also the wrap she was wearing when she was captured by the Termite worshippers, a garment that had been doused with the scent of their hideous ghost ants. It was the same wrap that had been stripped from her before she was pushed onto an auctioneers' stone at a slave market. Later, she had to hide the wrap from the nameless Hulkrite who had bought her with a basket full of arrowheads, a man who had his own ideas about what she should wear. Jakhuma sighed, felt tearful, and then dropped the wrap to the floor.

"Take it with you," said Kula.

"Why should I?"

"It's from a proud time. A reminder of the Beautiful Days."

"It's just a filthy, old . . ."

"If you don't, then I will," said Kula, folding it into her basket. "Besides, we may run out of changing rags."

They giggled before they strapped the baskets to their backs and the babies to their chests and then took careful steps down the shanty's ladder. Jakhuma was taking the last few rungs when she saw two men approaching in waxed, whole-body suits and breathing masks. On their backs were something like water sacks marked with a red skull to warn of toxicity. On the sides of their legs, they had thigh-buckets with lid-brushes.

"Don't be frightened, Jakhuma, but don't come any closer," said the man, and she recognized Sebetay's voice. She could see from the wrinkling around his eyes that he was happy to see her. He held a short hose with one hand and at its end was a diffuser-nozzle that would spray the liquid from the squeeze sack on his back.

"You have not come to see us off?"

"No, I am here to do my duty, but lucky for me I get to see you once more. Do you have everything you need from this shelter?"

"We do."

"Jakhuma, *your* duty is to leave now," he said. "For everyone's safety in your family."

"In *our* family," Jakhuma said, and realized from the tone of her voice that she had just suggested to Sebetay that he propose marriage to her. His eyes smiled again.

Kula jerked at Jakhuma's arm. "I told you we were late!" she reprimanded. "They are calling us!"

Jakhuma trotted off, then stopped, wanting one more look at Sebetay in case it was the last time she ever saw him, even if he was hidden inside some strange suit. He looked something like a freshly hatched termite grub and waddled as he walked, an image she would hold closely to her heart. She watched as he climbed the ladder, then took the lid-brush and slapped a black slash over the shanty's entry: a warning that had been painted on each treated shelter.

"That looks like dangerous work," Jakhuma said to Kula.

"Let's go!" Kula demanded, dragging her away as she mirrored her worry. "We can pray for him as we walk."

Taskmasters from the Bee-Jorite army waved little red flags that pointed them east. Jakhuma and Kula caught up with the other Ledackis and then all of them filtered into the great mass of people from Loobosh trekking east. Some trekkers were like them: newly arrived refugees who had been in Hulkren, but most were Looboshites of what had been the Great and Holy Slope. Some of the Looboshites were old and chubby eunuchs with strange little jars around their necks, and others were younger eunuchs who helped the elders along and carried their burdens. Behind them were an endless number of human-drawn sleds that were piled high with ancient boxes wrapped in waxed cloth.

Among the eunuchs were dark-complexioned and poor Looboshite women with many children; they were laborers with meager belongings that they carried on their heads and shoulders. A smaller number were fair-complexioned women, with just as many children. Most of these women had their noses turned up, trying to look haughty, but they were weeping and sneaking glances over their shoulders at the home they were abandoning. None of these yellow-complected had dressed for a long march, but rather were wearing heavy dresses and multiple skirts with jackets and wraps of bee and wasp fuzz. Most were without antennae on their heads, and they let their freckle-faced servants walk ahead, ready to negotiate passage with ants that no longer existed. The light-skinned ladies had male servants as well: men who trudged behind them to lug sleds loaded with ornate nut chests, picture rugs, and even furniture carved out of amber!

A command came from the taskmasters and everyone came to a slow halt. All of them were murmuring about what was next when Jakhuma noticed thick cables from underground spools were raising up what looked like six sand-covered lids of some enormous chests. The taskmasters were waving everyone forward again. Slowly, the Ledackis took short, quiet steps towards the darkness of the central lid.

"I am not at all scared," said Kula.

"Not for a moment," said Jakhuma just as Chance began to cry and triggered the same in Hopeful. The Ledackis looked left and right in caution as they stepped into the darkness, then down an incline to what they realized was a tunnel, one with walls that were reinforced by scaffolding and netting. A taskmaster handed Kula a little torch of glow-fungus from a vat—one torch for every sixth person entering.

"I would feel better if I knew where we were going," said Kula as their entry converged into one great tunnel.

"I think we'll be all right," said Jakhuma, looking at the torch. "They have given us a little light to see."

"**A**re we sure about this?" Terraclon asked inside the shelter at the top of Loobosh's central watchtower. He looked around its walls, which had been thickly padded, then covered with tightly glued strips of roach chitin. Velvet ant chitin, weirdly, was the recommended material in the weapons manual, but it was unavailable at the time of the shelter's construction.

But if things go well, we'll have plenty of that, he thought. He looked out the shelter's back window and at the taut cable of greased and shining spider silk, the lower end of which was tied to the base of a scrub oak in the distance.

"I am *most* sure about this," said Nuvao, staring west. "Just look at them, Pious. That's tens of thousands of warriors out there . . . on the backs of these impenetrable land wasps with the most venomous stingers on the Sand—and this is just what we can see of them from here."

As focused as Terraclon was, he was distracted for a moment by the bright colors and the satiny sheen of the velvet ants, what Anand called "land wasps," that had amassed on Loobosh's outskirts.

"I must confess that I . . . I am not so sure." Terraclon's voice quavered before it broke. "This is not the approach the Dranverites would have taken—from what Anand has told me of them."

"We are not the Dranverites, most unfortunately. We are not an unimaginably huge and sophisticated nation with endless resources and an army of millions. We are but a crippled little country who has lost our ants and is doing what we can in order to survive."

Terraclon nodded his head in silence, overwhelmed with deep feelings he could not identify. He looked at Nuvao, and even in this moment, on the verge of a deadly attack, Terraclon was taken with the beauty of the priest-king's face, in the resolve and calm he saw in his perfect profile. Against his will and for reasons unknown, Terraclon was sniffling and dabbed at a tear.

"No one is watching, Pious," Nuvao said. "Cry if you need to until the urge passes. Of course, the moment the Greeyas start crawling here, we will need you to pull yourself together."

"Most certainly," said Terraclon. "Whatever that was, well, it has passed now, swept away by a southern breeze. We will not speak of it again."

"Can I tell you something? And please, do not take offense."

"What?"

Don't take offense? What have I said? What have I done?

"It is very flattering to be imitated," said Nuvao. "But you really must stop speaking like me."

"Oh! I'm sorry, I . . ."

Nuvao chuckled. "Be at ease, friend. I was just trying to make you laugh. But you do know you can be yourself around me . . . as I wish to be myself around you."

He just called me "friend"!

"I hadn't realized," said Terraclon through a nervous laugh. "It's just I . . . I do like the way you speak."

Nuvao looked away from the gathering enemy and directly at Terraclon.

"Since we *are* waiting, I would like to tell you something, Ter, if you will allow me to be completely honest. It is something that might relieve your apprehensions about this moment that is approaching."

Now he's calling me "Ter"!

"Of course."

Just don't look me directly in the face when you do . . . it's too much . . . and we have a battle to fight.

"Before I ever had my say, it was decided that I should be a priest," said Nuvao. "I was . . . *sensitive*, to use the euphemism. I took no pride or joy in inflicting pain, but others took pleasure in hurting me. My brothers were my constant tormentors. They not only tortured me with their cruel words, but they beat me in secret and threatened to kill me if I ever told anyone. One of the reasons I wanted to be a priest was so that I could shave my head. My brothers would hold me down and pull out every last hair of my scalp and would beat me if I screamed. I begged my mother to bend the rules and send me to Venaris before I was of age to begin my training: my transition to the holy life."

"I am . . . I'm sorry, Nuvao. It's not at all what I imagined as life in the palace."

"I am sorry too, Ter."

"For what?"

"I have some idea of what you have suffered. It is far more than I ever did . . . or ever will."

"How could you possibly know?"

"We are not so different, you and I. But you suffered being 'sensitive' in the brutality of the midden. You did not have the choice of leaving to become a priest . . . of becoming anything other than a dung worker among a people who have been kept in misery for centuries."

Terraclon felt a growing stone in his throat that was hard and dry. He was wordless as buried feelings burst through his body in explosions that dislodged the stone just as it was choking him. He fell into tears as his body shook. A strange rush of relief and grieving coursed through him, and for the first time ever in his life, there was an end of something, some constant pain he had lived with all his life. For this single, golden moment, his *loneliness* was gone—all of it! Nuvao looked at him as if he understood and tenderly clasped Terraclon at the back of his arm. Terraclon yanked his arm away, thinking this was all some humiliating prank.

"Don't touch me!" Terraclon said. "I . . . I can't . . . I'm not . . ." He doubled over and struggled to breathe as he felt cramping in his gut and his head pulse with fear.

"I understand, Terraclon, I do. You are safe with me."

Nuvao slowly, gently, placed his hand on the small of Terraclon's back where there was an opening in his armor and just the thin cloth of his under-suit. This slight touch made Terraclon tremble.

"And I know others like us," continued Nuvao as Terraclon's sobbing subsided and he was filled with something else unknown—a pure and pristine joy. "And all of us talk now, among ourselves," Nuvao continued. "About Dranveria, about this place where they would accept us without question . . . where they know that what we are is as natural as sunlight and air."

Terraclon nodded. He couldn't bring himself to look at Nuvao, who had taken his hand away and clasped it with his other behind his back as he raised his chin and rocked on his feet. They stared in silence at the masses of velvet ants and at the war beetles crawling up to the front of the Greeyas' line. Anand had told them this would be to disperse food and ammunition to the warriors as well as to bring nectar for their insects. It meant they were readying their attack.

"But I have not told you my real secret," said Nuvao, turning to look at Terraclon again. He, who had faced Hulkrites and ghost ants, had to gather his courage to look Nuvao in the face.

"You . . . you haven't?"

"I have not. And it is something I have never told anyone. You promise me you will keep this secret?"

"I swear it to all the gods."

"Such as they are," said Nuvao, with a little grin that quickly disappeared. "I have had certain . . . fantasies," he said quietly. He paused a moment, dropped his head, and closed his eyes.

"As I grew older and my brothers grew crueler, I had fantasies about killing them—stabbing them in their sleep or bashing their skulls in with a mace when they were passed out from drink. When I learned my brothers were dead in the war with the Hulkrites, I was not just relieved, I . . . I was happy."

Nuvao looked at Terraclon, gauging his reaction.

"My brothers used to brag of their kills, of the

foreign women they had ravaged on their return home. These are stories with details so ugly I will never repeat them to you or to anyone else. One night my eldest brother, Jepeblo, came into my bed-chamber, drunk as a fruit fly, after a skirmish with the Carpenters. He woke me by throwing an open sack on my mattress. 'Nuvao, I promised you a gift from the Pine Lands,' he said. The sack spilled . . . and out rolled five severed heads."

Nuvao was heaving now as he relived the memory. "Then my brother said, 'Father asked me for six. I need a sixth head so I am thinking of taking yours. He won't miss you, little daisy-bottom.' And then he took his sword and swung it at me, grazing my neck and opening that largest of arteries that gushes with blood. When I fainted, I was sure I had died."

Nuvao pulled down his collar where it met his helmet to show Terraclon a scar. Terraclon struggled to find the right words to say. He watched as tears spilled over the thrust of Nuvao's cheekbone and then down to the square of his chin.

"Those men down there on the backs of those 'velvet ants,' those wingless wasps," said Nuvao as he stiffened himself and found his determination. "Those men are *all* like my brothers. They're like most men when eyes are averted. They have come here to kill and rape and plunder because it pleases them . . . not for some noble cause or to defend their families. Do you understand me now . . . Pious Terraclon . . . why I tell you all of this?"

"I think I do," said Terraclon, gulping hard as the stone lodged in his throat again.

"So you know that this is no time for us to be . . ."

"Sensitive," said Terraclon.

CHAPTER 35

A WALL OF OLD CLOTHES

"The Setcha asks if that is the banner of Mound Loobosh," said Ulatha to Trellana after hearing it from Queestra. They were seated on a saddle meant for three behind the Setcha and the driver of his blue velvet ant as they passed under a directional post. From his facial features, Trellana had decided that the driver must be the Setcha's oldest son, someone he smiled at once in a while and patted on the back.

"Why doesn't he just ask the two of you?" Trellana said, squirming in pain on the seat where her waist and arms were bound to a stiff board. "The Britasytes have dragged their tawdry little carnival to every mound on the Slope including this one—

they know their names and placements better than I do."

"He does not trust us because we are roach people."

"Tell him 'yes,' that is the banner of Loobosh and that he is attacking the right mound," said Trellana. "Loobosh! Loobosh!" she repeated, loud and drawn out, as if the Setcha were both hard of hearing and stupid. He scowled at her, spitting and screaming in the Carpenters' tongue with words the roach-women chose not to translate.

Loobosh's crystal palaces were not yet in sight, but as Trellana remembered them, they were taller and thinner with a jar-like shape and had ornamental lids. Trellana had only been to Loobosh once in her life, as a twelve-year-old, to meet a young king, Puptap the 11th, who was as round and ugly as a tick and who had a strange split at the end of his tongue. Puptap's first wife had killed herself and his second one had attempted to kill *him*. Rather hurtfully, Puptap had rejected Trellana before she could refuse him, taking to his sickbed and canceling a reception dinner after a brief meeting on her arrival. She looked up at the post and at Loobosh's short, broad banner with its split tail and it reminded her of Puptap's cloven tongue. The banner had a painting of a jar in its middle, the insignia of the Learned Eunuchs: creatures she detested almost as much as the Greeyas.

The sun was at its peak when they got a faint

glimmer of the mound in the distance. After a passage through some unkempt mullein weeds that were as hairy as the velvet ants, the elegant, jar-shaped palaces came into view. Trellana dreaded the days ahead, sure that it would all be a tormenting repeat of the conquest and transformation of Ospetsek, with all of it conducted before her eyes. As she sank further into despair, the masses of velvets slowed to a stop.

Seated up high on the Setcha's ant, Trellana saw something strange yet familiar in the distance when the blue ants crawled up a low boulder for a clearer view. Coming into sight on the fringes of Loobosh's hunting weeds was a kind of long, yellow barrier. As bright and as strange as the barrier appeared, it did not look formidable and it seemed to ripple in the breeze. And then Trellana remembered what it reminded her of, something once described to her: a Dranverish banner, sighted before the Fission Trek, with a painting of a stiff hand. That banner was a warning not to enter, to turn back; it was something that Dolgeeno had dismissed as a cowardly gesture from whatever primitives were squatting on Trellana's new queendom. Squinting, Trellana tried to see what was painted on this chain of banners ahead of her but they were too distant.

The smaller multicolored velvets that surrounded the Setcha and his captains were parting to allow a party of riders to approach from the East. The arriving Greeyas were men riding on insects whose longer velvet had been painted with splotches of dark and light green to blend into the weeds—these men were scouts. As they shouted up to the Setcha, Trellana was struck with how familiar they were with their ruler, with their lack of protocol. They spoke before being spoken to and looked directly in the Setcha's eyes.

The Setcha shouted at Trellana, staring into her face with his dark and loathing eyes until the translation reached her. "He has questions for you, expects truthful answers, and is taking you to the border for your observations," said Queestra. "We are to wait here and will translate on your return."

The Setcha shouted to his captains, informed them of his plans, and they tapped their foreheads in acknowledgment. Trellana was lifted off the stiff back of her chair and thrown to the scout below her, who caught her in his arms. She screamed as she was hoisted over his shoulder and felt a painful tension through her pregnant belly. The scout climbed back onto the saddle of his camouflaged ant and ordered his driver to ride east, holding Trellana with one arm and the horn of his saddle with the other. The Setcha rode alongside them on his own camouflaged ant, driving it himself. As he passed his men, they showed their respect with a simple nod of the head.

It was three or four thousand breaths before they

weaved through masses of velvet ants when they finally reached a typical Slopeish border: a combination of dung pellets dropped by leaf-cutter ants and a coinciding barrier of sand grains assembled by humans. Trellana was carried up to the top of the loose barrier and positioned to look just over it. The sight startled her as she had never seen anything like it: a wide, pristine clearing that was covered in some whitish powder that stretched all along the border. The Setcha was shouting at her as he pointed to the banners—clearly, they were all images of death and a warning to stay away. And they were not just a few banners, but there were thousands of them, stretched on poles from north to south for as far as she could see.

Trellana was stunned by the strange emptiness between the border wall and the banners in the distance. Every weed in this immaculate strip had been cleared, but what was this covering of rough powder? Was it just another warning, a territorial marker? Was it some Dranverish poison, or was it just a ruse? One of the scouts had been ordered down to the strip where he slid to it, then swept some of the powder into a sack with his gloved hands. As he scrambled back up, the Setcha stared up at the central watchtower and at what looked like a shelter atop its platform. The structure had a pitched roof and a loop at its peak. The Setcha had to be wondering, as Trellana was, who was inside it? Was it Anand? And how did its occupants pass messages, if they were—and to who?

The Setcha was squinting and noticed that there was another watchtower farther north and another in the south, near the Weedlands. And then, like some message from the gods, new banners unrolled from all three towers, banners as tall as the mound itself. The banner before them had an enormous painting of Goddess Bee with Her six claws holding cones of honey. Her stinger had been exaggerated to a sword-like point and at its end was a black drop of venom. The Setcha backed away from the image before he began shouting at his scouts. He ordered the one who manhandled Trellana to bring her back to the camp. Within moments, they had turned around and were returning to the blue velvet ants. She was interrogated as soon as she was reseated with the roach-women.

"The banners are obviously warnings!" she shouted for the third time after the Setcha rejected her answers. "But again, I have no idea what they are warning of. Perhaps there is an army of a hundred thousand behind them. Perhaps the banners are nothing more than the cloth they are made of."

"The Setcha said you lied to him—you said Loo-bosh was a Slopeish mound."

"It was. It has been stolen by Bee-Jor in the last moon."

The Setcha ordered the scout below him to open his sack and reveal the powder.

"What is this white powder?"

"Hmm. Well, I am not quite sure. But I would say that it is *white powder*," Trellana answered.

"'Yes, it is white powder, you mosquito-turd! Is it poisonous?'"

"You will not know until you eat some," she said. "Please give it a go."

The Setcha ordered his scout to do exactly that. He hesitated before he dipped in a finger and licked up some of the smaller crystals, which dissolved in his mouth. He shrugged after doing so—whatever it was, it was not offensive tasting, and it did not immediately sicken him.

"The Setcha asks why no ants have attacked us yet," said Ulatha. Both interpreters were looking at Trellana with tight mouths and cocked heads, knowing full well why there were no ants.

"Because we have denied them our powers," said Trellana. "The Sorceress Queen of Loobosh, Her Majesty Hathleem the 18th, has denied the ants her magic essence. The Bee-Jorites have likely slaughtered all the leaf-cutters to make food of them before the Yellow Mold could turn them into a noxious goop."

The Setcha grinned at her, spoke more softly.

"The Setcha agrees with you about the banners," said Queestra. "He says they are just a silly woman's work, a wall made of old clothes. He thinks all the Bee-Jorites have to defend themselves with after wars with the Hulkrites and the Barley people is some paint and fabric."

The Setcha stood on his saddle and raised up his sword with the seven banners. He shouted to the circle of his six captains who were doing the same. The thousands of men surrounding them raised their own weapons.

Slowly, the Greeyas and their land wasps crawled east and into war, their insects chirping as they crowded each other.

Terraclon and Nuvao were looking downward as the mass of velvet ants was shifting again like the windswept waves of a lake when, finally, they surged forward.

"Now," Nuvao said. "They're attacking." He went to the back of the shelter to wave the red flag, a signal that only the Bee-Jorites in the rear of the tower could see.

"Not yet," said Terraclon. "We *must* wait."

"But they are coming!"

"Wait!" Terraclon ordered. "They must cross the border first. It must be unquestionable that they violated our boundaries. *That* is the Dranverish way."

Nuvao nodded. No sooner had he done so when they saw the first wave of fuzzy land wasps climbing up, then down, the tumbling sands of the border wall. They crawled onto the cleared strip where they stirred up its powder.

Sebetay's heart was pounding as he peered through a hole of the sand-covered barricade that hid him and the other *defenders*, as the Bee-Jorites called themselves, just behind the banners. He was sweating inside the bodysuit, eager to take it off and wondering if he should just pee down one of its legs when, at last, they received a signal from the watchtower, a single wave of its bloodred flag. He lowered his goggles over his eyes and pulled up the breathing mask from around his neck and tightened its strap. He already felt a little dizzy from sucking in air through its layers of silk filters and he could smell yesterday's spicy lunch inside it. Behind him stood his partner-defender, holding a shell of a small, sealed ant's skull filled with "the yellow powder." The Greeyas were advancing, a third of the way over the strip, when his squad's sergeant shouted, "Load!" Sebetay took a pair of handles at the banner's center and pulled them back as his partner loaded the slot with a shell that was already cracked and seeping.

"Release!" shouted the sergeant.

Sebetay looked between the banners and watched as the shells soared up, then fell on the velvet ants, hit their riders, or burst on the ground to spread their poison. The Greeyas were coughing and slumping, slipping from their saddles as they breathed in toxins that killed both them and their insects. The velvet ants were slowing, shaking and wobbly as they collided into each other before they altogether stilled.

"Load!" shouted the sergeant, and a moment later Sebetay's division had poisoned the next wave of soldiers and their mounts. His goggles were fogged, but he looked out and saw that more Greeyas were pressing forward, crawling over and through the corpses of their own army.

Why don't they just retreat? These men are brave . . . or stupid.

Or just doing what they are told.

A fresh pallet of shells was delivered to Sebetay's squad and they kept up their barrage even as their arms ached and they felt trapped behind their breathing masks. Above him, he heard a downpour of the Greeyas' arrows as they arced over the banners, then landed in the thick shield-roofs of straw that protected the defenders. The arrows that flew into the banners were deflected by their spider silk linings and they clattered as they fell into silly little piles.

This is not the Ledacki way of war! Not fair or noble! Sebetay thought as he watched the pileup of enemy casualties. *Then again, it's unfair to bring so many warriors. Not a fair battle on either side.*

He knew the same was happening all along the border of Loobosh, wherever the Greeyas attempted to break through. He looked out to see hundreds of invaders who struggled for breath, who couldn't call for help as they died along with their insects across the powdered strip. The most determined of the Greeyas were struggling forward on foot, their faces covered with cloths, as their trembling arms attempted to shoot arrows.

"Release!" shouted his sergeant. After he did, Sebetay massaged the ache in his arm as he watched these brave—or foolish—warriors succumb to the next bombardment of yellow powder.

The moment came when the last pallet emptied and there were no more shells and the battle went very quiet. Sebetay looked between the banners and saw the masses of dead and hoped the Greeyas had given up. He was alarmed when thousands of new warriors and their insects pushed forward again, almost vertically crawling down the corpses. A messenger boy with an ear painted on his smock arrived and spoke in Slopeish with the sergeant. From what Sebetay understood of it, the Bee-Jorites had yet to see the fabled blue ants of this Setcha Greeya and his captains—that meant the Greeyas still had a force of hundreds of thousands, that only a sliver of them had been slaughtered.

"Second position!" shouted the sergeant after receiving a two-wave signal from the tower. Sebetay and his squad backed away from the banners as the Greeyas got closer to them. Most of their insects were crippled, weakened by the launched poisons and their residues, but their riders were jumping from them and advancing on foot. They hacked at the thick ropes of spider silk that held the banners, but their blades could not cut through its unyielding fibers. Instead, the Greeyas hacked at the poles that held the banners up and then marched over their cloth when they fell.

As the Greeyas advanced under the shield-roofs that were thick with their arrows, Sebetay and his squad picked up distant ropes and yanked out their poles. As the ceilings collapsed on the Greeyas, membranes broke that released more of the deadly yellow powder. Sebetay watched as these men stumbled or crawled out from under the collapse, wiping at their burning eyes, choking on their own blood, and falling on their backs or faces to twitch and vomit. Before they died, their faces and hands erupted with giant blisters that burst and glistened with moisture.

"Third position!" shouted the sergeant as Sebetay and his squad ran to the stacked cubicles of a twig wall running north and south. The facade of the wall was covered with paper to conceal the cubicles' insides. Sebetay climbed up to the back of his fourth-story cubicle and removed the first of six man-sized arrows from the wall, each with a filled pouch around its head. He pulled back the bowstring of his accumbent missile launcher as he heard the war whoops of the Greeyas and the clicking of their insects.

"Fire!" shouted the sergeant from the side of the wall. Sebetay released his first missile, which tore through the paper concealment of his cubicle. He watched as the missile's blunt head of feldspar exploded into fragments when it hit a velvet ant, knocked it off its legs, and then sprayed its human riders with poisons. The cloths around the Greeyas' faces were useless as filters and they fell into a chaos of suffocation and retching as they sucked the powder into their lungs. Sebetay loaded his next missile when an enemy arrow pierced his chest plate and another ripped through his thigh panel. His screams were trapped in his breathing filter as he aimed his last missile at the next wave of Greeyas crawling over and through the jumble of their casualties. The missile's explosion blew back the first warriors along the front line but not the men behind them.

"Fourth position!" shouted the sergeant.

Sebetay and his squad jumped from their cubicles to join the tens of thousands of other defenders, all of them running east. He was slowed by the puncture in his thigh, worried that the enemies' arrow had been dipped in a poison of velvet ant venom. He ran past the dyed red pegs that thrust out of the ground and then onto a taut canvas with a camouflage of glued sand grains. Exhausted and panicked, he was tempted to pull off the breathing mask that made him so dizzy, but that would be deadly. He reached the next set of red pegs and took his position behind one as his mask filled with the poisons of his shallowing breath. *Breathe deep, blow out hard,* he reminded himself.

"Hack!" shouted the sergeant after all the defenders had crossed the canvas. Chopping with his sword, Sebetay destroyed one of the thousands of pegs that held the canvas in place. The canvas fell down to a long, curving trench that the Greeyas and their insects could easily cross.

"Fifth position!" shouted the sergeant. Sebetay looked down in the trench and saw something he had not seen when they had practiced this maneuver: a thick layer of the yellow poison at the bottom of the trench. As the Bee-Jorite defenders retreated east, Sebetay looked over his shoulder to see the Greeyas halting at the trench's edge. Most of them had arrived on foot, but some were mounted on wasps, which had yet to succumb to the poison. All the Greeyas were staring down at the trench's yellow powder.

"Keep running!" shouted the sergeants at their Bee-Jorite squads as the defenders combined into a mass of men and women racing east. The pain in Sebetay's thigh was slowing him and he stumbled, blacking out as his breathing got frantic again. Another defender helped him up, and then a second one, and they were running together, holding him up under his arms. Finally, all of them reached their destination: a clearing beyond some brambles. He was unsure of where he was and what had happened when he saw the bizarre sight of massive squares of sand rising up on one end to reveal the entries to the tunnel running east.

"Slow your pace! Deepen your breaths!" urged his sergeant, coming towards Sebetay as their squad regathered. "You're all right, Defender Sebetay, you done all right," the sergeant said in Slopeish, then in Hulkrish. The squad was walking down a decline into the vaguely illuminated tunnel—a place with a darkness and quiet that was somehow comforting. Along the sides of the tunnel were piles of bodysuits, all of them shed by the defenders who had arrived before them. After marching for a few thousand breaths, the sergeant called, "Halt," and Sebetay and his squad removed their suits, stripped off their underclothes, and then used fine bristled brushes to remove every last grain of powder from their skins.

"Keep marching now, defenders," said the sergeant. "Got a lot more behind you coming through. And when you get to the surface, you'll find a bath and someone to bathe you. It's a bath that everyone must take . . . before we rest up for the night, then head south to the next battle."

The next battle? How soon? And how many more after that?

Torvock-son-of-Koshvock, the Setcha Greeya of the United Land Wasp Tribes, was infuriated as he smelled it, that most detested of odors: the yellow powder. The odor was offensive and sickening, but more importantly, it was deadly. He knew what the message from the arriving scout was before he could speak it.

"Setcha," shouted the scout, drawing the attention of the six captains atop their blue-furred wasps. "The army of Bee-Jor has attacked us with the yellow powder. They have hurled it at us in shells from their banners. They have shot us with it on the ends of arrow-missiles. They have dug a trench pit around the mound and covered its bottom with it."

"Face cloths! Halt the advance!" the Setcha shouted to his captains, who shouted it in turn in every direction until the order spread through the united tribes. The Setcha tied a layered square of pine bark cloth around his face and nose, but he knew it would be of little help if he breathed in the powder. It was one of the few things that frightened him—he fought *not* to remember the son, the nephews, the uncles, and the brother who had been killed by it. He looked over his shoulder at the two roach-women and resisted the urge to stab them in the throat. Both looked ill and were wheezing. The Slopeish queen looked even more ill—her yellowish complexion had turned to a waxy white and her chin was covered with clots of coughed-up mucus.

"So the killing powder makes even roach-women sick," he said to Queestra in the Pine people tongue.

"Why wouldn't it?" she asked, her voice weakened by the pain in her throat.

"Because roach people make it! Out of roaches!"

"We do no such thing."

"You lie! Roach sorcerers scrape the dust from fallen stars and mix it with roach blood and the magic piss of Slopeish queens!"

Queestra said nothing as her eyes darted.

"You *do* know what I'm talking about," shouted the Setcha. "Roach riders trade the killing powder to the Pine people. And now they have traded it to the Slopeites, who used it to kill my men!"

"You invaded *their* country," said Queestra, trying to shout.

He hated that the roach tramp no longer had any deference in her voice, that she was tempting death and expected no mercy from him. "And it is *Bee-Jor* now, not the Slope," she continued. "What did you expect when you attacked this mound? A parade of dancing girls with flower garlands and kegs of barley ale?"

The Setcha pondered killing her right at this moment, of finally doing it . . . but first he would kill her cousin to torment her. He reached for his dagger when he felt a hand on his wrist.

"No, Father," said Shlovock, his eldest son. "The roach-women may have their uses yet. And at some point, we can ransom them—if the roach people have something we need."

The Setcha paused, then returned the dagger to his sheathe. He stroked his son's back, smiled at him. "You are wise beyond your years, Shlovock.

"Loobosh is our mound now," said the Setcha, turning to Queestra and speaking in a quieter voice in the Pine tongue. "It is made out of the holy sands of Greeya-Tepic. No one else will pollute it again— not Slopeites, not Bee-Jorites, not Britasytes. When Mound Loobosh is secured, it will be time again to use your tongues to tell the dark-skinned females that they have been freed to marry Greeya warriors. You will tell the dark-skinned men that they are no longer slaves but have the honor to fight in our army as Greeya descendants."

"Listen to me or do not, *Setcha*," said Queestra, mustering all her contempt. "Loobosh is part of Bee-Jor now. And Bee-Jorites have already been freed from slavery."

The urge to kill the woman was burning again. Torvock stared at her, heaving in rage. "If the lost sons of the Greeyas are still living among the Jaundiced Usurpers, they have not been freed. They are unclean!" he shouted. "We will have this mound. It is the will of Gree Dari-Ekh!"

"Not if the Bee-Jorites poison all of you first," said Queestra in open contempt.

Shlovock retied his cloth around his chin sprouting whiskers. "Father, what if these honey eaters have more poison?" he asked in their own tongue. "What if they have enough to kill us all?"

"No one has that much poison, Shlovock. If they did, the Pine tribe would have destroyed us long ago. The powder at the bottom of this trench may be just a trick—it may be nothing but crushed chalk and yellow dye."

"Setcha! Listen to my words!" shouted Veltfock. The captain of the Red Wasp tribe was shouting at him again from atop his blue mount, his red-dyed beard flapping left and right as he spoke. "We were not prepared for the killing powder! We should have been! Our scouts cannot count the tens of thousands of men we have lost! Half of those lost were riders of red wasps!"

The Setcha fixed his gaze on Veltfock, enraged by his rebuke. Veltfock had broken an agreement in stating a grievance for his red-bearded tribe instead of as a grievance for all. The other captains looked at the two, staring sideways, in the tense silence.

"Veltfock, did you know these Bee-Jorites would have the killing powder?" asked the Setcha, his voice rising. "Did you know that these bee worshippers would be here at Loobosh instead of Mushroom Eaters? What else did you know, Veltfock, that you did not tell me . . . or anyone else?"

The Setcha stood on his saddle, slipping the ends of his boots into its side loops to face his captains. "Who knew this mound would have the killing powder? Which of you captains warned me that this mound would be annexed by Bee-Jor? Can any of you make these claims? If you can, then take your sword and thrust it through my heart to become the rightful Setcha Greeya. Do you make that claim, Captain Veltfock?"

Veltfock dropped his head as all eyes turned to him. "No, Setcha."

The Setcha looked up at the late-noon sun, which was high and bright. "These cowards will run out of poison if they have not already. Then they will hide instead of fight like real men. We will push forward, draw them out, and deplete their poison. We will fill this trench with enough sand to make a bridge over it. Mound Loobosh will be ours by tomorrow and its dwellings will be filled with Greeya families at day's end."

His captains tapped their foreheads in agreement. Torvock was comforted when Shlovock turned around and grinned at him in admiration, his eyes crinkling as he smiled through the cloth around his face.

"Forward!" the Setcha shouted, and Veltfock and the other captains shouted it in return. "And rip out whoever is inside that watchtower, and feed him to the beetles."

A roar of cheers went up and, slowly, the great mass of Greeyas and land wasps resumed their advance on Loobosh.

"Well, well, Pious Terraclon. It is a very fine start," said Nuvao as they surveyed a sprawling mass of Greeya corpses and insects from above.

"Not fine enough," said Terraclon as he pointed to what looked like a flood of Greeyas mounted on land wasps in the distance. "That was just a rain shower. The storm is still approaching."

"I know. And I'm worried for her," Nuvao said.

"Polexima?"

"No, not Mother. Trellana. She may still be out there as the Greeyas' prisoner."

Terraclon grimaced, looked away.

"Of course you should hate her," Nuvao said. "But she is my sister."

"I have a secret too . . . Nuvao," said Terraclon. "Since we appear to have a moment."

"Please. As I was just about to become the slightest bit bored." Both of them chuckled and Terraclon smiled, then regretted revealing the teeth that he thought were too large.

"When everyone in my family is dead, including my aunts and older sisters," said Terraclon, falling into his midden accent and a deeper, louder voice that came from the back of his throat. "I'll be happy too. I'll be relieved when I never have to see them, smell them, or hear their sickening voices again. Few were the days that my father didn't hit me while he called me names—names I won't repeat for you or anyone else. And few were the days that I didn't want to kick his teeth out of his face and then his brain out of his skull. And my mother, well, she never tried to stop him, so I hate her just as much."

Nuvao sighed, nodded his head. They watched in silence as the new mass of warriors on land wasps reached the border wall and then parted to let their war beetles through. At first there were ten, then twenty, then fifty, then more of the beetles. They kicked up the borax powder with their claws as they pushed aside the corpses to clear a route to the watch-tower. When the path was cleared, Greeya warriors on velvet ants crossed over the strip. One velvet had already reached the base of the tower and was climb-ing up its girders.

"Very sensible of them to try and attack us up here," said Terraclon. He looked down at the faces of the Greeya warriors hanging tight to their saddles as their insects climbed up the girders of the tower. "I'm afraid we're within their reach and one of them is loading an arrow in his bow. Shall we abandon our post, Your Majesty?"

"Indeed," said Nuvao.

"I'll need your help," said Terraclon as the two went to the back of the hut and reached for a loop-latch in the ceiling. "On three," Terraclon said. "One, two, *three!*"

They yanked hard at the loop-latch, then pulled harder to loosen the shelter up from its platform. Once the shelter was loose, the two leaned on its back wall and it tilted and fell off the platform. At the shelter's top, a loop carved from the hard wood of an oakwood knot contacted with the taut cable of greased spider silk. The shelter slid down the cable and soon it was racing—racing at an alarming speed. Terraclon looked over at Nuvao as they sat with their backs against the wall.

"It's going awfully fast," Nuvao said. "You did test this?"

"Yes, but . . . just by myself."

"Shit!"

They were sliding faster and faster when they heard a high-pitched whistling sound. The shelter began to vibrate, threatening to blow apart, when it reached ground and skidded over a leaf-strewn runway leading to a shallow pit. The shelter plunged into a cushion of dried oak leaves that flew up as fragments that floated back down, blanketing the shelter in a quiet darkness. Terraclon wobbled as he stood, grasping the window ledge to steady himself.

Thank Cricket I can stand.

"Are you all right, Nuvao?"

"I believe so."

"I'm sorry. Really! Anand said something about . . . *velocity* . . . some Dranverish word—speed being affected by the weight of the descending object. I should have listened!"

Nuvao was quiet.

"Let me clear these leaves, get us out of here!" said

Terraclon. "I can squirm through the window and push my way out."

"Not just yet," said Nuvao, who sounded . . . blissful. "It's so peaceful here. I'm sure someone up there is already working at extracting us. Help me stand, would you?"

Terraclon felt Nuvao's royal hands reaching up to him.

He's reaching up to me, an untouchable!

Terraclon took Nuvao's hands, felt the warmth of his palms, and then pulled Nuvao to his feet. Nuvao did not take away his hands once he was standing but held Terraclon's. They stood, facing each other, their armor creaking as their breathing got louder in the darkness. Terraclon felt his heart pumping at the ends of his fingers and heard it like thunder in his ears. He sensed Nuvao was coming closer to him, and he could smell his sweet breath, when both of them were thrown to the floor.

"Oof!" Nuvao said. The two tangled in each other as the shelter was pulled onto its side and out of the leaves.

"We've been rescued," said Terraclon, in search of something to say.

"Yes, we have," said Nuvao, standing. "And it is a good thing as I suppose we really should get back to the . . . to the defensive measure."

"Yes, we certainly should," said Terraclon, "if we do not want to be entirely destroyed."

"Terraclon . . ."

"Yes?"

"You're doing it again."

"What?"

"Imitating me. Up we go."

Terraclon gasped when Nuvao reached for his hands to pull him to his feet and then into something that was just short of an embrace. Men in pilots' armor were clearing the leaves from around the shelter and peering inside it to make sure that the two were still alive.

"Good Defenders! Thank you," said Nuvao out the window.

Nuvao climbed out of the shelter's window and then helped pull Terraclon out. They turned to look to the western sky.

"Ter, we've just enough daylight," Nuvao said.

"Just enough if we hurry," said Terraclon. They ran with the pilots to two docked locusts. The four had just climbed onto their saddles, ready for takeoff, when an arrow whizzed past Terraclon's face with its fletching tickling his nose.

"Up and spiral!" he shouted to the pilot, and the locust jumped, then spread its wings. He looked down at Nuvao as his locust spluttered, pivoted, then stilled. Ter could see the pilot below was shifting his grip when he got the locust into a jump, a leap, and then finally into flight as more arrows flew.

"Thank Cricket," Terraclon said, relieved to see Nuvao waving at him as they flew east.

"Circle around once," Terraclon commanded his pilot, "but go no lower." As Terraclon looked down, he could just see the shooters of the arrows: Greeya scouts on land wasps that had been painted with splotches of green. He could just make out their young faces as they closed one eye to aim.

Very young faces. They're almost children.

"East, pilot," Terraclon ordered, and the locust caught up with that of Nuvao. Terraclon felt elated—he and Nuvao had escaped, and so, it appeared, had everyone else at Loobosh.

On the flight east, Terraclon felt as if he and Nuvao had some magic knife that allowed them to cut themselves open and fuse together their inner worlds.

I will savor this feeling for as long as I can. But nothing this beautiful can last for long.

That thought turned Terraclon towards remorse, to pity for whoever these Greeyas were, even as they had just tried to kill him. In glimpsing their faces, they were no longer monsters in tales told on rainy nights. They weren't hairy giants with six arms or red-furred monsters with a single eye.

They look like people from the midden—like children from the midden.

Whoever they are, I hope tonight is the best night of their lives.

Terraclon shook his head and scolded himself.

Boy, you are too damn sensitive.

Nothing could have been more humiliating than to be bathed in public, but Trellana was glad for the suds and the clean scent that came from the fibrous plug of fresh soapberry that scraped over her skin. Somehow, the Setcha had the decency to let the camp women be the ones to bathe Trellana, but this did not prevent her from becoming an open spectacle for the men in the last of the day's light. The dark-as-night women scrubbed her as hard as a tiled floor but they treated her tender parts with a modicum of respect. The scrubbers avoided eye contact with her and seemed altogether repulsed to be bathing a light-skinned foreigner, which she found to be a rather strange reversal. While they scrubbed, the Greeya men pointed at Trellana and made jokes about her in their tongue that sounded like failed whistles and clicks.

When Trellana was rinsed with a soaked cloth of multiple loops, she saw that her skin was restored to its palest yellow. They had even combed and washed her hair and scraped some mites from her scalp. And then they wrapped her bottom in a stiff, fresh diaper, the greatest humiliation of all.

That means I am going back on that saddle, she realized as they tied her arms in back of her again and then threw something like a rough cape over her head: a sheet of common pine cloth with a hole in its middle.

The roach-women had also been bathed and were being returned to the back of the saddle on the Setcha's blue velvet when a man and woman arrived in a bizarre-looking sand-sled. The sled was painted blue, like the sky, and had a sun-hood that was topped with a thick pile of fluff that resembled a cloud. It was drawn by a pair of velvet ants, one white and one black, each with a young child to drive them. The man was dressed in bright white trousers and a cape of green fringes. The woman was dressed in a black tunic with panels down the front that resembled the underside of a cricket. On her head was something remarkable—the first pair of antennae that Trellana had seen on a Greeya person as they did not need to negotiate passage with their ants. The long, thin antennae rose up from the woman's head and then fell down her back, like those of a cricket.

Like a cricket! Trellana thought, and it disturbed her. The Greeya warriors and their camp women were folding their hands towards these two, and when they shook rattles at the ends of their staffs, the people nodded as if to thank them for a blessing.

"Who do you think they are?" Trellana asked the roach-women.

"Someone that intercedes with their god. Or

their gods, perhaps," said Ulatha, pausing. "It looks like they have at least two gods—one male and one female. I don't know. Britasytes never traded with Greeyas."

"Why not?"

"They don't trade. They take."

The Setcha, his son, and the two holy people conversed for a moment before they shook their rattles again and sang a harsh, screechy song while raising their free hands to the sky in a pleading motion.

Trellana was surprised when the Setcha took his driver and held him by his shoulders to speak softly to him. They kissed each other on the cheek and then patted each other's backs as they exchanged smiles. The son jumped from their saddle and then lowered his head before the holies, who shook their rattles over him. They set an amulet around his neck—a small, tied bag—before he joined them on their sled and rode off. A different boy of twelve or so years, perhaps another of the Setcha's sons, climbed up the ladder and assumed the job as driver.

"Where do you think they are taking the Setcha's son?" Trellana asked.

"We've seen those two before, at Ospetsek. They're going up to the top of Loobosh, likely to vanquish its ghosts and bless it before it's occupied. I don't know. But it looks like the Setcha's son is going with them to pick out his palace."

"So Loobosh has been lost," Trellana said. The

thought made her sicker at heart than she expected, and she wasn't sure why. And then she realized that Loobosh was far to the North, on the way to Mound Imclotta and then to . . . Cajoria.

"Not Cajoria!" she said aloud, and then fell into a dark pit of longing and grief as she imagined the ravaging of her home mound, the extermination of the last of its nobles, and its occupation by a people more loathsome than Anand and his untouchables.

This night will be very long . . .

CHAPTER 36

THE DAY AFTER

Torvock and his captains were beside their insects washing their faces and hands in the morning dew. None of them had slept well. The night had been loud with coughing . . . and so was the morning. The camp women were coughing as they set out the first meal of the day: pickled pine seeds and sticky-aphids, sent directly from Emperor Sinsora's pantries. Also arrived from the Pine Lands was an imperial war beetle hauling a fresh vat of thickened aphid nectar for their land wasps. The camp's women and children turned from the feeding of the Setcha and his captains to the nourishing of their majestic blue insects.

A party of scouts approached from the East.

Their thirsty and hungry insects were uncontrollable once they had sniffed the nectar being squeezed from the nearby vat and they crowded into the clicking blue wasps to feed. "Forgive us, Setcha," shouted Esnock, the senior scout whose face drooped like his long mustache. "We did not have time to feed/water our mounts at the border. We needed to bring you our report."

"Speak," said the Setcha, licking his sticky fingers after consuming half an aphid. Esnock took a moment to turn away and cough.

"Throughout the night, our Greeya warriors filled the poison-covered trench with enough sand to make a safe and sturdy bridge, one that reaches the mound's main artery. Shlovok-son-of-Torvok reached the western palace at the top of the mound near midnight. He found it sound and said he would inspect it and the other three palaces in the light of day. The warriors who won Loobosh have staked out homes in all but its lowest dwellings. The fighting over the better and larger houses at the mound's top has ended with only a few deaths—but quite a number of woundings."

Esnock went silent.

"What? Speak, Esnock."

He coughed again before resuming.

"All the Looboshites who lived at this mound have fled. All of them. All dwellings, from crystal palaces at the top to pitched shanties in the lowest rings, were empty of both light- and dark-skinned people.

We found no trace of living ants or any other insects. No one hides inside this mound . . . or we have yet to find them."

The Setcha was startled.

"What about their goods, their clothes? The tools of their trade and their means of making things?"

"They left little behind. They took all that can be carried."

"Has anyone sighted them?"

"No, and our scouts have wandered far to the East, near to this next mound, Imclotta, which is populated. We have not seen any signs of a migration, nor can we detect any trunk trails left by ants. If the people of Loobosh rode leaf-cutters to some other mound, they did it well before we arrived. We have found thousands of corpses of leaf-cutter ants—but only their shells, their legs, and their feelers. Every last ant corpse has been scraped for its meat and blood."

The Setcha Greeya fumed in silence.

I have been insulted by these fools at Loobosh! It is one thing for the yellow-skinned to run, but another for the sons and daughters of Greeyas to run from their own people!

Veltfock was glaring at him sideways, his mouth twisted to the left of his face.

"Speak, Veltfock!"

"Setcha, I have nothing to say," he said, looking down and coughing.

"You are angry with me! Your face does not lie!"

"No, Setcha, I am angered by the . . . by what has happened. We promised women and fine shelters to our warriors. They have the shelters. If the women here have fled to the next mound, we will drag them back. This problem is small."

"Yes," said the other captains, nodding in agreement around the leaf platter, hoping to soften the Setcha's anger.

"Setcha, this victory at Loobosh is strange and hollow," said Captain Zalavock of the Yellow Wasp tribe as he wiped a bit of egg from his beard dyed as bright as a mustard flower. "But it *is* a victory. These Bee-Jorites are cowards . . . or they are just too small and weak to fight us."

"That must be true," said Ovoglock, the captain of the Orange Wasp tribe who, as usual, spoke with his mouth full. His thick eyebrows, dyed a bright orange, flapped like the wings of a milkweed butterfly when he chewed or spoke. "We had reports of women in their ranks—always a sign of weakness. Wasp-waisted women," he said, and smiled. "With milk makers that got in the way of aiming their missiles."

The Setcha forced a grin as his captains chuckled.

"They may be luring us in," said the Setcha as his grin turned to a grimace. "They could be raising their forces. They could spring like trapdoor spiders when our backs are turned. We must never be brash, no matter our numbers. These are clever people even if they are cowards who fight with potions instead of swords and arrows. Captains, after we eat, our warriors will go to the poisoned trench around this mound to fill it with our dead and bury them. We will offer their blood to Mother Blood-fly and their flesh to Father Dead-Eater. Then we will fill the trench with wheat seeds to grow and offer to the Gree Dari-Ekh when She wakes this spring, holy be Her name."

"Holy be Her name," repeated the captains.

"Setcha," said the coughing scout with an unmanly shake in his voice. Torvock had forgotten he was still there.

"Speak, Esnock."

"The scouts . . . we scouts think . . ."

"Speak! Or you will lose your tongue and your teeth and will never speak again!"

Esnock attempted to control his worst coughing fit yet.

"Setcha, the scouts think you should see what has happened to our wasps at the front—before we move on to Mound Imclotta."

Trellana's mouth and face were crusty with the breakfast that the Setcha's wife or whoever she was had almost smashed into her face—something both sticky and crumbly that vaguely resembled food. Afterwards, the woman cheated Trellana out of her usual ration of water by plucking the bag from her mouth before she could quench the most awful thirst. She felt weaker than usual as she had spent most of the night rocking atop the shifting insect while coughing from some windblown poison that the Looboshites had used against the Greeyas. The roach-women looked to be as sick as she was, and after eating her breakfast, Ulatha threw it up, where it would likely remain, drying on her chest for the day.

Below her, she had heard the Setcha and his captains as they spoke in loud voices on this morning, after an annexation, it appeared, that had gone wrong. Last night they had not celebrated with pine liquors, wrestling matches, and the disembowelment of yellow-skinned Slopeites stretched between poles that were butchered and eaten. This morning they were arguing. Something had happened, something related to this poison that had them all coughing their lungs out. Now the army's leaders were leaving the center of the camp to take a look.

"What went wrong here?" she asked Ulatha. "Have they taken this mound or not?"

"We don't know," said Ulatha. "And we are not going to ask the Setcha for an update."

The boy of twelve appeared again and crawled up the ladder to sit with the Setcha on his saddle. The boy was wearing some fuzzy armor now and had risen in status. With gloved hands, he reached for the ropes that pulled back the velvet's antennae until he could grip them with his palms. The Setcha climbed up and took his seat and gently corrected his son's grip when the ant lurched forward. As the ant smoothed its crawl, the Setcha yelled at Queestra and then glared at Trellana as the words were translated.

"The Setcha says we are going to the top of Mound Loobosh," said Ulatha. "And you will explain to him what the Bee-Jorites have done."

"I am not a Bee-Jorite!" Trellana protested. "And I can never explain what they do."

The Setcha's velvet ant seemed sluggish and so did those of his captains riding in back of him. The dense crowd of mounted velvets they passed through were also slow and bumbling. As they reached the border wall, Trellana noticed that some of the velvets were quivering in place. As they got closer, she saw that many of the ants were dead. Many of the Greeyas were off their mounts, coughing as they coaxed the sickened war beetles to push the dead velvets into piles that allowed for freer passage.

The Setcha and his captains stopped before one of these piles of ant corpses and stared at it in silence. Finally, he spoke to some of the men below who hung their heads and whose faces looked darker and longer than usual. As they were questioned, the warriors shook their heads and shrugged their shoulders. Some of the youngest ones seemed on the verge of tears.

The Setcha turned and glared at Trellana, as if this were all her fault. He shouted something at her that sounded like an accusation.

"The Setcha wants to know why his wasps are dying," wheezed Ulatha.

"His wasps? I don't know anything about his wasps. I didn't know he even had wasps."

"'You are riding on a wasp, you stupid flea-shit!'" shouted the Setcha.

"Am I? I thought they were ants—velvet ants."

"'They are wasps—wingless, female land wasps, you ignorant bagworm.'"

The Setcha spit in her face and then slapped her.

When the dead "wasps" had been cleared—she would never make the mistake of calling them "ants" again—the Setcha and his men drove their blue mounts up the barrier wall for a look across the powdered clearing. Trellana saw the strip was spotted with thousands of dead insects, nearly all of them land wasps with their different-colored furs. Some of the insect corpses were carrion beetles, drawn to the wasps in the attempt to eat them, but the beetles had died as well. Their dark corpses circled the wasps like the petals of some strange black flowers.

The Setcha was heaving, shuddering, as he surveyed the bizarre landscape, his rage evident in his trembling hands that turned to fists. He shouted at his captains, who shouted back at him. One of the captains, with a bleached white beard, was urging the other captains to follow him as he drove his own blue wasp into the powder. The other captains screeched at him, arguing with a violence, until the white beard and his wasp stepped back over the border, the white powder clinging to his wasp's claws and the fur of its underside. When their arguing ended, they all fell into coughing, covering their mouths as if it were weak and shameful.

As the captains coughed, Trellana noticed a scouting party coming down the main artery of the mound and crawling over the powdered strip. The green spatters of the wasps they were riding came into view when one of them slowed, then stilled, and the rider abandoned her. The rider was helped onto the saddle of another wasp just as the third wasp stopped to shake, then die. Finally, four scouts on two dying wasps just reached the border wall. The wasps were too weakened to climb so the scouts jumped off them to scramble up. The scouts also looked ill, struggling to climb up the short wall, and tumbling down its other side. They were barely able to stand before the Setcha to give their report and wobbled as they did.

The scouts were hesitant, fearful, and avoiding eye contact, but as one of them spoke, his voice got higher and louder until he burst into a tearful wailing that drew every ear. The other scouts with him had collapsed, unable to rise, and laid on the ground coughing as water bags were brought to them, though they were too weak to drink.

The Setcha screamed his orders, fury in his voice as he pointed, shook his fists, and then shouted at Mound Loobosh as if his voice could make it implode.

The sickened scouts were hoisted over shoulders to take away to die. The Setcha continued his rant when his voice broke. He fell into a coughing fit that turned into a sobbing he failed to hide with the fuzzy muff of his sleeve. The son, his driver, was crying and hugging him, burying his face in the fur of his father's armor to hide the shame of his tears.

"Someone up there has died," whispered Trellana.

"Not *someone*. *Every*one up there, you stupid she-slug," whispered Ulatha. "Including the Setcha's oldest son."

The Setcha turned and glared at the women, his eyes bloodshot with tears. He reached for Ulatha's neck and gouged his fingers into it, shaking her head back and forth as she gasped for breath, then lost it.

CHAPTER 37

A GOOD REPORT

It was a relief to be out of the hot, stinky bodysuit, but Sebetay had not escaped it—it was stuffed into his backsack with his goggles and breathing mask, and the weight of it chafed him as he held on to the waist of a strange light-skinned woman who spoke to him in Hulkrish. At the same time, she was holding the waist of a yellow-skinned man, a Dneeper from the Grasslands, who was driving all three of them west—on a cockroach!

The Dneeper would not allow Sebetay to sit directly in back of him and make physical contact; he would only drive once this strange hairless woman volunteered to sit as the cushion between them. The woman had been sharp with the Dneeper, scolding him as she was helped up to the saddle by women dressed in robes of brown and orange with crinkled antennae on their heads. "No offense, Good Defender," the woman had said to Sebetay from under the hood that covered her head. "I should have asked if you will allow me to share this saddle."

"Of course," he had answered. The other light-skinned women who accompanied the woman were all doing the same as her: getting on the saddles of other roach drivers who would not tolerate the touch of a dark-skinned rider.

Why? Sebetay wondered. *What would happen if I touched this Dneeper? Would he spout blood from punctures? Would his skin peel away from his bones? Would he dry up and float away?*

The driver would not speak directly to Sebetay but only through the bald woman, even as Sebetay understood most of what he said. "Tell him we are stopping for a break," the Dneeper snapped in Slopeish.

"Tell him yourself," said the woman as the roach was halted for a moment at a cluster of dried hair sedge. As they waited for the driver to relieve himself, the woman unwrapped some oven-baked mushroom chips with a filling of whipped pond scum and handed one to Sebetay. "If you are hungry," she said.

"Very kind of you, thanks," he said in Slopeish.

"Where are you from?" she asked with a smile, intrigued by his accent.

"I was born in Ledack," he said.

"The people of the meat ants. Welcome to Bee-Jor."

"Thank you. Can you tell me why we go to this Mound Zilpot?"

"I am told the Greeyas are crawling towards the South for their next attack. We are preparing a defense of some kind at Zilpot."

When the Dneeper returned from the hair sedge, the woman frowned at him. She did not offer him any of her food even as he eyed it with hunger. As their roach reentered the mass of them crawling west, Sebetay coughed again, a fit of it he could not contain, and he turned his head over his shoulder. He heard others on the roaches doing the same. What had made them ill as well as made their lungs ache? Was it the stinking oil of the roaches? Was it the extract of mushroom poison he had sprayed inside the shelters of Loobosh? Perhaps in the battle against the Greeyas, he had breathed in the yellow powder. He looked at the wax-encased yellow barrels of the supply-sleds and wondered if that's what was inside them.

What if this war with the Greeyas is never over? he wondered. *What if Bee-Jor wars again with these Seed Eaters who want their mounds back? And what if these*

Dneepish roach riders—who have demanded and gotten Palzhad—ask for even more?

What if these Bee-Jorites are like Hulkrites: a people who are always at war and provoke their neighbors by pushing into their land? And as for land, where will we Ledackis live . . . and how? Have we come here as soldier-slaves to fight in endless wars?

And where, in the name of Meat Ant, are the bees of Bee-Jor and all this promised honey?

He looked above him at the formation of blue locusts that guided the roach swarm to Mound Zilpot. The locusts were circling now as the mound came into view. Zilpot looked little different from Palzhad, Loobosh, or the other human-inhabited ant mounds they had passed. As he got closer, he saw Zilpot was just another noisy, filthy city where people crowded together to quarrel and elbow each other. It was one more mound in Bee-Jor without any ants to protect or provide its working people with food. And now thousands more humans, hungry refugees like himself, were arriving for a stay at Zilpot with the "honor" of defending it.

Maybe someday we can get back to Ledack.

As the roaches came to a slow halt, they parted to allow Sebetay's roach to continue riding. It crawled up to the edge of the mound's outermost ring where thousands of people with crude, hastily made banners of Bee-Jor were waiting. More shaven-headed women, reeking of sage perfume, were coming towards the roach. Two of them carried a little staircase to allow the woman to step down from the roach in safety. She struggled as she did so, but was handed a staff, which she used to stand erect as another removed the cloak she was wearing. Still another set a pair of long, crinkled antennae on her head while one more handed her a harp and a plectrum. The crowd was cheering her as she was helped up to a pyramid-type structure that was under construction, something with strange and unfinished decorations carved into its facade. An amplifying-cone was pushed before her as she struck her harp to silence the people.

"People of Zilpot," she shouted in a rich and golden voice. "You are our newest Bee-Jorites. Please welcome these other new Bee-Jorites, brave men and women, who like me were prisoners in Hulkren. These are the heroes who turned back the Greeyas at Loobosh!"

The crowd cheered and turned to applaud those who had arrived on roaches. Children pushed through the crowd with basins of dried and shredded flower petals that they threw over the arrivals.

"We welcome these men and women who fight with us to live in peace, who fight to be equal, who fight to lead lives of their own agency!"

The people of Zilpot cheered even louder. When the woman repeated it in Hulkrish for the new arrivals, the cheers that followed were an uproar that filled Sebetay's ears and it warmed and excited him. "Po-lex-ima! Po-lex-ima," the crowd chanted as they clapped in unison.

"Polexima!" said Sebetay to himself. "Queen Polexima!"

A chill, like the falling of little stars, ran down his back. He took up the chant as the locusts broke their circle and flew west.

Torvock-son-of-Koshvock, the First Setcha Greeya, wanted to get away from his army, his camp, and his captains in order to find a place where he could hide and sleep and grieve all alone. He needed a place where he would be free to remember Shlovock, the beautiful boy, his firstborn, and the boy who was to be the Second Setcha and rule the resurrected country of Greeya-Tepic. Instead, brave little Shlovy was dead in a Slopeish palace, a victim of a sorcerer's spell or a witch's brew. Making it worse, his body was unretrievable, left to rot, then shrivel without any rites. And as for rites, the Divinely Chosen of Gree Dari-Ekh and the High Priest of Father Dead-Eater were also corpses inside that palace—as was everyone else who had slept on Loobosh. How had these cowardly Bee-Jorites killed tens of thousands of his men and their families—as well as his son and heir?

I will never see Shlovock again, Torvock thought, even as he could see his son all too well inside his head. There he was, running towards him, with a broad smile and proudly holding the tooth that had just fallen out. There he was **again**, fiercely proud of the first time his arrow had made its mark: a robber fly hanging on the underside of a white meadow-foam. And there he was, at his most beautiful, grinning as he held up the first head he had ever taken in battle: a yellow-skinned Slopeite who had leapt on him from the flower top of a vinegar-weed.

"Setcha, I said we should send scouts to the South," repeated Veltfock.

"The South," said Torvock, nodding his head as if he had been listening. His captains had gathered on their blue wasps in a circle to confer. "How far south?"

"To wherever this strip of white poison ends . . . if it does."

"What if it doesn't end?" shouted Captain Ovoglock. "What if they have poisoned the entire border, all the way to the Dead Lands?"

"And poisoned every dwelling of every mound," added Zalavock.

The Setcha was quiet and searched his feelings. "What if they haven't?" he asked. "What if they are weak and open in the South and have spent all their poisons in the North?"

"What if the Pine people sent us here knowing we would be poisoned and slaughtered?" questioned Veltfock. "What if this is some trick of Sinsora's?"

Torvock could hear the keening of his kinswomen as they mourned for Shlovock. The sound was mad-making and distracting. "Enough weeping, women!" he scolded them. "These tears without end will shame my son! He is up above, in the Blue Sky Kingdom where he flies with clear wings and hunts with Grandfather Locust!"

The women quieted, muffling their mouths as the Setcha looked into each of his captains' eyes. In back of him, Trellana and the roach-women were weakly coughing.

"We will attack no mound unless we know it is occupied and safe," said the Setcha. "These Bee-Jorites forfeited Loobosh. But they cannot give up all their mounds."

He turned to the Britasytes. Queestra was crying for her sister, who was barely alive.

"Roach-woman. Will these Bee-Jorites sacrifice all their mounds?"

Queestra slitted her eyes and her mouth tightened. "They will sacrifice *everything*," she said. "Including their own lives before they surrender to a foreign master."

"Then their ears have been poisoned!" Torvock shouted. "We are not foreigners! This is our land!"

As he looked at the roach-woman, he knew she was lying.

Never trust a Britasyte. This poisoning of Loobosh was a trick!

"Captains," he shouted to them. "We will send our scouts ahead. And we will follow them south until they find a place where these Bee-Jorites are weak and open. The Gree Dari-Ekh is with us . . . and we will fulfill Her will. Let us promise Father Dead-Eater one thousand hearts for every Greeya who gave his life at Loobosh."

From atop a locust in a small squadron, Terraclon looked down at the thousands of defenders arrived at Zilpot, their presence hopefully signaling to the Greeyas that what the Bee-Jorites had done at Loobosh, they would do here.

And everybody would lose.

He looked over at Nuvao on his locust as they surveyed the progress of the mound's preparation. Nuvao shrugged and then so did Terraclon. The warning banners were still being pitched and a white powder had been layered over the cleared strip. It was too bright and white and did not resemble borax on closer examination; it looked like what it was, crushed chalk, and some of it had not been crushed very well. In back of the banners, he saw the defenders practicing with this newest contraption, a catapult, the efficacy of which was uncertain.

The squadron veered southwest to Mound Escarte, an older, poor, and sparsely populated mound next to a grove of dead and dying bortshus. Terraclon saw that the border strip along Escarte was still being cleared of its weeds and the largest and toughest of them were still standing. The parts of the strip that had been cleared had little in the way of the decoy powder. It was just a small crew that was working below, spreading a thin layer of crushed chalk. Farther south, where the strip connected to the mound's main artery, it was wide open and free of any powder.

If the Greeya scouts have seen this, they will accept it as an invitation.

Nuvao made the circling motion with fingers up to order a return. The locust squadron veered around to fly east with enough sunlight to get them back to Zilpot. Terraclon signaled to the two locusts in back of him that they were to leave the squadron and follow him north for a last reconnaissance. He had to see how close the Greeyas were, if they still numbered in the hundreds of thousands, and if it was true that more of them were gushing out of the Pine Lands.

He looked over at Nuvao, who mouthed, "Be careful." Terraclon understood his concern and was warmed by it just at the moment the winds grew chilly. The days were getting shorter and cooler. Soon it would be difficult to fly locusts and then impossible to breed and transform them out of grasshoppers.

But the Greeyas are a people without a code. They don't wait through the winter moons, thought Terraclon, remembering what Anand had learned from his Dranverish books. *And when the weather is too cold and their insects die, the Greeyas will attack on foot—and we'll have neither ants nor defenders to stop them.*

It was all too soon before Terraclon saw the edges of the Greeyas' army. He knew that land wasps crawled more swiftly than ants, but they were only a day or two from Zilpot's border and three, maybe four days from Escarte if they marched at night. Terraclon's heart thumped inside him when he saw their uncountable numbers in the North—they might have been a million or more. He was stunned again by the colorfully eerie beauty of a massive spread of furry insects and the giant black beetles that serviced them.

Bee-Jor is too small for all these Greeyas! They would attack the Seed Eaters after us!

Moist, gray clouds were drifting across the western horizon. The locust stopped beating its wings and went into a glide as it got darker sooner than expected. Terraclon had hoped for a glimpse of the bright blue land wasps that carried the Setcha and his captains at their army's center, but they were too far away. He signaled to the pilots behind him to dip lower and head east where they might find a more favorable current. With the help of the south-blowing wind, they might just reach the outskirts of Zilpot in the very last of the dying light.

I won't be sleeping tonight, he thought.

I may never sleep again.

It was under a patchy sky in the late afternoon when the scouts returned from the South with their shoulders pinned back and a gleam in their eyes. They were eager to report to the Setcha.

"Our scouts report what I thought," said the Setcha to his captains in the orange light of the setting sun. They had gathered on the ground and waited for the evening meal. "The Bee-Jorites have laid out a white powder along the borders of Zilpot and Escarte. But it is not the powder that dried and killed our wasps at Loobosh."

The Setcha opened a bag and emptied its bright white powder. "This is powdered chalk, a ruse! A stupid ruse that anyone would see through! Farther south, at this dying mound of Escarte, they don't even have this *decoy* powder!"

"Then we should have attacked in the South at Escarte," said Veltfock.

Torvock glared at Veltfock.

I should have replaced him long ago.

"We should have, Captain," said the Setcha. "And

you should have told us that before we warred on Loobosh."

Veltfock lowered his head, gritted his teeth.

"Bee-Jor is weak," said Oglovock. "We should attack them now, before they regroup at Escarte."

"They may be out of the white powder, but what if they have the yellow?" asked Veltfock.

I should have killed him long ago!

"At Escarte, we will send forth our bravest and see what these Escartites can throw at them," said the Setcha. "And after we take Escarte, we will take these southern mounds of Caladeck, Palzhad, and Rinso. From there we will march to Venaris and then to Cajoria—where Quegdoth will scream like a woman when I rip his bones out, one by one, starting with his toes."

"Setcha, when do we leave?" asked Veltfock.

"Tomorrow at dawn."

The captains tapped their heads in agreement. Around them, the women erected the sleeping tents of felted velvet on their wooden floating rings as they sensed a coming rain. They chanted their prayers to Lady Moon Roach and asked for Her protection. They tossed the Lady scraps of the evening meal before they laid out the captains' eating leaf.

"Listen," said the Setcha, smiling when the dark of the night was complete. A three-quarter moon glowed behind the gray gossamers of fleeting clouds. "Can you hear them?"

A slow, faint chirping was coming from distant trees.

"Autumn crickets in the South," said the Setcha, bowing his head. "She comes."

"I don't hear them," whispered Veltfock.

CHAPTER 38

THE TAKING OF ESCARTE

The roach-woman was dying of thirst and her breath was a terrible stink.

And I cannot even pinch my own nose, thought Trellana.

"Water," said Ulatha hoarsely as she came out of sleep or stupor. "I need water!"

"She needs water!" Trellana shouted in her first attempt at the Carpenters' tongue. The Setcha looked over his shoulder in contempt. After a short discussion with this younger, beardless son and heir apparent, the Setcha turned and thrust his uncapped squeeze bag into Ulatha's mouth and let her drink. Trellana and Queestra opened their own mouths in hopes of water but the bag was emptied and the Setcha used it to slap their faces.

"Where do you think we're going?" Ulatha asked Trellana.

"South," she said, shrugging her shoulders.

"Why south?"

"I will assume it is because the League of Velvet Ant Peoples will attempt to invade Bee-Jor from a point that is more favorable to them."

"I have been dreaming," said Ulatha. "A long and terrible daymare."

"What daymare could be worse than this?"

"I saw the end of the Britasyte tribe, the deaths of the last of our people," said Ulatha as her voice got stronger. "We were fleeing to the North with Anand, on our way to Dranveria, when we were captured by tree cannibals. They tore us into pieces to feed their children."

"Sounds rather lovely," said Trellana.

"In some ways it was," said Ulatha after a pause. "You were with us. They took you first, but after everyone bit into you, they spit you out and said you were bitter and greasy. You were still alive when they did."

The Setcha turned to them and shouted at Queestra, jutting his chin from under his beard streaked with the paints of the league's colors. Queestra whispered the translation to Ulatha, who whispered it to Trellana. "The Setcha says we are to speak when spoken to . . . and not to each other."

Trellana sighed. The weather had turned cooler. Clouds were filling the afternoon sky and turning it a heavy gray.

Please, Father Grasshopper, drown me in a flood. Better yet, strike me dead with lightning.

Sebetay stood with his squad behind the banners stretched along Zilpot's frontier where he waited. The defenders had been allowed to take off their goggles and breathing masks as the powder bombs were far behind them and covered with tarps. Farther back were these new devices, the catapults: a weapon that could result in massive casualties for the enemy. Their idle operators were playing on these devices, riding up and down on their weighted ends, before they were scolded by the sergeant.

The defenders were not allowed to chat but whispered when they had to. They knew the Greeyas, their wasps, and their war beetles were just west of them, crawling south down a rock-strewn decline to avoid a lengthy patch of dried and dangerous bur weeds. The Greeyas had been on the move since yesterday, and though the defenders of Bee-Jor could not see their migration, they could hear it. Their marching sounded like distant rain, similar to windblown leaves and a bit like the rattle-song of cicadas.

"Stay awake, defenders!" said the sergeant in a low voice as he passed a platter with globs of chewing sap rolled in kwondle powder. "The Greeyas may attack when we least expect it."

Sebetay looked between the banners as the clouds smothered Father Sun Beetle. He emerged, briefly, shining one last moment before sinking into His bed in the Great Ant Nest to be fed and comforted by His wife, Meat Ant, who had spent the day hunting for His dinner with Her tens of thousands of children.

Sebetay nodded a quick prayer to both his gods for Jakhuma's safety and then coughed again. He spit up something darkly red. Around him, he saw similar splats, spit out by the other defenders.

Our lungs are bleeding, he thought as his panic pulsed inside him. *Bleeding lungs are more frightening than the threat of any Greeya!*

Greeya scouts on their camouflaged wasps struggled northwest through an endless maze of wasps crawling south when at last they reached the Setcha and his captains. Their blue wasps had just arrived to establish their center of command not under but near a grove of dead and dying oak trees just west of Mound Escarte. A wealth of glow-fungus grew on fallen logs, within the grove, that were infested with fat termites to be harvested for a celebratory dinner. Much of the army was settled for the night in a clearing south of the grove that was safe from falling acorns and twigs while a third of the army was still arriving from the East.

"Setcha," shouted up Esnock, the young scout with his beard shaved into seven separate locks. "The people of Escarte have fled. As soon as they saw our approach, they abandoned their banners and the powdering of their border. They have no ants and fled on foot."

The other captains searched each other's faces and looked doubtful.

"They could have poisoned their dwellings before they left," said Veltfock. The other captains nodded.

"Let us send some Slopeish prisoners up this mound of Escarte," said the Setcha. "Let us place them in rooms of the palaces and in the shanties of the laborers and in all the shelters in between. If these prisoners live through the night, only then will we settle this mound."

A short time later, cramped wicker cages of yellow-skinned prisoners from the conquered Slopeish mounds were dragged before the Setcha for his approval. He rejected the prisoners who looked old and sickly and sent those that were younger and healthy. "Feed and water these prisoners well before leaving them for the night," he said before they were tossed into supply-sleds and hauled away by beetles.

The air felt wetter once it was dark. Gray clouds dimmed the light of Lady Moon Roach and Her millions of glistening eggs.

Rain is coming, thought the Setcha. *It will be a comfort, gods willing, to take this mound before it does.*

Punshu looked down from the end of a branch of a sickly oak tree with a mix of other defenders. All of them lay quietly on their stomachs as they watched Greeya women gathering glow-fungus from fallen branches and make torches of it. They did not leave any fungus behind to regrow, stupidly, but scraped off every glowing bit, which they speared on the ends of sticks hewn out of the wood. He watched as the torches were passed through the vast lake of the Greeyas' army and it was a beautiful but disturbing sight to see their thousands of bobbing flickers.

Punshu looked behind him and gasped. "Sweet Roach Lord!" he muttered when the torches concentrated farther west at what had to be the center of their command—within that circle was the fearsome Setcha Greeya and the captains of the united tribes who rode on their blue velvet land wasps. Someone shushed Punshu and he turned to see Putree, the tree dweller, and Odwaznee with fingers pressed to their mouths, urging him to keep mum.

When the wind blew, the dry, fragile branches of the tree shifted with creaks and crackles. Punshu used the toe spikes of his boots and the grasping hooks on his fingers to dig into the bark of the branch to cling tight. The obsidian tools in his backsack added their weight to keep him steady, but he feared a harsh blast of wind could blow them out of the tree and all the others that were occupied.

And was rain coming?

"Save us, Madricanth," he mouthed, "from demon rains and Greeya warriors." As they waited through the night, Punshu went in and out of a shallow sleep and longed for the hammock in his father's sand-sled. He was in a deeper sleep when he dreamt of a moon roach nibbling on his ankle. He woke to realize Odwaznee was tugging on his foot.

"Look!" Odwaznee whispered, and pointed. Punshu turned to the watchtower and saw a torch float up and glow inside its windows. His heart was pounding as he looked to the East but saw and heard nothing.

Nothing yet.

The Greeyas had seen the torch too. He could hear their murmurs, and the warnings they shouted as thousands of them roused to leave their round tents of wasp felt. They were untethering their insects from a vast web of ropes, gathering weapons, and climbing onto saddles to prepare for an attack.

A glimmer in the Northeast caught Punshu's eye. He turned to see faint little lights getting closer on the traveling route outside Escarte. It was twenty or thirty insects of some kind, and with torches of glow-fungus glued to their heads they were announcing themselves! The insects had no riders on their backs but were racing down the flat of the artery. They headed straight for the Greeyas, then fanned out against their front line.

In back of these insects, Punshu could see other arrivals, and from their gait, he knew they were roaches. They were also lit up with torches glued to their heads but they had riders kneeling in saddles. The roaches had herded this first group of insects into the Greeyas—and to certain death.

Those must be ants if they've fled from roaches.

Punshu heard the swelling voices of the Greeyas and the louder click/chirping of their wasps. The Greeyas were aiming bows at the ants, their arrows flying at these easy targets with lights glued to their skulls. The roaches that had driven the bitters had completely disappeared.

To where?

An ant exploded, its glowing head flying from its body. Moments later, the other ants had detonated, their heads flying up and rolling when they landed.

"Bitter ants!" Punshu whispered.

But why so few?

The great mass of Greeyas were alert and ready for battle, shouting a war chant that was great and terrifying and reverberated between them and the palaces of the mound. But no more bitter ants had followed and the few that did had not come close enough to harm the Greeyas. The scattered parts of the ants were being examined by men on foot who had run out to see what had attacked them.

"Look," said Putree, and pointed to the watchtower where a second torch had risen to join the first.

The Setcha and his captains had left their tents and gathered under torch lights as they waited for a report from the front. The Setcha ordered the untethering of the blue wasps in preparation for an attack and impatiently joined in the work, throwing off the ropes of his own mount. A relay messenger on foot finally reached him.

"Setcha, twenty or thirty ants from the East have been . . . have been destroyed. Or they . . . they have destroyed themselves."

"They what? What kind of ants?"

"Black ants, large enough to ride, but none of them mounted. All are dead. They . . . they flew apart."

"Flew apart?"

"Yes, Setcha, or they *blew* apart. When the arrows hit them, there was a whistling sound and then a loud pop. Their blood sprayed and their parts broke and flew into pieces."

The Setchas was wordless . . . as were his captains.

"What kind of sorcery is this?" asked Veltfock.

"I will ride to see these ants," said the Setcha. He turned to his captains. "This may be a trick, a lure of some kind. Zalavock, Ovlogock, and Hawjud, come with me. The rest of you stay here to protect my son and our families. Lead from the back if we don't return."

"Yes, Setcha," said the remaining captains, tapping their foreheads.

"Yes, Setcha," followed Veltfock, later than the rest and barely tapping his head.

I will kill Veltfock on my return, thought the Setcha.

Crawling slowly in the darkness through his spooked warriors and the clicking wasps, the time grew long before the Setcha reached the eastern edge of his camp. He stared at the remnants of these bizarre ants that had blown apart. Under torch lights, his men were kicking their pieces over and examining them for clues, when one of them, using his naked hands, screamed in pain. The blood of these ants was eating the man's skin and they heard it sizzle. He screamed as he ran in circles, then dropped to his knees to scrape his palms over the edges of sand grains and left smears of his own blood.

The Setcha was startled.

This is just a warning! They are telling us to leave!

"Look," said Zalavock, and pointed up to the watchtower to see a second torch glowing in its windows.

"Let us tear this tower down now and see who raises lights inside it!" said the Setcha as he pressed his sword and a torch together and raised them. "To the watchtower! Attack!" he shouted.

"Attack!" shouted his men, and as the command was passed, they drove their wasps east.

The Setcha was leading them to the watchtower when he saw a third torch join the other two. As the Greeyas advanced, they heard a clattering rumble. Behind him, the wasps' clicking got louder and faster as they raised their abdomens and extended their stingers—their antennae were waving and had sensed something. Their mandibles pulsed as they waited for an assault.

The wasps would not turn their backs and run from whatever was coming, but Torvock wished he could when he saw a gushing river of ants racing towards him—massive ants that were as clear as crystals. The ants were lit up with garlands of glow-fungus around their head joints. They had drivers kneeling on their skulls and bowmen standing behind them in upright stirrups.

The bowmen were shooting arrows in rapid fire. Around him, the Setcha heard the sickening crunch of arrows piercing Greeyan armor.

How?

An arrow burst through the Setcha's shoulder panel and lodged under his clavicle. He yanked it out to see an arrowhead of black obsidian. As the ghost ants came closer, their riders switched to a mouth pipe with a flap that fed it darts. The Setcha saw that the men to his left and right had been targeted in the face. They dropped their bows and screeched in pain only to fall from their saddles to shake on the sand. Captain Hawjud had fallen and lay crushed under his wasp, the head of which had been shattered with arrows.

Darts hit the Setcha's chest plate and fell from it. "Advance!" he shouted to his army, but the front lines of warriors had lost control of their wasps. "Ghost ants! Ghost ants!" he heard shouted behind him. The camp women and children screamed and huddled in their tents as the wasps bunched up, unable to advance.

As the Setcha urged his own wasp forward, he saw that the ghost ants with their garlands of lights had split into two streams. They were no longer rushing forward but had crawled to the right and left of the main artery. Like lighted gates that had opened, they released a greater, thicker stream of unmounted ghosts that spread over the Greeyas' army in a vast, devouring blanket.

Tens of thousands of Greeyas and their wasps collided with ghost ants in a panicked tangle. Other Greeyas fled to the open spaces under the trees of the grove.

Punshu pulled up his breathing mask and lowered his goggles after the command was passed by his sergeant through the tree. He turned to see Putree and Odwaznee had done the same. They looked down at the Greeyas and their insects as they scattered south by the thousands in a chaotic crawl toward spaces under trees.

"Now!" shouted the sergeant at a platform on the trunk. Punshu and the others on his branch crawled back and clustered at the place where the branch joined the trunk. They set to work with their obsidian axes and hacked at the last segment of the precut branch that held it in place when it snapped.

Punshu stepped back and watched the branch fall. It seemed to gently float before it crashed. He heard the pops of the poison bombs attached to its underside and then the screams of the Greeyas who were crushed under it yet still alive. As the yellow powder was inhaled, he heard their shrieks of panic.

Punshu followed Odwaznee and Putree up a ladder to the next branch, chopping at its end while they listened to the fall of branches in the surrounding trees and the wails of agony from the Greeyas below. When all the branches had fallen, they heard a maddening din of coughing, choking, and cries for help. Some of the Greeyas attempted a weak retreat to the north on foot, but they were met with wave after wave of ghost ants that sucked them up and swallowed them whole. Ghost ants that had fed returned to the trunk trail and ran east, back to their nest, weaving in and out of more and more arriving ghosts that were hungry.

Punshu watched as some Greeyas, mounted on their land wasps, attempted to flee south. They crawled over or around the severed branches or fallen logs on the grove's floor but turned back north when they were met with a new onslaught. The Dneepers who had been waiting for them with their recumbent bows on sand-sleds were advancing. Their broad arrows with black-glass heads sliced through Greeyan armor to sever its wearer in two. Some missiles lifted both men and land wasps off the ground and slammed them into fallen logs where they were nailed into the wood.

The Setcha and his warriors attempted to shoot at the ghost ants with arrows or hack at them with swords, but they were just too many and just too large. The ghosts crawled over the wasps and used their mandibles to pluck the Greeyas from their saddles, toss them up, and swallow them down. Sated ghosts turned around to race home just as new ghosts entered to feed.

The Setcha's captains gripped their saddles with their legs and used their swords to cut into the ghosts' skulls or thrust into the bulges of their enormous eyes and managed to fell the smaller ones. When the ghosts could not tear Captain Ovoglock from his saddle, they snipped his head off his neck. Zalavock slashed off the ghosts' antennae, but it made the ants more erratic—they spun in circles and knocked both wasps and Greeyas onto their sides. When Zalavock's own wasp stumbled and fell, he struggled to disengage from his saddle as ants and wasps stepped over him, dragging their claws across his face.

Wasps that had lost their riders responded when attacked, but they were too small to dominate the ghosts and kill them. The wasps attempted to use their mandibles to grab at the ghosts' heads and curl up their abdomens to sting them, but the ghosts were lubricated—the Setcha could see they were slick with oil that made them impossible to grab and hard to pierce. The ghosts' sharp, thick mandibles could not break into the wasps' chitin, but they grabbed the wasps by the head to shake and flip them away.

The Setcha heard screaming behind him and turned to see a Greeya family of women and children who had been exposed. They were screaming inside a prison of shifting insect legs. As the children crawled away, the women were swallowed or cut into two before they were eaten. The children who had made it into a felt tent were screaming when a ghost's mandibles pierced the roof, then picked up the tent to shake it and hurl it away.

The Setcha was exhausted as he slashed and thrust and dodged when the ghost ants suddenly backed away. The war beetles were trudging to the front, crawling over and through the piles of carnage as they sprayed their stink. As his own mount pivoted,

the Setcha saw the ghosts were running from the beetles, repelled by their odors, and heading west.

We have a clearing to retreat north!

"North!" the Setcha shouted. "Retreat north!"

The command to retreat was passed through the
Greeyas and their mass made the slow pivot north.
The wasps picked up speed as the route freed up but
slowed when they reached the long incline leading
to the bur patch. Some of them, sick with the yellow
powder, were stopping to quiver and die. Their
riders abandoned them and jumped off their saddles
to hitch rides. The Setcha looked behind him when
he reached the peak of the incline and was shattered
when he could see the end of their column.

We have lost so many!

He looked northwest and saw the vague glimmer
of distant torches and felt his stomach fall out of him.

My army has been split in two!

Trellana and the roach-women were in a panicked
weep as they heard and smelled the foul mixture of
ghost ants, the stink of the yellow power, and the
stench of the war beetles. The captains the Setcha
had left behind were arguing over what to do and
who was in charge. The red-bearded scowler stood
on his saddle and shouted the loudest. The wasps
crowded each other, their clicking getting louder

and faster as they were pressed by an attack from the front.

"What do you think he's saying?" Trellana asked as the scowler ranted.

"I'm not sure," said Ulatha through her sobbing. "But it sounds like 'escape' . . . or 'retreat' . . . I heard the words 'west' and 'forest.'"

The three captains had come to an agreement. All three stood on their mounts, two on blue velvets, and the one on a white one since he had lost his blue to the powder. They shouted to the south, west, and north, and their command was spread through their army.

Slowly and awkwardly, the mass of Greeyas and their wasps turned to face west. Women and children collapsed their tents, then climbed onto saddles as all began a western crawl in retreat. The wasps were bumbling, bumping into each other as they trudged in a jam towards the Pine Lands. Trellana was ravaged with chills when she heard the screaming of thousands in the east—the ghost ants had not finished feeding.

The screams were getting closer.

Half of the Setcha's army was nearing the patch of bur weeds in their flight north. He looked right, and in the dim moonlight he could see the banners of Mound Zilpot and the broad swath of the strip they had covered with powder. Not taking any chances, the Setcha signaled with his left hand to veer west and ride flush against the bur weeds and avoid contact with the strip.

Maybe that powder is more than chalk.

In the darkness, Torvock heard the sound of what might have been the banners pulling inwards and then the whistling of flying bombs. The stench of the yellow powder filled his nose again as his wasp slowed and he heard the soft crash of powder bombs. The riders in back of him were screaming, gasping, and shouting as more of the bombs landed. Torvock had the urge to ride straight into these cowards who flung their poisons in the night and shoot each one through the eye with arrows—though he had no arrows left.

Keep going. The end of these bur weeds is near.

The bombing continued when he sighted the end of the burs and a clearing where the procession could veer northwest and evade the bombs.

"Thank you, Goddess!" he shouted to Gree Dari-Ekh when he heard the whoosh of something arcing, then falling. Just as he turned to look right, a bomb smashed into the shoulder plate of his armor and coated his face with the yellow powder. It got in his eyes and nose, and he sucked it into his mouth. He coughed as his lungs felt as if someone had ripped them from his chest. A pressure was building inside his head as if his brain was squirting from his ears.

He heard himself scream and then the scream faded to a whisper. His insides shrank into a tiny pellet that rolled in the husk of his body before it shrank to nothing.

Terraclon and Nuvao shivered from the night's chill as they looked down at the dark, almost lightless night scape of Escarte's western frontier from atop the watchtower. Here and there, fallen torches illuminated the corpses of the Greeyas, their abandoned tents, and their land wasps who were dead on their backs or shaking from the poisoning. A squad of defenders was searching for Greeya survivors they could bring into Cajoria, and managed to pull one up from under the corpse of a blue wasp. "Looks like we've got one!" Terraclon shouted. The men looked at each other, their breathing masks clinking before they stepped away. Nuvao grabbed Terraclon's hand and squeezed it.

"Once again, Ter. You have done it."

"You are too lavish with your compliments, Nuvao. Your praise must be redirected elsewhere."

Terraclon felt that strange gush of feelings again as he looked out at the grimness in the dark. He felt his tears building up in his goggles.

"You are crying again," said Nuvao.

"I am."

"Such a sensitive boy."

"Nuvao . . . do you think we will ever know peace?"

"No. But maybe our children will. I mean . . . not *our* children. The next generation. Of children, that is."

Terraclon lifted his torch up to the ceiling where there was a release loop. "Shall we try this again? I do believe I have it fixed. Some break knots along the cable will slow it down. And we are to stand on the other side, hanging on to these loops, for something called *equilibrium*."

"You are as clever as you are sensitive."

As the shelter glided down the cable, Nuvao and Terraclon removed their goggles and their breathing masks. They reached for the pairs of antennae that hung on the walls and strapped them to their heads. Outside the window they saw a circle of lights on the ground in the distance.

"Before we get there," Nuvao said, shouting over the noisy vibrations of the cable, "I want to do something."

"What?" said Terraclon, then he felt a warm hand at the back of his neck pulling him in. The shock of that moment gave way to the crushing sweetness of Nuvao's lips. Terraclon felt as if his heart was pumping an inner sunshine—the world had cracked open and revealed an unknown and staggering beauty. The two pulled apart, chuckling quietly as the shelter slowed its descent and came to a smooth stop in a shallow basin filled with cushioning leaves. They crawled out of the window and walked to the cluster of ghost ants garlanded with lights and the riders who waited.

"Terraclon!" shouted Anand, laughing with joy and relief. As his driver assumed the antennae, Anand slid down the skull of his massive, glassy ant and then onto its mandible before jumping to the ground. He ran with his arms open to hug Terraclon. Some of the ghost ants crawled towards Nuvao and probed him for kin-scent—he stepped back with a look of disgust and shock on his face.

Terraclon was wordless, stunned, still lost in the aura of his first kiss, when he looked over Anand's shoulder and noticed a woman descending from a ghost ant and coming towards them. Even in the soft glow of the torch she carried, he thought she was the most astoundingly beautiful woman he had ever seen—the most beautiful *human* he had ever seen. He wondered how Anand had befriended a demigoddess. She took off her helmet, and from the mass of ginger braids that fell out, he realized she was a Seed Eater.

"Greetings," she said. "You must is Terraclon."

"H-h-hello," Terraclon finally managed to say.

"Why you keep stare at me, Terraclon?" she asked in her broken Slopeish. "Anand told me you like boys."

Terraclon felt his eyes pop open and he glared at Anand. Nuvao chuckled.

"Anand! Really!"

"It's all right, Ter. This is Muti," Anand said. "I told you about her."

"Did you? I'm at a loss."

"I thought I did."

"No, you didn't."

"Yes, Ter. She's my . . . wife."

"Your *what*?"

"Well, one of my wives. We were married at Fadtha-dozh. Muti conducted our ceremony."

"Oh, really. She conducted her own wedding ceremony?"

"Yes, Ter. And yes, she is aware of my other two. Wives, that is."

Terraclon stared at Anand in wordless shock.

"Let me remind you," Anand said in their low-caste accent. "Marriages are made for practical reasons."

"She doesn't look so practical," Terraclon jested.

"Speaking of your wives," said Nuvao as he stepped forward. "I believe your second one might still be out there, a prisoner of the Greeyas."

"Yes," said Anand with a sigh. "The other woman who is . . . pregnant with my children."

A raindrop fell between them and domed before it broke and sank between the sand grains. Others followed.

"Thank Madricanth," Anand said. "The rain waited until after the battle."

"I told you," said Muti as she brushed back his hair with her fingers and looked at him with a lusty admiration. "Was all my doing."

"Your doing?" squeaked Terraclon, cocking his head.

"I held storm back," said Muti, raising her hands and splaying her fingers.

"Muti is . . . Muti *believes* in sorcery," said Anand with the straightest face he could muster.

"Oh, *really*," said Terraclon as a raindrop fell on Muti and soaked her in its dome before she shook free of it. The ghost ants shifted, made anxious by the rain, when Terraclon heard a thorn horn in the distance that blasted three times.

"That's a messenger down there, a Britasyte," said Anand. "He can't come any closer without his roach spooking these ants."

"Send someone else," said Muti.

"I am the only one who speaks Britasyte," Anand shouted over his shoulder.

"Hurry back," shouted Terraclon. "Rain is here."

Anand ran off into the darkness with a torch. Muti shook herself dry by shaking her head, then her shoulders, then her torso, then her hips before she shook each of her legs and feet dry. Terraclon was mystified by the ugly, gray crystal she wore around her neck, something unbefitting such a beauty.

"I brought you present," she said, and reached inside her jacket to offer him a necklace with a pendant of the same ugly jewel.

"Thank you," he said, working up his best priestly manners. "But I am unfamiliar with this . . . jewel."

"Lightning glass," she said. "Gift from Goddess Ghost Ant. You will wear it and show Her devotion."

"Oh, *really*," said Nuvao, his eyes shifting left and right when Terraclon went quiet.

Anand was returning, the torch bobbing in his left hand while the right was in a fist. As he got closer, Terraclon saw that look on Anand's face, when his teeth were gritted and his brows hooded his eyes. He was shaking with rage, heaving as he trembled, when he grabbed Terraclon by the shoulders, pulled him into his chest, and burst into tears.

"What's wrong?"

"I have to get back to Cajoria. Now."

"Right now, you're going into a shelter! It's about to rain!"

Anand was shaking, unable to control his sobbing. Everyone atop of their ghost ants was staring. Muti was coming forward, turning Anand towards her to comfort him, when lightning, like fast-growing roots of fire, fractured the sky and sent it tumbling.

"Everyone to shelters, now!" Terraclon shouted as winds raced up and thunder shook the ground.

CHAPTER 39

A DAY OF SIGHS

Anand looked down from Escarte's central watch-tower to see that banner-slings painted with warnings had been erected all along the extended border, and behind them, catapults were either being tested or were under construction. Behind the banners, the excavation of a deep, wide trench had begun, one that would be reinforced with scaffolding and nettings of spider silk to keep its walls intact. Once it was completed, Anand would order its bottom to be covered with enough borax to poison any insect that fell in it or attempted to crawl up out of it.

All of this will hold back the Greeyas . . . for a little while, he thought, and sighed.

As he descended the ladder, he saw the workers were not just Bee-Jorites of Slopeish stock but that they were a variety of peoples who had been captives in Hulkren and some had resumed the native garb of distant lands. Largely, they were women and he heard some of their different tongues, but mostly they spoke Hulkrish to each other—it would be their common tongue for a while. After he mounted the ghost ant that was waiting for him at the tower's bottom, the workers nearby stopped to gather around him and fold their hands above their heads as they praised him.

"Hail Commander Quegdoth!" the crowd shouted in Hulkrish, that harsh, glottal tongue—something that chilled him as he rode on a ghost ant and struggled to remember the correct hand placements on the antennae.

On his way to the airfield, Anand passed through more adoring crowds, some of them grating a delivery of acorns, until he reached the Meat Ant people. They were making cables out of spiderwebs and they carefully scraped the dots of glue from the fibers for other uses. The Ledackis turned to him and smiled, all of them looking strong and well fed even as most of their men were absent; they were likely up in the palaces, still recovering from coughing fits.

Hopefully these rains have washed most of that poison away. And it should degrade in a few moons, he thought. One of the Ledackis, the queenly beauty with her bright green eyes, was coming forward. "Thank you, Quegdoth," she shouted in Slopeish. She raised the chubby little baby from the pouch around her chest and waved his hand.

"Thank you," he said in Slopeish. "Welcome to . . . Bee-Jor."

Bee-Jor. I hesitated to say that.

At the airfield, Terraclon was waiting for him and inspecting his locust and its rigging. "Here, Anand," he said, void of the usual sarcasm as he handed Anand a water bag and a food pouch with shoulder straps. "She's all ready for you. I'd leave now since you've got a south-blowing wind. The sun sinks quickly in the twelfth moon."

Terraclon dropped his head and turned away and Anand knew he was hiding his tears.

"You were good to my father," Anand said, and fought the urge not to join him in crying. "Thank you, Ter."

"We were good each to other. And you were always good to me, Anand," said Terraclon, his eyes on the ground. "Now get your butt on that saddle, Commander, and get out of here. We're expecting sled-cages with our new ant queen from Fadtha-dozh any day now. I have a lot to do today."

"From the sounds coming out of your bedchamber it sounds like you've got a lot to do at night."

Terraclon looked startled but then bit his lip.

"Why, Terraclon," Anand said through a grin. "If you didn't have dark skin I believe I could see you blushing."

Polexima was chanting her afternoon prayers on a bead chain when Anand entered what had been her old bedchamber.

"Anand," she said. "I am so terribly sorry."

"Polly, thank you," he said as they embraced. The smell of vinegar was sharp and strong in the room. Mulga entered with a tea bowl and some mushroom biscuits. She set it down and went to Anand to take his hands in hers and look into his eyes—something that was a pleasant startle. "I am sorry, Commander Quegdoth," she said as her chin trembled. "So deeply sorry . . . Anand."

He nodded, unable to speak as she teared up. Her hands were warm as she squeezed his—something in her had changed.

"If you're thirsty, I brought you something," Mulga said. "Do you mind if I put this room back together?"

Anand looked around the chamber and saw the drawers that had been pulled out and tossed and the chests that had been opened and overturned.

"Please do," Anand said, and sighed. It was time, finally, to turn towards the bed.

"As soon as we found him, we wrapped him in

vinegar-soaked cloth, per your instructions," said Polexima. "And then wrapped him again in waxed silk."

Anand went to the bed and saw a royal coffin of chiseled quartz on the mattress. Something like a cocoon was inside it when he lifted up its lid. He unfolded the layers of sharp-smelling sheets to reveal his father's corpse. Yormu's cloudy eyes were open and looking up. His mouth was agape to reveal his missing teeth and the jagged scar of what had been his tongue. Anand pushed the chin up and saw the purple-black marks of strangulation on the throat and the flesh that had been gouged at the back of the neck. The hair was full of dark, crystalized blood. Anand probed through the back of the head with his fingers and sensed through the broken skin that his father's skull had been shattered.

Anand was sobbing again when he folded back the sheets. Polexima handed him a cloth dipped in cleaning spirits to wipe his hands. Mulga went about neatening, throwing the remains of some rotten and moldy food into a bin. She picked up some scratching paper from the table where Yormu had sat and then crumpled it into a ball before dropping it in the trash bin.

"Wait," Anand said. "Let me see that."

"See what, Commander?" said Mulga.

"That scratching paper."

"This?" she said, picking up the ball. "They're all

alike. He never drew anything. He just made these funny little scratchings."

She threw Anand the ball. He opened it up to see words on a page. Up in the top corner Yormu had written the numeral for "one."

"Got more over here," she said, and went to the other side of the bed to pull up multiple sheets that had fallen behind the night table. Anand sorted through them. In the corners were the Dranverish numerals for 3, 7, and 9.

These are drafts!

With each draft, Yormu's penmanship improved. Draft fourteen was the last one and looked to be incomplete, but draft thirteen filled the entire page. The words were misspelled, and instead of the proper punctuation, his sentences ended with a slash. Anand cleared his eyes of sudden tears and read.

*anand/my tongue and teeth torn from mouth
before you were ever born/i could never say i love
you/how you made me happy/most proud father
in holy slope now is beejor/proud proud proud/my
son is most great of all/ love love love my anand/
love/ i write that now if i can not say/*

*know this anand/ know know know this what i
saw/day of war with brown ant people/keel and
sons keel and 7 sons 7 sons took pleckoo out/keel
and 7 sons took pleckoo out of cage/pleckoo out of*

*cage ran/pleckoo ran north to place with no magic
of priests/ i saw/i saw this/and tal killed boy with
bad arm guard of cage/kick teeth out of face of boy/
know this anand what keel and sons did/you not
safe from keel and sons/*

*prayer for you/prayer for anand stay safe/love my
son/love/*

Anand trembled. *Dad was found in that cage! And accused of freeing Pleckoo! And of killing the boy left to guard
him! Of course it was Keel and Tal and the rest of those
inbred monsters!*

Anand fell to his knees and shouted, "Those vicious bloodsucking chiggers! Why did I let them live?
Why should any of them live?"

His shouting gave way to angry crying that he
muffled with his cupped hands. Polexima placed her
hand on his shoulder.

"Anand . . . tell me what's wrong."

"It's all here," he said, raising the page. "I know
who freed Pleckoo. And one of them killed my father."

"What will you do?"

A messenger appeared at the door, out of breath
and waiting to be recognized. The boy looked deeply
concerned, shifting on his feet as his forehead wrinkled. Embarrassed, Anand stood and resumed his
composure.

"Can you come back?" Polexima said to the messenger. "This is not a good time."

"No," said Anand. "He wouldn't be here if it weren't important."

"Commander," said the messenger. "I have been sent to tell you that something has appeared at our northernmost border."

"What?"

"A triple dome structure, something like the ones you are building over the borders of New Dneep and the Barley Lands. Someone, a man with skin as white as a daisy, threw this tube to a border guard and said it was for Vof Quegdoth. He spoke in our tongue. Behind him was an army of hundreds . . . on red hunter ants."

Polexima and Anand looked at each other.

"Commander Quegdoth—are we going to war again?" asked the boy, a quaver in his voice. "A war with Dranveria?"

"No, Good Messenger. I don't believe we are," said Anand, and then sighed with relief. He looked at the stoppered tube with its coating of shiny red paint and his actual name written on it: Anand son of Yormu and Corra of the Free State of Bee-Jor.

Thank Madricanth. I'm no longer Lick-My-Testicles.

CHAPTER 40

AN UNFINISHED LETTER

Anand looked out of a clear, quartz window in his new bedchamber on a sunny spring morning on an Eighth Day of Rest. The Cajorites were out strolling and were both drawn to and fearful of the multiplying ghost ants. Most of the ghosts were still inside the mound, emerging only at night to hunt, but a few were scattered up and down the rings to quietly keep guard. Some of the ants pivoted in place, but most were just resting, with their antennae gently twitching as they probed the air.

The humans that approached the ants used their new antennae to make contact; the pairs were longer but more flexible than those they had worn for the leaf-cutters. Some of the probed ants regurgitated their food, and a few Cajorites dipped their fingers to taste the offering: a greenish pulp of oak moth caterpillars. Some daring youths were climbing up the spikes of the ghosts' legs and onto their skulls in an attempt to prod their antennae for a ride. One of these would-be riders succeeded in getting some short, listless movements, but the boys would need proper instructions and scented gloves before they could get some speed.

Anand turned from the window to reread Dwan's latest letter and then took up a stylus and scratch paper to respond.

> *Cherished friend Dwan,*
>
> *As warmth returns to the Sand, it has yet to return to my heart. My wife, who likely carries twins inside her, remains in the Barley Lands, and as my roach tribe is no longer able to travel in the East, I have no news of her. Each day grows heavier with the weight of that worry.*
>
> *What does warm me is knowing that the first mission scholars from Dranveria are arriving soon to establish schools. We are agreed that the scholars should start here at Cajoria and then spread to our other mounds when their safety can be assured. The scholars should know that the archives of Mound Loobosh have been relocated to Cajoria, something that may be of great interest to them.*
>
> *As for the battle at Loobosh, you are right to be*

concerned about our use of floral and fungal poisons, but we had no other defense against an uncountable horde of Greeyas. As you know, their land wasps are nearly impenetrable and can be driven with precision for coordinated assaults that can be overwhelming. The poisons' effectiveness was both chemical as well as emotional as the people of the Carpenter Nation have used them against the Greeyas for centuries. Of course, these poisons will be less of a threat when the Greeyas learn to make breathing masks.

With no ability to communicate with the League of Velvet Ant Peoples, we made every attempt to warn them that crossing our border would be deadly. Our frontier was lined with thousands of sling-banners that were painted with images of death by poisoning. Since the repulsion of both the Greeyas and the Barley people, we have surrounded our border with a deep strip of borax powder that is safe for humans but deadly to insects. The borax is something that we always have to replenish for as long as we have access to its source . . . and until it runs out.

Yes, I celebrate the arrival of Dranveria's educators, but more importantly, I await the arrival of the Dranverish forces. The moment will come, all too soon, when we are invaded again by one of three hostile nations on our

"Commander!" shouted someone who appeared at the doorway in a Britasyte costume, someone with thousands of freckles on his light skin and with fuzzy, ginger whiskers.

"Odwaznee! Good travels! What brings you here?" said Anand in Britasyte.

"Best of good news!" he said with his newly deepened voice. "At last, they have come to Diplomacy Dome. Royal man with message from Barley Lands!"

"What?"

Anand dropped his stylus and stood. He was lightheaded, and before he could stop himself he was laughing. "You said a royal person with a message from the Barley Lands?"

"Yes. Is man who is requests to speak with you, has message coming from Volokop the emperor. Man says he has someone with him who is your person, who he returns to you. Wants someone in return."

Anand shuddered with ecstasy. "Daveena!" he shouted. "If Volokop wants his son back, he can have him!"

This could be a trap. But I'll risk it to get my wife.

A short time later, Anand arrived on a ghost ant at Cajoria's cathedral to find Muti and her priestesses in a heated argument with Polexima and her Cricket sisters. Most of them had their arms crossed as they faced each other before the altar. The priestesses were in the green glow of the first torches of lightning-fly eggs while the Cricket sisters were in the blue light of fungus torches.

"Listen to my every word, Muti," Polexima said in

Hulkrish. "You did not marry the king of Bee-Jor so you are not queen here. I am! Do not rearrange my cathedral's idols to your liking—and never set cricket meat before that abominable demoness!"

Anand saw that an idol of Ghost Ant had been set on the altar and had been bejeweled and dressed. An offering of food had been left on a platter at Her feet.

"Cricket is weak goddess!" said Muti. "Cricket is easily caught and eaten. She cannot defend Bee-Jor."

Muti's priestesses were bringing out a second idol, wrapped with a cloth, and were pushing aside Cricket to set it next to Locust.

"And just what is that?" Polexima shouted. "Remove that cloth!"

"No!" Muti shouted. "Not until night!"

Cricket sisters and Ghost Ant priestesses grabbed at the cloth until it tore in two to reveal the idol. Polexima gasped.

"How dare you!" she screamed. "That's a termite! You will not disgrace our altar with idols of Hulkro and Ghost Ant!"

"Ghost Ant is married to Hulkro," said Muti. "Do not offend Ghost Ant, who blesses mounds of Bee-Jor with Her daughters!"

"I won't have it!" Polexima shouted. "We won't have ghost ants for long—or *you* here either, you daft, brazen slut!"

Muti noticed Anand coming forward and shouted

at him. "Anand! You let this old, lame woman speak like this to me, to your wife?"

Anand was quiet. He nodded to Polexima, acknowledging their deeper bond. "This altar is crowded," he said. "But each of its idols have their devotees. We have other places within this mound—places where mushrooms were grown that are empty now. These can be places for new cathedrals . . . and new gods."

The women were quiet, tension leaving their faces.

"Muti, we will explore some of these places," said Anand as he took her arm. "Places for you to beautify and make your own, but at this moment, I need you to come with me."

"For what?"

Anand chuckled with joy as he looked at Polexima.

"Some Barley people, at last, have entered into the Diplomacy Dome! Volokop has sent a messenger, a royal from his palace!"

Polexima gasped. "And . . . and what about Daveena?"

"Yes. What about . . . Daveena," said Muti as she pouted.

"She is alive . . . it seems, and perhaps the time has come to return her! Muti, come with me, to be our two-tongued."

"No," she said. "You have Britasytes who can do this. Or Odwaznee, strange boy who wants to be Britasyte."

"No, what remains of the Britasytes are all in the South, trading, it appears, with Dneepers in hopes of building a bridge between us. Odwaznee will be with me, but he is . . . he is an offense, I am told, to the nobles of your old country and considered . . . rustic."

"No, not going," Muti said, and set her hands under her belly. "I am not well feeling."

Anand noticed that her belly and her breasts looked bigger.

"You're sick?" he said.

"No, stupid. I am pregnant."

Riding east on a roach, Anand was reeling from Muti's news and unsure of whether it was true.

And if it is true, am I really the father of this baby?

Push those thoughts aside, Anand.

He had decided that riding a roach to the Diplomacy Dome was a better choice than a ghost ant; the Seed Eaters' harvesters had repulsed Pleckoo's ghosts on the War of One Night, but they would always run in fear of roaches. And it was on the backs of roaches that Bee-Jor's force had turned back Volokop's army. Marching behind Anand's roach was an infantry of thousands of defenders. More and more of them were joining as volunteers, dedicated to his protection.

Good, in case the Seed Eaters try something.

Thirteen guards with blow-guns around their necks and black-glass swords at their sides preceded

Anand and Odwaznee as they entered the first of the three crystal domes from Bee-Jor's side. Anand was wearing his blue flying armor under a loose jacket and pants of yellow silk from King Sahdrin's wardrobe. On his face was a foundation of white-yellow paint and then a dusting of lily pollen to disguise himself in case he was recognized from his time as Volokop's prisoner. Odwaznee strutted proudly beside him in his Britasyte garb with his cape flung open. He wore a bright green tunic with a raised pattern of copulating roaches that was sure to offend whatever Barley royal had come to humble himself before Commander Quegdoth of Bee-Jor.

Anand and Odwaznee followed the thirteen guards into the central dome. The guards parted to let Anand step through and face a small guard of six Seed Eater soldiers in ceremonial armor of rainbow chitins. The guards stood on stilt shoes and had wings on their backs creating somewhat of a living fence. They stepped to the side to reveal a tall man wearing a heavily embroidered coat that likely covered his own armor. His pale, orange-tinged face was handsome but had a stern expression and his ginger beard was closely clipped to a strong chin. A cloth tube was stretched around his forehead, which allowed hundreds of his hair braids to droop out its end. He looked at Anand, nodded, then spoke. Odwaznee pursed his mouth in contempt and squinted at the man before making his translation.

"'I am Crown Prince Lagoradny, firstborn of Volo-kop, Holy Emperor of the Barley People at the Center of the World.'"

"Commander Vog Quegdoth," said Anand in Bri-tasyte, making a shallow bow. "I welcome you to this dome in hopes of an everlasting friendship between our two nations."

The prince made the slightest nod of his head again.

"'My father understands that you want the return of someone that we hold as a guest in Worxict.'"

Anand paused a moment. "We understand there are a number of prisoners held captive in Worxict—some Slopeites from eastern mounds as well as one Britasyte woman."

"'No, as prisoners we hold only the Britasyte woman as our . . . guest.'"

The prince smiled knowingly. Anand's face fell when he realized the captured Slopeites had been ex-ecuted. He paused a moment.

"And we have the emperor's third son as our *guest*," said Anand. "The Treti Korolsyn is treated well. He lives in the palace and is learning our language. We will gladly exchange him for the prisoner you hold and can bring him this day."

The prince was staring at Anand with an annoy-ing little grin when he snapped an order to a guard at his back who left for the eastern dome. Anand urged himself to breathe and fought to maintain calm as he expected the guard to return with Daveena. The guard returned a moment later with a lacy bundle in his arms and extended it to Anand.

Stunned, Anand could not move. The guard pushed the bundle into his chest until Anand raised his arms to take it. He looked down at the dark face of a brown-eyed baby who sucked on her thumb.

The prince spoke again and Odwaznee looked shocked. He turned to Anand and spoke directly to him.

"Commander, the prince says this is your daughter."

Anand felt his guts fall out of him as he looked at the little face and knew it was true. The prince looked in Anand's teary eyes and spoke to him, loudly, in the Britasyte tongue. The words hit like punches to his ears.

"Anand of the Britasytes, Commander Quegdoth of Dranveria," the prince recited. "You can keep my half brother, the emperor's third son, or return him if you please. But if you want to meet your son and to see your Daveena again, you will return something my father needs."

"What?" said Anand.

"His wife."

"His wife?"

"The witch. Muti."

"You lied to me!" Anand shouted.

"What lie?" said Muti.

"You never told me you were married to Volokop!"

"Never said I was not married to Volokop."

Muti had taken up residence in Trellana's old chambers and was more interested in going through what remained of her abandoned wardrobe than in talking to Anand. Her priestesses were tearing the clothes into pieces at the seams to rework and embroider. They pretended not to listen to the argument.

"You should have told me!"

"You got what you want, Anand," Muti said, and shrugged. "And I got what I want."

"You cannot be married to two men!"

"You are married to three women. Volokop is married to seven."

"But the woman I love is Volokop's prisoner. In order for me to get her back, he wants *you*!"

Muti held up the garment she was working on and examined it in the fading light, reconsidering its beauty.

"As soon as I am returned to Volokop, he will kill me—sacrifice me to Lumm Korol."

"Why would he do that?"

She shook her head, frowning at him. "You think he want me back because I am biggest prize on Sand, most beautiful woman he lost. No, Anand. He want me back to break spell."

"What spell?"

"The one that turned him into ugly, swollen monster."

Anand's rage was building.

THE GHOST ANTS OF GRYLLADESH 541

This anger must be contained. Choose your words carefully, Anand.

"Muti, you did not do anything to cause Volokop's condition. It is not the result of a spell or any magic. He was attacked by a mosquito that transmitted the swelling disease."

"Anand," she said, as if he was the stupidest child. "Who do you think sent that mosquito?"

She looked at him, slowly flapping her eyelids as she tilted her head. He was struck anew with her beauty . . . and hated her for it.

"Perhaps," she whispered when he turned his back. "I send mosquito for you."

Anand went to bed with hatred festering inside him. The night alone in his bedchamber had been long and sleepless, but every day in Bee-Jor had its demands and today would be very demanding. As he waited for Mulga to bring him more tea at breakfast, he resumed his letter to Dwan.

the moment will come, all too soon, when we are invaded by one of the three hostile nations on our borders, one of which has a credible claim to our territory and the other which has a tenuous one dating to a grievance from centuries ago.

After the Greeyas retreated, we managed to bring a few of their injured warriors into Bee-Jor to teach them our language and to learn theirs. Hopefully we will return them as envoys with an offer of cooperation between our nations. One of our guests is a Greeya Agu, which translates closely to tribal leader. Known as Hawjud, he was one of the Setcha Greeya's six captains that makes up their league of seven. The Setcha, or Great Greeya, we believe is dead from the personal effects found on one of many corpses near our western border. From what we can observe, the remainder of Greeyas occupy former Slopeish mounds and someday they will resume their invasion.

Physically, the Greeyas have black hair and brown skin—they look very much like me. We have discovered linguistic and cultural similarities that give credence to their claim that they are the descendants of a people who occupied the Slope and what are now the Dustlands. For centuries, the Greeyas have attempted to reclaim the Slope from the yellow-skinned conquerors who enslaved its dark-skinned inhabitants, a tribe of

"Creet-creet," Anand heard outside his door.

"Majesty?"

"Yes," said Polexima, and entered in her garb of iridescent green to honor the first meadow crickets of spring. Behind her were two dark-skinned women that Anand recognized but who averted his gaze.

"Good morning, Commander Quegdoth," Polexima said, exaggerating her formality. "I have a few things I should like to discuss with you this evening.

Would you be kind enough to join me for the evening meal in my apartments?"

"I would be very pleased, Majesty," Anand said. "But I am afraid my services are required at Mound Shishto where they report movements of Seed Eaters beyond our border." Anand looked at the women behind her who stooped under their cowls. "May we reschedule?"

"We certainly may," said Polexima. "Allow me to introduce you to Citizen Splooga and her daughter, Jizzlane. They were middenites at Cajoria during the days of caste, but at my invitation, they have shown an interest in joining the Order of Sisters of Cricket. Today I am showing them the ways of our devotion. Splooga's husband and her sons fought bravely against the Seed Eaters."

"Well, well," said Anand in a royal accent. "I am familiar with Splooga's husband and her sons." He looked at Splooga and her only surviving daughter and felt an immense sorrow for them. Growing up in the midden, Anand had seldom ever seen the two, but at night he had heard their screams when they were beaten.

"I do believe Keel is still foreman and likely it is his eldest, Tal, who will assume his duties someday?"

"Right," said Splooga as she finally looked up. Her nose had been broken a few times and her lips had never properly healed after being split by too many fists. Anand could see some beauty in her daughter's face, but Jizzlane was too shy to look at him; she shrank from men as men were dangerous.

"We thank your husband and all seven of his sons for their service," said Anand.

"Anand," said Splooga, suddenly familiar. "We hear this house we're getting today is large enough. But it's low on the mound. The men in my family risked their lives, all of them did, and my oldest boy lost his eye. We deserves us a house somewhere up near the barracks with all them other veterans."

"Citizen Splooga, the barracks are quite filled now, with heroes who fought both the Hulkrites as well as the Seed Eaters. The places that remain available will be for those who fought against the Greeyas as well."

"Are they now," she said, and frowned.

"Come along," said Polexima, coaxing the women. "The Sisters await and we have a full day ahead of us— one that won't end until the first chirps of evening."

As Splooga and Jizzlane walked off, Polexima turned over her shoulder. "Commander Quegdoth," she said, raising her eyebrows. "May you have a very fulfilling day."

"You as well, Majesty."

Anand was anxious as he waited inside a large, fragrant house of white sand grains glued with pine resin. It was a well-made dome and unfurnished except for a privy booth that Terraclon had modified. The two of them sat on its floor of interlocking tiles of rose quartz; near the end of the day, they had run out of things to discuss. It was annoyingly quiet as the nearby houses had all been emptied and awaited to be reassigned. Terraclon was doing needlework, and in the silence, Anand could hear the sound of his stitching.

"How is it so quiet here?" Terraclon asked.

"Lots of people left Cajoria for the southwestern mounds—for even bigger houses on higher rings."

"But those mounds are closer to the Greeyas. And the Dneepers—they'll be the first to be attacked."

"Doesn't matter. Looking down on someone is more important than safety . . . or happiness."

Terraclon looked up and raised his eyebrows. "I suppose you're right," he said after a very long pause. He turned the embroidery hoop to Anand. "What do you think?"

"What is that? A pink roach?"

"Yes."

"Pink?"

"It's for your daughter. A blanket. I mean, she is a Britasyte."

"Oh. Right. Thanks. It's lovely. Perfect, really."

"Anand, what's her name?"

"Who?"

"Your *daughter!*"

"Oh. I don't know."

"You *don't know?*"

"Shh! They're coming," Anand whispered as they heard the loud, coarse voices of men outside the house's portal with its diaphragm of waxed canvas. The men were arguing, unsure if this was the correct house. They continued to argue until they heard a new voice, that of a Slopeish priest-turned-clerk who had been assigned to granting the housing deed. Outside the portal, they heard the clerk speak with the long vowels and musical voice of a priest. Anand and Terraclon went into the privy booth, quietly closed its door, and locked it with a sliding bolt.

"Have I the pleasure of addressing Keel, foreman of the midden of Cajoria?" said the clerk.

"Right. I'm him."

"It is my duty and honor to extend to you the grant to this dwelling, number 3,423 on the thirty-fourth ring of Cajoria as well as the square it occupies by the grace of her Majesty Queen Polexima of Bee-Jor and her Royal Commander Vof Quegdoth in recognition of your efforts to defend our nation against foreign intrusion. Upon acceptance of this property, do you and all in your family swear to abide by the Eight Laws and all laws which will descend from them?"

"We do," Keel grunted.

"And you accept that the breaking of the Eight Laws may result in the forfeiture of this property?"

"I suppose we do."

"Sir," said the clerk. "No supposing. Yes or no."

"Yes, yes, no guess."

"Is your eldest son present, Tal of the midden, who will inherit this dwelling upon your demise?"

"I am," said Tal.

"Please, the two of you, stamp the corner of this deed and its copy with your thumbs dipped in ink and keep the original for yourselves. Guard this deed and never let it get wet or moldy."

Anand and Terraclon quieted their breathing inside the privy booth and looked out its tiny viewing holes as Keel and his sons pushed through the portal to enter the house they had won. "And her Royal Commander, Vof Quegdoth," Keel said in a poor attempt at mocking the priestly accent.

"Someday we'll kick her Royal Commander's teeth out of his face—and then take over his palace," said Tal.

"What do we think, boys?" Keel asked as they looked around the handsome, round room with a soft light coming through its walls. "We've made it up the mound."

"It's not a shit shack," said Dumbree. "We could fit three of our old houses in here. But what's that up in the ceiling?" He pointed to a cluster of dried insect eggs held by a fine mesh.

"I don't know," said Keel. "I never been in a house."

Anand nudged Terraclon and the two of them

pulled goggles over their eyes and breathing masks up to their faces. Terraclon yanked hard on a cord and Anand watched as shells burst in the ceiling and sprayed their contents in a mist. Anand kicked down the wall of the booth and stepped out with his black-glass sword in hand. Keel and his sons were coughing as they unsheathed their swords and stumbled towards Anand, trying to hold their breath. As they attempted an attack on Anand, Terraclon stepped out of the booth with his bow and arrow to shoot them through the back, the face, the neck, and chest. Shimus reached Terraclon before he could reload, but he jabbed the arrow through Shimus's throat, then thrust it to snap his spinal cord. The rest fell and jittered before they died from the arrowheads' poisons—all of them but Keel and Tal.

Father and son staggered towards Anand as they weakly swung their swords. As their blades clashed, Anand darted and danced between the bulk of the two as they slowed and succumbed to the poisoning. As Tal raised up his sword to strike Anand, he kicked Tal in his testicles; he bent in pain as he sucked in toxic air. Keel, pinching his nose, swiped at Anand with his Hulkrish sword, but the moment came when he had to breathe. He rushed at Anand, sword thrust before him, but Anand leapt to the side to let Keel stumble. Keel's hands trembled as he got to his knees and crawled towards the portal.

"You freed Pleckoo!" Anand shouted through his

mask. "You and all your sons! And Tal killed the boy who guarded him—a poor, crippled boy!"

"We did no such thing," wheezed Keel as he reached the portal.

"I'm freeing you from your misery," Anand said as he ripped the back of Keel's collar off to reveal his neck. Keel thrust a hand through the portal's diaphragm and then screamed and pulled back a stump—his hand had been severed by someone outside the house. Anand picked up Keel's heavy Hulkrish sword and looked at it in contempt before he took the handle with both hands and then hacked through the bulk of Keel's neck. Blood, flesh, and fat spattered until the head was severed.

Anand walked towards Tal, who attempted to rise but fell to his knees before he collapsed face-down. "Give me a hand, Ter," Anand said. "He's a big boy."

"Gladly," smirked Terraclon, and the two grabbed Tal's limbs and jerked him onto his back. Tal's eyes were darting with fear as he coughed.

"You wanted to kick my teeth out of my face, huh?" said Anand. "The way you kicked them out of that boy that guarded Pleckoo?"

Anand raised the sharp end of his boot, threw back his leg and thrust it with all his force into Tal's cheek. His screams were loud and pathetic as he choked on the poisonous air. Anand looked down at Tal, raising his blood-covered boot over his face to taunt him.

Tal's teeth lay scattered on his neck and chest and in blood on the floor.

"I got me a few teeth," Anand said in the guttural voice of his old caste. "Let's see if I can get me some more."

Anand kicked again and again as years of rage exploded and consumed him. Tal's head became a bloody mass of shredded flesh and broken bone. Anand was howling as he kicked, lost in hatred and immersed in the impulse to kill.

"Anand," he heard faintly. "Anand! Stop! That's enough! You're turning into one of them!"

Someone had grabbed Anand's arm. He turned to attack, cocking a fist, when he realized it was Terraclon.

"Come back from wherever you are, Anand! They're dead. We have to get out of here."

Anand tried to catch his breath, but the breathing mask was full of stale air. He pivoted, dizzy and wobbling, when he remembered where he was and why he was there.

"Let's go," Terraclon said.

"Wait," said Anand. "Wait!"

"What?"

"Count them," Anand said. "I have to count them."

"I already have," Terraclon said. "Eight corpses. One father and seven sons . . . and not a beauty among them. Wipe your boots off and put this on."

Anand was suddenly, overwhelmingly, exhausted

as Terraclon handed him a rag and a plain cloak with a hood to cover his head and face.

"We're coming out," Terraclon shouted through the portal's cloth. He pushed out of the opening and then pulled Anand out and onto his feet. Nuvao was waiting for them with an ant-drawn sled.

"Where is it?" Anand asked.

"Here," said Nuvao as he handed Anand a sheet of paper with Keel's and Tal's thumbprints in the corner. Anand took the sled's torch from its sconce and held the sheet to the light.

"Read it to me," Terraclon said.

"I, Keel, foreman of the midden of Cajoria, confess to the following crimes that I and my sons committed in order that my wife, Splooga, and my daughter, Jizzlane, may retain ownership of the dwelling granted to our family by Queen Polexima. First offense: the freeing of Pleckoo the Hulkrite after murdering the child who was left to guard him. Second offense: the murder of Yormu the Mute by my son Tal who . . ."

Anand stopped reading. "I wasn't sure how this would feel when it was over," he said.

"How does it feel?" Nuvao asked.

Anand paused.

"It's . . . it's strangely peaceful."

Anand gulped down a liquid supper and fell straight into bed to sleep deeply through the night. He woke only once from a dream in which he was back in the midden, drowning at the bottom of a shit vat, when hands reached in and yanked him up. He saw Tal's face, heard his cruel laughter, and then watched as his mouth opened wider and wider. Tal lifted Anand up and stuffed him down his throat where he drowned again in a wet darkness, trying and failing to claw his way out.

Anand did not wake again until well after sunrise. Mulga had already left him tea and a sun-steamed grating of the season's first barley seeds for breakfast. Today was a seventh day, when Bee-Jorites from every mound would queue up to accuse each other of crimes and beg for a bigger house on a higher ring. Anand sighed and picked up his stylus, determined to finish his letter to Dwan before it was time to leave for court.

For centuries, the Greeyas have attempted to reclaim the Slope from the yellow-skinned conquerors who enslaved its dark-skinned inhabitants, a tribe of cricket ranchers, many of which escaped the Slopeites and fled west to the Scrublands. The Greeyas are likely correct about their claim. They have similar deities to ours; their creator/sky god is Grandfather Locust and their chief goddess is Lady Cricket, known as Gree Dari-Ekh in their tongue. The name of their tribe derives from the worship of Cricket.

The land She bestowed on them is known as Greeya-Tepic, or Place of the Crickets.

Which leads me, dear Dwan, to an admission. It was, of course, a terrible mistake to call our new nation Bee-Jor. As was predicted, the name drew hundreds of thousands of disparate Hulkrish refugees into our land with unmeetable expectations. It is now a struggle to incorporate all of them and it will be for decades. The reality of our situation is that Bee-Jor has no bees nor any bee people. The ones we invited, the Bulkokans, were a vile and amoral tribe who were convinced of their own superiority. They were destroyed after they demolished the colony of an unknown tree tribe.

So we must change the name of our new nation. This will cast doubt on my leadership and end all foolish notions of my infallibility as the Son of Locust. I have learned from one of our educated eunuchs, Brother Moonsinger, that the name of this land before its conquest was Grylladesh. That name, like Greeya-Tepic, means "Place of the Crickets." I have discussed this with Queen Polexima and others and we have decided

The first messenger of the day appeared at Anand's portal and called, "Creet-creet." Just as crickets do.

"Yes, Good Messenger."

"Commander Quegdoth," said the boy as he extended a white message tube from Dranveria, the color marking an urgent matter.

Anand, I am on the way to Bee-Jor but I must relay something before my arrival. I will be coming from our southern lake city of Porata Delth where I learned of a man who was rescued from tree cannibals and brought to a healing center by our Humanitarian Border Patrol. After he was rehabilitated, our scholars realized the language he spoke, Hulkrish, was closely related to Slopeish, which he speaks as well. The man arrived in Porata with a clipped ear and a missing nose. When the scholars reviewed your testimony of life in Cajoria, they concluded that this may be your cousin Pleckoo, the man who came to be known as the Second Prophet of the Hulkrites. He managed to escape just as we were planning to arrest him for crimes committed in Porata. I urge you to send a bulletin to all parts of Bee-Jor to stay on the alert for him. Included is a recent sketch of his current appearance.

> *Stay safe and well,*
> *Dwan*

"Pleckoo," Anand said aloud as he looked at the drawing of a handsome young man with an intact nose. Anand felt a pang of joy and a shiver down his spine.

Pleckoo has his nose back!

And then, for the first time in moons, Anand felt that strange, chaotic mixture of brotherly love and a hatred that raged like fire. His lungs were irritated and he coughed—was it the shock of this news or was it poison exposure? His mind raced in a spiral of panic where thoughts and feelings crashed into heaps of broken glass.

"Just where are you, Cousin Pleckoo?"

ABOUT THE AUTHOR

CLARK THOMAS CARLTON is an award-winning novelist, playwright, journalist, screen and television writer, and a producer of reality TV. He was born in the South, grew up in the East, went to school in the North, and lives with his family in the West. As a child he spent hours observing ants and their wars and pondered their similarity to human societies.

Discover great authors, exclusive offers, and more at hc.com.